Jack London
Jules Verne
Harriet Beecher-Stowe
Daniel Defoe
Bret Harte
Karl May
Rudyard Kipling

Illustrated by
Zdeněk Burian

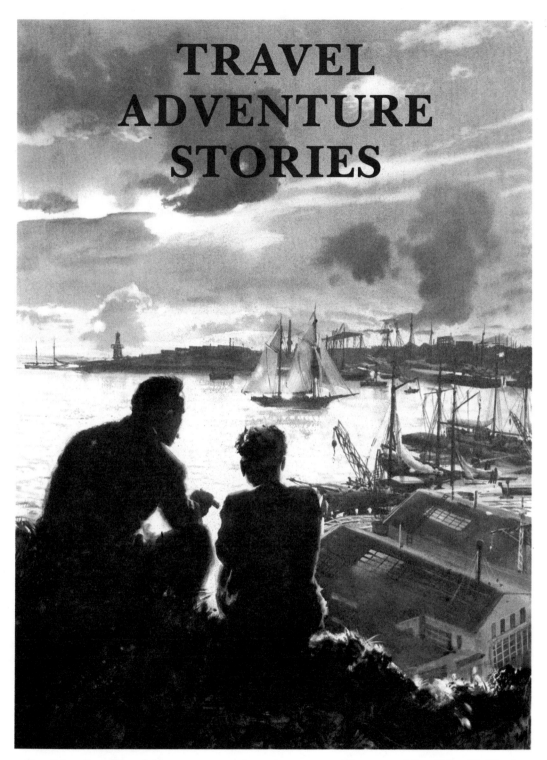

TRAVEL ADVENTURE STORIES

edited by Jan Hendriks   illustrated by Zdeněk Burian

GALLEY PRESS

THE SPRING RUNNING
from THE SECOND JUNGLE
BOOK by Rudyard Kipling is reprinted by
permission from The National Trust for
Places of Historic Interest or Natural
Beauty.

The publishers wish to acknowledge the use
of illustrations kindly provided by the
Museum of National Literature and by
Mr. M. Šmerhovský.

Edited by Jan Hendriks
Illustrated by Zdeněk Burian
The texts Matthew Sandorf
and The Sands of Destruction
translated by Stephen Finn
Graphic design by Jiří Schmidt
First published 1983 by
Galley Press
59 Grosvenor Street
London Wl
ISBN 0 7064 1969 3
© 1983 Artia, Prague
Printed in Czechoslovakia by TSNP Martin
1/18/06/51-01

CONTENTS

LOVE OF LIFE

JACK LONDON

This out of all will remain —
They have lived and have tossed:
So much of the game will be gain,
Though the gold of the dice has been lost.

They limped painfully down the bank, and once the foremost of the two men staggered among the rough-strewn rocks. They were tired and weak, and their faces had the drawn expression of patience which comes of hardship long endured. They were heavily burdened with blanket packs which were strapped to their shoulders. Head straps, passing across the forehead, helped support these packs. Each man carried a rifle. They walked in a stooped posture, the shoulders well forward, the head still farther forward, the eyes bent upon the ground.

'I wish we had just about two of them cartridges that's layin' in that cache of ourn,' said the second man.

His voice was utterly and drearily expressionless. He spoke without enthusiasm; and the first man, limping into the milky stream that foamed over the rocks, vouchsafed no reply.

The other man followed at his heels. They did not remove their footgear, though the water was icy cold — so cold that their ankles ached and their feet went numb. In places the water dashed against their knees, and both men staggered for footing.

The man who followed slipped on a smooth boulder, nearly fell, but recovered himself with a violent effort, at the same time uttering a sharp exclamation of pain. He seemed faint and dizzy and put out his free hand while he reeled, as though seeking support against the air. When he had steadied himself he stepped forward, but reeled again and nearly fell. Then he stood still and looked at the other man, who had never turned his head.

The man stood still for fully a minute, as though debating with himself. Then he called out:

'I say, Bill, I've sprained my ankle.'

Bill staggered on through the milky water. He did not look around. The man watched him go, and though his face was expressionless as ever, his eyes were like the eyes of a wounded deer.

The other man limped up the farther bank and continued straight on without looking back. The man in the stream watched him. His lips trembled a little, so that the rough thatch of brown hair which covered them was visibly agitated. His tongue even strayed out to moisten them.

'Bill!' he cried out.

It was the pleading cry of a strong man in distress, but Bill's head did not turn. The man watched him go, limping grotesquely and lurching forward with stammering gait up the slow slope towards the soft sky line of the low-lying hill. He watched him go till he passed over the crest and disappeared. Then he turned his gaze and slowly took in the circle of the world that remained to him now that Bill was gone.

Near the horizon the sun was smouldering dimly, almost obscured by formless mists and vapours, which gave an impression of mass and density without outline or tangibility. The man pulled out his watch, the while resting his weight on one leg. It was four o'clock, and as the season was near the last of July or first of August — he did not know the precise date within a week or two — he knew that the sun roughly marked the north-west. He looked to the south and knew that somewhere beyond those bleak hills lay the Great Bear Lake; also he knew that in that direction the Arctic Circle cut its forbidding way across the Canadian Barrens. This stream in which he stood was a feeder to the Coppermine River, which in turn flowed north and emptied into Coronation Gulf and the Arctic Ocean. He had never been there, but he had seen it, once, on a Hudson's Bay Company chart.

Again his gaze completed the circle of the world about him. It was not a heartening spectacle. Everywhere was soft sky line. The hills were all low-lying. There were no trees, no shrubs, no grasses — naught but a tremendous and terrible desolation that sent fear swiftly dawning into his eyes.

10

'Bill!' he whispered, once and twice. 'Bill!'

He cowered in the midst of the milky water, as though the vastness were pressing in upon him with overwhelming force, brutally crushing him with its complacent awfulness. He began to shake as with an ague fit, till the gun fell from his hand with a splash. This served to rouse him. He fought with his fear and pulled himself together, groping in the water and recovering the weapon. He hitched his pack farther over on his left shoulder, so as to take a portion of its weight from off the injured ankle. Then he proceeded, slowly and carefully, wincing with pain, to the bank.

He did not stop. With a desperation that was madness, unmindful of the pain, he hurried up the slope to the crest of the hill over which his comrade had disappeared — more grotesque and comical by far than that limping, jerking comrade. But at the crest he saw a shallow valley, empty of life. He fought with his fear again, overcame it, hitched the pack still farther over on his left shoulder, and lurched on down the slope.

The bottom of the valley was soggy with water, which the thick moss held, spongelike, close to the surface. This water squirted out from under his feet at every step, and each time he lifted a foot the action culminated in a sucking sound as the wet moss reluctantly released its grip. He picked his way from muskeg to muskeg, and followed the other man's footsteps along and across the rocky ledges which thrust like islets through the sea of moss.

Though alone, he was not lost. Farther on, he knew, he would come to where dead spruce and fir, very small and wizened, bordered the shore of a little lake, the *titchin-nichilie,* in the tongue of the country, the 'land of little sticks'. And into that lake flowed a small stream, the water of which was not milky. There was rush grass on that stream — this he remembered well — but no timber, and he would follow it till its first trickle ceased at a divide. He would cross this divide to the first trickle of another stream, flowing to the west, which he would follow until it emptied into the river Dease, and here he would find a cache under an upturned canoe and piled over with many rocks. And in this cache would be ammunition for his empty gun, fishhooks and lines, a small net — all the utilities for the killing and snaring of food. Also he would find flour — not much — a piece of bacon, and some beans.

Bill would be waiting for him there, and they would paddle away south down the Dease to the Great Bear Lake. And south across the lake they would go, ever south, till they gained the Mackenzie. And south, still south, they would go, while the winter raced vainly after them, and the ice formed in the eddies, and the days grew chill and crisp, south to some warm Hudson's Bay Company post, where timber grew tall and generous and there was grub without end.

These were the thoughts of the man as he strove onward. But hard as he strove with his body, he strove equally hard with his mind, trying to think that Bill had not deserted him, that Bill would surely wait for him at the cache. He was compelled to think this thought, or else there would not be any use to strive, and he would have lain down and died. And as the dim ball of the sun sank slowly into the northwest he covered every inch — and many times — of his and Bill's flight south before the downcoming winter. And he conned the grub of the cache and the grub of the Hudson's Bay Company post over and over again. He had not eaten for two days, for a far longer time he had not had all he wanted to eat. Often he stooped and picked pale muskeg berries, put them into his mouth, and chewed and swallowed them. A muskeg berry is a bit of seed enclosed in a bit of water. In the mouth the water melts away and the seed chews sharp and bitter. The man knew there was no nourishment in the berries, but he chewed them patiently with a hope greater than knowledge and defying experience.

At nine o'clock he stubbed his toe on a rocky ledge, and from sheer weariness and weakness staggered and fell. He lay for some time, without movement, on his side. Then he slipped out of the pack straps and clumsily dragged himself into à sitting posture. It was not yet dark, and in the lingering twilight he groped about among the rocks for shreds of dry moss. When he had gathered a heap he built a fire — a smouldering, smudgy fire — and put a tin pot of water on to boil.

He unwrapped his pack and the first thing he did was to count his matches. There were sixty-seven. He counted them three times to make sure. He divided them into several portions, wrapping them in oil paper, disposing of one bunch in his empty tobacco pouch, of another bunch in the inside band of his battered hat, of a third bunch under his shirt on the chest. This accomplished, a panic came upon him, and he unwrapped them all and counted them again. There were still sixty-seven.

He dried his wet footgear by the fire. The moccasins were in soggy shreds. The blanket socks were worn through in places, and his feet were raw and bleeding. His ankle was throbbing, and he gave it an examination. It had swollen to the size of his knee. He tore a long strip from one of his two blankets and bound the ankle tightly. He tore other strips and bound them about his feet to serve for both moccasins and socks. Then he drank the pot of water, steaming hot, wound his watch, and crawled between his blankets.

He slept like a dead man. The brief darkness around midnight came and went. The sun arose in the northeast — at least the day dawned in that quarter, for the sun was hidden by grey clouds.

At six o'clock he awoke, quietly lying on his back. He gazed straight up into the grey sky and knew that he was hungry. As he rolled over on his elbow he was startled by a loud snort, and saw a bull caribou regarding him with alert curiosity. The animal was not more than fifty feet away, and instantly into the

man's mind leaped the vision and the savour of a caribou steak sizzling and frying over a fire. Mechanically he reached for the empty gun, drew a bead, and pulled the trigger. The bull snorted and leaped away, his hoofs rattling and clattering as he fled across the ledges.

The man cursed and flung the empty gun from him. He groaned aloud as he started to drag himself to his feet. It was a slow and arduous task. His joints were like rusty hinges. They worked harshly in their sockets, with much friction, and each bending or unbending was accomplished only through a sheer exertion of will. When he finally gained his feet, another minute or so was consumed in straightening up, so that he could stand erect as a man should stand.

He crawled up a small knoll and surveyed the prospect. There were no trees, no bushes, nothing but a great sea of moss scarcely diversified by grey rocks, grey lakelets, and grey streamlets. The sky was grey. There was no sun nor hint of sun. He had no idea of north, and he had forgotten the way he had come to this spot the night before. But he was not lost. He knew that. Soon he would come to the land of the little sticks. He felt that it lay off to the left somewhere, not far — possibly just over the next low hill.

He went back to put his pack into shape for travelling. He assured himself of the existence of his three separate parcels of matches, though he did not stop to count them. But he did linger, debating, over a squat moose-hide sack. It was not large. He could hide it under his two hands. He knew that it weighed fifteen pounds — as much as all the rest of the pack — and it worried him. He finally set it to one side and proceeded to roll the pack. He paused to gaze at the squat moose-hide sack. He picked it up hastily with a defiant glance about him, as though the desolation were trying to rob him of it; and when he rose to his feet to stagger on into the day, it was included in the pack on his back.

He bore away to his left, stopping now and again to eat muskeg berries. His ankle had stiffened, his limp was more pronounced, but the pain of it was as nothing compared with the pain of his stomach. The hunger pangs were sharp. They gnawed and gnawed until he could not keep his mind steady on the course he must pursue to gain the land of the little sticks. The muskeg berries did not allay this gnawing, while they made his tongue and the roof of his mouth sore with their irritating bite.

He came upon a valley where rock ptarmigan rose on whirring wings from the ledges and muskegs. *Ker — ker — ker* was the cry they made. He threw stones at them but could not hit them. He placed his pack on the ground and stalked them as a cat stalks a sparrow. The sharp rocks cut through his pants legs till his knees left a trail of blood; but the hurt was lost in the hurt of his hunger. He squirmed over the wet moss, saturating his clothes and chilling his body; but he was not aware of it, so great was his fever for food. And always the ptarmigan rose, whirring, before him, till their *ker — ker — ker* became a mock to him, and he cursed them and cried aloud at them with their own cry.

Once he crawled upon one that must have been asleep. He did not see it till it shot up in his face from its rocky nook. He made a clutch as startled as was the rise of the ptarmigan, and there remained in his hand three tail feathers. As he watched its flight he hated it, as though it had done him some terrible wrong. Then he returned and shouldered his pack.

As the day wore along he came into valleys or swales where game was more plentiful. A band of caribou passed by, twenty and odd animals, tantalizingly within rifle range. He felt a wild desire to run after them, a certitude that he could run them down. A black fox came towards him, carrying a ptarmigan in his mouth. The man shouted. It was a fearful cry, but the fox, leaping away in fright, did not drop the ptarmigan.

Late in the afternoon he followed a stream, milky with lime, which ran through sparse patches of rush grass. Grasping these rushes firmly near the root, he pulled up what resembled a young onion sprout no larger than a shingle nail. It was tender, and his teeth sank into it with a crunch that promised deliciously of food. But its fibres were tough. It was composed of stringy filaments saturated with water, like the berries, and devoid of nourishment. He threw off his pack and went into the rush grass on hands and knees, crunching and munching, like some bovine creature.

He was very weary and often wished to rest — to lie down and sleep; but he was continually driven on, not so much by his desire to gain the land of little sticks as by his hunger. He searched little ponds for frogs and dug up the earth with his nails for worms, though he knew in spite that neither frogs nor worms existed so far north.

He looked into every pool of water vainly, until, as the long twilight came on, he discovered a solitary fish, the size of a minnow, in such a pool. He plunged his

15

arm in up to the shoulder, but it eluded him. He reached for it with both hands and stirred up the milky mud at the bottom. In his excitement he fell in, wetting himself to the waist. Then the water was too muddy to admit of his seeing the fish, and he was compelled to wait until the sediment had settled.

The pursuit was renewed, till the water was again muddied. But he could not wait. He unstrapped the tin bucket and began to bail the pool. He bailed wildly at first, splashing himself and flinging the water so short a distance that it ran back into the pool. He worked more carefully, striving to be cool, though his heart was pounding against his chest and his hands were trembling. At the end of half an hour the pool was nearly dry. Not a cupful of water remained. And there was no fish. He found a hidden crevice among the stones through which it had escaped to the adjoining and larger pool — a pool which he could not empty in a night and a day. Had he known of the crevice, he could have closed it with a rock at the beginning and the fish would have been his.

Thus he thought, and crumpled up and sank down upon the wet earth. At first he cried softly to himself, then he cried loudly to the pitiless desolation that ringed him around; and for a long time after he was shaken by great dry sobs.

He built a fire and warmed himself by drinking quarts of hot water, and made camp on a rocky ledge in the same fashion he had the night before. The last thing he did was to see that his matches were dry and to wind his watch. The blankets were wet and clammy. His ankle pulsed with pain. But he knew only that he was hungry, and through his restless sleep he dreamed of feasts and banquets and of food served and spread in all imaginable ways.

He awoke chilled and sick. There was no sun. The grey of earth and sky had become deeper, more profound. A raw wind was blowing, and the first flurries of snow were whitening the hilltops. The air about him thickened and grew white while he made a fire and boiled more water. It was wet snow, half rain, and the flakes were large and soggy. At first they melted as soon as they came in contact with the earth, but ever more fell, covering the ground, putting out the fire, spoiling his supply of moss fuel.

This was a signal for him to strap on his pack and stumble onward, he knew not where. He was not concerned with the land of little sticks, nor with Bill and the cache under the upturned canoe by the river Dease. He was mastered by the verb *to eat*. He was hunger mad. He took no heed of the course he pursued, so long as that course led him through the swale bottoms. He felt his way through the wet snow to the watery muskeg berries, and went by feel as he pulled up the rush-grass by the roots. But it was tasteless stuff and did not satisfy. He found a weed that tasted sour and he ate all he could find of it, which was not much, for it was a creeping growth, easily hidden under the several inches of snow.

He had no fire that night, nor hot water, and crawled under his blanket to sleep the broken hunger sleep. The snow turned into a cold rain. He awakened many times to feel it falling on his upturned face. Day came — a grey day and no sun. It had ceased raining. The keenness of his hunger had departed. Sensibility, as far as concerned the yearning for food, had been exhausted. There was a dull, heavy ache in his stomach, but it did not bother him so much. He was more rational, and once more he was chiefly interested in the land of little sticks and the cache by the river Dease.

He ripped the remnant of one of his blankets into strips and bound his bleeding feet. Also he recinched the injured ankle and prepared himself for a day of travel. When he came to his pack he paused long over the squat moose-hide sack, but in the end it went with him.

The snow had melted under the rain, and only the hilltops showed white. The sun came out, and he succeeded in locating the points of the compass, though he knew now that he was lost. Perhaps, in his previous days' wanderings, he had edged away too far to the left. He now bore off to the right to counteract the possible deviation from his true course.

Though the hunger pangs were no longer so exquisite, he realized that he was weak. He was compelled to pause for frequent rests, when he attacked the muskeg berries and rush-grass patches. His tongue felt dry and large, as though covered with a fine hairy growth, and it tasted bitter in his mouth. His heart gave him a great deal of trouble. When he had travelled a few minutes it would begin a remorseless thump, thump, thump, and then leap up and away in a painful flutter of beats that choked him and made him go faint and dizzy.

In the middle of the day he found two minnows in a large pool. It was impossible to bail it, but he was calmer now and managed to catch them in his tin bucket. They were no longer than his little finger, but he was not particularly hungry. The dull ache in his stomach had been growing duller and fainter. It seemed almost that his stomach was dozing. He ate the fish raw, masticating

17

with painstaking care, for the eating was an act of pure reason. While he had no desire to eat, he knew that he must eat to live.

In the evening he caught three more minnows, eating two and saving the third for breakfast. The sun had dried stray shreds of moss, and he was able to warm himself with hot water. He had not covered more than ten miles that day; and the next day, travelling whenever his heart permitted him, he covered no more than five miles. But his stomach did not give him the slightest uneasiness. It had gone to sleep. He was in a strange country, too, and the caribou were growing more plentiful, also the wolves. Often their yelps drifted across the desolation, and once he saw three of them slinking away before his path.

Another night; and in the morning, being more rational, he untied the leather string that fastened the squat moose-hide sack. From its open mouth poured a yellow stream of coarse gold dust and nuggets. He roughly divided the gold in halves, caching one half on a prominent ledge, wrapped in a piece of blanket, and returning the other half to the sack. He also began to use strips of the one remaining blanket for his feet. He still clung to his gun, for there were cartridges in that cache by the river Dease.

This was a day of fog, and this day hunger awoke in him again. He was very weak and was afflicted with a giddiness which at times blinded him. It was no uncommon thing now for him to stumble and fall; and stumbling once, he fell squarely into a ptarmigan nest. There were four newly hatched chicks, a day old — little specks of pulsating life no more than a mouthful; and he ate them ravenously, thrusting them alive into his mouth and crunching them like eggshells between his teeth. The mother ptarmigan beat about him with great outcry. He used his gun as a club with which to knock her over, but she dodged out of reach. He threw stones at her and with one chance shot broke a wing. Then she fluttered away, running, trailing the broken wing, with him in pursuit.

The little chicks had no more than whetted his appetite. He hopped and bobbed clumsily along on his injured ankle, throwing stones and screaming hoarsely at times; at other times hopping and bobbing silently along, picking himself up grimly and patiently when he fell, or rubbing his eyes with his hand when the giddiness threatened to overpower him.

The chase led him across swampy ground in the bottom of the valley, and he

came upon footprints in the soggy moss. They were not his own — he could see that. They must be Bill's. But he could not stop, for the mother ptarmigan was running on. He would catch her first, then he would return and investigate.

He exhausted the mother ptarmigan; but he exhausted himself. She lay panting on her side. He lay panting on his side, a dozen feet away, unable to crawl to her. And as he recovered she recovered, fluttering out of reach as his hungry hand went out to her. The chase was resumed. Night settled down and she escaped. He stumbled from weakness and pitched head foremost on his face, cutting his cheek, his pack upon his back. He did not move for a long while; then he rolled over on his side, wound his watch, and lay there until morning.

Another day of fog. Half of his last blanket had gone into foot-wrappings. He failed to pick up Bill's trail. It did not matter. His hunger was driving him too compellingly — only — only he wondered if Bill, too, were lost. By midday the irk of his pack became too oppressive. Again he divided the gold, this time merely spilling half of it on the ground. In the afternoon he threw the rest of it away, there remaining to him only the half blanket, the tin bucket, and the rifle.

A hallucination began to trouble him. He felt confident that one cartridge remained to him. It was in the chamber of the rifle and he had overlooked it. On the other hand, he knew all the time that the chamber was empty. But the hallucination persisted. He fought it off for hours, then threw his rifle open and was confronted with emptiness. The disappointment was as bitter as though he had really expected to find the cartridge.

He plodded on for half an hour, when the hallucination arose again. Again he fought it, and still it persisted, till for very relief he opened his rifle to unconvince himself. At times his mind wandered farther afield, and he plodded on, a mere automaton, strange conceits and whimsicalities gnawing at his brain like worms. But these excursions out of the real were of brief duration, for ever the pangs of the hunger bite called him back. He was jerked back abruptly once from such an excursion by a sight that caused him nearly to faint. He reeled and swayed, doddering like a drunken man to keep from falling. Before him stood a horse. A horse! He could not believe his eyes. A thick mist was in them, intershot with sparkling points of light. He rubbed his eyes savagely to clear his vision, and beheld not a horse but a great brown bear. The animal was studying him with bellicose curiosity.

The man had brought his gun halfway to his shoulder before he realized. He lowered it and drew his hunting knife from its beaded sheath at his hip. Before him was meat and life. He ran his thumb along the edge of his knife. It was sharp. The point was sharp. He would fling himself upon the bear and kill it. But his heart began its warning thump, thump, thump. Then followed the wild upward leap and tattoo of flutters, the pressing as of an iron band about his forehead, the creeping of the dizziness into his brain.

His desperate courage was evicted by a great surge of fear. In his weakness, what if the animal attacked him? He drew himself up to his most imposing stature, gripping the knife and staring hard at the bear. The bear advanced clumsily a couple of steps, reared up, and gave vent to a tentative growl. If the man ran, he would run after him; but the man did not run. He was animated now with the courage of fear. He, too, growled, savagely, terribly, voicing the fear that is to life germane and that lies twisted about life's deepest roots.

The bear edged away to one side, growling menacingly, himself appalled by this mysterious creature that appeared upright and unafraid. But the man did not move. He stood like a statue till the danger was past, when he yielded to a fit of trembling and sank down into the wet moss.

He pulled himself together and went on, afraid now in a new way. It was not the fear that he should die passively from lack of food, but that he should be destroyed violently before starvation had exhausted the last particle of the endeavour in him that made towards surviving. There were the wolves. Back and forth across the desolation drifted their howls, weaving the very air into a fabric of menace that was so tangible that he found himself, arms in the air, pressing it back from him as it might be the walls of a wind-blown tent.

Now and again the wolves, in packs of two and three, crossed his path. But they sheered clear of him. They were not in sufficient numbers, and besides, they were hunting the caribou, which did not battle, while this strange creature that walked erect might scratch and bite.

In the late afternoon he came upon scattered bones where the wolves had made a kill. The debris had been a caribou calf an hour before, squawking and running and very much alive. He contemplated the bones, clean-picked and polished, pink with the cell life in them which had not yet died. Could it possibly be that he might be that ere the day was done! Such was life, eh? A vain and fleeting thing. It was only life that pained. There was no hurt in death. To die was to sleep. It meant cessation, rest. Then why was he not content to die?

But he did not moralize long. He was squatting in the moss, a bone in his mouth, sucking at the shreds of life that still dyed it faintly pink. The sweet meaty taste, thin and elusive almost as a memory, maddened him. He closed his jaws on the bones and crunched. Sometimes it was the bone that broke, sometimes his teeth. Then he crushed the bones between rocks, pounding them to a pulp, and swallowed them. He pounded his fingers, too, in his haste, and yet found a moment in which to feel surprise at the fact that his fingers did not hurt much when caught under the descending rock.

Came frightful days of snow and rain. He did not know when he made camp, when he broke camp. He travelled in the night as much as in the day. He rested wherever he fell, crawled on whenever the dying life in him flickered up and burned less dimly. He, as a man, no longer strove. It was the life in him, unwilling to die, that drove him on. He did not suffer. His nerves had become blunted, numb, while his mind was filled with weird visions and delicious dreams.

But ever he sucked and chewed on the crushed bones of the caribou calf, the least remnants of which he had gathered up and carried with him. He crossed no more hills or divides, but automatically followed a large stream which flowed through a wide and shallow valley. He did not see this stream nor this valley. He saw nothing save visions. Soul and body walked or crawled side by side, yet apart, so slender was the thread that bound them.

He awoke in his right mind, lying on his back on a rocky ledge. The sun was shining bright and warm. Afar off he heard the squawking of caribou calves. He was aware of vague memories of rain and wind and snow, but whether he had been beaten by the storm for two days or two weeks he did not know.

For some time he lay without movement, the genial sunshine pouring upon him and saturating his miserable body with its warmth. A fine day, he thought. Perhaps he could manage to locate himself. By a painful effort he rolled over on his side. Below him flowed a wide and sluggish river. Its unfamiliarity puzzled him. Slowly he followed it with his eyes, winding in wide sweeps among the bleak, bare hills, bleaker and barer and lower-lying than any hills he had yet encountered. Slowly, deliberately, without excitement or more than the most casual interest, he followed the course of the strange stream towards the sky line and saw it emptying into a bright and shining sea. He was still unexcited. Most unusual, he thought, a vision or a mirage — more likely a vision, a trick of his disordered mind. He was confirmed in this by sight of a ship lying at anchor in the midst of the shining sea. He closed his eyes for a while, then opened them. Strange how the vision persisted! Yet not strange. He knew there were no seas or ships in the heart of the barren lands, just as he had known there was no cartridge in the empty rifle.

He heard a snuffle behind him — a half-choking gasp or cough. Very slowly, because of his exceeding weakness and stiffness, he rolled over on his other side. He could see nothing near at hand, but he waited patiently. Again came the snuffle and cough, and outlined between two jagged rocks not a score of feet away he made out the grey head of a wolf. The sharp ears were not pricked so sharply as he had seen them on other wolves; the eyes were bleared and bloodshot, the head seemed to droop limply and forlornly. The animal blinked continually in the sunshine. It seemed sick. As he looked it snuffled and coughed again.

This, at least, was real, he thought, and turned on the other side so that he might see the reality of the world which had been veiled from him before by the vision. But the sea still shone in the distance and the ship was plainly discernible. Was it reality after all? He closed his eyes for a long while and thought, and then it came to him. He had been making north by east, away from the Dease Divide and into the Coppermine Valley. This wide and sluggish river was the Coppermine. That shining sea was the Arctic Ocean. That ship was a whaler, strayed east, far east, from the mouth of the Mackenzie, and it was lying at anchor in Coronation Gulf. He remembered the Hudson's Bay Company chart he had seen long ago, and it was all clear and reasonable to him.

He sat up and turned his attention to immediate affairs. He had worn through the blanket wrappings, and his feet were shapeless lumps of raw meat. His last blanket was gone. Rifle and knife were both missing. He had lost his hat somewhere, with the bunch of matches in the band, but the matches against his chest were safe and dry inside the tobacco pouch and oil paper. He looked at his watch. It marked eleven o'clock and was still running. Evidently he had kept it wound.

He was calm and collected. Though extremely weak, he had no sensation of pain. He was not hungry. The thought of food was not even pleasant to him, and whatever he did was done by his reason alone. He ripped off his pants legs to the knees and bound them about his feet. Somehow he had succeeded in retaining the tin bucket. He would have some hot water before he began what he foresaw was to be a terrible journey to the ship.

His movements were slow. He shook as with a palsy. When he started to collect dry moss he found he could not rise to his feet. He tried again and again, then contented himself with crawling about on hands and knees. Once he crawled near to the sick wolf. The animal dragged itself reluctantly out of his way, licking its chops with a tongue which seemed hardly to have the strength to curl. The man noticed that the tongue was not the customary healthy red. It was a yellowish brown and seemed coated with a rough and half-dry mucus.

After he had drunk a quart of hot water the man found he was able to stand, and even to walk as well as a dying man might be supposed to walk. Every minute or so he was compelled to rest. His steps were feeble and uncertain, just

24

as the wolf's that trailed him were feeble and uncertain; and that night, when the shining sea was blotted out by blackness, he knew he was nearer to it by no more than four miles.

Throughout the night he heard the cough of the sick wolf, and now and then the squawking of the caribou calves. There was life all around him, but it was strong life, very much alive and well, and he knew the sick wolf clung to the sick man's trail in the hope that the man would die first. In the morning, on opening his eyes, he beheld it regarding him with a wistful and hungry stare. It stood crouched, with tail between its legs, like a miserable and woebegone dog. It shivered in the chill morning wind and grinned dispiritedly when the man spoke to it in a voice that achieved no more than a hoarse whisper.

The sun rose brightly, and all morning the man tottered and fell toward the ship on the shining sea. The weather was perfect. It was the brief Indian summer of the high latitudes. It might last a week. Tomorrow or next day it might be gone.

In the afternoon the man came upon a trail. It was of another man, who did not walk, but who dragged himself on all fours. The man thought it might be Bill, but he thought in a dull, uninterested way. He had no curiosity. In fact

sensation and emotion had left him. He was no longer susceptible to pain. Stomach and nerves had gone to sleep. Yet the life that was in him drove him on. He was very weary, but it refused to die. It was because it refused to die that he still ate muskeg berries and minnows, drank his hot water, and kept a wary eye on the sick wolf.

He followed the trail of the other man who dragged himself along, and soon came to the end of it — a few fresh-picked bones where the soggy moss was marked by the foot pads of many wolves. He saw a squat moose-hide sack, mate to his own, which had been torn by sharp teeth. He picked it up, though its weight was almost too much for his feeble fingers. Bill had carried it to the last. Ha-ha! He would have the laugh on Bill. He would survive and carry it to the ship in the shining sea. His mirth was hoarse and ghastly, like a raven's croak, and the sick wolf joined him, howling lugubriously. The man ceased suddenly. How could he have the laugh on Bill if that were Bill; if those bones, so pinky-white and clean, were Bill?

He turned away. Well, Bill had deserted him; but he would not take the gold, nor would he suck Bill's bones. Bill would have, though, had it been the other way around, he mused as he staggered on.

He came to a pool of water. Stooping over in quest of minnows, he jerked his head back as though he had been stung. He had caught sight of his reflected face. So horrible was it that sensibility awoke long enough to be shocked. There were three minnows in the pool, which was too large to drain; and after several ineffectual attempts to catch them in the tin bucket he forbore. He was afraid, because of his great weakness, that he might fall in and drown. It was for this reason that he did not trust himself to the river astride one of the many drift logs which lined its sandspits.

That day he decreased the distance between him and the ship by three miles; the next day by two — for he was crawling now as Bill had crawled; and the end of the fifth day found the ship still seven miles away and him unable to make even a mile a day. Still the Indian summer held on, and he continued to crawl and faint, turn and turn about; and ever the sick wolf coughed and wheezed at his heels. His knees had become raw meat like his feet, and though he padded them with the shirt from his back it was a red track he left behind him on the moss and stones. Once, glancing back, he saw the wolf licking hungrily his bleeding trail, and he saw sharply what his own end might be — unless —unless he could get the wolf. Then began as grim a tragedy of existence as was ever played — a sick man that crawled, a sick wolf that limped, two creatures dragging their dying carcasses across the desolation and hunting each other.

Had it been a well wolf, it would not have mattered so much to the man; but the thought of going to feed the maw of that loathsome and all but dead thing was repugnant to him. He was finicky. His mind had begun to wander again and to be perplexed by hallucinations, while his lucid intervals grew rarer.

He was awakened once from a faint by a wheeze close in his ear. The wolf leaped lamely back, losing its footing and falling in its weakness. It was ludicrous, but he was not amused. Nor was he even afraid. He was too far gone for that. But his mind was for the moment clear, and he lay and considered. The ship was no more than four miles away. He could see it quite distinctly when he rubbed the mists out of his eyes, and he could see the white sail of a small boat cutting the water of the shining sea. But he could never crawl those four miles. He knew that, and was very calm in the knowledge. He knew that he could not crawl half a mile. And yet he wanted to live. It was unreasonable that he should die after all he had undergone. Fate asked too much of him. And, dying, he declined to die. It was stark madness, perhaps, but in the very grip of death he defied death and refused to die.

He closed his eyes and composed himself with infinite precaution. He steeled himself to keep above the suffocating languor that lapped like a rising tide through all the wells of his being. It was very like a sea, this deadly languor that rose and rose and drowned his consciousness bit by bit. Sometimes he was all but submerged, swimming through oblivion with a faltering stroke; and again, by some strange alchemy of soul, he would find another shred of will and strike out more strongly.

Without movement he lay on his back, and he could hear, slowly drawing near and nearer, the wheezing intake and output of the sick wolf's breath. It drew closer, ever closer, through an infinitude of time, and he did not move. It was at his ear. The harsh dry tongue grated like sandpaper against his cheek. His hands shot out — or at least he willed them to shoot out. The fingers were curved like talons, but they closed on empty air. Swiftness and certitude require strength, and the man had not this strength.

The patience of the wolf was terrible. The man's patience was no less terrible. For half a day he lay motionless, fighting off unconsciousness and waiting for the thing that was to feed upon him and upon which he wished to feed. Sometimes the languid sea rose over him and he dreamed long dreams; but ever through it all, waking and dreaming, he waited for the wheezing breath and the harsh caress of the tongue.

He did not hear the breath, and he slipped slowly from some dream to the feel of the tongue along his hand. He waited. The fangs pressed softly; the pressure increased; the wolf was exerting its last strength in an effort to sink teeth in the food for which it had waited so long. But the man had waited long, and the lacerated hand closed on the jaw. Slowly, while the wolf struggled feebly and the hand clutched feebly, the other hand crept across to a grip. Five minutes later the whole weight of the man's body was on top of the wolf. The hands had not sufficient strength to choke the wolf, but the face of the man was pressed close to the throat of the wolf and the mouth of the man was full of hair. At the end of half an hour the man was aware of a warm trickle in his throat. It was not pleasant. It was like molten lead being forced into his stomach, and it was forced by his will alone. Later the man rolled over on his back and slept.

There were some members of a scientific expedition on the whale ship *Bedford*. From the deck they remarked a strange object on the shore. It was moving down the beach toward the water. They were unable to classify it, and, being scientific men, they climbed into the whaleboat alongside and went ashore to see. And they saw something that was alive but which could hardly be called a man. It was blind, unconscious. It squirmed along the ground like some monstrous worm. Most of its efforts were ineffectual, but it was persistent, and it writhed and twisted and went ahead perhaps a score of feet an hour.

Three weeks afterwards the man lay in a bunk on the whale ship *Bedford*, and with tears streaming down his wasted cheeks told who he was and what he had undergone. He also babbled incoherently of his mother, of sunny southern California, and a home among the orange groves and flowers.

The days were not many after that when he sat at table with the scientific men and ship's officers. He gloated over the spectacle of so much food, watching it anxiously as it went into the mouths of others. With the disappearance of each mouthful an expression of deep regret came into his eyes. He was quite sane, yet he hated those men at mealtime. He was haunted by a fear that the food would not last. He inquired of the cook, the cabin boy, the captain, concerning the food stores. They reassured him countless times; but he could not believe them, and pried cunningly about the lazaret to see with his own eyes.

It was noticed that the man was getting fat. He grew stouter with each day. The scientific men shook their heads and theorized. They limited the man at his meals, but still his girth increased and he swelled prodigiously under his shirt.

The sailors grinned. They knew. And when the scientific men set a watch on the man they knew. They saw him slouch for'ard after breakfast, and, like a mendicant, with outstretched palm, accost a sailor. The sailor grinned and

passed him a fragment of sea biscuit. He clutched it avariciously, looked at it as a miser looks at gold, and thrust it into his shirt bosom. Similar were the donations from other grinning sailors.

The scientific men were discreet. They let him alone. But they privily examined his bunk. It was lined with hardtack; the mattress was stuffed with hardtack; every nook and cranny was filled with hardtack. Yet he was sane. He was taking precautions against another possible famine — that was all. He would recover from it, the scientific men said; and he did, ere the *Bedford's* anchor rumbled down in San Francisco Bay.

MATTHEW SANDORF

JULES VERNE

The Prison above the Abyss

Pisino Castle is one of the most remarkable of medieval buildings. It is as picturesque from without as it is within. Its long, vaulted halls were once the meeting-place of knights in armour, who would gaze from their gothic windows at the ladies of the court in their brocaded gowns and lace caps. On the towers and battlements and beyond the drawbridge, archers and crossbowmen would stand at the ready. The stonework stood as it had in the Middle Ages, but the brightly coloured costumes of that era had given way to the sober blue uniforms of the Austrian army.

It was from the watchtower of this castle that Count Matthew Sandorf and his friends intended to escape in the last hours before their execution. The attempt was a bold one, almost foolhardy, for the condemned men did not even know where they were.

Perhaps it was just as well they did not. Had they known more about the situation of the castle, the difficulty, not to say impossibility, of escape from their tower prison would surely have undermined their resolve. Not that the lie of the land was unfavourable, for a fugitive must soon reach the coast, whichever way he turned his steps. Nor were the streets of Pisino so closely guarded as to prevent an escaped prisoner from passing through the town. But to escape from the tower in which Matthew Sandorf was held had always been considered impossible, and it had never even occurred to anyone that a prisoner might accomplish such a feat.

How, then, was the tower situated?

The castle is built on a headland, which comes to an abrupt end in that place. It looks down on a deep abyss, whose walls are completely vertical, and covered with climbing plants. The precipice is quite uninterrupted. There is not the tiniest ledge on which to rest one's foot, nor the merest crevice in which to place a hand. In short, it is a chasm which induces vertigo, and promises never to return what it has once swallowed.

This chasm — the local folk call it Buco — forms a sort of small reservoir for the waters of a stream known as Foiba. From it the water flows through an underground tunnel which the stream has bored through the cliff. No one knows the route it takes beneath the town. Nor had anyone ever found out where its waters gushed out again into the light of day. None could tell either the length or the height of this channel, which it had taken the stream thousands of years to cut through the solid rock. No one knows whether the waters do not lap against a thousand underground pillars, supporting the headland and the whole town

with it. Once, long ago, a group of bold adventurers tried to follow the stream's course in a small boat, but the roof of the passage became so low that they had to turn back, and it remained a mystery whether the water might flow into the sea in some invisible spot far below the surface.

Such, then, was the abyss which yawned beneath the castle tower — and Count Sandorf had no notion of it. But since the only window through which the condemned men could make good their escape overlooked the chasm, their flight meant certain death, just as if they had stood before the firing squad which was to carry out their sentence the next morning.

Count Ladislas Zathmar and Stephen Bathory were now waiting only for the right moment to accomplish the deed. They were willing to remain prisoners, if that would have facilitated Sandorf's escape, but it had been decided that they would accompany him, since it would in no way hamper the count in his flight.

'We shall flee together,' Sandorf had said. 'But as soon as we are free, each shall go his own way.'

From the town below they heard a clock strike eight. They had only another twelve hours to live.

Darkness fell. And what a darkness it was. Black and heavy, motionless clouds obscured the sky. A violent storm was gathering. There was no lightning as yet, but the dull rolling of thunder could be heard from somewhere beyond the mountains.

These conditions would have offered some hope of a successful escape, had not the gaping chasm awaited them below. The dark night and the din of the storm provided ideal cover for their flight.

Count Sandorf realized at once that the only escape lay through the window of the cell. To break open the heavy oaken door was unthinkable, quite apart from the guard, whose footsteps the prisoners could constantly hear outside. And even if they were to overcome these obstacles, how were they to make their way out of a completely strange building? And how would they get past the sentries? On the side of the abyss there were no sentries, for this natural barrier was more effective than a whole troop of soldiers. But Count Sandorf was not to know this, as he planned his escape.

The window was ninety centimetres high and sixty wide. On the outside of the wall, which was very thick, the opening was somewhat broader. It was covered by a stout iron grille, sunk into the walls. It had no wooden ledge, nor was any required, since the window was sunk in such a way that the chasm beneath could not be seen from it. Thus, if the grille were removed, it would be a simple matter to crawl through the hole, which looked more like a loop-hole than a window.

And how were the prisoners to descend a vertical wall if they did get out? There was nothing from which they could make a rope ladder. The escape seemed impossible. But then the count noticed a steel cable stretched across the wall close to the window. It was the wire of the lightning conductor, which led down the side of the tower nearest the gorge. 'See that cable,' the count told his friends. 'With a little courage, it shall help us to escape.'

'We have the courage,' replied Count Zathmar, 'but do we have the strength?'

'What difference does it make?' interjected Bathory. 'If our strength fails, then we shall merely die a few hours sooner. That is the worst that can happen.'

'There is no need for us to die,' replied Count Sandorf. 'Listen to my plan. If we had a rope, we should certainly not hesitate to throw it from the window and climb down it. But that cable is better than a rope, for it will not twist or sway. It will be a simple matter to climb down it, for it is certainly attached to the wall with iron pegs, which will support our legs. We need not fear vertigo, since it is dark, and we shall see nothing beneath us. The window invites us to freedom; all that is required is a little courage and cold blood, and we shall escape. I do not deny that we are risking our lives, but we have no choice. Certain death awaits us here.'

'Let it be so,' said Count Zathmar.

'But what is at the end of the cable?' asked Stephen Bathory.

'Probably some well; but it is certainly beyond the tower, and that is all we ask,' Sandorf replied. 'All I know now is that our liberty awaits us at the end of that cable.'

Count Matthew Sandorf was right in thinking that the cable was attached to the wall with pegs, which made their task easier. What the prisoners did not know, was that the lightning conductor was no longer fixed from the lip of the gorge, but swung freely against the rock. Nor did they know that the end of it plunged into the vicious waves of the Foiba, swollen by the recent rains. They were unaware that, where they expected to find solid earth, there was in fact a savage rush of water and fierce eddies, or that the wild waters plunged headlong into the ground. Would they have abandoned their escape, had they known all this, or what a tiny chance they had of succeeding? Indeed, no!

'What does it matter how we meet our deaths?' said Sandorf. 'Let us die, if must be: but first we shall try to win our freedom.'

But first they must get through the window. They would have to wrench away the grille. But how were they to do that without chisel, lever, or other implement?

'I do not suppose we shall succeed,' said Matthew Sandorf, 'but we shall try, for the rest is easy.'

Having spoken these words, Sandorf climbed up to the window and took hold of the bars. He soon realized that it would require no great effort to wrench out the grille, for the iron bars were loosened in the stonework. Maybe this was the work of time, or perhaps a discharge from the lightning conductor had jumped onto the grille.

It would be enough to free the ends of the bars by picking away at the spongy masonry which surrounded them; then they could simply force the grille from its anchorages and send it hurtling down from the tower. No one would hear it fall amid the roar of the thunder, which was now almost continuous.

'But we cannot do it with our hands,' pointed out Count Zathmar.

'Indeed not,' Sandorf replied. 'We must find a piece of metal, a chisel or something like it.'

Their fingers were truly not enough to dig out the masonry. A simple nail would probably have sufficed, but some piece of metal was needed.

Matthew Sandorf felt around the walls of the cell to see whether there might be any nail driven into one of them. He found nothing.

Then it occurred to him that it might be possible to break off a leg from one of the iron beds. They all began to examine their beds, and Stephen Bathory was soon calling them to him.

One of the tie-rods which joined together the bars of his bed had given way. It would be enough to take hold of the end of the bar and bend it back and forth, and it would break off.

Soon they had done this, and Count Sandorf had in his hands a good-sized piece of iron, some fifteen centimetres long and about three centimetres wide. He wound a scarf round it at one end to protect his hands, then swung himself up to the window and began to chip and scrape away at the stone.

He was making a good deal of noise, but it was drowned by the din of thunder. Whenever the latter died down, Sandorf would leave off for a moment, only to continue with renewed vigour when the thunder began to roll again.

Stephen Bathory and Ladislas Zathmar were listening at the door, in order to warn Sandorf of the guard's approach.

'Pssst!' hissed Zathmar suddenly.

Sandorf interrupted his work at once.

'What is it?' asked Stephen Bathory.

'Listen!' Zathmar told them.

He moved towards the focal point of the vaulting, where they had overheard the words which brought to their attention their betrayal. Again they could hear snatches of a conversation:

'Tomorrow...released...freedom...'

'Yes...as soon...'

'...meet Zirone in Sicily...is to wait for me there...'

'You weren't here long...'

It seemed that Sarcany was speaking to someone who was probably a police official. He mentioned the name Zirone, another of the traitors. For this reason Matthew Sandorf took good note of it.

Unfortunately, the following words, undoubtedly giving the name of the town where the two adventurers were to meet, did not reach the prisoners' ears. Towards the end of the last sentence there was a deafening clap of thunder, and an electric current shot along the lightning conductor.

Nor did they hear the name of the town in which they were prisoners. This would have been a help to them, for they would then have known the best direction to take in order for their flight to be successful.

Count Sandorf set to work again. In three places the stonework was broken enough to prise the bars out. The count worked away at a fourth end, as the lightning criss-crossed outside.

At half-past ten the work was finished. The grille could be forced out of the window. It was enough to strike it a hard blow, and it would fall out. This they did, as soon as Count Zathmar had ensured that the sentry was at the other end of the passage.

The iron bars tumbled down into the darkness.

Just at that moment, the thunder held off. Count Sandorf listened carefully to see if he could hear the grille strike the ground, but he heard nothing.

'The tower is probably built on a high rock overlooking a valley,' said Stephen Bathory.

'The height does not matter,' said Sandorf, 'for if it is to serve its purpose, the lightning conductor must reach to the ground. So we shall also reach the ground. We need have no fear of falling.'

The logic of his words was sound enough, but incomplete, since in this case the cable of the lightning conductor ended in the waves of the Foiba.

The window was passable. The moment of escape had come.

'Friends, we shall proceed as follows,' decided Sandorf. 'I am the youngest and, I think, the strongest. I shall therefore go first. If I come upon some insurmountable obstacle, and cannot reach the ground, I shall climb back up, provided my strength suffices. Stephen will follow two minutes after me, then in another two minutes you will go, Ladislas. We shall meet at the foot of the tower.'

'We shall do as you have decided, Matthew, but we do not want you to have the most dangerous task,' objected Stephen Bathory.

'My life is less precious than yours,' offered Zathmar.

'All our lives are of equal worth in the face of the righteous task we have before us,' replied Matthew Sandorf. 'Whoever survives shall mete out justice to the traitors. Let us embrace, my friends.'

They threw their arms about each other, which seemed to lend strength to their courage. Count Zathmar returned to his post by the door, while Sandorf squirmed through the window.

Soon he was dangling over the abyss. Closing his knees tightly and clutching the cable, with one foot he felt for a peg, in order to gain a moment's rest.

The storm raged full force. It was not raining, but a strong wind was blowing and flash after flash of lightning pierced the darkness. They criss-crossed above the tower, whose great height and isolated position drew them towards it. The point of the lightning conductor was enveloped in pale light, and the cable shook violently in the gusting wind.

It is easy enough to imagine the perils of hanging from a cable constantly charged with electricity. Provided the lightning conductor was in good condition, there was no fear of the lightning killing a man, since the fact of the metal's much higher conductivity in comparison with that of the human body would necessarily preserve him from a fatal discharge. But should the cable be poorly earthed, the bold fugitive was in mortal danger even if the lightning did not strike the conductor direct. The electricity accumulated in the cable would suffice.

Count Sandorf was well aware of the danger which threatened him. But the desire for revenge was stronger than the fear of death. Slowly and carefully, he descended. His feet groped gingerly for the support of the pegs, and whenever a streak of lightning lit up the gorge Sandorf tried in vain to judge its depth.

When he had climbed down some eighteen metres, his feet suddenly came to rest on a firmer base. It was some sort of ledge, jutting out a few centimetres from the stonework.

But it was not the end of the cable, which continued downwards, and from this point on — though Count Sandorf was not to know it — was no longer attached to the wall, but swung freely beside the cliff face, touching only an occasional projection from the side of the abyss.

Sandorf paused for a moment on the ledge to recover his breath. He rested both his feet on it and kept hold of the cable with his hands. Now he realized that he was standing on the foundations of the tower. He was, however, unable to perceive the distance to the foot of the cliff.

'It must be quite a drop,' he thought to himself.

Some large birds, scared by the lightning's brilliance, were flying about beneath him; they did not, however, rise into the air, but glided down into the darkness below him. This told the count that a deep gorge yawned beneath his feet.

Just then he heard a faint sound somewhere above his head. The next flash revealed a dark form beside the window.

It was Stephen Bathory, setting out to make the dangerous descent. Taking the cable in his hands, he climbed down slowly towards his companion. Sandorf waited for him, his feet firmly planted on the ledge. There Stephen Bathory would have to wait until the other set off.

In a few moments the two friends were standing side by side.

As soon as the din of the thunder had died away they were able to speak.

'What of Ladislas?' Sandorf asked.

'He will join us presently,' replied Bathory.

'Is all well?'

'All is well.'

'I shall make room for him here, and you, Stephen, shall wait for him.'

'Very well.'

Just then there was another flash of lightning. It felt as if the electricity penetrated to their very marrow.

'Matthew! Matthew!' cried Bathory, unable to control his fear.

'Keep your head... I shall climb down, and you follow me in a little while!'

Matthew Sandorf took hold of the cable more firmly, intending to descend to the nearest peg and to wait there until Zathmar arrived.

Then the sound of voices reached them from above. They were coming from the window of the cell they had just left. Now they heard quite clearly: 'Flee for your lives!'

It was Zathmar's voice.

At the same time a tongue of fire shot along the wall, followed by a sharp report without echo.

This time it was neither the zigzag of a lightning flash, nor the clap of thunder. Someone had fired a shot from the window of the tower. Whether it was merely a signal that some prisoners had escaped, or was aimed at the fugitives, it was clear that their flight was discovered.

The sentry in the corridor had heard suspicious noises from the cell and given the alarm. Half a dozen men burst into the cell, realizing immediately that two of the prisoners were missing. The window clearly indicated their escape route. Before they could stop him, Ladislas Zathmar had thrust his head out of the window to shout a warning to his friends.

'Poor fellow!' called Bathory. 'Are we to leave him? Matthew... Leave him?'

Another shot rang out, this time half drowned by a new peal of thunder.

'He may already be dead!' replied Sandorf. 'We must flee — if only to avenge him! Onward, Stephen, onward!'

There was not a moment to lose. By now the firing had become regular, as windows began to open on the lower floors. The sound of many voices could also be heard. The guards must be approaching across the ground at the foot of the tower, in order to cut off the fugitives' retreat. There was also the danger of being hit by shots fired from another part of the tower.

'Hurry!' called Sandorf for the last time.

And he descended as fast as he could. Bathory followed him. It was only now that they discovered that the cable was hanging in mid air. There were no more pegs securing it, so there was nothing on which the two could rest to catch their breath. They hung from the swaying cable, which tore the flesh of their hands. Their knees closed tight, unable to stop, they slid on down. All the while, bullets were whizzing about them.

In the space of a minute, they had dropped some twenty-five metres. The gorge seemed bottomless, but they could now hear the rush of the waters beneath them as they dashed against the rocks. They realized now that the cable ended in a wild torrent. But even if they had wanted, they could not have climbed back up, notwithstanding the certain death awaiting them above.

Just then a deafening roar smote their ears and for a few seconds they were blinded by a searing light. Though the lightning conductor was not struck direct, so intense was the discharge that the whole length of the cable was shrouded in white light, as if glowing with heat. Crying out with pain, Stephen Bathory let go of the cable.

Sandorf saw him hurtle past, arms outstretched.

But he, too, was obliged to release his grip on the cable, as it scorched his hands, and he fell more than twelve metres into the unfathomed abyss, into the turbulent waters of the Foiba.

The Underground Torrent

It was eleven o'clock in the evening. A heavy downpour began, the rain mixed with hailstones, which bounced off the rocks and lashed the waters of the Foiba. The shots from the tower had died down. Why waste bullets? If the Foiba ever gave them up, it would be as corpses.

The moment Sandorf plunged into the water, he felt himself being carried away rapidly by the current. Soon he was engulfed in darkness, now no longer pierced by the flashes of lightning. The din of the thunder was lost in the water's howling roar.

He had been carried into an unknown cave, where neither sound nor light could penetrate.

'Over here!' a faint voice called. It was Stephen Bathory. The cold water had brought him to his senses, but he could not stay afloat. The waves would surely have swallowed him up, had not a strong arm supported him as he went down again.

'Do not be afraid, Stephen — I am here!'

With one arm Count Sandorf drew him to his side, while he tried to swim with the other.

Their plight seemed hopeless. Bathory had almost lost control of his movements, still paralyzed by the electric shock. Though his torn hands no longer burned so fiercely, he had not the strength to swim. For Sandorf to abandon him even for a moment would have been to condemn him to certain death in the savage stream, though he was hard put to save himself.

Moreover, he was filled with foreboding as to where the underground torrent was taking them, where it flowed to, or into what river or sea it emptied. Even if Sandorf had known that the stream was called the Foiba, his position would have been equally hopeless, since no one knew where the waves of the savage watercourse came to rest. They had once thrown a sealed bottle into the water, but it was never found, either in the sea or in any river. It had probably been smashed against the rocks, or had become caught in some fissure.

The fugitives were carried off at tremendous speed. This at least meant that it was easier to stay above water.

Stephen Bathory was now quite unconscious, and his body went limp in Sandorf's arms, so that the latter was obliged to struggle on behalf of both. But he knew that before long he would be at the end of his strength.

To the danger of being smashed against one of the rocks or a low part of the ceiling was added the further and more pressing peril of being caught up in the whirlpools which formed wherever the waters struck the rocks. Should they ever be drawn into such a whirlpool, they would not have the strength to get out again, and would be battered helplessly against the stone.

This terrible swim, whose every minute threatened death, had already been in progress for a full half hour.

Matthew Sandorf had not yet come to the end of his strength, for his stamina and will-power were almost superhuman. In fact he was glad that his companion was senseless: had Bathory regained consciousness, he would surely have resisted. Then Sandorf would have had to struggle not only against the elements, but against his friend as well; he would probably have been obliged to abandon him to the savage waters. But Sandorf could not keep up his efforts much longer, and Bathory might at any time come to his senses. At times, as he raised Bathory's head above the water, his own head would plunge beneath the waves, so that he was becoming short of breath and starting to suffocate.

Several times, he was obliged to release his companion, who would immediately sink beneath the surface. Somehow Sandorf always managed to catch hold of him again. And all this went on amid the thunderous din of the waters, as they smashed against the rocky walls confining them. By now Sandorf was convinced that his struggle was in vain. Bathory's limp body slipped from his grasp and disappeared altogether. He made a last desperate effort to find his friend... But his groping hands found nothing, and he himself sank to the bottom.

At that moment Sandorf was brought to his senses by a sharp blow to his shoulder. As he instinctively thrust out a hand to protect himself, his fingers closed on some sort of clump of tendrils trailing in the water.

It was the roots of a tree which had been carried away by the stream. Taking hold of its trunk, Sandorf pulled himself out of the water. Then, holding onto the treetrunk with one arm, he used his free hand to feel for the body of his friend.

At last he managed to find him and draw him up against the trunk.

43

Thus they almost miraculously escaped death by drowning; but their salvation was far from being assured. Their own fate depended entirely on the fate of this tossing lump of wood. They were at the mercy of the underground torrent. For a moment Sandorf again lapsed into unconsciousness. As soon as he came round, his first thought was to see to it that Bathory's senseless body did not slip from the treetrunk.

As a precaution, he shifted his companion's limp form to a position in which he was better able to keep hold of it. Then he gazed intently ahead of him, trying to discern whether some glimmer of daylight might penetrate the darkness of the underground cavern. But there was no sign of an end to the dark passage.

Nonetheless, their situation had certainly improved a little. The treetrunk was almost four metres long, and its spreading roots kept it from overturning. It floated along steadily, and at no mean speed.

Before very long Count Matthew Sandorf had regained his composure. He tried to bring round his friend, whose head was now resting on his knees. He found that Bathory's heart was still beating, though his breathing was weak.

Bending over the motionless body, Sandorf began to rub Bathory's temples and neck. Sure enough, in a little while the body gave a shudder and Bathory's chest began to heave gently as his breathing became stronger.

At last a few words broke from the pallid lips.

'My wife...! My child...! Matthew...!'

These words summed up the whole of Stephen Bathory's life, all he lived for.

'Stephen! Can you hear me...? Can you hear me?' asked Sandorf, shouting over the roar of the waters.

'Yes...Yes...I hear...Only speak...Give me your hand...'

'Stephen, the worst is behind us,' Sandorf reassured him. 'We are floating on a treetrunk — where I cannot say, but we shall not fall.'

'And the tower, Matthew?'

'Far behind us. Our captors are sure to suppose that we have drowned in these underground waters: they will not pursue us. But wherever this stream may end, we shall get out alive. Take courage, Stephen. I shall watch over you. Rest now, and save your strength until you need it. In a few hours we shall be saved: we shall be free!'

'And Ladislas?' Bathory whispered.

Sandorf made no answer. What could he say? Any hope which Zathmar may have had of escaping, he had lost when he called out a warning to his friends. Now he would be guarded more closely than ever, and there was nothing they could have done to help him if they had tried.

Stephen Bathory's head had again sunk back; he had neither the strength, nor even the will, to fight his faintness.

But Sandorf kept watch, ready if need be to leap from the log, should it be in

danger of smashing to pieces against some unavoidable obstruction lurking ahead in the dark.

It was about two in the morning when the current began to slow down appreciably. It was clear that the underground channel was widening, so that the waters could flow more freely. This must mean that the exit from the cave was not far away.

But though the walls of the cavern were receding, the ceiling was getting lower. With his raised hand, Sandorf was able to feel the layers of slate which formed the roof here. From time to time, too, there was a scraping sound as the tree's roots rubbed against the rock above. The tree shuddered under the

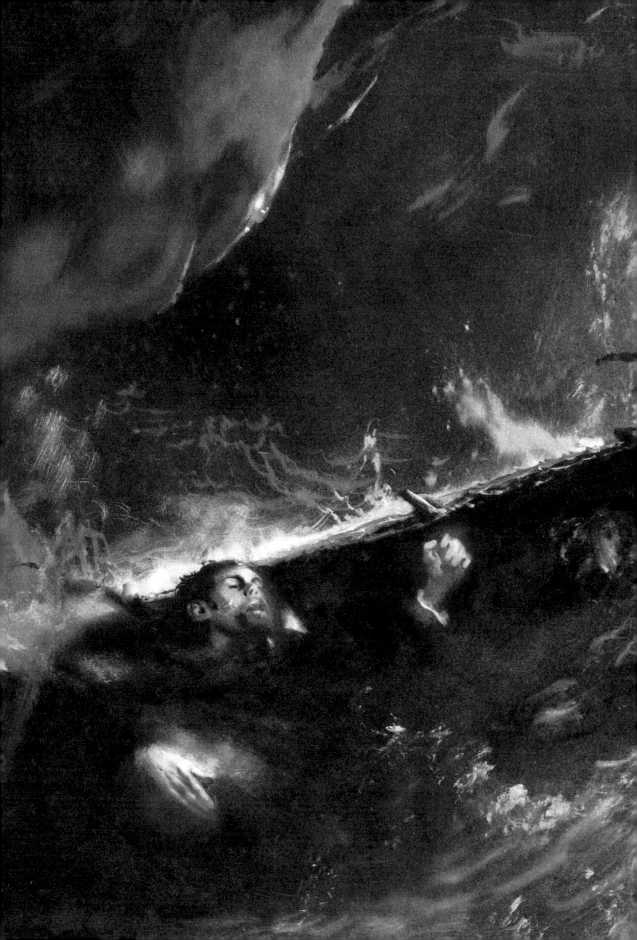

frequent shocks, and would come to a stop and spin round, threatening to throw the two companions in the water.

Though they managed to hold on to the trunk, another danger now appeared, which the count was well aware of. The roof of the cave was still getting lower all the time. Sandorf had several times avoided banging his head at the last minute only by ducking quickly.

Would they be obliged to take to the water once more? He could manage well enough himself, but could he still find the strength to save Stephen? And how was he to survive himself, should the ceiling get so low that he was obliged to swim a great distance under water? No; then they would not escape. The death they had managed to evade so long would catch up with them.

Though Matthew Sandorf had exceptional courage, this thought was enough to seize his heart with anxiety. He felt he was approaching the decisive moment of his life. The tree's roots were now striking the ceiling more and more often, and sometimes the trunk was pushed so far down in the water that the waves washed over them.

'But we must be close to the end of the cave,' Sandorf said to himself.

Again he strained his eyes for a glimpse of light entering the underground gloom. It must be dawn by now, he thought, so that it cannot be entirely dark outside. Some light must get through into the cave.

But there was not the merest glimmer of light: only the selfsame darkness and the endless din of the waters, whose foam was also quite black.

Suddenly, there was a sharp impact. The front end of the log had struck against a piece of the roof which reached down low into the water. The treetrunk turned right over, but Sandorf managed to keep hold of it. With one hand he grasped the roots firmly, while with the other he grabbed hold of Bathory just as the waves were carrying him off.

Then he released his grip on the wood, and allowed himself to be taken along by the current. He was forced to dive beneath the water, which was now lapping against the rocky ceiling.

This went on for about a minute. Sandorf felt that the end had come; his lungs ached, and he could hold his breath no longer. Then, suddenly, even through his closed lids, he was aware of a bright light coming through the water. There was a flash of lightning, followed by a clap of thunder.

Light at last!

The stream had indeed emerged from its underground course, and was now flowing through the open countryside. But to which shore did it flow; into which sea did it empty?

That was the question which remained unanswered: a question which remained unanswered: a question of life and death.

The treetrunk surfaced close by; Sandorf was still holding on to Bathory's body, and with a great effort he managed to haul his friend up onto the log.

Then he looked above and about him. Behind him he could make out a tall, dark mass. It was the huge rock from which the stream flowed. A rosy glow in the sky signalled the coming of the dawn; it was still outshone by occasional flashes of lightning, followed at ever-increasing intervals by the roll of thunder. The storm was retreating, having vented its anger on the land; now it seemed to be fleeing the approaching daybreak.

With deep disquiet, Sandorf looked from side to side. He saw that the stream was still flowing very rapidly along a narrow, rocky gorge.

The fugitives were again carried along past whirlpools and through narrows between the rocks, though there was no longer the low ceiling to threaten to smash their skulls. Nonetheless, there was nowhere they might easily go ashore with their log.

The tall cliffs on either side confined the stream just as had the walls of the cavern.

The cold waters into which they had plunged as they emerged from the cave had brought Stephen Bathory to his senses again. He felt for Sandorf's hand. The count leaned over him and whispered:

'We are saved!'

Had he the right to speak such words? Were they indeed saved, when they did not yet know where the waves would take them, or when they might let go of the log? But his faith and strength of will were now stronger than all else. He sat upright on the treetrunk and called out at the top of his voice:

'Saved! Saved! Saved!'

No one was likely to hear his cries. On cliffs where there was not enough earth to support the tiniest bush, no human being was likely to be found. Nor was the countryside about much more hospitable.

The region where the stream flows between these granite walls is a sad sight. There is no other watercourse running into it, and no birds fly above its waves, which roll along so fiercely that not even fish dare to come here. There were occasional boulders whose tops rose above the waves and were drying. This fact indicated that it was only after heavy rain that the stream grew so wild, when its waters were swollen beyond their usual volume. At other times only an ordinary mountain stream flowed along this deep channel.

The fugitives saw that they need have no fear of the log colliding with a rock. It avoided them of its own accord, following the course of the stream.

But there was also no chance of steering the log to the shore, or of slowing it down enough for the pair of them to get to the bank.

This state of affairs continued for a full hour, without the two of them making a move. Far off on the horizon the last of the lightning flickered, and from time to time the clouds still rumbled. Daylight was coming, and the sky, cleared of its stormclouds, was brightening. It was about four o'clock in the morning.

Bathory slept in Count Sandorf's arms, while the latter kept watch for both.

Suddenly, the sound of a distant shot could be heard.

'What can that be?' The count asked himself. 'Perhaps the signal to open some harbour? And which port might it be? Could it be Trieste? No; the shot came somewhere from the south-west. Perhaps Pola, at the southern tip of Istria? But then...?' There was a second shot, followed closely by a third.

'Three cannon shots,' said Sandorf to himself. 'That means the harbour is closed, and vessels are forbidden to sail. Could it be connected with our escape?'

His fears were well-founded. The authorities were sure to try to recapture the prisoners, who were bound to make for the coast.

The steep cliffs alongside the stream became gradually lower, and the distance between them increased. But it was still impossible to see what lay beyond. The horizon was cut off by quite tall hills, reducing visibility to a few hundred paces.

The bed of the stream widened, slowing the waters down. They were carrying along a number of trunks and tree-stumps, torn up somewhere along its upper reaches.

The June morning was very cool. In their wet clothes they shivered with cold.

It was becoming expedient to find some sort of shelter, so that they might at least dry off.

At around five o'clock the last of the hills disappeared from view, and the uplands gave way to a deserted plain. Here the Foiba became so broad that it seemed like a lake. Westwards, a number of sails appeared; it was clear that this 'lake' was in fact a broad estuary, reaching deep inland. The sea could not be far away. There was nothing for it but to try to get there as soon as possible. But there was no chance of asking the sailors for refuge. If they already knew of the prisoners' escape, then they would hand them over to the Austrian gendarmes, who were sure to be seeking them.

Sandorf was unsure what they should do. Then the log snared on some underwater object, and came to rest. It lay as still as a ship at anchor.

He went ashore carefully. His main concern was to make sure they were not being watched.

Whichever way he looked, there was not a soul to be seen. Nevertheless, not two hundred paces away there was a man who was able to observe the fugitives without being seen, for he was lying in the sand.

Perceiving no danger, Sandorf returned to the treetrunk and carried his companion ashore. He did not know where they were, or which direction they should take.

The large stretch of water into which the stream flowed was a bay which filled at high tide. The stream which flowed into the sea here on the west coast of Istria, between Orsera and Rovigno, was known as the Lème canal, since no one knew that it was actually the Foiba, which disappeared into the ground.

Not far from the spot where they had landed was a fisherman's hut. When he had made sure it was not occupied, Sandorf went towards it. Bathory had recovered somewhat, and was able to accompany him. When they reached the hut, they took off their wet clothes, laid them out to dry in the sun, and waited.

The fishing boats had by now left the canal, and the place was quite deserted.

Then the man who had observed their arrival stood up, approached the hut as if to make sure of something, and disappeared southwards over a low rise.

Three hours later, Sandorf and Bathory put on their clothes, which were still somewhat damp. It was time to set off.

'We cannot stay in the hut,' said Bathory.

'Are you strong enough to walk?' Sandorf asked him.

'I am weak with hunger, but I can walk.'

'We must make for the coast; there we can perhaps get something to eat, and maybe even get on a vessel. Let us go, Stephen!'

So, more weakened by hunger than by exhaustion, they left the hut.

Pursuit

Sandorf intended walking along the estuary until they reached the shore. Though the region was a deserted one, it was cut across by numerous streams which flowed into the bay.

This network of watercourses served to transform the land into one large morass, without firm ground. So the fugitives made south, a direction they deduced from the course of the climbing sun.

For two hours Sandorf and Bathory walked without meeting a soul. They were half dead with hunger.

Finally they found themselves in countryside which was less deserted. They came to a road running from east to west, and on it they found a milestone, though they were unable to deduce from it where they were. But some rows of mulberry trees and fields of millet allowed them to stave off their hunger for a while at least.

Now they would be able to reach the coast sooner, and need not fear that they might collapse from hunger. But the cultivated fields showed that they were now walking through inhabited country, and they must be prepared to meet people there.

Around midday, they did indeed spot a group of some five or six people, coming towards them on foot. Sandorf was resolved to avoid them. Fortunately, they spotted a dilapidated farm not far from the road. Making their way to it before they had been seen, they hid in a cellar, where they were obliged to remain until nightfall.

The travellers were peasants and workers from the salt-works. The peasants were driving a flock of geese, undoubtedly to market in the town, which could not have been far away. Both men and women were wearing the local costume, with beads, medallions and decorative pendants. The workers were dressed much more simply, carrying sacks on their backs and holding sticks in their hands.

Some of them stopped close to the deserted farm, and two of them even came to sit down on the threshold. They spoke loudly, but only about their work.

The two fugitives, crouched in a corner, listened intently. Perhaps these people had heard of their escape, and would speak about it. Or maybe they would speak of something which would help Sandorf to deduce which part of Istria they were in.

But no such words were spoken, and the two escapees were left with their assumptions.

'These country folk said nothing of our escape, so they have certainly not yet heard of it,' supposed Sandorf.

'Which means that we are already some distance from the fortress,' replied Bathory. 'Which does not surprise me, when I think of how fast was the current which carried us off.'

'I think you are right,' the count agreed.

But after some two hours they heard some more workers passing. They were speaking about a troop of gendarmes which they had seen in front of the gates of the town.

But in front of the gates of what town? The workers did not mention this important item of information.

But what they had heard was enough. If troops of gendarmes were patrolling the countryside, then they were looking for them.

'But they might well have supposed from the circumstances of our escape, that we had been killed,' said Bathory. 'Is it not strange that they are searching for us?'

'They will be satisfied that we are dead only when they find our bodies,' Sandorf replied.

Be that as it may, there was no doubt that the police were going to considerable pains to search for the pair. For this reason they resolved to remain hidden at the farm until nightfall. They were sorely tried with hunger, but they did not dare leave their hiding-place — which was just as well.

At about five in the afternoon they heard the clatter of horses' hooves along the road, and a troop of horsemen approached the farm.

Count Sandorf, who had crawled right up to the gate of the farm, hurried back

to their hiding-place and drew his companion into the darkest corner of the cellar. There they hid beneath a heap of dry leaves and kept quite still. Six gendarmes and their sergeant were heading eastwards along the road. Would they stop at the farm? thought Sandorf to himself, not a little anxious: if the gendarmes were to search the place, they would be sure to discover them.

The troop did indeed stop. The sergeant and two of his men dismounted, while the others remained in the saddle. They received orders to patrol the surrounding area and return to the farm, where they would be expected at seven o'clock.

When the four had ridden off, the sergeant and the other two tied their horses to the fence which surrounded the farmstead. Then they sat down outside and began to speak. The fugitives could hear everything they said.

'This evening we shall return to the town, where we shall get fresh information,' the sergeant replied to the question of one of his men. 'There should be new orders from Trieste by then.'

Then the nearby town was not Trieste. Sandorf took good note of the fact.

'Might not the prisoners have gone in the opposite direction, and reached the Bay of Quarnero?' asked the other gendarme.

'That may be so,' replied the first gendarme, 'for they would find greater safety there than here.'

'If they reach that coast, they will be recaptured anyway,' the sergeant added, 'for the whole coastline is guarded.'

Count Sandorf thus discovered that they were still on the west coast of Istria.

'The fugitives will certainly be sought in the salt-works of Pirano and Capo d'Istria,' the sergeant went on. 'There they may easily hide, then try to steal a fishing boat and sail across to Venice or Rimini.'

'They would have done better to stay in prison,' declared one of the gendarmes, wisely.

'Indeed, for they will surely be found sooner or later, if their bodies do not turn up first. I wish it were so to be, for we should not have to search for them in this heat.'

'Who knows if they are not indeed already dead?' replied the sergeant. 'The abyss has probably already carried out the death sentence. The prisoners could not have chosen a worse escape route, with the Foiba swollen by the rains.'

Thus it was that Sandorf learnt the name of the stream which had carried them into the underground cavern. Then they must have been taken to Pisino Castle after their capture, and it was there they had been condemned. It was from the tower of that castle that they had escaped. There, too, they would have been executed. Count Sandorf knew Pisino well; he knew now where they were,

and would no longer have to flee blindly across Istria. If they were still able to
flee at all, that was.

The gendarmes said no more, but the fugitives had learnt all they needed to
know, except for the name of the nearby town.

The sergeant rose to his feet. He took a stroll around the garden to see if he
could spot his men returning from their search. Two or three times he entered

the crumbling buildings and examined the rooms there. It was more a question
of habit than of any real suspicion that the escapees might be hidden there. Thus
he also came into the cellar where the two lay hidden, and even thrust the point
of his bayonet into the pile of leaves beneath which the pair had taken refuge.

Bathory and Sandorf were seized with fear for a moment, but were resolved to
sell their lives dearly, were they to be discovered.

They considered leaping on the sergeant, taking advantage of surprise to disarm him, and killing both him and the two gendarmes outside before they could kill them.

But just at that very moment the two gendarmes called to the sergeant, who left the cellar without finding anything suspicious. The rest of the troop were returning. They had found no trace of the fugitives anywhere.

But they were not alone. With them was a man.

It was a Spaniard who worked in the nearby salt-works. He had been on his way back from the town when the gendarmes met him. Since he had told them he had come from the town, the gendarmes had decided to take him to the sergeant for questioning, and the man had not resisted.

The sergeant asked him if anyone from the salt-works had seen two suspicious strangers.

'No, but after leaving the town this morning I saw two men come ashore at the end of the canal.'

'Two men, you say?' asked the sergeant.

'Yes, sergeant; but I did not take much note of them, for no one knew of the escape, and we thought they had already been executed. I have only now learnt who they might have been; I should not be surprised if they were indeed the ones.'

Count Sandorf and Stephen Bathory, lying in their hiding-place, heard every word of this conversation, so important to them. So they had indeed been observed as they went ashore.

'What is your name?' asked the sergeant.

'Carpena. I work in the salt-works.'

'Would you recognize the men you saw by the canal?'

'Yes...I think so.'

'You shall go to the town now, and inform them of what you have seen. You shall help the police.'

'I shall obey your orders.'

'Did you know that there is a reward of five thousand guilders for him who leads us to the fugitives?'

'Five thousand!'

'And that it will be penal servitude for anyone who hides them?'

'I hear this for the first time from you.'

'Then go!' the sergeant told him, releasing him.

The effect of the Spaniard's evidence was that the gendarmes left the farmstead. The sergeant gave orders to mount and to search along the banks of the canal more carefully, even though night was at hand.

Carpena set off, hoping he might receive a reward of five thousand guilders.

Sandorf and Bathory remained hidden in the cellar a little while longer. Now they knew that the gendarmes had picked up their trail, that they had been seen, and might be recognized. In short, Istria was no longer a safe place for them to be. They must flee its shores at the first opportunity.

Italy seemed to offer the best chance of escape, but only if they were to manage to steal some sort of boat, or to force some fishermen to carry them across the Adriatic.

At about half past eight, when darkness fell, Sandorf and his companion set off westwards towards the coast.

They could not leave the road if they were not to sink into the mire. By keeping to it, however, they would come to the town from which the road led into the hinterland. This brought with it a good deal of danger, but they had no choice.

At about half past nine they saw the silhouette of the town on the horizon. They were unable, however, to make out any details. All they could see was a group of houses perched on a huge cliff. In fact this cliff offers a sheltered anchorage, and a harbour lies below it. A tall bell tower rises above the town, and in the dark it seemed taller than ever.

Sandorf had no intention of entering the town, where the presence of two strangers was bound to arouse immediate suspicion. They would be obliged to skirt around it to get to the sea.

This they did, but they had been observed for some time — by the same man who had seen them in the morning. It was Carpena, whom they had heard giving evidence to the sergeant.

On his way home, the Spaniard had hidden by the roadside to see who went by. Thus he had chanced to pick up the trail of the two fugitives anew.

Almost at the same moment they were threatened from the front by a troop of police who had left the gate of the town, effectively blocking their path. It was high time for them to leave the road and move sideways.

They thus came to the shore, where a small fisherman's house stood. The windows were lit and the door ajar. If the escapees found no refuge there, then they were lost.

But to seek refuge was to risk all. However, they could not afford to hesitate.

Sandorf and his companion hurried to the door of the cottage, halting at the threshold.

In the parlour a man was mending a net by the light of a lantern.

'What is the name of this town, my friend?' asked Sandorf.

'Rovigno!'

'And what is your name?'

'I am Andrea Ferrato, a fisherman.'

'Would you give us shelter for the night?'

Ferrato looked at the two men, stepped over to the door, and saw the troop of gendarmes. He must have guessed who was asking for his hospitality, and that they would be lost if he refused.

'Come in,' he said.

The fugitives hesitated.

'My friend,' said Sandorf. 'There is a reward of five thousand guilders for him who gives up the escaped prisoners: we are they.'

'I know that.'

'And penal servitude for any who shelters them.'

'I know that, too.'

'You have the opportunity to hand us over...'

'I told you to come in; then come in!' said the fisherman.

And Andrea Ferrato closed the door behind the two fugitives just as the knot of policemen approached the cottage.

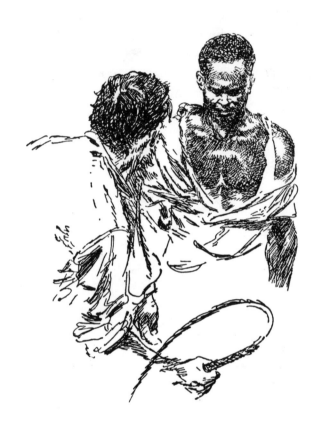

UNCLE TOM'S CABIN

HARRIET BEECHER-STOWE

The Unprotected

We hear often of the distress of the negro servants, on the loss of a kind master; and with good reason, for no creature on God's earth is left more utterly unprotected and desolate than the slave in these circumstances.

The child who has lost a father has still the protection of friends, and of the law; he is something, and can do something, — has acknowledged rights and position; the slave has none. The law regards him, in every respect, as devoid of rights as a bale of merchandise. The only possible acknowledgment of any of the longings and wants of a human and immortal creature, which are given to him, comes to him through the sovereign and irresponsible will of his master; and when that master is stricken down, nothing remains.

The number of those men who know how to use wholly irresponsible power humanely and generously is small. Everybody knows this, and the slave knows it best of all; so that he feels that there are ten chances of his finding an abusive and tyrannical master, to one of his finding a considerate and kind one. Therefore is it that the wail over a kind master is loud and long, as well it may be.

When St. Clare breathed his last, terror and consternation took hold of all his household. He had been stricken down so in a moment, in the flower and strength of his youth! Every room and gallery of the house resounded with sobs and shrieks of despair.

Marie, whose nervous system had been enervated by a constant course of self-indulgence, had nothing to support the terror of the shock, and, at the time her husband breathed his last, was passing from one fainting fit to another; and he to whom she had been joined in the mysterious tie of marriage passed from her forever, without the possibility of even a parting word.

Miss Ophelia, with characteristic strength and self-control, had remained with her kinsman to the last, — all eye, all ear, all attention; doing everything of the little that could be done, and joining with her whole soul in the tender and impassioned prayers which the poor slave had poured forth for the soul of his dying master.

When they were arranging him for his last rest, they found upon his bosom a small, plain miniature case, opening with a spring. It was the miniature of a noble and beautiful female face; and on the reverse, under a crystal, a lock of dark hair. They laid them back on the lifeless breast, — dust to dust, — poor

mournful relics of early dreams, which once made that cold heart beat so warmly!

Tom's whole soul was filled with thoughts of eternity; and while he ministered around the lifeless clay, he did not once think that the sudden stroke had left him in hopeless slavery. He felt at peace about his master; for in that hour, when he had poured forth his prayer into the bosom of his Father, he had found an answer of quietness and assurance springing up within himself. In the depths of his own affectionate nature, he felt able to perceive something of the fullness of Divine love; for an old oracle hath thus written, — 'He that dwelleth in love dwelleth in God, and God in him'. Tom hoped and trusted, and was at peace.

But the funeral passed, with all its pageant of black crape, and prayers, and solemn faces; and back rolled the cool, muddy waves of every-day life; and up came the everlasting hard inquiry of 'What is to be done next?'

It rose to the mind of Marie, as, dressed in loose morning-robes, and surrounded by anxious servants, she sat up in a great easy-chair, and inspected samples of crape and bombazine. It rose to Miss Ophelia, who began to turn her thoughts towards her northern home. It rose, in silent terrors, to the minds of the servants, who well knew the unfeeling, tyrannical character of the mistress in whose hands they were left. All knew, very well, that the indulgences which had been accorded to them were not from their mistress, but from their master; and that, now he was gone, there would be no screen between them and every tyrannous infliction which a temper soured by affliction might devise.

It was about a fortnight after the funeral, that Miss Ophelia, busied one day in her apartment, heard a gentle tap at the door. She opened it, and there stood Rosa, the pretty young quadroon, whom we have before often noticed, her hair in disorder, and her eyes swelled with crying.

'O, Miss Feely,' she said, falling on her knees, and catching the skirt of her dress, '*do, do go* to Miss Marie for me! do plead for me! She's goin' to send me out to be whipped, — look there!' And she handed to Miss Ophelia a paper.

It was an order, written in Marie's delicate Italian hand, to the master of a whipping-establishment, to give the bearer fifteen lashes.

'What have you been doing?' said Miss Ophelia.

'You know, Miss Feely, I've got such a bad temper; it's very bad of me. I was trying on Miss Marie's dress, and she slapped my face; and I spoke out before I thought, and was saucy; and she said that she'd bring me down, and have me know, once for all, that I wasn't going to be so topping as I had been; and she wrote this, and says I shall carry it. I'd rather she'd kill me, right out.'

Miss Ophelia stood considering, with the paper in her hand.

'You see, Miss Feely,' said Rosa, 'I don't mind the whipping so much, if Miss Marie or you was to do it; but, to be sent to a *man!* and such a horrid man, — the shame of it, Miss Feely!'

Miss Ophelia well knew that it was the universal custom to send women and young girls to whipping-houses, to the hands of the lowest of men, — men vile enough to make this their profession, — there to be subjected to brutal exposure and shameful correction. She had *known* it before; but hitherto she had never realized it, till she saw the slender form of Rosa almost convulsed with distress. All the honest blood of womanhood, the strong New England blood of liberty, flushed to her cheeks, and throbbed bitterly in her indignant heart; but, with habitual prudence and self-control, she mastered herself, and, crushing the paper firmly in her hand, she merely said to Rosa,

'Sit down, child, while I go to your mistress.'

'Shameful! monstrous! outrageous!' she said to herself, as she was crossing the parlour.

She found Marie sitting up in her easy-chair, with Mammy standing by her, combing her hair; Jane sat on the ground before her, busy in chafing her feet.

'How do you find yourself, to-day?' said Miss Ophelia.

A deep sigh, and a closing of the eyes, was the only reply, for a moment; and then Marie answered, 'O, I don't know, Cousin; I suppose I'm as well as I ever shall be!' and Marie wiped her eyes with a cambric handkerchief, bordered with an inch deep of black.

'I came,' said Miss Ophelia, with a short, dry cough, such as commonly introduces a difficult subject, — 'I came to speak with you about poor Rosa.'

Marie's eyes were open wide enough now, and a flush rose to her sallow cheeks, as she answered, sharply,

'Well, what about her?'

'She is very sorry for her fault.'

'She is, is she? She'll be sorrier, before I've done with her! I've endured that child's impudence long enough; and now I'll bring her down, — I'll make her lie in the dust!'

'But could not you punish her some other way, — some way that would be less shameful?'

'I mean to shame her; that's just what I want. She has all her life presumed on her delicacy, and her good looks, and her lady-like airs, till she forgets who she is; — and I'll give her one lesson that will bring her down, I fancy!'

'But, Cousin, consider that, if you destroy delicacy and a sense of shame in a young girl, you deprave her very fast.'

'Delicacy!' said Marie, with a scornful laugh, — 'a fine word for such as she!

I'll teach her, with all her airs, that she's no better than the raggedest black wench that walks the streets! She'll take no more airs with me!'

'You will answer to God for such cruelty!' said Miss Ophelia, with energy.

'Cruelty, — I'd like to know what the cruelty is! I wrote orders for only fifteen lashes, and told him to put them on lightly. I'm sure there's no cruelty there!'

'No cruelty!' said Miss Ophelia. 'I'm sure any girl might rather be killed outright!'

'It might seem so to anybody with your feeling; but all these creatures get used to it; it's the only way they can be kept in order. Once let them feel that they are to take any aim about delicacy, and all that, and they'll run all over you, just as my servants always have. I've begun now to bring them under; and I'll have them all to know that I'll send one out to be whipped, as soon as another, if they don't mind themselves!' said Marie, looking around her decidedly.

Jane hung her head and cowered at this, for she felt as if it was particularly directed to her. Miss Ophelia sat for a moment, as if she had swallowed some explosive mixture, and were ready to burst. Then, recollecting the utter uselessness of contention with such a nature, she walked out of the room.

It was hard to go back and tell Rosa that she could do nothing for her; and, shortly after, one of the man-servants came to say that her mistress had ordered him to take Rosa with him to the whipping-house, whither she was hurried, in spite of her tears and entreaties.

A few days after, Tom was standing musing by the balconies, when he was joined by Adolph, who, since the death of his master, had been entirely crest-fallen and disconsolate. Adolph knew that he had always been an object of dislike to Marie; but while his master lived he had paid but little attention to it. Now that he was gone, he had moved about in daily dread and trembling, not knowing what might befall him next. Marie had held several consultations with her lawyer; after communicating with St. Clare's brother, it was determined to sell the place, and all the servants, except her own personal property, and these she intended to take with her, and go back to her father's plantation.

'Do ye know, Tom, that we've all got to be sold?' said Adolph.

'How did you hear that?' said Tom.

'I hid myself behind the curtains when Missis was talking with the lawyer. In a few days we shall all be sent off to auction, Tom.'

'The Lord's will be done!' said Tom, folding his arms and sighing heavily.

'We'll never get another such a master,' said Adolph, apprehensively; 'but I'd rather be sold than take my chance under Missis.'

Tom turned away; his heart was full. The hope of liberty, the thought of distant wife and children, rose up before his patient soul, as to the mariner shipwrecked almost in port rises the vision of the church-spire and loving roofs of his native village, seen over the top of some black wave only for one last farewell. He drew his arms tightly over his bosom, and choked back the bitter tears, and tried to pray. The poor old soul had such a singular, unaccountable prejudice in favour of liberty, that it was a hard wrench for him; and the more he said, 'Thy will be done,' the worse he felt.

He sought Miss Ophelia, who, ever since Eva's death, had treated him with marked and respectful kindness.

'Miss Feely,' he said, 'Mas'r St. Clare promised me my freedom. He told me that he had begun to take it out for me; and now, perhaps, if Miss Feely would be good enough to speak about it to Missis, she would feel like goin' on with it, as it was Mas'r St. Clare's wish.'

'I'll speak for you, Tom, and do my best,' said Miss Ophelia; 'but, if it depends on Mrs. St. Clare, I can't hope much for you; — nevertheless, I will try.'

This incident occurred a few days after that of Rosa, while Miss Ophelia was busied in preparations to return north.

Seriously reflecting within herself, she considered that perhaps she had shown too hasty a warmth of language in her former interview with Marie; and she resolved that she would now endeavour to moderate her zeal, and to be as conciliatory as possible. So the good soul gathered herself up, and, taking her knitting, resolved to go into Marie's room, be as agreeable as possible, and negotiate Tom's case with all the diplomatic skill of which she was mistress.

She found Marie reclining at length upon a lounge, supporting herself on one elbow by pillows, while Jane, who had been out shopping, was displaying before her certain samples of thin black stuffs.

'That will do,' said Marie, selecting one; 'only I'm not sure about its being properly mourning.'

'Laws, Missis,' said Jane, volubly, 'Mrs. General Derbennon wore just this very thing, after the General died, last summer; it makes up lovely!'

'What do you think?' said Marie to Miss Ophelia.

'It's a matter of custom, I suppose,' said Miss Ophelia. 'You can judge about it better than I.'

'The fact is,' said Marie, 'that I haven't a dress in the world that I can wear; and, as I am going to break up the establishment, and go off, next week, I must decide upon something.'

'Are you going so soon?'

'Yes. St. Clare's brother has written, and he and the lawyer think that the servants and furniture had better be put up at auction, and the place left with our lawyer.'

'There's one thing I wanted to speak with you about,' said Miss Ophelia. 'Augustine promised Tom his liberty, and began the legal forms necessary to it. I hope you will use your influence to have it perfected.'

'Indeed, I shall do no such thing!' said Marie, sharply. 'Tom is one of the most valuable servants on the place, — it couldn't be afforded, any way. Besides, what does he want of liberty? He's a great deal better off as he is.'

'But he does desire it, very earnestly, and his master promised it,' said Miss Ophelia.

'I dare say he does want it,' said Marie; 'they all want it, just because they are a discontented set, — always wanting what they haven't got. Now, I'm principled against emancipating, in any case. Keep a negro under the care of a master, and he does well enough, and is respectable; but set them free, and they get lazy, and won't work, and take to drinking, and go all down to be mean, worthless fellows. I've seen it tried, hundreds of times. It's no favour to set them free.'

'But Tom is so steady, industrious, and pious.'

'O, you needn't tell me! I've seen a hundred like him. He'll do very well, as long as he's taken care of, — that's all.'

'But, then, consider,' said Miss Ophelia, 'when you set him up for sale, the chances of his getting a bad master.'

'O, that's all humbug!' said Marie; 'it isn't one time in a hundred that a good fellow gets a bad master; most masters are good, for all the talk that is made. I've lived and grown up here, in the South, and I never yet was acquainted with a master that didn't treat his servants well, — quite as well as is worth while. I don't feel any fears on that head.'

'Well,' said Miss Ophelia, energetically, 'I know it was one of the last wishes of your husband that Tom should have his liberty; it was one of the promises that he made to dear little Eva on her death-bed, and I should not think you would feel at liberty to disregard it.'

Marie had her face covered with her handkerchief at this appeal, and began sobbing and using her smelling-bottle, with great vehemence.

'Everybody goes against me!' she said. 'Everybody is so inconsiderate! I shouldn't have expected that *you* would bring up all these remembrances of my troubles to me, — it's so inconsiderate! But nobody ever does consider, — my trials are so peculiar! It's so hard, that when I had only one daughter, she should have been taken! — and when I had a husband that just exactly suited me, — and I'm so hard to be suited! — he should be taken! And you seem to have so little feeling for me, and keep bringing it up to me so carelessly, — when you know how it overcomes me! I suppose you mean well; but it is very inconsiderate, — very!' And Marie sobbed, and gasped for breath, and called Mammy to open the window, and to bring her the camphor-bottle, and to bathe her head, and unhook her dress. And, in the general confusion that ensued, Miss Ophelia made her escape to her apartment.

She saw, at once, that it would do no good to say anything more; for Marie had an indefinite capacity for hysteric fits; and, after this, whenever her husband's or Eva's wishes with regard to the servants were alluded to, she always found it convenient to set one in operation. Miss Ophelia, therefore, did the next best thing she could for Tom, — she wrote a letter to Mrs. Shelby for him, stating his troubles, and urging them to send to his relief.

The next day, Tom and Adolph, and some half a dozen other servants, were marched down to a slave-warehouse, to await the convenience of the trader, who was going to make up a lot for auction.

The Slave Warehouse

A slave warehouse! Perhaps some of my readers conjure up horrible visions of such a place. They fancy some foul, obscure den, some horrible *Tartarus* *"informis, ingens, cui lumen ademptum."* But no, innocent friend; in these days men have learned the art of sinning expertly and genteely, so as not to shock the eyes and senses of respectable society. Human property is high in the market; and is, therefore, well fed, well cleaned, tended, and looked after, that it may come to sale sleek, and strong, and shining. A slave-warehouse in New Orleans is a house externally not much unlike many others, kept with neatness; and where every day you may see arranged, under a sort of shed along the outside, rows of men and women, who stand there as a sign of the property sold within.

Then you shall be courteously entreated to call and examine, and shall find an abundance of husbands, wives, brothers, sisters, fathers, mothers, and young children, to be 'sold separately, or in lots to suit the convenience of the purchaser;' and that soul immortal, once bought with blood and anguish by the Son of God, when the earth shook, and the rocks rent, and the graves were opened, can be sold, leased, mortgaged, exchanged for groceries or dry goods, to suit the phases of trade, or the fancy of the purchaser.

It was a day or two after the conversation between Marie and Miss Ophelia, that Tom, Adolph, and about half a dozen others of the St. Clare estate, were turned over to the loving kindness of Mr. Skeggs, the keeper of a depot on — street, to await the auction, next day.

Tom had with him quite a sizable trunk full of clothing, as had most others of them. They were ushered, for the night, into a long room, where many other men, of all ages, sizes, and shades of complexion, were assembled, and from which roars of laughter and unthinking merriment were proceeding.

'Ah, ha! that's right. Go it, boys, — go it!' said Mr. Skeggs, the keeper. 'My people are always so merry! Sambo, I see!' he said, speaking approvingly to a burly negro who was performing tricks of low buffoonery, which occasioned the shouts which Tom had heard. As might be imagined, Tom was in no humour to join these proceedings; and, therefore, setting his trunk as far as possible from the noisy group, he sat down on it, and leaned his face against the wall.

The dealers in the human article make scrupulous and systematic efforts to promote noisy mirth among them, as a means of drowning reflection, and rendering them insensible to their condition. The whole object of the training to which the negro is put, from the time he is sold in the northern market till he arrives south, is systematically directed towards making him callous, unthinking, and brutal. The slave-dealer collects his gang in Virginia or Kentucky, and drives them to some convenient, healthy place, — often a watering place, — to be fattened. Here they are fed full daily; and, because some incline to pine, a fiddle is kept commonly going among them, and they are made to dance daily; and he who refuses to be merry — in whose soul thoughts of wife, or child, or home, are too strong for him to be gay — is marked as sullen and dangerous, and subjected to all the evils which the ill will of an utterly irresponsible and hardened man can inflict upon him. Briskness, alertness, and cheerfulness of appearance, especially before observers, are constantly enforced upon them, both by the hope of thereby getting a good master, and the fear of all that the driver may bring upon them, if they prove unsaleable.

'What dat ar nigger doin here?' said Sambo, coming up to Tom, after Mr. Skeggs had left the room. Sambo was a full black, of great size, very lively, voluble, and full of trick and grimace.

'What you doin here?' said Sambo, coming up to Tom, and poking him facetiously in the side. 'Meditatin', eh?'

'I am to be sold at the auction, to-morrow!' said Tom, quietly.

'Sold at auction, — haw! haw! boys, an't this yer fun? I wish't I was gwine that ar way! — tell ye, wouldn't I make em laugh? But how is it, — dis yer whole lot gwine to-morrow?' said Sambo, laying his hand freely on Adolph's shoulder.

'Please to let me alone!' said Adolph, fiercely, straightening himself up.

'Law, now, boys! dis yer 's one o' yer white niggers, — kind o' cream colour, ye know, scented!' said he, coming up to Adolph and snuffing. 'O, Lor! he'd do for a tobaccer-shop; they could keep him to scent snuff! Lor, he'd keep a whole shope agwine, — he would!'

'I say, keep off, can't you?' said Adolph, enraged.

'Lor, now, how touchy we is, — we white niggers! Look at us, now!' and Sambo gave a ludicrous imitation of Adolph's manner; 'here's de airs and graces. We's been in a good family, I specs.'

'Yes,' said Adolph; 'I had a master that could have bought you all for old truck!'

'Laws, now, only think,' said Sambo, 'the gentlemens that we is!'

'I belonged to the St. Clare family,' said Adolph, proudly.

'Lor, you did! Be hanged if they ar'n't lucky to get shet of ye. Spects they's gwine to trade ye off with a lot o' cracked tea-pots and sich like!' said Sambo, with a provoking grin.

Adolph, enraged at this taunt, flew furiously at his adversary, swearing and striking on every side of him. The rest laughed and shouted, and the uproar brought the keeper to the door.

'What now, boys? Order, — order!' he said, coming in and flourishing a large whip.

All fled in different directions, except Sambo, who, presuming on the favour which the keeper had to him as a licensed wag, stood his ground, ducking his head with a facetious grin, whenever the master made a dive at him.

'Lor, Mas'r, 'tan't us, — we's reglar stiddy, — it's these yer new hands; they's real aggravatin', — kinder pickin' at us, all time!'

The keeper, at this, turned upon Tom and Adolph, and distributing a few kicks and cuffs without much inquiry, and leaving general orders for all to be good boys and go to sleep, left the apartment.

While this scene was going on in the men's sleeping room, the reader may be curious to take a peep at the corresponding apartment allotted to the women. Stretched out in various attitudes over the floor, he may see numberless sleeping forms of every shade of complexion, from the purest ebony to white, and of all years, from childhood to old age, lying now asleep. Here is a fine bright girl, of ten years, whose mother was sold out yesterday, and who to-night cried herself to sleep when nobody was looking at her. Here, a worn old negress, whose thin arms and callous fingers tell of hard toil, waiting to be sold to-morrow, as a cast-off article, for what can be got for her; and some forty or fifty others, with heads variously enveloped in blankets or articles of clothing, lie stretched around them. But in a corner, sitting apart from the rest, are two females of a more interesting appearance than common. One of these is a respectably-dressed mulatto woman between forty and fifty, with soft eyes and a gentle and pleasing physiognomy. She has on her head a high-raised turban, made of a gay red Madras handkerchief, of the first quality, and her dress is neatly fitted, and of good material, showing that she has been provided for with a careful hand. By her side, and nestling closely to her, is a young girl of fifteen, — her daughter. She is a quadroon, as may be seen from her fairer complexion, though her likeness to her mother is quite discernible. She has the same soft, dark eye, with longer lashes, and her curling hair is of a luxuriant brown. She also is dressed with great neatness, and her white, delicate hands betray very little acquaintance with servile toil. These two are to be sold tomorrow, in the same lot with the St. Clare servants; and the gentleman to whom they belong, and to whom the money for their sale is to be transmitted, is a member of a Christian church in New York, who will receive the money, and go thereafter to the sacrament of his Lord and theirs, and think no more of it.

These two, whom we shall call Suzan and Emmeline, had been the personal attendants of an amiable and pious lady of New Orleans, by whom they had been carefully and piously instructed and trained. They had been taught to read and write, diligently instructed in the truths of religion, and their lot had been as happy an one as in their condition it was possible to be. But the only son of their protectress had the management of her property; and, by carelessness and extravagance involved it to a large amount, and at last failed. One of the largest creditors was the respectable firm of B. & Co., in New York. B. & Co. wrote to their lawyer in New Orleans, who attached the real estate (these two articles and a lot of plantation hands formed the most valuable part of it), and wrote word to that effect to New York. Brother B., being, as we have said, a Christian man, and a resident in a free State, felt some uneasiness on the subject. He didn't like trading in slaves and souls of men, — of course, he didn't; but, then, there were thirty thousand dollars in the case, and that was rather too much money to be lost for a principle; and so, after much considering, and asking advice from those that he knew would advise to suit him, Brother B. wrote to his lawyer to dispose of the business in the way that seemed to him the most suitable.

The day after the letter arrived in New Orleans, Suzan and Emmeline were attached, and sent to the depot to await a general auction on the following morning; and as they glimmer faintly upon us in the moonlight which steals through the grated window, we may listen to their conversation. Both are weeping, but each quietly, that the other may not hear.

'Mother, just lay your head on my lap, and see if you can't sleep a little,' says the girl, trying to appear calm.

'I haven't any heart to sleep, Em; I can't; it's the last night we may be together!'

'O, mother, don't say so! perhaps we shall get sold together, — who knows?'

'If 't was anybody's else case, I should say so, too, Em,' said the woman; 'but I'm so feard of losin' you that I don't see anything but the danger.'

'Why, mother, the man said we were both likely, and would sell well.'

Suzan remembered the man's looks and words. With a deadly sickness at her heart, she remembered how he had looked at Emmeline's hands, and lifted up her curly hair, and pronounced her a first-rate article. Suzan had been trained as a Christian, brought up in the daily reading of the Bible, and had the same horror of her child's being sold to a life of shame that any other Christian mother might have; but she had no hope, — no protection.

'Mother, I think we might do first rate, if you could get a place as cook, and I as chamber-maid or seamstress, in some family. I dare say we shall. Let's both look as bright and lively as we can, and tell all we can do, and perhaps we shall,' said Emmeline.

'I want you to brush your hair all back straight, tomorrow,' said Suzan.

'What for, mother? I don't look near so well, that way.'

'Yes, but you'll sell better so.'

'I don't see why!' said the child.

'Respectable families would be more apt to buy you, if they saw you looked plain and decent, as if you wasn't trying to look handsome. I know their ways better 'n you do,' said Suzan.

'Well, mother, then I will.'

'And, Emmeline, if we shouldn't ever see each other again, after to-morrow, — if I'm sold way up on a plantation somewhere, and you somewhere else, — always remember how you've been brought up, and all Missis has told you; take your Bible with you, and your hymn-book; and if you're faithful to the Lord, he'll be faithful to you.'

So speaks the poor soul, in sore discouragement; for she knows that to-morrow any man, however vile and brutal, however godless and merciless, if he only has money to pay for her, may become owner of her daughter, body and soul; and then, how is the child to be faithful? She thinks of all this, and she holds her daughter in her arms, and wishes that she were not handsome and attractive. It seems almost an aggravation to her to remember how purely and piously, how much above the ordinary lot, she has been brought up. But she has no resort but to *pray;* and many such prayers to God have gone up from those same trim, neatly-arranged, respectable slave prisons, — prayers which God has not forgotten, as a coming day shall show; for it is written, 'Who causeth one of these little ones to offend, it were better for him that a mill-stone were hanged about his neck, and that he were drowned in the depths of the sea.'

The soft, earnest, quiet moonbeam looks in fixedly, marking the bars of the grated windows on the prostrate, sleeping forms. The mother and daughter are singing together a wise and melancholy dirge, common as a funeral hymn among the slaves:

'O, where is weeping Mary?
O, where is weeping Mary?

'Rived in the goodly land.
She is dead and gone to Heaven;
She is dead and gone to Heaven;
'Rived in the goodly land.'

These words, sung by voices of a peculiar and melancholy sweetness, in an air which seemed like the sighing of earthly despair after heavenly hope, floated through the dark prison rooms with a pathetic cadence, as verse after verse was breathed out:

'*O, where are Paul and Silas?*
O, where are Paul and Silas?
Gone to the goodly land.
They are dead and gone to Heaven;
They are dead and gone to Heaven;
'Rived in the goodly land.'

Sing on, poor souls! The night is short, and the morning will part you forever!

But now it is morning, and everybody is astir; and the worthy Mr. Skeggs is busy and bright, for a lot of goods is to be fitted out for auction. There is a brisk look-out on the toilet; injunctions passed around to every one to put on their best face and be spry; and now all are arranged in a circle for a last review, before they are marched up to the Bourse.

Mr. Skeggs, with his palmetto on and his cigar in his mouth, walks around to put farewell touches on his wares.

'How 's this?' he said, stepping in front of Suzan and Emmeline. 'Where's your curls, gal?'

The girl looked timidly at her mother, who, with the smooth adroitness, common among her class, answers.

'I was telling her, last night, to put up her hair smooth and neat, and not havin' it flying about in curls; looks more respectable so.'

'Bother!' said the man, peremptorily, turning to the girl; 'you go right along, and curl yourself real smart!' He added, giving a crack to a rattan he held in his hand, 'And be back in quick time, too!'

'You go and help her,' he added, to the mother. 'Them curls may make a hundred dollars difference in the sale of her.'

Beneath a splendid dome were men of all nations, moving to and fro, over the marble pave. On every side of the circular area were little tribunes, or stations, for the use of speakers and auctioneers. Two of these, on opposite sides of the area, were now occupied by brilliant and talented gentlemen, enthusiastically forcing up, in English and French commingled, the bids of connoisseurs in their various wares. A third one, on the other side, still unoccupied, was surrounded by a group, waiting the moment of sale to begin. And here we may recognize the St. Clare servants, — Tom, Adolph, and others; and there, too, Suzan and Emmeline, awaiting their turn with anxious and dejected faces. Various spectators, intending to purchase, or not intending, as the case might be, gathered around the group, handling, examining, and commenting on their various points and faces with the same freedom that a set of jockeys discuss the merits of a horse.

'Hulloa, Alf! what brings you here?' said a young exquisite, slapping the shoulder of a sprucely-dressed young man, who was examining Adolph through an eye-glass.

'Well, I was wanting a valet, and I heard that St. Clare's lot was going. I thought I'd just look at his —'

'Catch me ever buying any of St. Clare's people! Spoilt niggers, every one. Impudent as the devil!' said the other.

'Never fear that!' said the first. 'If I get 'em, I'll soon have their airs out of them; they'll soon find that they've another kind of master to deal with than Monsieur St. Clare. 'Pon my word, I'll buy that fellow. I like the shape of him.'

'You'll find it'll take all you've got to keep him. He's deucedly extravagant!'

'Yes, but my lord will find that he *can't* be extravagant with *me*. Just let him be sent to the calaboose a few times, and thoroughly dressed down! I'll tell you if it don't bring him to a sense of his ways! O, I'll reform him, up hill and down, — you'll see. I buy him, that's flat!'

Tom had been standing wistfully examining the multitude of faces thronging around him, for one whom he would wish to call master. And if you should ever be under the necessity, sir, of selecting, out of two hundred men, one who was to become your absolute owner and disposer, you would, perhaps, realize, just as Tom did, how few there were that you would feel at all comfortable in being made over to. Tom saw abundance of men, — great, burly, gruff men; little, chirping, dried men; long-favoured, lank, hard men; and every variety of stubbed-looking, commonplace men, who pick up their fellow-men as one picks up chips, putting them into the fire or a basket with equal unconcern, according to their convenience, but he saw no St. Clare.

A little before the sale commenced, a short, broad, muscular man, in a checked shirt considerably open at the bosom and pantaloons much the worse for dirt and wear, elbowed his way through the crowd, like one who is going actively into a business; and, coming up to the group, began to examine them systematically. From the moment that Tom saw him approaching, he felt an immediate and revolting horror at him, that increased as he came near. He was evidently, though short, of gigantic strength. His round, bullet head, large, light-grey eyes, with their shaggy, sandy eye-brows, and stiff, wiry sun-burned hair, were rather unprepossessing items, it is to be confessed; his large, coarse mouth was distended with tobacco, the juice of which, from time to time, he ejected from him with great decision and explosive force; his hands were immensely large, hairy, sun-burned, freckled, and very dirty, and garnished with long nails, in a very foul condition. This man proceeded to a very free personal examination of the lot. He seized Tom by the jaw, and pulled open his mouth to inspect his teeth; made him strip up his sleeve, to show his muscle; turned him round, made him jump and spring, to show his paces.

'Where was you raised?' he added, briefly, to these investigations.

'In Kentuck, Mas'r,' said Tom, looking about, as if for deliverance.

'What have you done?'

'Had care of Mas'r's farm,' said Tom.

'Likely story!' said the other, shortly, as he passed on. He paused a moment before Adolph; then spitting a discharge of tobacco-juice on his well-blacked boots, and giving a contemptuous umph, he walked on. Again he stopped before Suzan and Emmeline. He put out his heavy, dirty hand, and drew the girl towards him; passed it over her neck and bust, felt her arms, looked at her teeth, and then pushed her back against her mother, whose patient face showed the suffering she had been going through at every motion of the hideous stranger.

The girl was frightened, and began to cry.

'Stop that, you minx!' said the salesman; 'no whimpering here, — the sale is going to begin.' And accordingly the sale began.

Adolph was knocked off, at a good sum, to the young gentleman who had previously stated his intention of buying him; and the other servants of the St. Clare lot went to various bidders.

'Now, up with you, boy! d'ye hear?' said the auctioneer to Tom.

Tom stepped upon the block, gave a few anxious looks round; all seemed mingled in a common, indistinct noise, — the clatter of the salesman crying off his qualifications in French and English, the quick fire of French and English bids; and almost in a moment came the final thump of the hammer, and the clear ring on the last syllable of the word *'dollars'*, as the auctioneer announced his price, and Tom was made over. — He had a master!

He was pushed from the block; — the short, bullet-headed man seizing him roughly by the shoulder, pushed him to one side, saying, in a harsh voice, 'Stand there, *you*!'

Tom hardly realized anything; but still the bidding went on, — rattling, clattering, now French, now English. Down goes the hammer again, — Suzan is sold! She goes down from the block, stops, looks wistfully back, — her daughter stretches her hands towards her. She looks with agony in the face of the man who has bought her, — a respectable middle-aged man, of benevolent countenance.

'O, Mas'r, please do buy my daughter!'

'I'd like to, but I'm afraid I can't afford it!' said the gentleman, looking, with painful interest, as the young girl mounted the block, and looked around her with a frightened and timid glance.

The blood flushes painfully in her otherwise colourless cheek, her eye has a feverish fire, and her mother groans to see that she looks more beautiful than she ever saw her before. The auctioneer sees his advantage, and expatiates volubly in mingled French and English, and bids rise in rapid succession.

'I'll do anything in reason,' said the benevolent-looking gentleman, pressing in and joining with the bids. In a few moments they have run beyond his purse.

He is silent; the auctioneer grows warmer; but bids gradually drop off. It lies now between an aristocratic old citizen and our bullet-headed acquaintance. The citizen bids for a few turns, contemptuously measuring his opponent; but the bullet-head has the advantage over him, both in obstinacy and concealed length of purse, and the controversy lasts but a moment; the hammer falls, — he has got the girl, body and soul, unless God help her!

Her master is Mr. Legree, who owns a cotton plantation on the Red river. She is pushed along into the same lot with Tom and two other men, and goes off, weeping as she goes.

The benevolent gentleman is sorry; but, then, the thing happens every day! One sees girls and mothers crying, at these sales, *always!* it can't be helped, &c.; and he walks off, with his acquisition, in another direction.

Two days after, the lawyer of the Christian firm of B. & Co., New York, sent on their money to them. On the reverse of that draft, so obtained, let them write these words of the great Paymaster, to whom they shall make up their account in a future day: *'When he maketh inquisition for blood, he forgetteth not the cry of the humble!'*

The Middle Passage

'Thou art of purer eyes than to behold evil, and canst not look upon iniquity: wherefore lookest thou upon them that deal treacherously, and holdest thy tongue when the wicked devoureth the man that is more righteous than he?'

— HAB. 1 : 13.

On the lower part of a small, mean boat, on the Red river, Tom sat, — chains on his wrists, chains on his feet, and a weight heavier than chains lay on his heart. All had faded from his sky, —moon and star; all had passed by him, as the trees and banks were now passing, to return no more. Kentucky home, with wife and children, and indulgent owners; St. Clare home, with all its refinements and splendours, the golden head of Eva, with its saint-like eyes; the proud, gay, handsome, seemingly careless, yet ever-kind St. Clare; hours of ease and indulgent leisure, − all gone! and in place thereof, *what* remains?

It is one of the bitterest apportionments of a lot of slavery, that the negro, sympathetic and assimilative, after acquiring, in a refined family, the tastes and feelings which form the atmosphere of such a place, is not the less liable to become the bond-slave of the coarsest and most brutal, − just as a chair or table,

which once decorated the superb saloon, comes at last, battered and defaced, to the bar-room of some filthy tavern, or some low haunt of vulgar debauchery. The great difference is, that the table and chair cannot feel, and the *man* can; for even a legal enactment that he shall be 'taken, reputed, adjudged in law, to be a chattel personal,' cannot blot out his soul, with its own private little world of memories, hopes, loves, fears, and desires.

Mr. Simon Legree, Tom's master, had purchased slaves at one place and another, in New Orleans, to the number of eight, and driven them, handcuffed, in couples of two and two, down to the good steamer Pirate, which lay at the levee, ready for a trip up the Red river.

Having got them fairly on board, and the boat being off, he came round, with that air of efficiency which ever characterized him, to take a review of them. Stopping opposite to Tom, who had been attired for sale in his best broadcloth suit, with well-starched linen and shining boots, he briefly expressed himself as follows:

'Stand up.'

Tom stood up.

'Take off that stock!' and, as Tom, encumbered by his fetters, proceeded to do it, he assisted him, by pulling it, with no gentle hand, from his neck, and putting it in his pocket.

Legree now turned to Tom's trunk, which, previous to this, he had been ransacking, and, taking from it a pair of old pantaloons and a dilapidated coat, which Tom had been wont to put on about his stable-work, he said, liberating Tom's hand from the handcuffs, and pointing to a recess in among the boxes,

'You go there, and put these on.'

Tom obeyed, and in a few moments returned.

'Take off your boots,' said Mr. Legree.

Tom did so.

'There,' said the former, throwing him a pair of coarse, stout shoes, such as were common among the slaves, 'put these on.'

In Tom's hurried exchange, he had not forgotten to transfer his cherished Bible to his pocket. It was well he did so; for Mr. Legree, having refitted Tom's handcuffs, proceeded deliberately to investigate the contents of his pockets. He drew out a silk handkerchief, and put it into his own pocket. Several little trifles, which Tom had treasured, chiefly because they had amused Eva, he looked upon with a contemptuous grunt, and tossed them over his shoulder into the river.

Tom's Methodist hymn-book, which, in his hurry, he had forgotten, he now held up and turned over.

'Humph! pious, to be sure. So, what's yer name, — you belong to the church?'

'Yes, Mas'r,' said Tom, firmly.

'Well, I'll soon have *that* out of you. I have none o' yer bawling, praying, singing niggers on my place; so remember. Now, mind yourself,' he said, with a stamp and a fierce glance of his grey eye, directed at Tom, *'I'm* your church now! You understand, — you've got to be as I say.'

Something within the silent black man answered *No!* and, as if repeated by an invisible voice, came the words of an old prophetic scroll, as Eva had often read them to him, — 'Fear not! for I have redeemed thee. I have called thee by my name. Thou art MINE!'

But Simon Legree heard no voice. That voice is one he never shall hear. He only glared for a moment on the downcast face of Tom, and walked off. He took Tom's trunk, which contained a very neat and abundant wardrobe, to the forecastle, where it was soon surrounded by various hands of the boat. With much laughing, at the expense of niggers who tried to be gentlemen, the articles very readily were sold to one and another, and the empty trunk finally put up at auction. It was a good joke, they all thought, especially to see how Tom looked after his things, as they were going this way and that; and then the auction of the trunk, that was funnier than all, and occasioned abundant witticisms.

This little affair being over, Simon sauntered up again to his property.

'Now, Tom, I've relieved you of any extra baggage, you see. Take mighty good care of them clothes. It'll be long enough 'fore you get more. I go in for making niggers careful; one suit has to do for one year, on my place.'

Simon next walked up to the place where Emmeline was sitting, chained to another woman.

'Well, my dear,' he said, chucking her under the chin, 'keep up your spirits.'

The involuntary look of horror, fright and aversion, with which the girl regarded him, did not escape his eye. He frowned fiercely.

'None o' your shines, gal! you 's got to keep a pleasant face, when I speak to ye, — d'ye hear? And you, you old yellow poco moonshine!' he said, giving a shove to the mulatto woman to whom Emmeline was chained, 'don't you carry that sort of face! You 's got to look chipper, I tell ye!'

'I say, all on ye,' he said, retreating a pace or two back, 'look at me, — look at me, — look me right in the eye, — *straight,* now!' said he, stamping his foot at every pause.

As by a fascination, every eye was now directed to the glaring greenish-grey eye of Simon.

'Now', said he, doubling his great, heavy fist into something resembling a blacksmith's hammer, 'd'ye see this fist? Heft it!' he said, bringing it down on Tom's hand. 'Look at these yer bones! Well, I tell ye this yer fist has got as hard as iron *knocking down niggers*. I never see the nigger, yet, I couldn't bring down with one crack,' said he, bringing his fist down so near to the face of Tom that he winked and drew back. 'I don't keep none o' yer cussed overseers; I does my own overseeing; and I tell you things *is* seen to. You 's every one on ye got to toe the mark, I tell ye; quick, — straight, — the moment I speak. That's the way to keep in with me. Ye won't find no soft spot in me, nowhere. So, now, mind yerselves; for I don't show no mercy!'

The women involuntarily drew in their breath, and the whole gang sat with downcast, dejected faces. Meanwhile, Simon turned on his heel, and marched up to the bar of the boat for a dram.

'That's the way I begin with my niggers,' he said, to a gentlemanly man, who had stood by him during his speech. 'It's my system to begin strong, — just let 'em know what to expect.'

'Indeed!' said the stranger, looking upon him with the curiosity of a naturalist studying some out-of-the-way specimen.

'Yes, indeed. I'm none o' yer gentlemen planters, with lily fingers, to slop round and be cheated by some old cuss of an overseer! Just feel of my knuckles, now; look at my fist. Tell ye, sir, the flesh on 't has come jest like a stone, practising on niggers, — feel on it.'

The stranger applied his fingers to the implement in question, and said, ''T is hard enough; and, I suppose,' he added 'practice has made your heart just like it.'

'Why, yes, I may say so,' said Simon, with a hearty laugh. 'I reckon there's as little soft in me as in any one going. Tell you, nobody comes it over me! Niggers never gets round me, neither with squalling nor soft soap, — that's a fact.'

'You have a fine lot there.'

'Real,' said Simon. 'There's that Tom, they told me he was suthin' uncommon. I paid a little high for him, tendin' him for a driver and a managing chap; only get the notions out that he's larnt by bein' treated as niggers never ought to be, he'll do prime! The yellow woman I got took in in. I rayther think she's sickly, but I shall put her through for what she's worth; she may last a year or two. I don't go for savin' niggers. Use up, and buy more, 's my way; — makes you less trouble, and I'm quite sure it comes cheaper in the end;' and Simon sipped his glass.

'And how long do they generally last?' said the stranger.

'Well, donno; 'cordin' as their constitution is. Stout fellers last six or seven years; trashy ones gets worked up in two or three. I used to, when I fust begun, have considerable trouble fussin' with 'em and trying to make 'em hold out, — doctorin' on 'em up when they 's sick, and givin' on 'em clothes and blankets, and what not, tryin' to keep 'em all sort o' decent and comfortable. Law, 't wasn't no sort o' use; I lost money on 'em, and 't was heaps o' trouble. Now, you see, I just put 'em straight through, sick or well. When one nigger 's dead, I buy another; and I find it comes cheaper and easier, every way.'

The stranger turned away, and seated himself beside a gentleman, who had been listening to the conversation with repressed uneasiness.

'You must not take that fellow to be any specimen of Southern planters,' said he.

'I should hope not,' said the young gentleman, with emphasis.

'He is a mean, low, brutal fellow!' said the other.

'And yet your laws allow him to hold any number of human beings subject to his absolute will, without even a shadow of protection; and, low as he is, you cannot say that there are not many such.'

'Well,' said the other, 'there are also many considerate and humane men among planters.'

'Granted,' said the young man; 'but, in my opinion, it is you considerate, humane men, that are responsible for all the brutality and outrage wrought by these wretches; because, if it were not for your sanction and influence, the whole system could not keep foot-hold for an hour. If there were no planters except such as that one,' said he, pointing with his finger to Legree, who stood with his back to them, 'the whole thing would go down like a mill-stone. It is your respectability and humanity that licenses and protects his brutality.'

'You certainly have a high opinion of my good nature,' said the planter, smiling; 'but I advise you not to talk quite so loud, as there are people on board

the boat who might not be quite so tolerant to opinion as I am. You had better wait till I get up to my plantation, and there you may abuse us all, quite at your leisure.'

The young gentleman coloured and smiled, and the two were soon busy in a game of backgammon. Meanwhile, another conversation was going on in the lower part of the boat, between Emmeline and the mulatto woman with whom she was confined. As was natural, they were exchanging with each other some particulars of their history.

'Who did you belong to?' said Emmeline.

'Well, my Mas'r was Mr. Ellis, — lived on Levee-street. P'raps you've seen the house.'

'Was he good to you?' said Emmeline.

'Mostly, till he tuk sick. He's lain sick, off and on, more than six months, and been orful oneasy. 'Pears like he warnt willin' to have nobody rest, day nor night; and got so curous, there couldn't nobody suit him. 'Pears like he just grew crosser, every day; kep me up nights till I got farly beat out, and couldn't keep awake no longer; and cause I got to sleep, one night, Lors, he talk so orful to me, and he tell me he'd sell me to just the hardest master he could find; and he'd promised me my freedom, too, when he died.'

'Had you any friends?' said Emmeline.

'Yes, my husband, — he's a blacksmith. Mas'r gen'ly hired him out. They took me off so quick, I didn't even have time to see him, and I 's got four children. O, dear me!' said the woman, covering her face with her hands.

It is a natural impulse, in every one, when they hear a tale of distress, to think of something to say by way of consolation. Emmeline wanted to say something, but she could not think of anything to say. What was there to be said? As by a common consent, they both avoided, with fear and dread, all mention of the horrible man who was now their master.

True, there is religious trust for even the darkest hour. The mulatto woman was a member of the Methodist church, and had an unenlightened but very sincere spirit of piety. Emmeline had been educated much more intelligently, — taught to read and write, and diligently instructed in the Bible, by the care of a faithful and pious mistress; yet, would it not try the faith of the firmest Christian, to find themselves abandoned, apparently, of God, in the grasp of ruthless violence? How much more must it shake the faith of Christ's poor little ones, weak in knowledge and tender in years!

The boat moved on, — freighted with its weight of sorrow, — up the red, muddy, turbid current, through the abrupt, tortuous windings of the Red river; and sad eyes gazed wearily on the steep red-clay banks, as they glided by in dreary sameness. At last the boat stopped at a small town, and Legree, with his party, disembarked.

Dark Places

"The dark places of the earth are full of the habitations of cruelty."

Trailing wearily behind a rude wagon, and over a ruder road, Tom and his associates faced onward.

In the wagon was seated Simon Legree; and the two women, still fettered together, were stowed away with some baggage in the back part of it, and the whole company were seeking Legree's plantation, which lay a good distance off.

It was a wild, forsaken road, now winding through dreary pine barrens, where the wind whispered mournfully, and now over log causeways, through long cypress swamps, the doleful trees rising out of the slimy, spongy ground, hung with long wreaths of funereal black moss, while ever and anon the loathsome form of the moccasin snake might be seen sliding among broken stumps and shattered branches that lay here and there, rotting in the water.

It is disconsolate enough, this riding, to the stranger, who, with well-filled pocket and well-appointed horse, threads the lonely way on some errand of business; but wilder, drearier, to the man enthralled, whom every weary step bears further from all that man loves and prays for.

So one should have thought, that witnessed the sunken and dejected expression on those dark faces; the wistful, patient weariness with which those sad eyes rested on object after object that passed them in their sad journey.

Simon rode on, however, apparently well pleased, occasionally pulling away at a flask of spirit, which he kept in his pocket.

'I say, *you!*' he said, as he turned back and caught a glance at the dispirited faces behind him. 'Strike up a song, boys, — come!'

The men looked at each other, and the *'come'* was repeated, with a smart crack of the whip which the driver carried in his hands. Tom began a Methodist hymn,

'Jerusalem, my happy home,
Name ever dear to me!
When shall my sorrows have an end,
Thy joys when shall —'

'Shut up, you black cuss!' roared Legree; 'did ye think I wanted any o' yer infernal old Methodism? I say, tune up, now, something real rowdy, — quick!'

One of the other men struck up one of those unmeaning songs, common among the slaves.

'Mas'r see'd me cotch a coon,

High boys, high!
He laughed to split, — d'ye see the moon,
Ho! ho! ho! boys, ho!
Ho! yo! hi — e! oh!'

The singer appeared to make up the song to his own pleasure, generally hitting on rhyme, without much attempt at reason; and all the party took up the chorus, at intervals,

'Ho! ho! ho! boys, ho!
High — e — oh! high — e — oh!'

It was sung very boisterously, and with a forced attempt at merriment; but no wail of despair, no words of impassioned prayer, could have had such a depth of woe in them as the wild notes of the chorus. As if the poor, dumb heart, threatened, — prisoned, — took refuge in that inarticulate sanctuary of music, and found there a language in which to breathe its prayer to God! There was a prayer in it, which Simon could not hear. He only heard the boys singing noisily, and was well pleased; he was making them 'keep up their spirits'.

'Well, my little dear,' said he, turning to Emmeline, and laying his hand on her shoulder, 'we're almost home!'

When Legree scolded and stormed, Emmeline was terrified; but when he laid his hand on her, and spoke as he now did, she felt as if she had rather he would strike her. The expression of his eyes made her soul sick, and her flesh creep. Involuntarily she clung closer to the mulatto woman by her side, as if she were her mother.

'You didn't ever wear ear-rings,' he said, taking hold of her small ear with his coarse fingers.

'No, Mas'r!' said Emmeline, trembling and looking down.

'Well, I'll give you a pair, when we get home, if you're a good girl. You needn't be so frightened; I don't mean to make you work very hard. You'll have fine times with me, and live like a lady, — only be a good girl.'

Legree had been drinking to that degree that he was inclining to be very gracious; and it was about this time that the enclosures of the plantation rose to view. The estate had formerly belonged to a gentleman of opulence and taste, who had bestowed some considerable attention to the adornment of his grounds. Having died insolvent, it had been purchased, at a bargain, by Legree, who used it, as he did everything else, merely as an implement for money-making. The place had that ragged, forlorn appearance, which is always produced by the evidence that the care of the former owner has been left to go to utter decay.

What was once a smooth-shaven lawn before the house, dotted here and there with ornamental shrubs, was now covered with frowsy tangled grass, with horse-posts set up, here and there, in it, where the turf was stamped away, and the ground littered with broken pails, cobs of corn, and other slovenly remains. Here and there, a mildewed jessamine or honeysuckle hung raggedly from some ornamental support, which had been pushed to one side by being used as a horse-post. What once was a large garden was now all grown over with weeds, through which, here and there, some solitary exotic reared its forsaken head. What had been a conservatory had now no window-sashes, and on the mouldering shelves stood some dry, forsaken flower-pots, with sticks in them, whose dried leaves showed they had once been plants.

The wagon rolled up a weedy gravel walk, under a noble avenue of China trees, whose graceful forms and ever-springing foliage seemed to be the only things there that neglect could not daunt or alter, — like noble spirits, so deeply rooted in goodness, as to flourish and grow stronger amid discouragement and decay.

The house had been large and handsome. It was built in a manner common at the South; a wide verandah of two stories running round every part of the house, into which every outer door opened, the lower tier being supported by brick pillars. But the place looked desolate and uncomfortable; some windows stopped up with boards, some with shattered panes, and shutters hanging by a single hinge, — all telling of coarse neglect and discomfort.

Bits of board, straw, old decayed barrels and boxes, garnished the ground in all directions; and three or four ferocious-looking dogs, roused by the sound of the wagon-wheels, came tearing out, and were with difficulty restrained from laying hold of Tom and his companions, by the effort of the ragged servants who came after them.

'Ye see what ye'd get!' said Legree, caressing the dogs with grim satisfaction, and turning to Tom and his companions. 'Ye see what ye'd get, if ye try to run off. These yer dogs has been raised to track niggers; and they'd jest as soon chaw one on ye up as eat their supper. So, mind yerself! How now, Sambo!' he said, to a ragged fellow, without any brim to his hat, who was officious in his attentions. 'How have things been going?'

'Fust rate, Mas'r.'

'Quimbo,' said Legree to another, who was making zealous demonstrations to attract his attention, 'ye minded what I telled ye?'

'Guess I did, didn't I?'

These two coloured men were the two principal hands on the plantation. Legree had trained them in savageness and brutality as systematically as he had his bull-dogs; and, by long practice in hardness and cruelty, brought their whole nature to about the same range of capacities. It is a common remark, and one that is thought to militate strongly against the character of the race, that the negro overseer is always more tyrannical and cruel than the white one. This is simply saying that the negro mind has been more crushed and debased than the white. It is no more true of this race than of every oppressed race, the world over. The slave is always a tyrant, if he can get a chance to be one.

Legree, like some potentates we read of in history, governed his plantation by a sort of resolution of forces. Sambo and Quimbo cordially hated each other; the plantation hands, one and all, cordially hated them; and, by playing off one against another, he was pretty sure, through one or the other of the three parties, to get informed of whatever was on foot in the place.

Nobody can live entirely without social intercourse; and Legree encouraged his two black satellites to a kind of coarse familiarity with him, — a familiarity, however, at any moment liable to get one or the other of them into trouble; for, on the slightest provocation, one of them always stood ready, at a nod, to be a minister of his vengeance on the other.

As they stood there now by Legree, they seemed an apt illustration of the fact that brutal men are lower even than animals. Their coarse, dark, heavy features; their great eyes, rolling enviously on each other; their barbarous, guttural, half-brute intonation; their dilapidated garments fluttering in the wind, — were all in admirable keeping with the vile character of everything about the place.

'Here, you Sambo,' said Legree, 'take these yer boys down to the quarters; and here's a gal I've got for *you,*' said he, as he separated the mulatto woman from Emmeline, and pushed her towards him; — 'I promised to bring you one, you know.'

The woman gave a sudden start, and, drawing back, said, suddenly,

'O, Mas'r! I left my old man in New Orleans.'

'What of that, you —; won't you want one here? None o' your words, — go long!' said Legree, raising his whip.

'Come, mistress,' he said to Emmeline, 'you go in here with me.'

A dark, wild face was seen, for a moment, to glance at the window of the house; and, as Legree opened the door, a female voice said something, in a quick, imperative tone. Tom, who was looking, with anxious interest, after Emmeline, as she went in, noticed this, and heard Legree answer, angrily, 'You may hold your tongue! I'll do as I please, for all you!'

Tom heard no more; for he was soon following Sambo to the quarters. The quarters was a little sort of street of rude shanties, in a row, in a part of the plantation, far off from the house. They had a forlorn, brutal, forsaken air. Tom's heart sunk when he saw them. He had been comforting himself with the thought of a cottage, rude, indeed, but one which he might make neat and quiet, and where he might have a shelf for his Bible, and a place to be alone out of his labouring hours. He looked into several; they were mere rude shells, destitute of any species of furniture, except a heap of straw, foul with dirt, spread confusedly over the floor, which was merely the bare ground, trodden hard by the tramping of innumerable feet.

'Which of these will be mine?' said he, to Sambo, submissively.

'Dunno; ken turn in here, I spose,' said Sambo; 'spects thar's room for another thar; thar's a pretty smart heap o'niggers to each on 'em, now; sure, I dunno what I 's to do with more.'

It was late in the evening when the weary occupants of the shanties came flocking home, — men and women, in soiled and tattered garments, surly and uncomfortable, and in no mood to look pleasantly on new-comers. The small village was alive with no inviting sounds; hoarse, guttural voices contending at the hand-mills where their morsel of hard corn was yet to be ground into meal, to fit it for the cake that was to constitute their only supper. From the earliest dawn of the day, they had been in the fields, pressed to work under the driving lash of the overseers; for it was now in the very heat and hurry of the season, and no means was left untried to press every one up to the top of their capabilities. 'True,' says the negligent lounger; 'picking cotton isn't hard work.' Isn't it? And it isn't much inconvenience, either, to have one drop of water fall on your head; yet the worst torture of the inquisition is produced by drop after drop, drop after drop, falling moment after moment, with monotonous succession, on the same spot; and work, in itself not hard, becomes so, by being pressed, hour after hour, with unvarying, unrelenting sameness, with not even the consciousness of free-will to take from its tediousness. Tom looked in vain among the gang, as they poured along, for companionable faces. He saw only sullen, scowling, imbruted men, and feeble, discouraged women, or women that were not women, — the strong pushing away the weak, — the gross, unrestricted animal selfishness of human beings, of whom nothing good was expected and desired; and who, treated in every way like brutes, had sunk as nearly to their level as it was possible for human beings to do. To a late hour in the night the sound of the grinding was protracted; for the mills were few in number compared with the grinders, and the weary and feeble ones were driven back by the strong, and came on last in their turn.

'Ho, yo!' said Sambo, coming to the mulatto woman, and throwing down a bag of corn before her; 'what a cuss ye name?'

'Lucy,' said the woman.

'Wal, Lucy, yo my woman now. Yo grind dis yer corn, and get *my* supper baked, ye har?'

'I an't your woman, and I won't be!' said the woman, with the sharp, sudden courage of despair; 'yo go long!'

'I'll kick yo, then!' said Sambo, raising his foot threateningly.

'Ye may kill me, if ye choose, — the sooner the better! Wish't I was dead!' said she.

'I say, Sambo, you go to spilin' the hands, I'll tell Mas'r o' you,' said Quimbo, who was busy at the mill, from which he had viciously driven two or three tired women, who were waiting to grind their corn.

'And I'll tell him ye won't let the women come to the mills, yo old nigger!' said Sambo. 'Yo jes keep to yo own row.'

Tom was hungry with his day's journey, and almost faint for want of food.

'Thar, yo!' said Quimbo, throwing down a coarse bag, which contained a peck of corn; 'thar, nigger, grab, take car on 't, — yo won't get no more, *dis* yer week.'

Tom waited till a late hour, to get a place at the mills; and then, moved by the utter weariness of two women, whom he saw trying to grind their corn there, he ground for them, put together the decaying brands of the fire, where many had baked cakes before them, and then went about getting his own supper. It was a new kind of work there, a deed of charity, small as it was; but it woke an answering touch in their hearts, — an expression of womanly kindness came over their hard faces; they mixed his cake for him, and tended its baking; and Tom sat down by the light of the fire, and drew out his Bible, — for he had need of comfort.

'What's that?' said one of the women.

'A Bible,' said Tom.

'Good Lord! han't seen un since I was in Kentuck.'

'Was you raised in Kentuck?' said Tom, with interest.

'Yes, and well raised, too; never 'spected to come to dis yer!' said the woman, sighing.

'What's dat ar book, any way?' said the other woman.

'Why, the Bible.'

'Laws a me! what's dat?' said the woman.

'Do tell! you never hearn on 't?' said the other woman. 'I used to har Missis a readin' on 't, sometimes, in Kentuck; but, laws o' me! we don't har nothin' here but crackin' and awarin'.'

'Read a piece, anyways!' said the first woman, curiously, seeing Tom attentively poring over it.

Tom read, — 'Come unto ME, all ye that labour and are heavy laden, and I will give you rest.'

'Them 's good words, enough,' said the woman; 'who says 'em?'

'The Lord,' said Tom.

'I jest wish I know'd whar to find Him,' said the woman. 'I would go; 'pears like I never should get rested agin. My flesh is fairly sore, and I tremble all over, every day, and Sambo 's allers a jawin' at me, 'cause I doesn't pick faster; and

nights it's most midnight 'fore I can get my supper; and den 'pears like I don't turn over and shut my eyes, 'fore I hear de horn blow to get up, and at it agin in de mornin'. If I knew whar de Lor was, I'd tell him.'

'He's here, he's everywhere,' said Tom.

'Lor, you an't gwine to make me believe dat ar! I know de Lord an't here,' said the woman; ' 'tan't no use talking, though. I 's jest gwine to camp down, and sleep while I ken.'

The women went off to their cabins, and Tom sat alone, by the smouldering fire, that flickered up redly in his face.

The silver, fair-browed moon rose in the purple sky, and looked down, calm and silent, as God looks on the scene of misery and oppression, — looked calmly on the lone black man, as he sat, with his arms folded, and his Bible on his knee.

'Is God HERE?' Ah, how is it possible for the untaught heart to keep its faith, unswerving, in the face of dire misrule, and palpable, unrebuked injustice? In that simple heart waged a fierce conflict: the crushing sense of wrong, the foreshadowing of a whole life of future misery, the wreck of all past hopes, mournfully tossing in the soul's sight, like dead corpses of wife, and child, and friend, rising from the dark wave, and surging in the face of the half-drowned mariner! Ah, was it easy *here* to believe and hold fast the great password of Christian faith, that 'God Is, and is the REWARDER of them that diligently seek Him'?

Tom rose, disconsolate, and stumbled into the cabin that had been allotted to him. The floor was already strewn with weary sleepers, and the foul air of the place almost repelled him; but the heavy night-dews were chill, and his limbs weary, and, wrapping about him a tattered blanket, which formed his only bed-clothing, he stretched himself in the straw and fell asleep.

In dreams, a gentle voice came over his ear; he was sitting on the mossy seat in the garden by Lake Pontchartrain, and Eva, with her serious eyes bent downward, was reading to him from the Bible; and he heard her read,

'When thou passest through the waters, I will be with thee, and the rivers they shall not overflow thee; when thou walkest through the fire, thou shalt not be burned, neither shall the flame kindle upon thee; for I am the Lord thy God, the Holy One of Israel, thy Saviour.'

100

Gradually the words seemed to melt and fade, as in a divine music; the child raised her deep eyes, and fixed them lovingly on him, and rays of warmth and comfort seemed to go from them to his heart; and, as if wafted on the music, she seemed to rise on shining wings, from which flakes and spangles of gold fell off like stars, and she was gone.

Tom woke. Was it a dream? Let it pass for one. But who shall say that that sweet young spirit, which in life so yearned to comfort and console the distressed, was forbidden of God to assume this ministry after death?

It is a beautiful belief,
That ever round our head
Are hovering, on angel wings,
The spirits of the dead.

Cassy

"And behold, the tears of such as were oppressed, and they had no comforter; and on the side of their oppressors there was power, *but they had no comforter."*

— ECCL. 4 : 1.

It took but a short time to familiarize Tom with all that was to be hoped or feared in his new way of life. He was an expert and efficient workman in whatever he undertook; and was, both from habit and principle, prompt and

101

faithful. Quiet and peaceable in his disposition, he hoped, by unremitting diligence, to avert from himself at least a portion of the evils of his condition. He saw enough of abuse and misery to make him sick and weary; but he determined to toil on, with religious patience, committing himself to Him that judgeth righteously, not without hope that some way of escape might yet be opened to him.

Legree took silent note of Tom's availability. He rated him as a first-class hand; and yet he felt a secret dislike to him — the native antipathy of bad to good. He saw, plainly, that when, as was often the case, his violence and brutality fell on the helpless, Tom took notice of it; for, so subtle is the atmosphere of opinion, that it will make itself felt, without words; and the opinion even of a slave may annoy a master. Tom in various ways manifested a tenderness of feeling, a commiseration for his fellow-sufferers, strange and new to them, which was watched with a jealous eye by Legree. He had purchased Tom with a view of eventually making him a sort of overseer, with whom he might, at times, intrust his affairs, in short absences; and, in his view, the first, second, and third requisite for that place, was *hardness*. Legree made up his mind, that, as Tom was not hard to his hand, he would harden him forthwith; and some few weeks after Tom had been on the place, he determined to commence the process.

One morning, when the hands were mustered for the field, Tom noticed, with surprise, a new comer among them, whose appearance excited his attention. It was a woman, tall and slenderly formed, with remarkably delicate hands and feet, and dressed in neat and respectable garments. By the appearance of her face, she might have been between thirty-five and forty; and it was a face that, once seen, could never be forgotten, — one of those that, at a glance, seem to convey to us an idea of a wild, painful, and romantic history. Her forehead was high, and her eyebrows marked with beautiful clearness. Her straight, well-formed nose, her finely-cut mouth, and the graceful contour of her head and neck, showed that she must once have been beautiful; but her face was deeply wrinkled with lines of pain, and of proud and bitter endurance. Her complexion was sallow and unhealthy, her cheeks thin, her features sharp, and her whole form emaciated. But her eye was the most remarkable feature, — so large, so heavily black, overshadowed by long lashes of equal darkness, and so wildly, mournfully despairing. There was a fierce pride and defiance in every line of her face, in every curve of the flexible lip, in every motion of her body; but in her eye was a deep, settled night of anguish, — an expression so hopeless and unchanging as to contrast fearfully with the scorn and pride expressed by her whole demeanour.

Where she came from, or who she was, Tom did not know. The first he did know, she was walking by his side, erect and proud, in the dim grey of the dawn. To the gang, however, she was known; for there was much looking and turning of heads, and a smothered yet apparent exultation among the miserable, ragged, half-starved creatures by whom she was surrounded.

'Got to come to it, at last, — glad of it!' said one.

'He! he! he!' said another; 'you'll know how good it is, Misse!'

'We'll see her work!'

'Wonder if she'll get a cutting up, at night, like the rest of us!'

'I'd be glad to see her down for a flogging, I'll be bound!' said another.

The woman took no notice of these taunts, but walked on, with the same expression of angry scorn, as if she heard nothing. Tom had always lived among refined and cultivated people, and he felt intuitively, from her air and bearing, that she belonged to that class; but how or why she could be fallen to those degrading circumstances, he could not tell. The woman neither looked at him nor spoke to him, though, all the way to the field, she kept close at his side.

Tom was soon busy at his work; but, as the woman was at no great distance from him, he often glanced an eye to her, at her work. He saw, at a glance, that a native adroitness and handiness made the task to her an easier one than it proved to many. She picked very fast and very clean, and with an air of scorn, as if she despised both the work and the disgrace and humiliation of the circumstances in which she was placed.

In the course of the day, Tom was working near the mulatto woman who had been bought in the same lot with himself. She was evidently in a condition of great suffering, and Tom often heard her praying, as she wavered and trembled, and seemed about to fall down. Tom silently, as he came near to her, transferred several handfuls of cotton from his own sack to hers.

'O, don't, don't!' said the woman, looking surprised; 'it'll get you into trouble.'

Just then Sambo came up. He seemed to have a special spite against this woman; and, flourishing his whip, said, in brutal, guttural tones, 'What dis yer, Luce, — foolin' a'?' and, with the word, kicking the woman with his heavy cow-hide shoe, he struck Tom across the face with his whip.

Tom silently resumed his task; but the woman, before at the last point of exhaustion, fainted.

'I'll bring her to!' said the driver, with a brutal grin. 'I'll give her something better than camphire!' and, taking a pin from his coat-sleeve, he buried it to the head in her flesh. The woman groaned, and half rose. 'Get up, you beast, and work, will yer, or I'll show yer a trick more!'

The woman seemed stimulated, for a few moments, to an unnatural strength, and worked with desperate eagerness.

'See that you keep to dat ar,' said the man, 'or yer'll wish yer 's dead to-night, I reckin!'

'That I do now!' Tom heard her say; and again he heard her say, 'O, Lord, how long! O, Lord, why don't you help us?'

At the risk of all that he might suffer, Tom came forward again, and put all the cotton in his sack into the woman's.

'O, you mustn't! you donno what they'll do to ye!' said the woman.

'I can bear it!' said Tom, 'better 'n you;' and he was at his place again. It passed in a moment.

Suddenly, the stranger woman whom we have described, and who had, in the course of her work, come near enough to hear Tom's last words, raised her heavy black eyes, and fixed them, for a second, on him; then, taking a quantity of cotton from her basket, she placed it in his.

'You know nothing about this place,' she said, 'or you wouldn't have done that. When you've been here a month, you'll be done helping anybody; you'll find it hard enough to take care of your own skin!'

'The Lord forbid, Missis!' said Tom, using instinctively to his field companion the respectful form proper to the high bred with whom he had lived.

'The Lord never visits these parts,' said the woman, bitterly, as she went nimbly forward with her work; and again the scornful smile curled her lips.

But the action of the woman had been seen by the driver, across the field; and, flourishing his whip, he came up to her.

'What! what!' he said to the woman, with an air of triumph, 'YOU a foolin'? Go along! yer under me now, — mind yourself, or yer'll cotch it!'

A glance like sheet-lightning suddenly flashed from those black eyes; and, facing about, with quivering lip and dilated nostrils, she drew herself up, and fixed a glance, blazing with rage and scorn, on the driver.

'Dog!' she said, 'touch *me*, if you dare! I've power enough, yet, to have you torn by the dogs, burnt alive, cut to inches! I've only to say the word!'

'What de devil you here for, den?' said the man, evidently cowed, and sullenly retreating a step or two. 'Didn't mean no harm, Misse Cassy!'

'Keep your distance, then!' said the woman. And, in truth, the man seemed greatly inclined to attend to something at the other end of the field, and started off in quick time.

The woman suddenly turned to her work, and laboured with a despatch that was perfectly astonishing to Tom. She seemed to work by magic. Before the day was through, her basket was filled, crowded down, and piled, and she had several times put largely into Tom's. Long after dusk, the whole weary train, with their baskets on their heads, defiled up to the building appropriated to the storing and weighing the cotton. Legree was there, busily conversing with the two drivers.

'Dat ar Tom 's gwine to make a powerful deal o' trouble; kept a puttin' into Lucy's basket. — One o' these yer dat will get all der niggers to feelin' 'bused, if Mas'r don't watch him!' said Sambo.

'Hey-dey! The black cuss!' said Legree. 'He'll have to get a breakin' in, won't he, boys?'

Both negroes grinned a horrid grin, at this intimation.

'Ay, ay! let Mas'r Legree alone, for breakin' in! De debil heself couldn't beat Mas'r at dat!' said Quimbo.

'Wal, boys, the best way is to give him the flogging to do, till he gets over his notions. Break him in!'

'Lord, Mas'r'll have hard work to get dat out o' him!'

'It'll have to come out of him, though!' said Legree, as he rolled his tobacco in his mouth.

'Now, dar's Lucy, — de aggravatinest, ugliest wench on de place!' pursued Sambo.

'Take care, Sam; I shall begin to think what's the reason for your spite agin Lucy.'

'Well, Mas'r knows she sot herself up agin Mas'r, and wouldn't have me, when he told her to.'

'I'd a flogged her into 't,' said Legree, spitting, 'only there's such a press o' work, it don't seem wuth a while to upset her jist now. She's slender; but these yer slender gals will bear half killin' to get their own way!'

'Wal, Lucy was real aggravatin' and lazy, sulkin' round; wouldn't do nothin', — and Tom he tuck up for her.'

'He did, eh! Wal, then, Tom shall have the pleasure of flogging her. It'll be a good practice for him, and he won't put it on to the gal like you devils, neither.'

'Ho, ho! haw! haw! haw!' laughed both the sooty wretches; and the diabolical sounds seemed, in truth, a not unapt expression of the fiendish character which Legree gave them.

'Wal, but, Mas'r, Tom and Misse Cassy, and dey among 'em, filled Lucy's basket. I ruther guess der weight 's in it, Mas'r!'

'I do the weighing!' said Legree, emphatically.

Both the drivers again laughed their diabolical laugh.

'So!' he added, 'Misse Cassy did her day's work.'

'She picks like de debil and all his angels!'

'She's got 'em all in her, I believe!' said Legree; and, growling a brutal oath, he proceeded to the weighing-room.

Slowly the weary, dispirited creatures, wound their way into the room, and, with crouching reluctance, presented their baskets to be weighed.

Legree noted on a slate, on the side of which was pasted a list of names, the amount.

Tom's basket was weighed and approved; and he looked, with an anxious glance, for the success of the woman he had befriended.

Tottering with weakness, she came forward, and delivered her basket. It was of full weight, as Legree well perceived; but, affecting anger, he said,

'What, you lazy beast! short again! stand aside, you'll catch it, pretty soon!'

The woman gave a groan of utter despair, and sat down on a board.

The person who had been called Misse Cassy now came forward, and, with a haughty, negligent air, delivered her basket. As she delivered it, Legree looked in her eyes with a sneering yet inquiring glance.

She fixed her black eyes steadily on him, her lips moved slightly, and she said something in French. What it was, no one knew; but Legree's face became perfectly demoniacal in its expression, as he spoke; he half raised his hand, as if to strike, — a gesture which she regarded with fierce disdain, as she turned and walked away.

'And now,' said Legree, 'come here, you Tom. You see, I told ye I didn't buy ye jest for the common work; I mean to promote ye, and make a driver of ye; and to-night ye may jest as well begin to get yer hand in. Now, ye jest take this yer gal and flog her; ye've seen enough on 't to know how.'

'I beg Mas'r's pardon,' said Tom; 'hopes Mas'r won't set me at that. It's what I an't used to, — never did, — and can't do, no way possible.'

'Ye'll larn a pretty smart chance of things ye never did know, before I've done with ye!' said Legree, taking up a cowhide, and striking Tom a heavy blow across the cheek, and following up the infliction by a shower of blows.

'There,' he said, as he stopped to rest; 'now, will ye tell me ye can't do it?'

'Yes, Mas'r,' said Tom, putting up his hand, to wipe the blood, that trickled down his face. 'I'm willin' to work, night and day, and work while there's life and breath in me; but this yer thing I can't feel it right to do; — and, Mas'r, I *never* shall do it, — *never!*'

Tom had a remarkably smooth, soft voice, and a habitually respectful manner, that had given Legree an idea that he would be cowardly, and easily subdued. When he spoke these last words, a thrill of amazement went through every one; the poor woman clasped her hands, and said, 'O Lord!' and every one involuntarily looked at each other and drew in their breath, as if to prepare for the storm that was about to burst.

Legree looked stupefied and confounded; but at last burst forth, —

'What! ye blasted black beast! tell *me* ye don't think it *right* to do what I tell ye! What have any of you cussed cattle to do with thinking what's right? I'll put a stop to it! Why, what do ye think ye are? May be ye think ye'r a gentleman master, Tom, to be a telling your master what's right, and what an't! So you pretend it's wrong to flog the gal!'

'I think so, Mas'r,' said Tom; 'the poor crittur 's sick and feeble; 't would be downright cruel, and it's what I never will do, nor begin to. Mas'r, if you mean to kill me, kill me; but, as to my raising my hand agin any one here, I never shall, — I'll die first!'

Tom spoke in a mild voice, but with a decision that could not be mistaken. Legree shook with anger; his greenish eyes glared fiercely, and his very whiskers seemed to curl with passion; but, like some ferocious beast, that plays with its victim before he devours it, he kept back his strong impulse to proceed to immediate violence, and broke out into bitter raillery.

'Well, here's a pious dog, at last, let down among us sinners! — a saint, a gentleman, and no less, to talk to us sinners about our sins! Powerful holy critter, he must be! Here, you rascal, you make believe to be so pious, — didn't you never hear, out of yer Bible, "Servants, obey yer masters"? An't I yer master? Didn't I pay down twelve hundred dollars, cash, for all there is inside yer old cussed black shell? An't yer mine, now, body and soul?' he said, giving Tom a violent kick with his heavy boot; 'tell me!'

In the very depth of physical suffering, bowed by brutal oppression, this question shot a gleam of joy and triumph through Tom's soul. He suddenly stretched himself up, and looking earnestly to heaven, while the tears and blood that flowed down his face mingled, he exclaimed,

'No! no! no! my soul an't yours, Mas'r! You haven't bought it, — ye can't buy it! It's been bought and paid for, by one that is able to keep it; — no matter, no matter, you can't harm me!'

'I can't!' said Legree, with a sneer; 'we'll see, — we'll see! Here, Sambo,

Quimbo, give this dog such a breakin' in as he won't get over, this month!'

The two gigantic negroes that now laid hold of Tom, with fiendish exultation in their faces, might have formed no unapt personification of powers of darkness. The poor woman screamed with apprehension, and all rose, as by a general impulse, while they dragged him unresisting from the place.

ROBINSON CRUSOE

DANIEL DEFOE
adapted by J. V. Pleva

Fate decides that Robinson is not to return home from his travels.
A voyage to Africa and the Guinea coast.
Attack by pirates.
Robinson is taken prisoner.

Never before in his life had Robinson been in a city as big as London, and his wonder increased with every step he took. He said good-bye to Martin and his father as soon as they left the port. With the wreck of his ship, Captain Westlock had lost practically all he possessed. However, he had a wealthy brother who was a merchant in the city, and it was to his house that the two of them now turned their steps. As they parted, the Captain shook Robinson's hand and said: 'I am truly sorry, young fellow, that our voyage ended in such misfortune. When you get home, please pay my respects to your father; you need make no secret of the fate which has overtaken me, for such are the ways of the sea, and I do not despair. God willing, I shall meet with better fortune in the years to come. As for you, Master Crusoe, the best advice I can offer you is: return to York by stagecoach.'

Robinson took his leave of the Captain and his friend Martin. He rented a room not far from the harbour, and from it he set out to walk about London. He still had a sizable sum of money left over after putting down a deposit for his purchases.

The Captain had no need to advise me to travel by stagecoach, thought Robinson to himself. After all I have been through, I shall never board a ship again!

Robinson resolved to spend at least three more days in London, after which he would set off home. How pleased his father and mother would be when he told them of his decision never to go to sea again, when they found out that he had been cured of his longing to become a sailor on his very first voyage! His father would be sure to forgive him for setting off without his permission. Robinson genuinely looked forward to being reunited with his parents. How keenly he would attend to the business now; how hard he would work! His father was right: there was nothing better than a peaceful, ordered, merchant's life. He had, thank God, come off lightly in his adventure. But how closely death had passed him by...

For three days Robinson wandered the streets of London without a care. He saw imposing squares and busy embankments. On the fourth day he went to the stagecoach office to ask when there was a coach leaving for York. He was surprised to find that there was none that went there direct, and that he must first travel to Manchester. There he would have to wait for a coach to take him to York. But the stagecoach to Manchester chanced to have left just an hour ago, and it was another week before the next one was due. What is there to be done? Robinson thought to himself. So he arranged to leave on the next coach, put down a deposit, and returned to his hotel. He still had plenty of money for a week's stay in London and to pay his fare. With money enough, what was to prevent him from spending another week in the city? After all, when was he likely to have another opportunity to spend a few days in London without a care? His new-found resolve never again to journey by sea, to lead the life of a good citizen, had put him in an unusually good mood. He was cured for ever of the desire to become a sailor.

But the busy life of the harbour still lured Robinson back there, and the next day he set out to take a proper look around the huge Port of London. He spent the whole day wandering around the docks observing the hustle and bustle of the place. He was fascinated to watch the hundreds of people in long rows as they carried parcels and cases down into the bowels of the huge ships, while others unloaded vessels which had just docked, taking the goods off into the gigantic warehouses. He was unable to resist having his supper in one of the dockside taverns. After supper he ordered a glass of hot punch. Some sailors came to sit at his table. They began to recount their experiences from their last voyage, and one of them boasted of how many gold pieces he had brought back from a voyage to the distant shores of Africa. A little drunk from the punch, and allured by the vivid pictures of adventure conjured up by the sailors, Robinson joined in their conversation. Out of youthful vanity, he boasted of how he had lived through a terrible storm at sea, and survived a shipwreck. The sailors soon saw that they

were speaking to a guileless young lad. They ostentatiously expressed their wonder at his tale, and drank his health. As he had once done at home in York, so now, too, Robinson bought the sailors drinks, making a show of paying with a sovereign. After that they took more interest in him than ever. They soon learnt that he was the son of a wealthy merchant in York, that since his childhood he had wanted nothing more dearly than to be a sailor, to voyage far across the seas and to visit unknown lands, where he would have great adventures. Finally, he told them how, after his recent experience, he never wanted to go aboard a ship again, and that he was quite cured of his ambition to become a sailor. His companions laughed, and one of them cried out: 'There would be mighty few sailors and sea-captains in the world if they were all put off by the first storm like you, young fellow!' Then he raised his glass and drank to the health of all fearless seamen. After that the sailors tried to convince Robinson that Captain Westlock's ship had certainly been wrecked simply because her master had not handled her properly. They considered that the recent storm had not been a particularly severe one. They themselves had been caught in it in the English Channel, and had they not sailed safely home?

The sailors' words were enough to shake Robinson's resolution a good deal, as far as never going to sea again was concerned. In a while they began to throw dice, and invited Robinson to join them. They were experienced players, and at first they let the lad win a good sum of money once or twice. But then his luck changed, and within an hour the sailors had won all his money from him. He begged them to lend him at least one sovereign so that he might play on, hoping that his luck might return. Laughing, however, the sailors rose from the table, wished Robinson good-night and bon voyage, and left the tavern.

Robinson was alone again. He sat there full of contrition at this sudden turn of events. Too late, he reproached himself for his foolishness in bringing upon himself this unpleasant state of affairs. He had no choice but to return to his hotel, ask for credit, and write to his father to send him the money to pay his debts and his fare home. As he sat there, head in hands, musing on how, a short while before, he had been blessed with good fortune and full of cheer, a pair of well-dressed men sat down at his table and ordered themselves a fine supper. The older of the two observed Robinson discreetly, and in a while asked him straight out: 'What are you so sad about, young friend?' Lost in his thoughts,

Robinson turned to him with distrust. But when he spied the kindly face of a man of about forty, with a well-groomed beard and neatly-pressed necktie, he lost his suspicion, and before very long he had recounted to the stranger the whole tale of what had just befallen him.

'Just as I thought,' remarked the stranger. 'I could see at once that you are no Londoner. My dear young fellow, London is a great city, and sailors are often a band of rogues. You must be very careful here.' Having said these words, the stranger introduced himself as Captain Dubbley of York.

'Ah, then you are from York, Captain, sir?' In sheer surprise, Robinson almost shouted the words.

'Indeed,' replied the Captain, looking at Robinson searchingly. 'Could you be...'

'I am Robinson Crusoe, son of a merchant of that name, from York also.'

'Great Heavens! You are Mr. Crusoe's boy? Why, of course I know your father. Crusoe is one of the best merchants in York. Though I do not know him personally, I know well enough how well-respected is his house in that town. What a chance meeting this is! Your health, Master Crusoe!' And the captain and his younger companion, who introduced himself as Mr. Smith, helmsman of Grimsby, joined Robinson in raising their glasses.

Robinson also confided to Captain Dubbley that he had left home without his parents' consent.

'You should not have done that, Master Crusoe. Your father is sure to be very worried about you.'

'I wrote to him from Hull to say that I was going to London, and that I should be gone for some six weeks. But I was not to know what fate awaited me, thanks to my own foolishness and recklessness. I wanted to return home by stagecoach. I have already bespoken a seat on the coach and paid a deposit. But now I haven't a penny to my name. I shall write to my father to ask him to send me money, and until it arrives, I must stay here in London.'

'There is no need to write for money, Master Crusoe. I shall be pleased to lend you what you need to pay your fare and what debts you have incurred. When I return from the next voyage, you shall repay me. But do not worry on that account now. I shall be gone some three months at least. I shall sail for the Guinea coast, in Africa, where I am doing excellent barter with the natives.'

Then Captain Dubbley told Robinson how this was his third trip to Guinea. The first two had brought him a good return on his money. In London he had spent fifty sovereigns on various trifles — glass beads, looking-glasses, some gold-plated trinkets, silk ribbons, scissors, and other small tools of that sort. In Guinea he had received several hundredweight of ivory for such worthless baubles. It was possible to exchange tools or trinkets there for precious woods, rare spices — even for gold.

So carried away was Robinson by the Captain's story, that he forgot in an instant all his recent troubles, forgot all that he had been through in the past few days, and begged the Captain to take him to Guinea with him. He promised to write to his father about the trip, saying that as soon as he heard what a voyage he was making, with what an experienced captain, and a native of York at that, he would surely have no fear for his son. When Robinson returned from the voyage with his profits, his father was sure to forgive him for leaving without his permission. The lad was most surprised to see the enthusiasm with which the Captain agreed to his new idea. He willingly agreed to lend Robinson forty sovereigns with which to buy various trifles to barter in Africa.

Robinson returned from the tavern to his hotel, happy again, and full of bold plans for the future. His chance meeting that evening had further convinced him that it was the will of Fate that he should make at least one voyage to distant lands. But he was also drawn by the great profit which he supposed the journey would bring him. Foolishly, he already saw himself returning to his native town from distant Africa with great riches, which would ensure him a peaceful and carefree life. He wove himself beautiful dreams. When he returned from Africa, he would buy another house in York, get married; as a respected merchant he would become a member of the city council, one day perhaps even mayor. That would be far better than being a mere clerk of the King's Court.

In his hotel bed, Robinson fell into the deep and carefree sleep of a man for whom all these dreams had already been fulfilled. The next day he wrote to his father of the great good fortune he had met with in London. He begged forgiveness for leaving home without his consent, promising that on his return he would make up for everything by being twice as industrious, and that he would really give up all thought of travelling the seas again.

Before sending the letter, he asked Captain Dubbley to add a few lines to greet his father and to assure him that his son was undertaking the journey in his good charge.

Three days later Captain Dubbley's vessel sailed from the Thames Estuary out to sea. A favourable south-easterly wind was blowing. That night they passed through the Straits of Dover. To starboard shone the lighthouses of the English coast, while far off on the port beam they could see flashes from the shores of France. In the Channel the Captain was anxious about the fog which often came up there, but the night passed without event, and the dawn sun was reflected from the white Kentish cliffs, far astern.

On the fifth day out of the Port of London, the vessel was already out of sight of land, in the vast waters of the Atlantic Ocean. Here, too, the weather was kind to the sailors. A south-westerly breeze blew them on their way. The sky remained clear. Robinson noted that, while the waters of the North Sea had been greenish-blue in colour, the Atlantic had a deep blue hue, and the water was

very clear. In the depths he could see fish of many shapes and colours. It sometimes seemed to him that whole forests of some sort of sea plants grew tall from the ocean bed.

Off the Portuguese coast he also saw shells and beautiful starfish on the bottom of the sea. Near the Canary Islands a shoal of flying fish flew low across the deck. One night, when Robinson was unable to sleep on account of the heat, he went up on deck, and saw the strange phenomenon of the luminous sea. Flashes of lightning seemed to be coming from the surface of the water, each one followed by millions of tiny sparks dancing over the sea. A breaking wave shone with blue and red light, as if some invisible creature were setting off wonderful fireworks. The ship, too, left in its wake a luminous strip of water. In the place where the seething waters churned up by her hull fell back into the ocean, a patch of multi-coloured foam boiled from the surface.

The helmsman explained to Robinson that such a luminous sea was not unusual in and around the tropics. He said it was caused by millions of tiny marine animals close to the surface, shining in the water just as fireflies did on land. But it was also frequently caused by decaying seaweed, which luminesced like rotting wood in the forest.

Robinson would sit on the deck contentedly, pleased whenever the Captain or the helmsman came to sit beside him. He would ask them about everything to do with the voyage, and they always replied most willingly to all his questions.

The Canaries were behind them now, and the Captain was looking forward to completing the trip as smoothly as he had begun it. For several days they had been sailing down the African coast.

Early one morning Robinson was awakened by loud shouts of 'Ship Ahoy!' He hurried on deck, and was surprised to find the whole crew already busily at work. The watch at the crow's-nest was observing the unknown vessel through a telescope. The Captain had reason to be anxious. It could be a merchantman, but it might also be a pirate ship. In these waters there were many pirates.

To be on the safe side the Captain ordered his men to take up action stations and to maintain full speed ahead.

Half an hour later it became clear that the unknown vessel was indeed a pirate ship. She was much faster than Captain Dubbley's vessel, and was coming up on them rapidly.

118

'The devils are making straight for us,' Dubbley muttered, watching the pirates through his telescope. He ordered the cannon and muskets to be loaded. This upset the passengers a good deal. Then the Captain had all the men issued with muskets and sabres. He was expecting a cruel struggle with the pirates, for in those days such encounters usually came to a fight to the death. Robinson was given a sabre and a pistol. He felt most dispirited. God only knew what new fate awaited him now.

At about six o'clock in the morning the pirate vessel came within range. Dubbley was anxious to fire first, and he ordered a salvo from all guns. But the shots fell short, and before the sailors could reload the pirates returned their fire with all guns. Fortunately, little damage was done, though a few of the sailors were wounded. Dubbley's men fired off another salvo, but apparently to very little effect, for the pirates continued to come up abeam at great speed. It was

119

clear that their crew was much larger, and that they were much better armed. As they drew nearer, the two ships exchanged musket fire; when this had died down, for it took several minutes to reload, the pirates came alongside and attached grappling-hooks to Dubbley's vessel.

With great shouting the pirates swarmed onto the merchantman's deck, and a fierce battle ensued. Robinson, when he had fired his pistol twice, had no time to reload, and flung himself at the enemy with his sabre. But one of the pirates wrenched the sword from him and brought the stock of his musket down on the young man's head. Robinson lost consciousness. The brave sailors were unable to hold off the first attack, and the fate of Dubbley's craft was sealed.

Captain Dubbley fell, as did most of his crew; the rest were taken prisoner. The blow on his head had not been fatal, and Robinson came to his senses just as the pirates were tying the prisoners' hands. The injured young man was led off with the rest.

The pirates took Dubbley's ship in tow to the Moroccan port of Saleh, north-west of Casablanca, where they divided the spoils among themselves.

Robinson is made a slave. He escapes.
Rescue at sea. A voyage to Brazil.
Shipwreck

Because of his injuries, Robinson, instead of being led off at once with the other captives to the slave market to be sold into the interior, spent some time receiving treatment. He was kept in the pirate captain's house. Abd el Mami's men looked after him well; they healed his wound, gave him plenty to eat, and did not mistreat him. This was not because the pirates were especially kind-hearted or humane, but simply because a strong and healthy young slave fetched a much better price.

Captain Abd el Mami was a Moor and a mohammedan. He had a fine house on the clifftop at Saleh, decorated with marble. On the hillside above the house were terraced gardens filled with flowering bushes, especially roses. In the middle of one of these gardens, shaded by palm-trees, stood a summer-house on slender white marble pillars, with a remarkable onion-shaped dome. Inside were low, stone divans, covered with rare and expensive carpets. In front of the summer-house there was a timbered well, richly decorated with marble carvings. It was in this summer-house that Captain Abd el Mami liked to relax. There was a fine view not only of the town below, but also far out to sea.

Abd el Mami took a liking to Robinson, not only for his pleasant appearance, but especially because he was not Spanish. The Captain had a deep hatred of Spaniards, and regarded them as his arch-enemies. In those days all Moors harboured enmity for the Spanish. As Robinson was later to learn, Abd el Mami's grandfather had at one time been a powerful nobleman in Spain. The Spaniards had confiscated all his property and banished him from the land. The Moorish aristocrat's grandson, Abd el Mami, was taking his vengeance on them to this day.

Since Robinson had an excellent memory, he managed to learn the Moorish tongue surprisingly quickly. When he saw this, Abd el Mami decided to make him his personal servant. But he never took him to sea on his ship. While the Captain was away on his voyages of piracy, Robinson would work in the terraced gardens. There he and the other slaves tended their master's vines and the hundreds of rose bushes. While he was engaged upon this work, Robinson

121

had plenty of time to consider his fate. It was only here, ignominiously enslaved in a distant land, that he learned the real value of all those things whose worth he had once so little appreciated: home — living together with the two creatures on earth most dear to him, his mother and father. He recalled the companionship of his friends, the days he had spent with them at school and at play. How fine a place his school at York now seemed to him; how pleasant were the hours he had spent sitting in its benches! He now bitterly regretted that he had so disliked it at the time. Would he ever return to York? he wondered. Would he ever again walk along the riverbank, where he had once dreamed foolish dreams of travelling far across the sea? How he had hated to work with his hands! His father had once told him to help the gardener to weed the flower beds. He had made all sorts of excuses, and had been upset that his father should demand such lowly work of him — he, the son of a wealthy family, work with his hands in the soil, like some peasant! And here he had to do all the work of the garden, with spade and mattock, from morning till evening, in the unbearable heat. He could not straighten his back even for a moment while old Mulej, the slave driver, was in the gardens. The moment any of the slaves stopped work even for an instant to stand up and wipe the sweat from his brow, Mulej would yell at him and threaten him with his stick.

Whenever the Captain returned from his expeditions of piracy and spent some time at home, life was easier for Robinson. He would no longer have to labour in the gardens. Abd el Mami wished to have him close at hand whatever he was doing. He had taken good note of the fact that Robinson was a gifted young man, had a good memory and some learning, and that it was possible to converse with him as an educated person. He summoned an old Moor, and ordered him to teach Robinson every evening to read Moorish script. Within a year he had learnt to read so well that he was able to read Abd el Mami Moorish tales before he went to sleep.

In three years the Captain grew to like Robinson so much that he allowed him to move freely about the town without a guard, but he still did not take him to sea with him. Robinson was disappointed at this. If the Captain were to take him to sea, there was a chance that one day he would fall captive to Europeans, and be released from his slavery. He therefore pretended great loyalty to his master. Abd el Mami allowed him a privilege which none of his slaves had ever had — to accompany him on long trips in his small yacht. He also permitted him to take fishing trips with old Mulej.

When Abd el Mami stayed at home for some time, he would hold frequent banquets for his relatives and friends. He always required large amounts of food, especially fish and various birds. So he would send Robinson out fishing with old Mulej. Mulej used to take a negro lad called Xury along with them. Old Mulej would sit at the tiller, while Robinson and Xury took the oars.

'Perhaps one day I shall manage to escape from slavery in this boat,' thought Robinson. 'When I get the chance I shall get rid of Mulej and Xury, and sail off to Europe. In the meantime I must pretend loyalty to Mulej too, in order to gain his confidence. The Captain trusts Mulej. He would surely like to hear from him that Robinson is reliable, always, everywhere, and in everything. Then, perhaps, the Captain will one day send me out in the boat without the old man. It will be easy to persuade the negro boy to run away. He is a slave like myself. He hates old Mulej as I do, and he likes me.'

And old Mulej really did give Abd el Mami the best possible account of Robinson. Now the Captain took him more often on long trips in the yacht. Robinson would entertain him on the way. He would sometimes ask the young man to tell him about life in his far-off homeland... He listened with great interest to everything Robinson told him. He sometimes asked to hear English songs and tales. Abd el Mami was very fond of tales. He liked best to take such trips in a yacht with a small cabin at the stern, where there was also room for a helmsman. The boat had a lugsail, whose boom stretched back well over the cabin roof. The cabin itself was not very broad. No more than four people could move about in it comfortably. There was a low table, two bunks, a shelf and a coffee pot. Robinson very soon learned to handle the boat, and the Captain entrusted him with the work of the helmsman in the cabin.

Another year passed. One day in May, Abd el Mami ordered his yacht to be made ready for a trip. Two old friends, Moors of high birth, were to visit him. To entertain them he wished to sail across to the far shore to catch fish and shoot birds. They were to leave early and be gone all day. So as to make an early start, Abd el Mami ordered a supply of food and drink to be put aboard the night before. He also had three muskets and powder and shot made ready. The yacht was scrubbed from stem to stern, and the cabin smoked with fragrant spices and its floor covered with fine carpets. Gaily-coloured bunting was hung from the masthead, along with all manner of ornaments. Robinson, old Mulej and the boy Xury were to set off before dawn to await the Captain and his guests aboard the boat.

But in the morning Abd el Mami's steward came to tell them that, because of some pressing business, the guests would not arrive until evening, and that the three of them were to set sail at once to catch fish and shoot birds for supper, returning in the afternoon.

At once it occurred to Robinson that this might be an excellent chance to make good his escape. He would deal with Mulej and Xury somehow. But he would need a better supply of water, and perhaps also of food. When the steward had left them, he persuaded Mulej that it was not fitting for them to eat the provisions which their master had prepared for his honoured guests, and that they should have their usual ship's biscuits brought from the house, and a jug of water for each of them.

So old Mulej sent Robinson and Xury to fetch these things. Robinson stopped off in the servants' quarters, where he took a ball of string and some wax for making candles, after which he returned to the boat with the ship's biscuits and the water. He hid the wax and string in the bottom of the basket, so that Mulej did not see them.

Robinson was disappointed to note that a northerly wind was blowing, and that he would not be able to sail for the coast of Spain. Nonetheless, he was resolved to make his escape.

Mulej the slave-driver was a distant relative of his master's, and was completely faithful to him. He followed the Captain's orders to the letter; while fishing they were never to sail further than a mile away, so that the Captain could safely keep an eye on them through his telescope from the shore. Thus he rejected Robinson's suggestion that they should fish further out. So Robinson and Xury deliberately fished in such a manner as to catch nothing.

Three hours passed, and not a single fish had been landed. Robinson said to old Mulej: 'I do not know how our master will welcome us if we return empty-handed. We have yet to catch a single fish, and there are no birds to be seen either. Mulej, I know the master's orders as well as you do, and I know that they must be obeyed. But you must admit that it would indeed be wiser to move

126

to a place where I suppose there will be many more fish. Once, when I was out fishing with our most noble master, we sailed about a league, to a place where the fish were so plentiful that in the space of an hour we caught more than we had ever before taken in a whole day. I can remember well where it was. From that place a very high mountain with a pointed peak can be seen.'

'I know the place of which you speak, Robinson,' said Mulej. 'The peak of that mountain can indeed be seen from there. But when the master is aboard, it is a different matter. He gives the orders, and we sail where he wishes. But you know well enough how cruel is his wrath, and what harsh punishment he is wont to mete out for the slightest disobedience. I do not wish to make the master angry. He would shut me up in a dark chamber and leave me without food for three days. And you would each receive fifty lashes. It is not to be, Robinson. Our noble master is surely sitting in his arbour at this very moment and watching our boat through his telescope. If we sail too far away, he will send fast cutters in pursuit, and we shall not escape punishment. It would be better for us to return, and I shall ask the master if we may go to the place of which you speak.'

Robinson knew he must tread carefully with Mulej. He also knew that the old man was vain, that he liked to be flattered, especially for his own wisdom to be compared to that of his master.

'No, wise Mulej,' said Robinson. 'I do not advise you to return and to go before the master with such a request. It would distress him and arouse his anger. You know well enough how he was looking forward to taking a trip with his guests this morning. He could not, and his disappointment is great. See what a beautiful day it is. And then you come and tell him of our failure. Consider the wisdom of my words. I know that you are a wise man, and know what to do in order that our master may be pleased with us this evening.'

'There is some truth in what you say, Robinson. I must think of a way of resolving the matter without disobeying the master's orders.'

'Will you, wise Mulej, who are for me the first after my master himself, permit me, a poor slave, to offer you my humble advice?'

Old Mulej, who liked to listen to such words, especially coming from Robinson, the most preferred of all the slaves, thought for a moment, and then said: 'Speak, then, Robinson, and I shall consider the reason of your words.'

'The master's orders are not to sail more than a mile from the shore. But I know of nothing which forbids us to sail along the coast in either direction. You yourself recall, Mulej, that we once sailed over two miles along the shoreline, when the master sent us to shoot the fat razorbills along the cliffs.'

'You are right, Robinson. I remember. I hope that the master does not send cutters after us, when he sees us sail shorewards and turn to the north-west.'

At once Robinson began to persuade Mulej energetically that the wise master would at once realize why they were making north-westwards along the coast. 'Why, he knows well enough himself how many birds there are in those parts, and if he should send anyone after us, it will be easy to explain why we are sailing that way.'

So Mulej gave orders to sail along the coast to the north-west. The northerly wind took them forward briskly. In less than an hour they came to deserted cliffs. Flocks of birds circled above them. On low rocks jutting out of the water sat the razorbills. Robinson rejoiced. Here, among these lonely cliffs, no one was likely to witness what was about to happen.

Robinson handed Xury the helm and went forward to where Mulej stood at the bow. He crouched, as if wishing to rest his musket on the side of the boat in order to shoot at the birds. Then he quickly grabbed the unsuspecting Mulej's legs from behind, and flung him into the sea. He bobbed up again like a cork. Robinson levelled the musket at him and called out: 'Come no closer, or I shoot. Swim to the shore, and go and tell your master that he will never see me again. I am resolved to escape from slavery, whatever the price.'

But Mulej pleaded with him to take pity on him, promising that he would go where Robinson pleased. He said that his life was worthless anyway, that he could not return without yacht and without slaves to his master.

Robinson, though he felt truly sorry for Mulej, and was touched by his pleas, did not trust the old Moor, and repeated his warning. So Mulej turned around and swam to the shore. The negro lad, Xury, when he saw all this, began to tremble with excitement and fear. Robinson turned to him and said: 'Xury, if you obey my orders and are faithful to me, we shall be good friends. We shall sail to a land where my people live, and I promise that there you shall be a free man, as I am, and shall live well. I was once a free man, until Abd el Mami took me prisoner and made me a slave.'

Xury gladly promised to go with Robinson wherever he wished, and to show his loyalty he bowed deeply.

Robinson knew that Mulej would watch to see which way they went. In order to deceive him, he steered the boat to the north-west, towards the open sea. Mulej would be convinced that they were sailing towards the shores of Europe, and would tell Abd el Mami so. When the coast of Africa was lost from sight, he sailed due south for some time, then steered south-east again. With the wind behind them, they again approached the coast of Africa. Abd el Mami was scarcely likely to suppose that Robinson would flee southwards, thus leaving the continent of Europe even further behind him. Only a fool would make for the inhospitable and unknown shores of Africa.

The sea remained calm, and the favourable wind held for several days. The boat slid quietly and swiftly across the waves. Robinson was afraid to go ashore, wanting to sail on as long as their food and water lasted, always in the same direction. He took comfort from the hope that on the way they might come across some European ship sailing from the Guinea coast, or perhaps from distant India, round the Cape of Good Hope.

They had been sailing for many days. First they ran out of water. They suffered greatly from thirst, and had no choice but to go ashore in search of fresh water. At evening they came to the mouth of a small river. Afraid to step ashore, they decided to wait until dawn.

In the morning Robinson asked Xury if he were not afraid to go ashore in an unknown land. He was anxious lest the riverbanks were inhabited by wicked savages. Xury said: 'If come savages, Xury no afraid. We shoot and they run away.'

Robinson was pleased that the boy was in a good mood, that he was not afraid. They sailed quietly into the rivermouth. It was only just getting light. Flocks of birds flew up out of the bushes. But they saw no other creatures on the banks. Nor were there any human inhabitants in sight. A deep silence reigned. They dropped anchor by the bank. Robinson hesitated for a moment, unsure whether to step out onto the unknown shore. Then Xury said to him: 'Robinson stay in boat. Xury go fetch water himself.'

'Are you not afraid, Xury?'

'Xury no afraid. He find water and come back.'

'No, Xury, I shall go with you.'

'Robinson stay in boat. Xury go himself.'

'Why do you want to go alone?'

'If something eat Xury, it not eat you. You stay alive and sail away.'

Robinson was greatly touched by the boy's loyalty. He gave him a drink of the liquor which was left in Abd el Mami's bottle. Then they went ashore together. For half an hour they searched for water in vain. The river water was muddy and had an unpleasant smell. Exhausted, they returned to the riverbank. So desperate had their thirst become, that they drank the river water in spite of its evil odour. When they had quenched their thirst, they began to feel hungry. They ate some ship's biscuits, made themselves comfortable aboard the boat, and soon fell fast asleep.

When Robinson awoke, it was already afternoon. Xury was still asleep. The countryside was surely uninhabited, for if it were not, their boat would have been discovered while he and Xury had been asleep. This allayed Robinson's fears. He roused the boy and they set off again in search of water. This time they went further inland. After an hour's trek in the oppressive heat they came to a shallow valley with tall grass and a few trees and bushes.

Robinson was too tired to go on. He sat down to rest. Xury offered to go and look for water alone. Robinson was loath to let him go, lest he should get lost. But Xury assured him that he would return.

Half an hour later Robinson heard a musket-shot. He was afraid that Xury had been attacked by wild beasts or by savages. But after a further half hour the boy came running up, quite out of breath. Robinson was startled. Thinking that Xury was being pursued, he stood up quickly and prepared to fire his musket. But Xury smiled at him from afar, and when he reached Robinson he flung down in the grass an animal like a small goat, which he had been carrying on his back. It was a young gazelle. He had brought water, too. With great relish, Robinson took a draught of pure water. It was warm, but it tasted excellent, nonetheless. Afterwards they took all the vessels they had aboard the yacht to the place where Xury had found the water, and filled them up.

That evening they lit a fire by the waterside and roasted the gazelle. The meat was very tasty. After supper they raised anchor and sailed once more for the open sea.

After ten days at sea they had eaten all the ship's biscuits and the other food they had on board. The coast along which they were sailing was barren and deserted. Now Robinson and Xury suffered both hunger and thirst. They made several vain attempts to find water. They could not even sleep for thirst, and they were very weak from hunger. They both gazed seawards, vainly hoping for a ship to appear on the horizon. Their one piece of good fortune was that the sea remained calm, so that it required no great effort to sail their little craft.

After spending a troubled night, they saw in the light of dawn that the shore was overgrown with trees. Birds appeared. Where there were plants and animals, there must be water, too. They made for the land. Robinson's throat was so dry with thirst that he could not speak, and his cracked lips hurt terribly. They dropped anchor and stepped ashore. But they could find no water. Xury came upon a number of huge agaves and a group of cactuses. He cut into their leaves, and caught the juice which flowed from them. The agave and cactus juice

soothed their parched throats a good deal, but it did not quench their thirst. Robinson's head ached violently, and his feet were as heavy as lead. Xury was much fresher. He cut some agave leaves and took them aboard the boat. Then they sailed on for another day and night.

Towards morning of the next day, Robinson became delirious with fever. Xury steered the boat alone, anxiously surveying the shore. Suddenly he started to shout: 'Robinson! Robinson! Men, men on land! Shall Xury sail to land?'

Robinson wanted to ask Xury what kind of people they were, but from his dry throat no sound came. He waved a hand towards the shore and nodded his head. Xury understood. A few minutes later the boat grounded in the shallows some fifty yards from the beach.

A group of people were standing on the beach. Beyond them a cluster of huts was to be seen. There were women and children, too. The men held long, light spears in their hands. From this fact Xury deduced that they were about to go fishing. He gestured to the natives that they were hungry and thirsty. They answered with shouts in some unintelligible tongue, and indicated that Xury was to come to them. Xury was suspicious. But when he saw how the natives stayed on the beach, though they might easily have waded out to the boat had they been hostile, he ceased to be anxious. He went into the cabin and told Robinson everything. Robinson lay there helpless. He was too weak even to move. With Xury's help he dragged himself up to see what was happening ashore. He motioned to the natives that he wanted to drink. They understood. Two of them went into a nearby hut and returned with clay vessels. They stayed on the beach, lifting the water pots up high.

'Robinson, Xury go to them. Take gun, and if men bad, he shoot.'

Robinson indicated to the negro lad that there was no need to fear the natives, that he could go to them without a musket. So Xury jumped into the water and swam ashore. When he got to the beach the natives gave him one of the vessels of water at once. Xury drank thirstily. The natives clapped their hands and smiled. Refreshed by the water, Xury gained new strength, and gestured to the natives that they must give water to his companion, who was lying sick in the boat. They discussed the matter among themselves for a few moments. Xury saw that they were afraid of coming to some harm if they approached the boat. They did not trust white men. Xury gesticulated, persuading them that no one would be hurt.

To convince these good-natured folk, he indicated that he would stay ashore with them while some of them took water to the boat.

A pair of tall natives set off towards the boat, carrying the water on their heads. When they reached the yacht the sea came exactly up to their shoulders. The water had a truly miraculous effect on Robinson. He invited the two natives aboard. But they went away in silence. Refreshed, Robinson called out to Xury to help him to beach the craft. Then he came ashore. The natives brought dried meat from their huts, together with some sort of biscuits, and offered them to Robinson. He and Xury ate with relish. The natives then offered them coconuts, and brought some kind of grain which looked like millet, in a clay bowl. Robinson wondered what he might give them in return for gifts which were so precious to them. He remembered that they still had aboard the yacht Abd el Mami's small metal bowls, coffee cups, decorated knives and silver spoons.

He returned to the boat and brought these things for the natives. They showed great pleasure at the gifts, and passed them from hand to hand.

Robinson made gestures to tell the natives that he would like them to catch some fish. In a little while they had killed a fair number by stabbing them in the water with their spears.

Suddenly a large flock of birds came flying over from somewhere inland. They were larger than our partridges. Robinson and Xury grabbed their muskets and shot down five of the birds. The sound of gunfire had a dramatic effect on the natives. Some threw themselves on the ground, while others yelled and danced about in great fear; the women and children ran to their huts. Robinson and Xury showed them that there was no need to be afraid. From their behaviour Robinson judged that no Europeans had ever been to these parts before, since the people had apparently never heard gunfire.

It was a long time before the natives, encouraged by Robinson and Xury, hesitantly returned. Robinson asked them to roast the birds, and to prepare some of the fish.

It was of great interest to Robinson to see how the natives lit a fire by rubbing together two pieces of wood. One of them brought from a hut some small, dry twigs, dry grass, and three pieces of wood. Two pieces had a smooth depression in them, while the third was round, about eight inches long. The man placed the latter between two twisted thongs in the string of a bow, and inserted the ends of

133

it in the holes, between the other pieces of wood. He then moved the bow back and forth as if he were using a saw, and the stick moved rapidly in the holes. Soon there was a smell of burning wood, and smoke came out of the holes. The native placed a handful of dry grass around the bottom one; this soon caught fire. The man added the dry twigs, and soon had a good fire going.

Robinson and Xury spent the whole morning ashore with the natives. Inside the huts, where they were invited by these good people, they were given coconuts, fruit, biscuits, dried meat and ostrich eggs. They now had enough supplies for at least a fortnight. They took their leave of the natives gratefully. When they were accompanied to the shore by the inhabitants of the whole village, one of the men pointed to Robinson's musket. Robinson supposed that he wanted to hear it fired again. He and Xury reloaded their weapons and fired into the air. Their shots had the same effect on the natives as before. They were terribly afraid of the guns.

When the pair of sailors pushed their small craft off again, the natives stood on the shore for a long time, watching them until they disappeared from sight.

For another eleven days Robinson sailed southwards. On the twelfth day a strong easterly wind came up, blowing them out to sea. Just before midday they sighted a strip of land on the horizon to the south-west. Robinson pondered as to what land it might be. He remembered Captain Dubbley's saying that opposite Cape Verde were the Cape Verde Islands. The islands were still a great distance away, their conical mountains appearing on the horizon like splashes of light.

Robinson was worried. He was afraid the wind, which was getting stronger all the time, would turn into a gale and blow the small vessel far out to sea. By now they had food for only two days, and scarcely enough water for one.

Robinson endeavoured to hold the yacht on a southward course. Suddenly, Xury began to jump about the deck and shouted like a man possessed: 'Robinson, Robinson, ship, ship on horizon! Ship there!'

It was so. Far out to starboard the sails of a three-master had hove into view. She had the wind abeam, and was making good speed on a south-easterly course. Robinson and Xury did all they could to steer across her path, but the larger vessel was getting further way. Robinson loaded a musket and fired off a shot. Xury pulled out a carpet, fixed it to the mast, and waved it about.

Whether the shot had been heard, or they had been spotted through a telescope, the ship cut back some of her speed. Robinson fired twice more. The three-master slowed up still more, and finally dropped anchor. In less than an hour Robinson and Xury came up on her. She was a Spanish merchantman, bound for Brazil. The Spaniards invited them aboard. Robinson could speak no Spanish, but one of the sailors was a Scot, and he acted as an interpreter.

Robinson, delighted to be safe at last and once more among Europeans, offered the yacht and all it contained to the ship's captain. But he refused the gift, saying to Robinson: 'I rescued you because it was my duty to do so. I myself should be equally joyous, had someone extended me a helping hand in your situation. One never knows when misfortune may strike at sea. Therefore I cannot accept from you your magnanimous gift. If you will, I shall buy the vessel from you; I see that she is very well constructed. I shall be happy to give you a letter of credit for eighty Brazilian pieces-of-eight for the boat, if you are willing, for it is worth that. You may then buy some goods when we reach Brazil.' Then the Captain looked at Xury and said: 'I will also buy the negro boy from you, if you will take sixty pieces-of-eight for him. He is well-built, and I am sure he is strong.'

The blood came to Robinson's cheeks. He was surprised at the Captain's offer. He had forgotten that in Europe all those who had black skin were simply considered slaves, to be bought and sold like some piece of property.

He looked the Captain resolutely in the eye and said: 'I could never do any such thing. Xury is my best friend. I lived with him in slavery for almost five years. He has helped me to escape to freedom. In return I have promised him his freedom also. When I was sick he cared for me like a brother. He was willing to die for me if need be. He is a rare and good person. There are few like him even among us white men.'

The Captain raised his eyebrows. He was amazed that an Englishman should take the part of an ordinary negro, and even call him his friend. It was the Captain's opinion that no black man deserved such respect. Even if a negro risked his own life for a white man, it was no more than his duty; indeed, it was an honour for him to do so. The Spaniard shrugged his shoulders, and asked what the boy's religion was.

'He is a mohammedan,' Robinson replied.

'Very well; then I should advise you to have him christened at the first possible opportunity, or you will get into trouble with the authorities of the Church of Rome. I myself have no objection if your friend stays with you on my ship.'

The merchantman was sailing to Brazil to pick up rare wood, tobacco and other goods. The passage from Africa to South America was completed almost without event.

Three weeks had passed since Robinson and Xury had been taken aboard. The Captain predicted that they would sight land the next day. The weather was exceptionally close. The wind dropped completely. The vessel was becalmed, her sails hanging limply from the yards. Towards evening a wall of dark grey cloud appeared on the horizon to the west. Around six o'clock they were struck without warning by a sudden strong gust of wind, which caused the vessel to list steeply. A few minutes later the storm broke. The sky clouded over, it began to rain heavily, and flashes of lightning stabbed seawards. Thunder roared about them. The rain poured down like a waterfall, drenching the entire deck. The storm raged all night. It snapped two of the masts and carried away the bridge, compass and all. The gale blew the ship they knew not where.

At dawn the sailors cried: 'Land-ho!' But the Captain could not determine their position; he did not know if they had sighted the mainland, or some island. The gale blew them straight towards the shore. The crew did all they could to alter the course, but after several men had been swept overboard, the rest gave up the useless struggle.

Shortly before noon the ship was shaken by a violent shock. It was clear to everyone aboard what had occurred. The vessel had run aground. Water poured in through the side of the ship. The Captain ordered the lifeboats to be launched. The ship remained lodged in an underwater cleft in the rocks. This gave them some hope that she would not go down at once. The Captain ordered Robinson and Xury into the first boat. Scarcely had they pushed off, when a huge wave lifted the boat high in the air, overturned it, and engulfed all those aboard. Robinson swam desperately towards the shore. Each time he found himself above water, he took a deep breath, so as to hold out until the next wave broke. He must have been some dozen or so yards from the shore when a powerful wave caught him up and threw him down on the rocks. Robinson lost consciousness.

The impact of the next wave brought him round just in time. With his last vestiges of strength he clung to the rocks. When the wave had passed, he crawled up to a higher spot. He gripped the rock tightly so as not to be washed back into the sea by the thunderous surf. Finally he reached a point touched only by the seething foam. There he fell in a faint. He was saved.

Land, or an island?
First days as a castaway.

When Robinson returned to his senses, it was a while before he could remember what had happened. He felt pain in many different parts of his body. Low clouds still darkened the sky, but the wind had dropped and the rain was beginning to stop. Still, Robinson did not know whether it was day or night. Painfully, and with great effort, he sat up on the wet rock, and tried to stand. But the moment he got to his feet he began to totter, so he preferred to sit down again. His life-and-death struggle with the stormy sea had drained his strength. His stomach was turning over, for during his wave-swept swim he had swallowed a good deal of the evil-tasting sea water. He looked around him. The darkling sea roared, and sent its waves crashing against the rocks. He was alone, then. There was no sign of the ship or her crew.

It must have been a good hour or so before he recovered himself enough to stay on his feet. He made his way round the rock until he found a place where it was not too steep, and climbed gingerly down. By and by he found himself beneath the branches of spreading trees, and sat down on dry, rain-flattened grass. Resting his back against a huge treetrunk, he quickly fell into a deep sleep.

When Robinson awoke, the sun was already high in a clear sky. Leaving the shade of the tree, he was surprised at the blast of heat which struck him in the sun's direct rays. He took off his wet clothes to dry them. His deep sleep, which had lasted a good twelve hours, had refreshed him a great deal. He judged by the sun that it might be about nine in the morning. The grass and the leaves of the trees were already dry.

Robinson climbed a small hill by the seashore. The sea was calm now, its surface shining like a mirror. Far out to sea he observed the glimmer of a line of tiny waves. From the treetops came the cries of birds; otherwise there was a deep silence. Over the bushes, the trees and the whole landscape there was a bluish haze.

It was only now that Robinson realized that he had no shoes on — only his socks. He had lost his shoes in the sea, during his struggle with the waves. His short trousers and woollen tunic had now dried in the sun. He put them on. He decided to look for fresh water and to try to find some food. Not far away he could see a sizable mountain rising out of the haze. It would be a good idea to climb it, and to have a look around. He took himself to be on the coast of South America. He looked at the trees and bushes around him, but he could see no fruit. He went through his pockets in search of a piece of ship's biscuit. There was none; but in the pocket of his trousers he found a small knife in a leather case. He had taken it from the cabin of Abd el Mami's yacht. It was the only tool, the only piece of property, which he had saved. All the rest must be deep down on the seabed, along with his faithful friend Xury.

The land around the coast was overgrown with waist-high grass, out of which the crowns of trees and bushes poked upwards. Beyond these, at a distance of some five hundred yards, was a green wall of tall trees. It was the edge of a thick, impenetrable forest.

It was very humid, and Robinson was pestered by swarms of mosquitoes. He proceeded upwards through the long grass, and came to a strange tree, like

139

a palm, but quite low, whose leaves were some three yards long and maybe two feet across. He noted its beautiful red and yellow flowers. Just below these blossoms was some sort of fruit which looked like cucumbers, growing in large bunches. Robinson climbed up the pulpy and stalk-like trunk, a little more than six feet tall, to the crown, where he broke off a bunch of the fruit. It smelt wonderful. Beneath the leafy skin it was soft and sweetly-scented, and had a pleasant taste. Robinson was in a dilemma. Might not the fruit be poisonous? The pleasant taste and smell, and above all his cruel hunger, dispelled his doubts, and he began to eat. He did not know that these were bananas, nor that the banana tree is not a tree at all, but a tall, palm-like plant. The juicy fruit quelled his hunger and the worst of his thirst. The sun scorched him mercilessly. Robinson had no hat, so he broke off one of the long banana leaves and shaded himself with it like a parasol.

After a quarter of an hour he came to a stream, where he took a drink. But the water was warm, and stank of rotting vegetation. After driving away the worst pangs of hunger and quenching his thirst, Robinson made better progress, and after a walk of about an hour he reached the peak of the mountain.

From the top he had a glorious view. Down in the valley there was still a blanket of mist, but above the hilltops the air was clear, and he could see for miles. Robinson's heart sank. He saw that all around, as far as the eye could see, the land was surrounded by water, and that it was not the American continent, but some island close to it. He therefore named the mountain on which he stood Disappointment.

He thought bitterly of how differently all his childhood dreams had turned out. He was indeed in an unknown land, where, perhaps, no European had ever set foot before, at an immense distance away from home. But he was alone on an island. Alone and helpless — hopeless; a poor castaway.

He cast his gaze over the scene below in search of some sign of whether or not the island was inhabited. In the near distance there was no sign of human habitation, nor was there any smoke rising from the distant hills. He considered what animals might live on the island: whether there would be beasts of prey or poisonous snakes among them. What would he do if he met some large carnivore? He was quite unarmed.

On his way down again, Robinson surveyed the ground in front of him most attentively, in case he should tread on some sort of snake or scorpion. He started violently when a rabbit-like creature scurried off out of a bush. It had longer legs than a rabbit, especially the hind ones, and a much larger head, bald, and with hairless ears and big eyes. Its body-hair was flat, dark in colour, with a brownish green tinge to it and grey-green speckles on its hind quarters. It leapt from the bush with a piercing shriek, and fled. Robinson shook from head to foot. This was the first living creature he had met on the island. When he saw it take flight, his fear passed. The rabbit-like creature was in fact an agouti.

Not five minutes had passed, when he came to a halt with a start. His blood ran cold. There was an angry hissing coming from the grass. He had almost trodden on a horrible, ugly creature which looked like a fairytale dragon. It had a bumpy, scaly, green and yellow skin, and a comb-like crest ran from its neck to the tip of its long tail. Beneath its throat the animal had a golden red, scale-covered bag.

The monster opened its mouth, covered with green and golden yellow scales, to reveal rows of even, sharp teeth. Its eyes were as large as a cow's, bulging, and rolling angrily from side to side. On the top of its head the creature had five small, yellowy-brown, horn-like growths. Body and tail together were some five feet long. It crouched on short, stumpy legs with sharp claws. It was an iguana.

Shaking with fear, Robinson waited to see what this fearful creature would do. For a while it goggled at him, giving out short hissing sounds, then swished its tail fiercely and disappeared into the undergrowth. What ugly and horrible monsters there are on this island! thought Robinson to himself. If he had stepped on it, it would surely have bitten him!

He now thought of where he would sleep, when night fell and the whole island was steeped in darkness. Similar monsters were sure to come crawling out of every nook and cranny, and the beasts of prey would leave the forest. He had to consider where to spend the night. He had spent the first night beneath the trunk of a huge tree down by the shore. It was certainly only by good fortune that the predatory beasts on their nocturnal ramblings had not smelt him out there. Even now he trembled to think of the danger he had been in.

What if he were to try sleeping up a tree? It would be wise to find a suitable one at once. With these thoughts occupying his mind, he came to the shore. He hoped to see the wreckage of the ship or the yacht somewhere around. How much more pleasant life would be now, if only Xury had been saved, too. He surveyed the sea and the rocky coast, but there was nothing: not a sign of the fact that a large vessel had been wrecked there.

He walked round the cliffs and went along the sandy beach. In half an hour he came to a cove. Here, in the shallow water along the shore, were whole shoals of tiny, brightly-coloured fish. The sand was littered with gleaming shells. There are sure to be oysters around here somewhere, thought Robinson to himself. And, sure enough, in a while he came upon large numbers of these shellfish by the rocky shore. He did not like the flavour too much, but what was he to do when he was afflicted by such terrible hunger?

He continued his journey westward, and came to a clump of tall trees. They were hundreds of years old, with huge trunks. Their crowns consisted of thick, interwoven branches. He found one whose branches were very low above the ground, climbed up into it, and searched among the tangle of boughs for a suitable place to spend the night. Finally he settled down between two branches, resting his arms on a third. The spot seemed comfortable enough to him.

Tired out from his long trek and from the heat, he quickly fell asleep. The dense foliage provided pleasant shade, and a damp, cooling breeze blew occasionally off the sea.

When he awoke, he was surrounded by impenetrable darkness. It was some seconds before he remembered where he was. As soon as he moved, he felt pains all over his body. His feet had turned to wood, and his back was numbed. Each movement he made brought him new pain. But what could he do? He had to stay where he was. It was so dark that he could not see his hand in front of his face. Most painfully, he slowly changed his position, to try to get some relief, but to no avail. If only he knew what time it was, how long it would be till morning. His aching body kept him awake. Fear made him anxious. What if some lizard or snake were to crawl up there? From the heart of the island he could hear all manner of muffled sounds. It was the cries of the night animals and birds. Shorewards could be heard the steady threshing of the waves. The sky was pricked with countless stars. Time seemed to stand still. Not only did Robinson's limbs ache unbearably, but he was cold to boot. It seemed strange to him that the searing, tiresome heat of the day should give way to a night so chill. He longed for the dawn. At last he fell asleep again.

He woke with a great start. One of his legs had slipped off the branch in his sleep, and his body had lunged forward, bringing his forehead against a bough in front of him. His cry startled the birds which were sheltering in the treetop, and they flew off noisily right above his head, screeching loudly. Half asleep still, he thought he was being attacked by some beast of prey. Twilight lay around. The birds he had disturbed were parrots.

It took all of an hour for him to recover his body movements sufficiently to get down from the tree. He was extremely hungry and thirsty.

A beautiful day dawned on the island. The sky was again clear, and all was quiet. Large numbers of brightly coloured butterflies flitted about the grass. But the beauty of the morning meant nothing to Robinson. He was aching all over.

He could not spend another such night. Where was he to go? Where could he find safety? He decided to spend the day looking for a good, safe place to sleep. If he only had some shoes! His soles were painful from the previous day's walking. The skin of his feet burned like fire. A painful hunger gnawed at his innards. In spite of the pain, he set off in the direction of the stream. When he had quenched his thirst, he set off for the place where he had picked the bananas the day before. As he walked, the pain in his feet distressed him most. The soles of his stockings were torn to shreds.

He noticed rich growths of various bushes further upstream, and beyond them he could see the crowns of palm trees rising up. Perhaps there are bananas there, too, Robinson thought to himself.

He waded along the stream, whose bed was sandy, and whose water came up to his knees. The walk through the cool water was pleasant. But in a while he came to a place where his feet came down on rough and sharp stones. He therefore stepped out onto the bank. He was on the edge of the forest. The branches of huge trees formed a dense arch over the stream, and the light was poor. Creeping, rope-like lianas hung from the huge branches. He would scarcely find bananas here. He must go back. He looked around the bank of the stream for the place he could pass most easily between the dense treetrunks. Suddenly, the overhanging bank gave way beneath his feet, and Robinson found himself up to his waist in water. He took hold of one of the lianas and climbed back onto the bank. But he had scarcely taken a couple of steps when he froze with horror. Some five paces in front of him an enormous boa constrictor was crawling along a thick branch, slowly winding its fifteen-foot body from one bough to the next. Robinson was unable to move with fear. But the snake slid off quickly when it saw him. He was not to know that this species is neither venomous nor aggressive, and lives only on small animals.

When he had got over his shock, Robinson leapt into the stream, heedless of the sharp stones, and ran as fast as he could until he reached its mouth.

It was only when he reached the sandy beach that he sat down, exhausted by his flight. How dangerous it is to sleep in trees! he thought to himself. What good fortune that this huge snake had not climbed into the very tree in which he had slept! What was he to do now? Was he to lay down his weary body on some lonely rock out to sea?

Yesterday's encounter with the iguana and today's with the boa constrictor had made Robinson afraid to go further inland. But he had no wish to sleep on the shore, on the bare rock, with the incessant beating of the surf and splashed by the salt spray. He would walk along the coast, and perhaps he would find a more pleasant spot to take his rest.

The previous day, as he gazed down from the crest of Mount Disappointment, he had noted a conical mountain on the western side of the island, with deep inlets from the sea.

He set off westwards along the shore. After about an hour, he came to another inlet, whose eastern shore, by which he approached it, had a flat, sandy beach, while the far shore was overgrown with some kind of rich vegetation, bushes and trees, and rose steeply up to a huge, rocky mountain.

Robinson skirted the bay. In front of the steep rocks at the foot of the mountain the ground sloped more gently down to the sea for some fifty paces, and was overgrown with dense bushes right up to the cliff face.

Robinson searched for a place where he might pass through the wall of bushes to get to the foot of the mountain. He noticed that on the slope to the north side of the bay there rose a steep, rugged cliff. He thought to himself that he might find some suitable cleft there into which he could climb to spend the night.

He thrust his way through the bushes to the rocks. The bushes were covered with green berries. Robinson tasted them, but they had a sharp, bitter flavour. Parting the branches of the shrubs, he saw that there was some dark opening in the overhanging cliff at the foot of the mountain. The bushes were too dense at that place. He started to cut through their branches with his knife. But after a while his thumb and forefinger became blistered. He managed, however, to cut himself a narrow path, and pushed his way through to the rocks. Up above the boulders at its foot, about six feet above the ground, there was an opening leading into the cliff. It was about a yard high and less than two broad. Robinson looked inside. A roomy cave became visible, its entrance blocked by stones fallen from the rocky overhang. He rolled some of the smaller ones away, thus enlarging the entrance. More light entered the cave, and Robinson could see that the floor was quite flat, and covered with sand. The difficulty of getting to the cave attracted Robinson. This might indeed be a safe shelter, where he might sleep securely. The cave was grown round with impenetrable bushes, and its

145

entrance fortified with stones. He crawled inside, and in a while his eyes had become accustomed to the darkness enough for him to see the whole of the space in which he stood. As he had guessed, the cave was some eight paces deep. The ceiling sloped down towards the inside.

Robinson was joyful. At last he would have a safe refuge, a roof above his head. The cave's situation was excellent. The overhanging wall of rock was sure to keep out the water during heavy rain. The entrance was raised above the ground. At night it could easily be walled up with rocks. The cave looked directly out to sea. The one thing that Robinson regretted was that the bushes made it so difficult to get to it. He was sorry he did not have an axe, with which he might cut himself a more comfortable approach.

He crawled out of the cave and, tired, sat on a boulder. He considered what he should do next. It would be a good idea to explore the immediate vicinity of the cave.

On his way around the bay, Robinson had noticed a small stream flowing into it from a narrow valley to the west; it probably flowed round the mountain. The water in this brook was pure, and much cooler than that in the large stream he had waded along in the morning, when he had seen the huge boa constrictor. Then I shall also have drinking water close at hand, he thought with satisfaction.

The sun was high by now, and burned unremittingly. Robinson returned to the shade of the cave, but cruel hunger soon drove him out again. He went to see if he could find some fruit somewhere near.

Between the bushes and the cliff there was a clear path some two paces wide. The overhanging rock kept the rainwater off this strip of ground, so that nothing grew there. Robinson was able to walk along this path right down to the sea. Truly, he thought to himself, I could not have found a better spot. He was standing on the northern limb of the base of the mountain, which formed one arm of the bay. Here the band of bushy vegetation ended.

Robinson skirted the bushes and came right down to the sandy shore of the inlet. He walked round to the mouth of the stream. He named this stream the Small Stream, to distinguish it from the larger one which flowed out of the forest, which he decided to call the Big Stream. The inlets he named Big Stream Bay and Small Stream Bay.

At the mouth of the Small Stream he found some bananas. When he had eaten his fill, he stuffed his pockets with the fruit. Then he walked upstream along the bank of the Small Stream. The forest reached down to the right bank, while on the left bank there was the mountain slope with its sparse vegetation. There he found cobs of maize. After eating as much as he could manage, he returned to the cave. When he had rested, he set out for the northern shore, in order to walk round the seaward side of the mountain, and to see what was on the other side.

At the foot of the mountain the sandy beach was bordered to a length of some two hundred paces with a line of dry sea grass, about a foot and a half high and some three feet wide. It had been thrown up by the sea. This would make him an excellent bed in his cave, he thought.

The western slopes of the mountain formed a further inlet, reaching deep inland. Here, too, the shores were sandy, but the sands gave way suddenly to an impenetrable bamboo forest. For about twenty minutes Robinson walked around the bamboo thicket, until he came to a palm grove. They were coconut palms. In their crowns, beneath the fan-shaped spread of the long leaves, hung plentiful fruit. Robinson was tempted to shake one of the trees to bring down a few coconuts. But he decided against it. What if one of the large nuts was to fall on his head? And, anyway, what was he to use to crack open the hard shell? No; the palms were not far from his cave, and when they were ripe they would fall of their own accord, and he would only have to gather them up.

Beneath the direct rays of the sun, Robinson's head soon began to ache. Fortunately, bananas were plentiful along that part of the coast. He broke off one of the leaves and held it above his head. What if he were to make himself a hat from the leaves? He snapped off a few young ones, brought some long liana runners from the nearby forest, and plaited the latter into a wreath. Into the openings in the wreath he pushed the stalks of the banana leaves, and bound them tightly together with the fibres of stalks which he cut off. He trimmed the protruding leaves to make an edge as straight as possible, and thus managed to make himself a sort of cornet, which he put on his head. The hat fitted well. It had one shortcoming. The banana leaves soon became dry, and broke. It did not matter — he could make himself such a hat every day. A greater problem was footwear. His cut and battered feet hurt. Robinson had noticed that there were several big old trees lying uprooted on the edge of the forest, probably overturned by the gale. In many places the thick bark was peeling off the dry trunks. What if he were to tie a a piece of bark to each foot with lianas? He set to work at once.

The bark sandals were not terribly comfortable, but in them he could walk painlessly over the sharp grass and pebbles.

After half an hour's walk he came to the farthest point of the bay. Here a range of conical hills began. They were those he had seen the previous day from the summit of Mount Disappointment. Their steep slopes were covered with low bushes. Here and there tall, spreading trees grew among them. Robinson decided to climb one of the hills to take a look around. When he had taken a few steps, he heard a crackling in the bushes. He stopped. A goat and two kids ran out. Robinson was overjoyed to see an animal he knew so well from home.

Walking in his bark sandals was uncomfortable, and the climb up the hill's steep slope took him a long time. From the top he had a beautiful view of the hilly western side of the island. In the eastern half a plain stretched inland, overgrown with forest.

Robinson sat down on a boulder to rest. He was gazing north-eastwards, out towards an endless expanse of sea. There, thousands of miles away, was his homeland. He felt a cruel twinge of homesickness clutch his heart. How long would he be alone? Would some ship ever call at the island and rescue him? Or would he first be torn apart by wild beasts or killed by savages? He had no idea what the interior of the island concealed. Would he ever again see another European face? Home, parents... How his mother and father were probably even now grieving at his departure! In his mind's eye he could see his mother, sitting in the garden bower and weeping bitterly.

For a long time Robinson sat in painful contemplation. Finally, however, he rose, and set off back. He wished to prepare his bedding while it was still light. In those parts the evening twilight was short. The light of day passed rapidly into pitch darkness. He glanced once more towards the horizon, and noticed that to the south west, in the far distance, three hazy hillocks rose from the sea, enormously far off. What could it be? Some distant island, or the mountains of the American coast? He had taken them for small grey clouds. But they had not moved. If it was the coast of America, then there was after all some hope that, one day, some ship or fishing boat would sail to his island...

On the way back he picked as many bananas and ears of maize as he could carry. He placed them in the cave, and returned to fetch the dry sea grass. From this he made himself a soft, comfortable bed, which he then covered with a layer of banana leaves. He thought of how he was to block up the entrance to the cave for the night. The best thing to do would be to pile up stones there. So he took some rocks into the cave and blocked up the hole from the inside. It was late in the evening before he had finished. He was so worn out from his work and his travels that he could scarcely stand. The moment he lay down, he was asleep.

Robinson makes himself a calendar and a sundial.
Furnishing the cave.
Is the island inhabited?

The next morning Robinson awoke quite refreshed. The sun's rays were already probing through the cracks between the stones and into the cave. What time can it be? thought Robinson. And what is the date? He decided he must write down the date of his arrival on the island, and record the days which passed, so that he might know how long he had been there. He tried to remember the date of the shipwreck. He recalled that it had been Thursday, the first of July, 1666. This was the fourth day he had spent on the island, so it must be the fourth of July, and a Sunday. But how was he to record the date? He had neither paper, nor anything to write with. He might carve the date in the rock with his knife. But how was he to mark the passing of the days? If he were to make one mark in the rock each day with his knife, he would in time wear out that, his only implement, and such an important one at that. Then he recalled that there were several young trees growing close to the cave entrance. What if he were to gouge a mark in their bark each day? Yes, that would be far simpler.

Robinson now placed the stones he had used to block the entrance against the wall of the cave, so that he might secure the doorway again in the evening.

The opening into the cave faced eastwards. The full light of the sun's rays now fell inside the cave, and Robinson was able to examine it thoroughly. The ceiling sloped gently towards the rear, and after about eight paces continued at a height of about two and a half feet on into the heart of the mountain. Robinson got down on all fours and crawled a good eight paces further before he came up against the end wall. A pity, he thought; what a spacious dwelling this would be, if the ceiling were not so low. As he was returning, crawling backwards on his hands and knees, he bumped his head against some sort of sharp objects near the roof of the cave. Over his head he could feel large numbers of sharp, icicle-like stone projections, hanging vertically downward. They were stalactites. Robinson had never before in his life seen any such thing, and he vainly racked his brains to think how such a strange rock formation might come about. He lay on his back and examined the stalactites. The whole ceiling in this back part of the cave was covered in them. Some were as thick as his finger, others as slender as a goose quill and over four inches long. There were some that were even longer. They were a yellowish-grey colour, and some were almost transparent. But they were quite dry. The whole of the cave floor was covered with sand. Robinson found himself a sharp stone and dug into the sand to find out how deep it was. He discovered that the layer of sand was very thick. He had dug a hole some two feet deep, and was still digging in sand. It occurred to him that if he were to remove the sand he would increase not only the depth of the cave, but also its useful length. There would be enough space to store even large supplies of food.

That morning he made a disappointing discovery. He found that the bananas he had saved from the previous day were going bad, decaying. He now knew that bananas could not be stored for long. Otherwise, thanks to his long and peaceful sleep, Robinson was in a good mood, and was pleased to see what a glorious sunny day it was. Gloomy thoughts of loneliness no longer entered his mind as much as before. From the cave there was a fine view of the eastern part of the island, and of the whole bay. Reflected in its waters he could see the green of the treetops, and beyond them, shrouded in a light morning mist, the hills, with Mount Disappointment rising above the rest.

Robinson's gaze fell on the clump of slender trees beside the entrance, and he remembered that he wanted to make a calendar. For each day he made a short cut in the bark of one of the trees. On the seventh day, marking the passing of a week, he would make a line twice as long. At the end of the month, in this case of July, he would make a mark on the next tree. The second tree would record the months. When twelve of these had passed, he would cut a deep groove in the third tree. One tree for the days and weeks, a second for the months, and a third for the years. In the smooth bark of one of the young trees he cut the date he had landed on the island: *On the first day of July, a Thursday, in the Year of Our Lord 1666, I landed on this island.* Beneath this inscription he cut four grooves. While he was engaged in this work, it occurred to him that he might also make himself a sundial. Looking around him, he decided that the most suitable spot would be on a small patch of sand at the foot of the mountain on which the sun shone all day. It was only some fifty paces from the entrance to the cave, and the tide never came up so high.

He considered how he might denote the first hour of the morning. He supposed that at the moment the sun rose above the horizon beyond Mount

Disappointment it might be about six o'clock. He would therefore rise early in the morning, in order not to miss the moment the sun came up above the mountains to the east. He would mark the shadow thrown by a stick inserted in the ground, using another stick. When the sun was directly overhead, and the shadow was at its shortest, he would again mark the position of the shadow with a stick. That would be roughly twelve noon. In the evening, when the sun set behind the conical hills, he would mark six o'clock in the evening. By dividing the space between the first and the last stick into twelve equal parts, he would be able to denote all the hours of the day.

Robinson still did not dare venture inland. For one thing, he could not travel far in his bark sandals. He was also afraid of meeting up with wild beasts, perhaps even a settlement of some natives. Every day he anxiously examined the surface of the sand in the bay, in case he should find a human footprint.

In the afternoon he set off for the place the ship had foundered. He hoped to find at least some debris from the ship, or the wreck of the lifeboat. He scanned the rocky coastline, and, sure enough, among the rocks to a distance of up to five hundred yards from the shore, he spotted some fifteen planks and timbers of various lengths and thicknesses floating on the water. They were the remains of the deck and hull of the sunken ship.

Robinson took off his clothes and swam out among the rocks. Within a few hours he had managed to carry the pieces of wood to the shore and drag them out onto the sand. They were soaked with water, and were very heavy. He must first let them dry off in the sun, and then take them to a safe place, where the tide would not carry them out to sea again. Robinson was delighted to find a piece of a mast with many yards of rigging still attached to it, and part of a rope ladder. He cut away all the ropes with his knife. This was a valuable prize. He could unravel the thick ropes and provide himself with a good supply of string. When his work was completed, he went to the place where he had previously found oysters, and took a meagre lunch. The heat was unbearable. On the way back to the cave he picked himself some bananas.

As the afternoon shadows were lengthening, he returned to the bay for more bananas. While he was there he cut himself a thick bamboo cane, so that he might have some weapon at least. As he was walking back along the sandy shore, in one place something gave way beneath his tread. The sand had caved in a little. Robinson thrust his cane into the hole. When he pulled it out again, he saw that the tip was covered in some sort of yellow fluid. He scraped away the sand to find out what it was, and, lo and behold, under a shallow layer of sun-baked sand were almost fifty turtle's eggs, with tough, parchment-like shells. They were much smaller than hen's eggs, only about an inch and a half long, and more rounded. He had learned from sailors that turtle's eggs were edible, and indeed very tasty. He tried one at once, raw. It had an oily yolk and a green white. The taste was not bad, but it needed salting.

The next morning early, he returned to the place where he had fished out the flotsam from the wreck, in order to take it to the cave. In the meantime the planks had dried out well. Robinson noted that their surface was covered with tiny crystals. As he dusted them off with his hand, it suddenly struck him that they might be crystals of salt from the evaporating sea water. Licking his hand, he found that they were indeed salty, that it really was salt. Robinson became thoughtful. By evaporating sea water he could obtain salt. There were plenty of hollows in the rocks. But what was he to use to carry the water in?

As he was pondering over the idea, his glance fell on a group of coconut palms. If he were to knock down some of the nuts, he thought, he might make himself a vessel for carrying water. So he went towards the palms. Two of them had trunks which leaned over steeply, so that there was no danger of the coconuts falling on his head. Once, as a boy, he had been able to climb even the smoothest of elms. But the palm was no elm tree; the trunk was rough, and rather thin. It cost him a great deal of patience and effort to get half way up the trunk, from where he was able to wave the palm from side to side, and shake down almost all of the nuts.

It was only when he had climbed down that Robinson felt the skin on the inside of his thighs and calves burning. He had grazed his legs on the trunk of the palm. He took off his trousers and ran into the water. He nearly cried out with pain. In the salt water the grazes burnt like fire. But he soon forgot his pain when he considered his rich spoils. Now he had to find some way of breaking the coconuts open. First he used a sharp stone to remove the fibrous covering around the shell. On the shell he discovered light-coloured, round spots. Testing with his knife, he found that it was easy to make a hole through them. He bored into one of the coconuts. The white coconut milk came running out. It was cool and had an excellent taste. The flesh of the coconut was about half an inch thick. It took him a long time to dig it out, but the work was worthwhile. He obtained from the coconut a sturdy vessel. Off he went to the sea, and before too long he had filled all the hollows in the rocks with sea water.

Robinson spent the rest of the day carrying the wood off home. The next day he was awoken early, before sunrise, startled by strange screeches. He was afraid some monster had discovered his dwelling. With trembling hands he carefully moved away some of the uppermost stones, in order to take a look outside. On the hedge of bushes in front of the cave sat a flock of large, beautifully-coloured parrots. They were pecking the berries with their curved beaks, and making a terrible racket as they did so.

The sun was still hidden behind Mount Disappointment. Recalling that he wished to record the dawn on his sundial, Robinson removed the stones and went out. Through his nose and mouth he breathed delightedly the exhilarating, sweet-scented and still-cool morning air. When they caught sight of him, the parrots flew off, screeching, somewhere into the interior of the island.

156

On the shore he gazed wistfully for a moment at the surface of the sea. The tide was coming in, and every half minute or so a tall breaker would send white foam scurrying far across the sands of the bay. From the east he could hear the sombre roar of waves pounding against the cliffs. On the horizon to the north-east the surface of the sea shone like silver: the sun had already risen there. In a few minutes the first rays reached the spot where Robinson was standing. The

shadow of his wooden gnomon was outlined sharply on the sand; Robinson traced a line along it and drove a peg into the ground. He left this sticking out about four inches from the surface of the sand. Six o'clock, he thought to himself.

Throughout the morning he went back and forth, carrying the planks and timbers home. Only the longest pieces, which he was unable to carry, were left where they lay. When the shadow of his sundial was at its shortest, Robinson

157

marked twelve noon on its face. He was surprised to see that the midday sun threw a shadow which pointed slightly south. From this fact Robinson deduced that, though the island was still in the Northern Hemisphere, it was below the Tropic of Cancer. When the sun moved closer to the Tropic of Capricorn, the shadow would point northwards. Late in the afternoon, when the shadows were already lengthening, Robinson set off along the rocky headland to Shipwreck Head. The water he had brought from the sea and poured into the hollows in the rocks had already evaporated, leaving behind a thin layer of crystalline salt. He collected this and filled his pockets with it. He used his coconut shells to fill the hollows with sea water again.

In the evening, when the sun touched the surface of the sea, Robinson marked six o'clock in the afternoon on his sundial.

Over the next few days he made some improvements to the entrance to his cave. Using a longish timber as a lever, he moved some of the larger boulders out of the way and enlarged the entrance. Then he went to the shore and found some large shells to use as spades and shovels, with which he scraped away the sand and carried it out of the cave.

Inside a week he had managed to lower the floor of the cave by about a foot and a half. He was greatly worried to find a large number of bones beneath the sand. He wondered how they might have got there. At some time or other the cave had been occupied. The bones belonged to small animals, perhaps goats and rabbits. But who or what had lived there? Savages, perhaps? Where had the sand that covered the bones come from? He thought perhaps the occupants of the cave had dug them into the sand themselves. What if they were to return some day? The thought cost him one or two nights' restless sleep. Every noise in the night, the screeching of birds, the muffled crash of some rotten tree falling in the forest, would wake him up in such terror that he would remain anxiously wakeful, unable to wait for the sun to rise.

While he was digging out the sand from the rear of the cave, beneath the low, stalactite-covered roof, he frequently bumped his head on the stony points. If only he had a spade on a long handle! At first he wanted to break the stalactites off with a stone, but then it occurred to him that they might come in useful for hanging up fruit and meat. At last he thought of how to make a spade out of a large shell which was almost a foot wide. All he had to do was somehow affix the shell to some sort of wooden haft. He emerged from the cave to look for something suitable. At the foot of the cliff he found a tree which had been overturned in the gale. He laboriously cut a thick branch off it with his knife. He then set about boring four holes in the thick side of the shell with the point of the knife. The work was tedious, and it took him a whole two days. When he had finished, he attached the shell firmly to its handle with string.

His digging now proceeded so much more easily and rapidly that within another week he had lowered the cave floor by almost a yard. In doing so he discovered an alcove in the side wall of the cave, about a yard high and some two yards wide, sloping obliquely downwards. At first he thought it was a side-passage leading from the cave. But after three days' untiring work with his spade he uncovered a space about three yards long and some four feet wide. What an excellent larder and cellar this will make! he thought.

Robinson interrupted his work only to fetch fresh food and water. He had now been working for over a fortnight. Towards evening he would visit Shipwreck Head, whence he brought salt, which he collected in coconut shells. He often sat down on the rocky point and gazed for a long time out to sea, in case he should spot some ship on the horizon. But he always returned to his cave disappointed. The work in the cave took three weeks. It was taller and wider. He could also walk a full eleven paces upright along its length now.

During the following days he rolled away the remaining boulders, and found that the floor of the cave was now level with the ground outside. He no longer piled up stones in the entrance at night, but placed the planks and timbers across it. He left a gap about a yard wide above the wood, in order to let fresh air into the cave. How easy it would have been to make door-posts from the timbers and a door from the planks, if only he had an axe, a saw and a few nails!

When Robinson had cleared the whole of the cave, he decided to make himself a table and a bench. Among the rotten treetrunks beside the stream there were plenty of slender young trees growing, perhaps more than thirty feet tall. Robinson would climb up the tree high enough to bend the whole trunk down to the ground with the weight of his body. It would then snap, and he was able to cut through the splintered break with his knife. It took a long time for him thus to cut four posts of about the same size, to serve as the legs of his table. Inside the cave he rammed the ends of the posts into the hard earth with a large stone. On them he placed the broadest and thickest plank he had salvaged from the wreck. So that it would not fall off, he tied it to the posts with string. It looked more like a broad bench than a table, but Robinson was exceedingly pleased with the product of his hard toil. In a similar fashion he made a bench next to the table. The moment he had finished, he began to prepare his first lunch on the new table. He laid a banana leaf on the tabletop, and on it he set two turtle's eggs baked in the hot sand, a banana, a piece of flesh from a coconut, and some oysters. To drink he had coconut milk. How different this was from the first day he had spent on the island, when he had slept in a tree! Now he had a comfortable bed in a roomy, dry cave, and he could sit down cosily at his very own table.

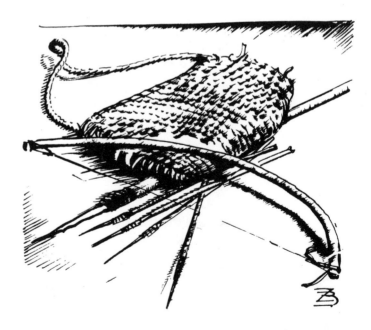

Robinson acquires weapons.
Vain efforts to light a fire. A sunshade.
A terrible storm. Fire. The rains arrive.

From his calendar tree, Robinson saw that he had already spent a month on the island. During all that time, though he had walked the length of the north coast, he had not found a single human footprint. He had several times climbed the mountain above his cave and carefully scanned the whole of the island. But he had never seen smoke rising from any human habitation.

Robinson regretted that he was not able to store up a larger supply of food in his cave, in case bad weather were to come. He pondered how to make some sort of bag, in which he might carry a larger amount of fruit to the cave.

When he worked on his hat, he always noticed how strong the fibres in the stalks of the banana leaves were. He brought a whole pile of banana leaves into the cave. He tried to weave a bag out of the fibres of their long stalks and ribs. As a child he had often watched the basket-makers at work in their street, making not only baskets, but also matting. They used a warp stretched tight on a wooden frame, across which they wove a weft of string. Instead of a wooden frame, Robinson used a pair of young trees standing close to each other, on which he stretched the twine he had obtained by unravelling the ship's ropes. He placed the pieces close to each other. Through these he then wove the fibres from the stalks of the banana leaves. He managed to weave a piece of rough matting some five feet long. When he had taken this down, he folded it in half and tied the ends of the pieces of string tightly together at each side. In this way he obtained a large bag. The sharp ends of the banana-leaf fibres were still sticking out at the top. He bent them back and tied them with string to the woven fabric of the bag. Instead of straps he tied a piece of stout string to the bag so that he could hang it from his shoulder.

The same day he set off to gather fruit. He brought a large supply of coconuts, maize cobs and bananas. On his trips to the surroundings of the cave, he noted that there were many birds thereabouts. There were pigeons, petrels, parrots, flycatchers, and many, many other small birds he did not know at all. In the evening an owl would also go flying quietly by his cave.

On the western side of the headland, which Robinson called Sundial Head, because his sundial lay at its northernmost point, he also saw many shy agoutis, and on the rocky, shrub-grown slopes above his cave, a number of wild goats.

He would have liked to introduce a little variety into his diet with some meat dishes. He recalled his meeting with the African natives, and thought he should try to make a bow and arrows and a spear. The Africans not only shot birds with a bow and arrow, but also small animals and fish. It would not be too difficult to make a bow. There were endless thickets of bamboo close by. He could make a bowstring from unravelled rope, and arrows from thin bamboo canes. It would be more difficult, however, to put sharp points on them. First he searched in the stream for a sharp stone, but found none. But as he was resting in the cave, the small stalactites caught his eye. He knocked off a few of the thinnest with a stone and sharpened them on a piece of hard rock. After several hours' grinding, he obtained a sharp point. He inserted the stone spike into a fork in the end of a bamboo cane and bound it securely. He ran out to try his first shot. He aimed at the nearest tree. The arrow flew, and stuck in the bark. Robinson clapped his hands with delight. He then practised shooting the arrow over and over again, until the stalactite broke. But he had time and patience enough to toil away for several hours in order to make a new one. He then ground a thicker stalactite to a point in order to make the spear.

Robinson now had two effective weapons, a bow and a spear. There was no need to be afraid of iguanas now. He could even venture inland. Now he lacked only fire. What use would it be to kill an animal, if he could not roast its meat? He should try to light a fire in the manner he had observed among the Africans.

He took two small planks and bored holes in the middle of them with his knife. He also constructed a bow with a double string. Into this he inserted a stick, one end of which he placed in the hole in the board which he placed on the ground. With his left hand he pressed the second board down on the stick. Then he drew the bow back and forth with his right hand like a saw. He turned the stick for half an hour, until he was dripping with sweat. But though the holes in the boards and the ends of the stick got very hot, no smoke came from them. Robinson took a rest and started again. During the next half hour the bowstring broke and the board he was using to press on the stick fell down and trapped his fingers. Not even this discouraged him. He replaced the bowstring and set to work again until he grew tired. Though the wood got very hot, it did not start to burn. He changed the bowstring twice more, but he was still unable to get a fire going. After three hours of exhausting work he was so tired that he trembled; his hands shook, and the sweat poured off him. Perhaps the natives use a different sort of wood, he thought to himself, or perhaps this wood is not dry enough. He placed the boards on the hot sand in front of the cave, to let the sun dry them out more.

Anxiously, Robinson surveyed his clothes. There were already several tears in his woollen tunic, and in his trousers too. His shirt was also in poor condition. What would he do when winter came? He therefore decided to go about without coat or shirt while the weather was sunny, wearing only his short underlinen. He must save his clothes for cold weather. But he gained new and very bitter experience from exposing his body to the searing rays of the sun. In the evening his head ached strongly. He lost his appetite, and felt bilious. Painful blisters came up on his arms, shoulders and back. In the night he had a fever, and trembled violently. His skin smarted from the waist upwards, so sharply that he could not even bear to touch it.

The next day he was obliged to stay in the cave. He felt very ill. He did not eat or drink. Only in the evening, when the sun went down, did he go down to the stream for water. His symptoms of sunstroke lasted a whole three days.

Following this harsh experience, Robinson made himself a sunshade from banana leaves. He found himself a long, thin cane in the bamboo grove, and bent it into a ring about a yard across. This he hung on pieces of string from a stout length of bamboo. He then bound banana leaves to the hoop in such a way that the stalks formed a rosette at the top of the pole. This sunshade worked very well, and was quite light in spite of its size.

Four days later he set off early in the morning for Banana Bay, to fill his bag with fruit and lay up a supply in the cave. He also searched for turtle's eggs, which he found tasty. He would also need some thickish bark, for he had to renew his sandals frequently. He equipped himself for the journey by hanging the bag, in which he placed his arrows, over his right shoulder, and his bow across his left; he leaned on his spear with his right hand, and in his left he held the sunshade. Not wishing to walk right round Sundial Head, he set off along the valley of the Small Stream. He knew that he could return to the bay along the south side of the mountain.

After about a quarter of an hour he came upon an impenetrable bamboo thicket. Skirting it, he found himself faced with a new obstacle. This time the slope was blocked by a wall of thorny bushes. He climbed higher and higher, in order to find a way round them. In a little while he smelt a pleasant scent like that of ripe strawberries. Lifting the sunshade, he looked around him. On a gently-sloping bank in the shade of some spreading trees, he saw some plants with low-spread leaves. Out of these grew a large, bulbous and scaly fruit, at the top of which there was another clump of leaves. They were pineapples. Robinson found the juicy fruit even tastier than bananas.

He climbed up the stony slope, pushing his way carefully between the cactuses and the prickly-leaved agaves. But the cactuses grew thicker and thicker. It was impossible to get through them. There was nothing for it but to return, and to seek a way down to the stream. The cactuses blocked his view. Robinson lost his bearings, and instead of heading south-east he walked further and further west. He put down the sunshade and looked about him to find out where he was. In front of him stood a conical hill, beyond which others were just visible. He realized he must be walking away from the cave. He sat down to rest. The weather was unpleasantly close. After a while he found himself sitting in the shade. He looked up. From over the mountain a tall, very dark cloud was appearing, with a silvery edge to it. That looks like a storm-cloud, thought Robinson, and he got up to continue his journey. He set off straight downwards. He walked round large boulders, pushed his way between cactuses. The sky darkened, and it began to rain heavily. Soon there was a stab of lightning, and a roll of thunder. A strong wind got up. The downpour soon broke through the dry banana leaves of his sunshade. Within minutes Robinson was soaked from head to foot. Lightning flashed upon lightning, and the thunder roared ceaselessly. Heedless of the thick bushes, heedless of the thorns, Robinson ran to the edge of the thicket. Suddenly a streak of lightning shot down in front of him, followed by a rumbling which shook the ground. He crawled into the bushes. In a while he smelled smoke and heard a strange crackling. He crawled out, and saw that the tall grass and the bushes some twenty paces in front of him had caught fire.

The lightning had struck a tree, split it open, and set light to it. In turn, it had ignited the bushes and grass. The flames spread rapidly.

Robinson ran up the slope, stopping only after some fifty paces at a large boulder. The rain had stopped, but the gale was growing fiercer. The fire was spreading across the whole of the mountainside. The grass beneath the boulder was already burning. Robinson ran as fast as his legs could carry him, up and up. Over his head parrots and many other birds were flying and screeching desperately. Right beside him, panic-stricken goats, agoutis, iguanas, troops of monkeys and other small animals were also fleeing from the flames.

Only now did Robinson realize the great danger he had been in. If he had remained deep in the bushes, he would have been unable to escape the fire, so quickly did it spread. It was a terrifying sight. But the catastrophe had brought him one great boon. It had given him fire.

After the storm Robinson returned to a place where the trees were still burning. There he took up a flaming branch and ran quickly back down to the cave with it. Beneath the overhanging rock, not far from the cave, he made a fire.

He thought how fortunate it was that he had already prepared dry grass and twigs when he had been trying to light a fire using the method of the African natives. Now the flames crackled merrily, and Robinson leaped about the fire with delight. He need no longer fear the cold. Now he could shoot some animal, and prepare tasty roast meat.

The fire quickly consumed the dry sticks, and he had to keep it going. So Robinson ran off to the nearby forest, whence he brought an armful of dry branches from old, dead trees. He built up the fire and returned for more wood. He spent the whole of the afternoon fetching fuel. Beside the rock face close to the cave entrance he piled up branches and dry stumps. Beneath the overhanging rock the rain would not soak the wood, and the greener pieces would soon dry there.

From the moment he lit the fire near the cave, his sleep once more became fitful and disturbed. He would wake up several times a night to hurry out and put wood on the fire. He was unable to sleep for fear it would go out in the night.

The fire lit up the area in front of the cave, thus keeping away the mosquitoes which had swarmed around it at night, spoiling Robinson's hours of rest.

Robinson sat in front of the fire for a long time that evening, feeding it with wood and gazing into the flames. It made his home cosier and merrier. He roasted cobs of corn and bananas. He was pleased to think that a fire on the coast would be visible from the sea, and might serve as a sign to any ship which happened to be passing that someone was living there.

The next morning it rained. How wise I was to lay in a good store of wood yesterday, Robinson thought to himself. Even at midday the rain had not stopped. He laid stones around the blaze. For lunch he roasted himself some cobs of corn. When, late in the afternoon, the rain stopped at last, he went hunting. He imagined that the animals, driven from the forest by the fire, would now stay close to the mountain. He went round the steep rock face beside the cave and began to climb upwards. He named the mountain above his cave Fire Mountain, since it had given him fire during the storm.

The fire had cleared a path along the mountainside due west as far as the bay. Where there had the day before been an impenetrable thicket of bushes, today there was an empty space, blackening with wet ashes. Robinson was amazed at how large an area the fire had consumed in so short a time. For a good twenty minutes he walked across scorched earth. From the western side of Fire Mountain, where the fire had not reached, there was now a fine view of the whole of Turtle Bay and the conical hills above it.

On the western slopes of Fire Mountain, he sat down on a stone under a tall bush, prepared his bow and an arrow, and waited. After some time an agouti hopped out from a bush about twenty paces away from him and, suspecting nothing, crouched to gnaw at a root. It had clearly not seen Robinson. His arrow swished through the air. The animal squealed, jumped a short distance, and then lay motionless. Robinson was highly pleased with his first hunting success, and proud at having brought down the agouti with his first shot. The arrow had pierced the creature's throat.

He quickly returned home, looking forward to a tasty supper. So as not to have to climb down the steep slope among the boulders above his cave, he made for the stream. When he was nearly there, he heard a noise like the bleating of a goat. He could not, however, see the animal. He noticed a huge tree, whose trunk had halted a landslide of rocks. He examined the strange tree carefully. It was enormous: perhaps a hundred feet tall. The trunk must have been a good three feet across. The huge boughs slanted downwards like those of a weeping willow, and young shoots hung down to the ground. On the branches was a fruit which Robinson had never seen before. It was nearly as big as coconuts. As he approached the tree he heard the bleating again. He climbed over the pile of rocks, and saw a goat down below. The moment it saw Robinson, it hopped off painfully on three legs towards the stream. Robinson put down his bag, laid his spear and his bow against the tree, and ran after the creature. After about fifty paces he caught up with it and took it by the horns. The goat was lame in its right foreleg. He dragged it to the place where he had left his bag. He saw a spring of water coming out from directly beneath the huge treetrunk and flowing in a narrow rivulet down to the stream. The goat must have been thirsty, which was why it was resting beside the spring. Beneath the tree were a few pieces of ripe, fallen fruit. Robinson put two of them in his bag so that he might take a closer look at them back at the cave. He always carried a piece of string in the bag in case he needed it, and now he tied it to the goat's horns so that he might lead it back to the cave.

167

Though the goat had an injured leg, it suddenly heaved so violently that Robinson, unready for such resistance, was thrown to the ground. The goat ran off, string and all. When Robinson caught up with it again, he tied the string around its neck, supposing he would be better able to control it in that fashion. But the string cut so deep into the struggling creature's throat that it began to choke.

Robinson untied the string. He had discovered that a wild goat cannot be led on a string. He took both its forelegs in his left hand and both its hind legs in his right, close to the hooves, pushed his head under the animal's belly, and lifted it onto his shoulders. The goat bleated mournfully all the way back to the cave.

When he arrived at the cave, Robinson tied the goat to a tree by the horns. He returned to fetch his bag, bow and spear. Taking a drink from the spring, he was surprised to find how cold the water was, and how pleasant it tasted. So he went back once again with his coconut shells and took some of this excellent water back to the cave. He had previously drunk only from the Small Stream. The water there was clean, but it had an unpleasant, muddy taste, and was never cold. Since the spring was not far away, he decided to go nowhere else for drinking water in future.

What a lucky day I have had, thought Robinson. He had shot an animal, caught a live goat, and found excellent spring water. The fire was waiting for him at home, and he could make himself a hot supper. In a single day a great change had come about in his circumstances.

When Robinson got back, he tended to the goat's injured leg. It had been scraped to the bone just above the hoof. The goat had probably been fleeing from the fire the previous day when it had injured itself on a sharp stone.

Robinson also noted that the animal's coat had been burnt away to the skin in several places on its left flank.

He went to a place nearby where aloes grew, cut off one of the leaves, and placed the pulp from it on the wound. Then he bound the wound with a piece of cloth torn from the tail of his shirt.

He then found a suitable post and drove it into the ground close to the cave entrance, near the bushes, and tethered the goat to it. So that the animal would not have to lie on the bare ground, he cleared a space near the post of small stones and strewed it with sea grass and banana leaves. Then he fetched an armful of fresh grass and green leaves from the Small Stream. He also gave the goat some water in a coconut shell. After seeing to the goat, he prepared supper.

Since he had never skinned an animal before, it took him some time. The agouti's skin was finer than that of a rabbit. He quartered and salted the meat, speared the pieces on a bamboo cane, and held them over the open fire. After a while it occurred to him that it would be better to turn the meat as on a spit, in

the manner he had seen it done at the house of Abḍ el Mami.

He raised the bank of stones around the fireplace, laid the cane across them, and turned the meat evenly. He kept the flames low, so as not to burn the outside of the meat. The charcoal glowed enough to roast it. It was soon giving off the appetizing smell of roasting flesh. In about an hour the meat was tender and came away easily from the bone.

The agouti tasted so good that Robinson felt he had never eaten anything so tasty in his life. After supper he examined the unknown fruit of the large tree. It was round, and had a very hard, woody skin, with a crack in the surface like a split chestnut. He thrust his knife into the crack and, lo and behold, the top came off to reveal strange, three-sided seeds inside. They were the size of walnuts, but very hard and rough. There were sixteen of them attached to a stalk which ran along the middle of the case. He took out the seeds and started to break them open with a stone. Inside were yellowish kernels which tasted rather like hazelnuts. To be on the safe side he ate only two of them. If they did not make him ill, then he had another food to add to his diet.

Robinson did not know that the large tree was called Bertholletia, and that its fruit is known as Brazil nuts.

In the night, when Robinson went to put more wood on the fire, it was again raining heavily. He was sorry for the goat, out in the rain, so he untethered it, and was surprised to see that it made for the entrance to the cave of its own accord. Inside he tied it up to the table leg, and the goat lay down contentedly.

The next day the rain had not stopped. It was only now that Robinson was able to appreciate just what a good place he had found to make his home in. The overhanging rock protected the fire from the downpour. Otherwise he would long since have been without fire. The rain streamed down incessantly. Robinson wondered what he would do if it rained like that for two days, and he used up his fuel supply.

In the morning he changed the dressing on the goat's leg. The wound was less inflamed now, and was beginning to heal. Since he had no fresh grass for the goat, he gave it a few cobs of corn. And, lo and behold, the goat ate them with relish. It even liked banana and pineapple skins.

The animal had already lost its initial shyness. It seemed to realize that Robinson was looking after it, and so was more affectionate. Robinson saw that its udder was growing in size. What if he were to milk it? He had seen this done often enough in the Yorkshire countryside when he was a boy. He took a coconut shell, sat down on the bench, and turned the goat sideways on to him. He held the shell in his left hand and took hold of a teat with his right. At that moment the goat swung its hind quarters round sharply and caught the crouching Robinson a sharp blow on the forehead. Before he knew it he had fallen from the bench onto the floor. The goat had kicked the coconut shell out of his hand and it had flown off somewhere to the back of the cave.

170

Thus Robinson found out that milking a goat is no easy task. His head was spinning, and he had scraped his back on the edge of the bench. He was seized with mild anger. He took hold of the goat and shoved it under the table. He tied its head to one of the legs. Then he fastened each of the goat's hind legs to another of the table's legs. Then he again set about his milking. The goat tossed and bleated terribly, but try as Robinson would, he could not get a single drop of milk out of the teats. The tabletop began to sway back and forth precariously. So Robinson decided he had better untie the goat and give up his milking.

After a few days he tried again to milk the goat, but again in vain. Perhaps it lost its milk when it was injured, he thought. But he was surprised that during those rainy days, when the creature ate nothing but dry grass and dry banana leaves, it was getting fatter. Its stomach was growing all the time.

Robinson was pleased to have a living creature as a companion. During the rainy days, when he went out only seldom, to fetch wood or to gather a minimum of food, he would sit in the cave and busy himself with small jobs. He ground some thin stalactites to make arrowheads.

He tried to make himself a pair of shoes from the agouti skin. But there was not enough of it to make two shoes. There was hardly enough for one. He would have to kill at least one more animal. There were plenty of agoutis in the vicinity of the cave.

Towards evening one day, the rain stopped for a while. Robinson set out hunting. He went to the spring, where he collected all the fallen fruit from the Brazil nut tree. Then he walked along the stream and turned his steps up along the burnt ground between the bushes, where he startled a flock of birds. They looked rather like small hens, and flew very low. They emitted strange sounds from their throats, a sort of *hock, hock, pew, meetoo* — something like a mixture between the squawking of a hen and the crowing of a cock. He managed to shoot one of them. Its feathers were greyish-brown, and it had a crest on its head.

He sat down among the boulders not far from the spring and waited to see if an agouti would appear. Steam was rising from the valley. It formed a fine mist, reducing visibility.

Robinson gave a violent start when, all of a sudden, there was a clatter of stones from behind him. He leapt up, and saw a whole herd of goats, with a large male at their head, thundering down the rocky hillside towards him. Their leader, when he saw Robinson, was unable to stop his headlong dash down the steep slope quickly enough. Robinson raised his spear with both hands and drove it into the animal's chest. The rest of the goats went dashing past him in terror. The dead leader of the herd was a sturdy fellow, and very heavy. Robinson was sweating profusely by the time he had dragged him back to the cave. But it was a fine prize. Without using a single arrow he had brought back enough meat to last him several days. And the goatskin would make him a far stronger pair of shoes than the agouti hide.

Scarcely had Robinson reached the cave, when it began to rain heavily again. During the night a storm broke.

He spent the whole of the next morning skinning and portioning the goat. Roast goat's meat was not nearly as tender or as tasty as agouti. Robinson cut the carcase into large pieces, so that the meat would not go bad. He salted them thoroughly and then roasted them on his spit.

Because he had no more dry wood, and had to use green, the fire gave off thick smoke. The roast meat had a smoked taste. If only I could make a chimney, and smoke meat properly, Robinson thought. Then it could be stored for much longer.

During the next few days, when it rained constantly, Robinson made himself some shoes. He wrapped the goatskin round his foot, with the hair inside, and trimmed the edges, which reached up over his ankles. He bored holes in the skin with his knife, threaded string through them, and tied the shoes up. He was looking forward to walking over the sharp grass and stones with his comfortable new footwear. When winter came, they would keep his feet warm. But at home he continued to go about barefoot.

The rain continued to pour down. This caused Robinson no little anxiety. Even in the wettest of weather he went to fetch wood and to find fodder for the goat.

Meanwhile, the goat had grown so accustomed to him that when he returned with an armful of banana leaves and green twigs from the bushes, it would greet him with joyous bleating. Its leg had healed, and it now walked on all four feet.

After a fortnight the rains began to leave off for short intervals, and Robinson was able to make longer expeditions for bananas, pineapples, Brazil nuts and maize. He was lucky that some one hundred and fifty paces from the cave there stretched the forest, an inexhaustible supply of wood. His ever-present fear of letting the fire out kept Robinson awake, so that he was often tired and sleepy. He soon noticed that green wood, especially in large pieces, burned much longer than dry wood, so in the evening he would put only good-sized lumps of the green on the fire.

One day he dragged a small uprooted tree back from the forest. There was still a large amount of earth clinging to its roots. Since he had nothing with which to chop it, he laid the tree across the hearth so that it would burn through near the roots. He would use the long logs he thus obtained to place on the fire at night.

Perhaps he was too tired from dragging the heavy treetrunk to the cave, but that night Robinson slept so soundly that dawn had broken when he awoke. Filled with anxiety, he leaped out of bed and ran up to the fire. The treetrunk, burnt through, lay beside the ring of stones, while the soil-covered roots covered the whole fireplace. There was not a wisp of smoke to be seen. The fire was out! The layer of earth on the base of the trunk, held together by the roots, was dry and hard, and covered the ashes of the fire. Robinson tried to lift it off. But he cried out in pain. Underneath the crust of dried earth, red-hot charcoal was smouldering. He took a handful of dry twigs and put them on the fire. Then he blew on the embers as hard as he could, and, lo and behold, the flames shot up once more.

Thus Robinson acquired new and very valuable experience. Beneath a layer of earth it was possible to keep charcoal alight for a long time. The next evening he put some thick branches on the fire, waited until they were burning well, and then covered the fireplace with sods of turf which he had brought from the banks of the stream.

When he went out at midnight to make sure the fire was still alight under the turf, and turned over one of the sods with a stick, flames at once leapt out from under it.

After that Robinson slept soundly till morning. All he had to do then was remove the sods and put some dry twigs on the fire, and it was soon burning again. At last he would be able to sleep peacefully at night, and to leave the fire untended for long periods during the day.

174

A WAIF OF THE PLAINS

BRET HARTE

I   A long level of dull grey that further away became a faint blue, with here and there darker patches that looked like water. At times an open space, blackened and burnt in an irregular circle, with a shred of newspaper, an old rag, or broken tin can lying in the ashes. Beyond these always a low dark line that seemed to sink into the ground at night, and rose again in the morning with the first light, but never otherwise changed its height and distance. A sense of always moving with some indefinite purpose, but of always returning at night to the same place — with the same surroundings, the same people, the same bedclothes, and the same awful black canopy dropped down from above. A chalky taste of dust on the mouth and lips, a gritty sense of earth on the fingers, and an all-pervading heat and smell of cattle.

This was 'The Great Plains' as they seemed to two children from the hooded depth of an emigrant waggon above the swaying heads of toiling oxen, in the summer of 1852.

It had appeared so to them for two weeks, always the same, and always without the least sense to them of wonder or monotony. When they viewed it from the road, walking beside the waggon, there was only the team itself added to the unvarying picture. One of the waggons bore on its canvas hood the inscription, in large black letters, 'Off to California!' on the other 'Root Hog, or Die', but neither of them awoke in the minds of the children the faintest idea of playfulness or jocularity. Perhaps it was difficult to connect the serious men, who occasionally walked beside them and seemed to grow more taciturn and depressed as the day wore on, with this past effusive pleasantry.

Yet the impressions of the two children differed slightly. The eldest, a boy of eleven, was apparently new to the domestic habits and customs of a life to which the younger, a girl of seven, was evidently native and familiar. The food was coarse, and less skilfully prepared than that to which he had been accustomed. There was a certain freedom and roughness in their intercourse; a simplicity that bordered almost on rudeness in their domestic arrangements, and a speech that was at times almost untranslatable to him. He slept in his clothes, wrapped up in blankets; he was conscious that in the matter of cleanliness he was left to himself to overcome the difficulties of finding water and towels. But it is doubtful if in his youthfulness it affected him more than a novelty. He ate and slept well, and found his life amusing. Only at times the rudeness of his companions, or, worse, an indifference that made him feel his dependency upon them, awoke a vague sense of some wrong that had been done to him which, while it was voiceless to all others, and even uneasily put aside by himself, was still always slumbering in his childish consciousness.

To the party he was known as an orphan put on the train at 'St. Jo' by some relative of his stepmother, to be delivered to another relative at Sacramento. As his stepmother had not even taken leave of him, but had entrusted his departure to the relative with whom he had been lately living, it was considered as an act of 'riddance', and accepted as such by her party, and even vaguely acquiesced in by the boy himself. What consideration had been offered for his passage he did not know; he only remembered that he had been told 'to make himself handy'. This he had done cheerfully, if at times with the unskilfulness of a novice; but it was not a peculiar or a menial task in a company where all took part in manual labour, and where existence seemed to him to bear the charm of a prolonged picnic. Neither was he subjected to any difference of affection or treatment from Mrs. Silsbee, the mother of his little companion, and the wife of the leader of the train. Prematurely old, of ill-health, and harassed with cares, she had no time to waste in discriminating maternal tenderness for her daughter, but treated the children with equal and unbiassed querulousness.

The rear waggon creaked, swayed, and rolled on slowly and heavily. The hoofs of the draught oxen occasionally striking in the dust with a dull report, sent little puffs like smoke on either side of the track. Within, the children were playing 'keeping store'. The little girl, as an opulent and extravagant customer, was purchasing of the boy, who sat behind a counter improvised from a nail keg and the front seat, most of the available contents of the waggon, either under their own names or an imaginary one as the moment suggested, and paying for them in the easy and liberal currency of dried beans and bits of paper. Change was given by the expeditious method of tearing the paper into smaller fragments. The diminution of stock was remedied by buying the same article over again under a different name. Nevertheless, in spite of these favourable commercial conditions, the market seemed dull.

'I can show you a fine quality of sheeting at four cents a yard, double width,' said the boy, rising and leaning on his fingers on the counter as he had seen the shopmen do. 'All wool, and will wash,' he added with easy gravity.

'I can buy it cheaper at Jackson's,' said the girl, with the intuitive duplicity of her bargaining sex.

'Very well,' said the boy. 'I won't play any more.'

'Who cares?' said the girl, indifferently.

The boy here promptly upset the counter; the rolled-up blanket which had deceitfully represented the desirable sheeting falling on the waggon floor. It apparently suggested a new idea to the former salesman. 'I say! let's play "damaged stock". See, I'll tumble all the things down here right on top o'the others, and sell 'em for less than cost.'

The girl looked up. The suggestion was bold, bad, and momentarily attractive. But she only said 'No', apparently from habit, picked up her doll, and the boy clambered to the front of the waggon. The incomplete episode terminated at once with that perfect forgetfulness, indifference, and irresponsibility common to all young animals. If either could have flown away or bounded off finally at that moment, they would have done so with no more concern for preliminary detail than a bird or squirrel. The waggon rolled steadily on. The boy could see that one of their teamsters had climbed up on the tailboard of the preceding vehicle. The other seemed to be walking in a dusty sleep.

'Kla'uns,' said the girl.

The boy, without turning his head, responded, 'Susy.'

'Wot are you going to be?' said the girl.

'Goin' to be?' repeated Clarence.

'When you is growed,' exclaimed Susy.

Clarence hesitated. His settled determination had been to become a pirate, merciless yet discriminating. But reading in a bethumbed 'Guide to the Plains' that morning of Fort Laramie and Kit Carson, he had decided upon the career of a 'scout', as being more accessible and requiring less water. Yet, out of compassion for Susy's possible ignorance, he said neither, and responded with the American boy's modest conventionality, 'President'. It was safe, required no embarrassing description, and had been approved by benevolent old gentlemen with their hands on his head.

'I'm goin' to be a parson's wife,' said Susy, 'and keep hens, and have things giv' to me. Baby clothes, and apples, and apple sass — and melasses! and more baby clothes! and pork when you kill.'

She had thrown herself at the bottom of the waggon with her back towards him and her doll in her lap. He could see the curve of her curly head, and beyond her bare dimpled knees which were raised, and over which she was trying to fold the hem of her brief skirt. 'I wouldn't be a President's wife,' she said, presently.

'You couldn't!'

'Could if I wanted to!'

'Couldn't!'

'Could now!'

'Couldn't!'

'Why?'

Finding it difficult to explain his convictions of her ineligibility, Clarence thought it equally crushing not to give any. There was a long silence. It was very hot and dusty. The waggon scarcely seemed to move. Clarence gazed at the vignette of the track behind them formed by the hood of the rear. Presently he rose and walked past her to the tail-board. 'Goin' to get down,' he said, putting his legs over.

'Maw says "No",' said Susy.

Clarence did not reply, but dropped to the ground beside the slowly turning wheels. Without quickening his pace he could easily keep his hand on the tail-board.

'Kla'uns.'

He looked up.

'Take me.'

She had already clapped on her sun-bonnet, and was standing at the edge of the tail-board, her little arms extended in such perfect confidence of being caught that the boy could not resist. He caught her cleverly. They halted a moment and let the lumbering vehicle move away from them as it swayed from

side to side as if labouring in a heavy sea. They remained motionless until it had reached nearly a hundred yards, and then with a sudden half real, half assumed, but altogether delightful trepidation, ran forward and caught up with it again. This they repeated two or three times until both themselves and the excitement were exhausted, and they again plodded on hand in hand. Presently Clarence uttered a cry.

'My! Susy — look there!'

The rear waggon had once more slipped away from them a considerable distance. Between it and them, crossing its track, a most extraordinary creature had halted.

At first glance it seemed a dog — a discomfited, shameless, ownerless, outcast of streets and byways, rather than an honest estray of some drover's train. It was so gaunt, so dusty, so greasy, so slouching, and so lazy! But as they looked at it more intently they saw that the greyish hair of its back had a bristly ridge, and there were great poisonous-looking dark blotches on its flanks, and that the slouch of its haunches was a peculiarity of its figure, and not the cowering of fear. As it lifted its suspicious head towards them they could see that its thin lips, too short to cover its white teeth, were curled in a perpetual sneer.

'Here, doggie!' said Clarence, excitedly. 'Good dog! Come.'

Susy burst into a triumphant laugh. 'Et taint no dog, silly; it's er coyote.'

Clarence blushed. It wasn't the first time the pioneer's daughter had shown her superior knowledge. He said quickly, to hide his discomfiture, 'I'll ketch him anyway, he's nothin' mor'n a ki yi.'

'Ye kant, tho,' said Susy, shaking her sun-bonnet. 'He's faster nor a hoss!'

Nevertheless Clarence ran towards him, followed by Susy. When they had come within twenty feet of him, the lazy creature, without apparently the least effort, took two or three limping bounds to one side and remained at the same distance as before. They repeated this onset three or four times with more or less excitement and hilarity, the animal evading them to one side, but never actually retreating before them. Finally, it occurred to them both that although they were not catching him they were not driving him away. The consequences of that thought were put into shape by Susy with round-eyed significance.

'Kla'uns, he bites.'

Clarence picked up a hard sun-baked clod, and, running forward, threw it at the coyote. It was a clever shot, and struck him on his slouching haunches. He snapped and gave a short snarling yelp and vanished. Clarence returned with a victorious air to his companion. But she was gazing intently in the opposite direction, and for the first time he discovered that the coyote had been leading them half round a circle.

'Kla'uns,' says Susy, with an hysterical little laugh.

'Well?'

'The waggon's gone.'

Clarence started. It was true. Not only their waggon, but the whole train of oxen and teamsters had utterly disappeared, vanishing as completely as if they had been caught up in a whirlwind or engulfed in the earth. Even the low cloud of dust that usually marked their distant course by day was nowhere to be seen. The long level plain stretched before them to the setting sun, without a sign or trace of moving life or animation. That great blue crystal bowl, filled with dust and fire by day, with stars and darkness by night, which had always seemed to drop its rim round them everywhere and shut them in, seemed to them now to have been lifted to let the train pass out, and then closed down upon them for ever.

II   Their first sensation was one of purely animal freedom!

They looked at each other with sparkling eyes and long silent breaths. But this spontaneous outburst of savage nature soon passed. Susy's little hand presently reached forward and clutched Clarence's jacket. The boy understood it, and said quickly, 'They ain't gone far, and they'll stop as soon as they find us gone.'

They trotted on a little faster; the sun they had followed every day and the fresh waggontracks being their unfailing guides; the keen cool air of the plains, taking the place of that all-pervading dust and smell of the perspiring oxen, invigorating them with its breath.

'We ain't skeered a bit, are we?' said Susy.

'What's there to be afraid of?' said Clarence, scornfully. He said this none the less strongly because he suddenly remembered that they had been often left alone in the waggon for hours without being looked after, and that their absence might not be noticed until the train stopped to encamp at dusk.

They were not running very fast, yet either they were more tired than they knew, or the air was thinner, for they both seemed to breathe quickly. Suddenly Clarence stopped. 'There they are now.'

He was pointing to a light cloud of dust in the far-off horizon, from which the black hulk of a waggon emerged for a moment and was lost. But even as they gazed the cloud seemed to sink like a fairy mirage to the earth again, the whole train disappeared, and only the empty stretching track returned. They did not know that this seemingly flat and level plain was really undulatory, and that the vanished train had simply dipped below their view on some further slope even as it had once before. But they knew they were disappointed, and that disappointment revealed to them the fact that they had concealed it from each other. The girl was the first to succumb, and burst into a quick spasm of angry tears. That single act of weakness called out the boy's pride and strength. There was no longer an equality of suffering; he had become her protector; he felt himself responsible for both. Considering her no longer his equal, he was no longer frank with her.

'There's nothin' to boo-hoo for,' he said, with a half-affected brusqueness. 'So quit now! They'll stop in a minit and send someone back for us. Shouldn't wonder if they're doin' it now.'

But Susy, with feminine discrimination detecting the hollow ring in his voice, here threw herself upon him and began to beat him violently with her little fists. 'They ain't! They ain't! They ain't! You know it! How dare you?' Then, exhausted with her struggle, she suddenly threw herself flat on the dry grass, shut her eyes tightly, and clutched at the stubble.

'Get up,' said the boy, with a pale, determined face that seemed to have got much older.

'You leave me be!' said Susy.

'Do you want me to go away and leave you?' asked the boy.

Susan opened one blue eye furtively in the secure depths of her sun-bonnet and gazed at his changed face.

'Ye-e-s.'

He pretended to turn away, but really to look at the height of the sinking sun.

'Kla'uns!'

'Well?'

'Take me.'

She was holding up her hands. He lifted her gently in his arms, dropping her head over his shoulder. 'Now,' he said cheerfully, 'you keep a good look-out that way, and I this, and we'll soon be there.'

The idea seemed to please her. After Clarence had stumbled on for a few moments, she said, 'Do you see anything, Kla'uns?'

'Not yet.'

'No more don't I.' This equality of perception apparently satisfied her. Presently she lay more limp in his arms. She was asleep.

The sun was sinking lower; it had already touched the edge of the horizon, and was level with his dazzled and straining eyes. At times it seemed to impede his eager search and task his vision. Haze and black spots floated across the horizon, and round wafers, like duplicates of the sun, glittered back from the dull surface of the plains. Then he resolved to look no more until he had counted fifty, a hundred — but always with the same result, the return of the empty, unending plains; the disc growing redder as it neared the horizon, the fire it seemed to kindle as it sank, but nothing more!

Staggering under his burden, he tried to distract himself by fancying how the discovery of their absence would be made. He heard the listless, half-querulous discussion about the locality that regularly pervaded the nightly camp. He heard the discontented voice of Jake Silsbee as he halted beside their waggon and said, 'Come, out o' that now, you two, and mighty quick about it.' He heard the command harshly repeated. He saw the look of irritation on Silsbee's dusky-bearded face that followed his hurried glance into the empty waggon. He heard the query, 'What's gone o' them limbs now?' handed from waggon to waggon. He heard a few oaths; Mrs. Silsbee's high, rasping voice, abuse of himself, the hurried and discontented detachment of a search party, Silsbee and one of the hired men, and vociferation and blame. Blame always for himself, the elder, who might have 'known better'! A little fear, perhaps, but he could not fancy either pity or commiseration. Perhaps the thought upheld his pride; under the prospect of sympathy he might have broken down.

At last he stumbled, and stopped to keep himself from falling forward on his face. He could go no further; his breath was spent; he was dripping with perspiration; his legs were trembling under him; there was a roaring in his ears; round red discs of the sun were scattered everywhere around him like spots of blood. To the right of the trail there seemed to be a slight mound where he could rest awhile and yet keep his watchful survey of the horizon. But on reaching it he found that it was only a tangle of taller mesquite grass, into which he sank with his burden. Nevertheless, if useless as a point of vantage, it afforded a soft couch for Susy, who seemed to have fallen quite naturally into her usual afternoon siesta, and in a measure it shielded her from a cold breeze that had sprung up from the west. Utterly exhausted himself, but not daring to yield to the torpor that seemed to be creeping over him, Clarence half sat, half knelt down beside her, supporting himself with one hand, and, partly hidden in the long grass, kept his straining eyes fixed on the lonely track.

The red disc was sinking lower. It seemed to have already crumbled away a part of the distance with its eating fires. As it sank still lower, it shot out long luminous rays, diverging fan-like across the plain as if, in the boy's excited fancy, it too were searching, with parted and extended fingers, for the lost estrays. And as one long beam seemed to linger over his hiding-place, he even thought that it might serve as a guide to Silsbee and the other seekers, and was constrained to stagger to his feet, erect in its light. But it soon sank, and with it Clarence dropped back again to his crouching watch. Yet he knew that the daylight was still good for an hour, and with the withdrawal of that mystic sunset glory, objects became even more distinct and sharply defined than at any other time. And with the merciful sheathing of that flaming sword which seemed to have waved between him and the vanished train, his eyes already felt a blessed relief.

III   With the setting of the sun an ominous silence fell. He could hear the low breathing of Susy, and even fancied he could detect the beating of his own heart in that oppressive hush of all nature. For the day's march had always been accompanied by the monotonous creaking of wheels and axles, and even the quiet of the night encampment had been always more or less broken by the movement of unquiet sleepers on the waggon-beds, or the breathing of the cattle. But here there was neither sound nor motion. Susy's prattle, and even the sound of his own voice, would have broken the benumbing spell. But it was part of his growing self-denial now that he refrained from waking her even by a whisper. She would awaken soon enough to thirst and hunger, perhaps; and then what was he to do? If that looked-for help would only come now — while she still slept. For it was part of his boyish fancy that if he could deliver her asleep, and undemonstrative of fear and suffering, he would be less blameful, and she less mindful, of her trouble. If it did not come — but he would not think of that yet. If she was thirsty meantime — well, it might rain, and there was always the dew which they used to brush off the morning grass — he would take off his shirt and catch it in that, like a shipwrecked mariner. It would be funny, and make her laugh. For himself he would not laugh, he felt he was getting very old and grown-up in this loneliness.

It was getting darker — they should be looking into the waggons now. A new doubt began to assail him. Ought he not, now that he was rested, make the most of the remaining moments of daylight, and before the glow faded from the west, when he would no longer have any bearings to guide him? But there was always the risk of waking her! — to what? The fear of being confronted again with *her* fear, and of being unable to pacify her, at last decided him to remain. But he crept softly through the grass, and in the dust of the track traced the four points of the compass, as he would still determine them by the sunset light, with a large printed W to indicate the west! This boyish contrivance particularly pleased him. If he had only a pole, a stick, or even a twig, on which to tie his handkerchief and erect it above the clump of mesquite as a signal to the searchers in case he should be overcome by fatigue or sleep, he would have been happy. But the plain was barren of brush or timber; he did not dream that this omission and the very unobtrusiveness of his hiding-place would be his salvation from a greater danger.

With the coming darkness the wind arose and swept the plain with a long-drawn sigh. This increased to a murmur, till presently the whole expanse — before sunk in awful silence — seemed to awake with vague complaints, incessant sounds, and low moanings. At times he thought he heard the holloing of distant voices, at times it seemed as a whisper in his own ear. In the silence that followed each blast he fancied he could detect the creaking of the waggon, the dull thud of the oxen's hoofs, or broken fragments of speech, blown and scattered even as he strained his ears to listen by the next gust. This tension of the ear began to confuse his brain, as his eyes had been previously dazzled by the sunlight, and a strange torpor began to steal over his faculties. Once or twice his head dropped.

He awoke with a start. A moving figure had suddenly uplifted itself between him and the horizon! It was not twenty yards away, so clearly outlined against the still luminous sky that it seemed even nearer. A human figure, but so

187

dishevelled, so fantastic, and yet so mean and puerile in its extravagance, that it seemed the outcome of a childish dream. It was a mounted figure, but so ludicrously disproportionate to the pony it bestrode, whose slim legs were stiffly buried in the dust in a breathless halt, that it might have been a straggler from some vulgar wandering circus. A tall hat crownless and brimless, a castaway of civilization, surmounted by a turkey's feather, was on its head; over its shoulders hung a dirty tattered blanket that scarcely covered the two painted legs, which seemed clothed in soiled yellow hose. In one hand it held a gun; the other was bent above its eyes in eager scrutiny of some distant point beyond and east of the spot where the children lay concealed. Presently, with a dozen quick noiseless strides of the pony's legs, the apparition moved to the right, its gaze still fixed on that mysterious part of the horizon. There was no mistaking it now! The painted Hebraic face, the large curved nose, the bony cheek, the broad mouth, the shadowed eyes, the straight long matted locks: it was an Indian! Not the picturesque creature of Clarence's imagination, but still an Indian! The boy was uneasy, suspicious, antagonistic; but not afraid. He looked at the heavy animal face with the superiority of intelligence, at the half-naked figure with the conscious supremacy of dress, at the lower individuality with the contempt of a higher race. Yet a moment after, when the figure wheeled and disappeared towards the undulating west, a strange chill crept over him. Yet he did not know that in this puerile phantom and painted pigmy the awful majesty of death had passed him by.

'Mama!'

It was Susy's voice, struggling into consciousness. Perhaps she had been instinctively conscious of the boy's sudden fears.

'Hush!'

He had just turned to the objective point of the Indian's gaze. There *was* something! A dark line was moving along with the gathering darkness. For a moment he hardly dared to voice his thoughts even to himself. It was a following train overtaking them from the rear! And from the rapidity of its movements a train with horses, hurrying forward to evening camp. He had never dreamt of help from that quarter. And this was what the Indian's keener eyes had been watching, and why he had so precipitately fled.

The strange train was now coming up at a round trot. It was evidently well appointed, with five or six large waggons and several outriders. In half an hour it would be here. Yet he restrained from waking Susy, who had fallen asleep again; his old superstition of securing her safety first being still uppermost. He took off his jacket to cover her shoulders, and rearranged her nest. Then he glanced again at the coming train. But for some unaccountable reason it had changed its direction, and instead of following the track that should have brought it to his side, it had turned off to the left! In ten minutes it would pass abreast of him a mile and a half away! If he woke Susy now he knew she would be helpless in her terror, and he could not carry her half that distance. He might rush to the train himself and return with help, but he would never leave her alone — in the darkness. Never! If she woke she would die of fright perhaps, or wander blindly and aimlessly away. No! The train would pass, and with it that hope of rescue. Something was in his throat, but he gulped it down and was quiet again, albeit he shivered in the night wind.

The train was nearly abreast of him now. He ran out of the tall grass, waving his straw hat above his head in the faint hope of attracting attention. But he did not go far, for he found, to his alarm, that when he turned back again the clump of mesquite was scarcely distinguishable from the rest of the plain. This settled all question of his going. Even if he reached the train and returned with someone, how would he ever find her again in this desolate expanse?

He watched the train slowly pass, still mechanically — almost hopelessly — waving his hat as he ran up and down before the mesquite as if he were waving a last farewell to his departing hope. Suddenly it appeared to him that three of the outriders who were preceding the first waggon had changed their shape. They were no longer sharp, oblong, black blocks against the horizon, but had become at first blurred and indistinct, then taller and narrower, until at last they stood out like exclamation points against the sky. He continued to wave his hat, they continued to grow taller and narrower. He understood it now — the three transformed blocks were the outriders coming towards him.

This is what he had seen —

■ ■ ■

This is what he saw now —

! ! !

He ran back to Susy to see if she still slept, for his foolish desire to have her

189

saved unconsciously was stronger than ever now that safety seemed so near. She was still sleeping, although she had moved slightly. He ran to the front again.

The outriders had apparently halted. What were they doing? Why wouldn't they come on?

Suddenly a blinding flash of light seemed to burst from one of them. Away over his head something whistled like a rushing bird, and sped off invisible. They had fired a gun; they were signalling to him, Clarence, like a grown-up man! He would have given his life at that moment to have had a gun. But he could only wave his hat frantically.

One of the figures here bore away and impetuously darted forward again. He was coming nearer, powerful, gigantic, formidable as he loomed through the darkness. All at once he threw up his arm with a wild gesture to the others; and his voice, manly, frank, and assuring, came ringing before him.

'Hold up! Don't fire! It's no Injin — it's a child!'

In another moment he had reined up beside Clarence and leaned over him, bearded, handsome, all-encompassing, and protecting.

'Hallo! What's all this? What are you doing here?'

'Lost from Mr. Silsbee's train,' said Clarence.

'Lost! How long?'

'About three hours. I thought they'd come back for us,' said Clarence apologetically to this big kindly man.

'And you kalkilated to wait here for 'em?'

'Yes, yes — I did — till I saw you.'

'Then why in thunder didn't you light out straight for us, instead of hanging round here and drawing us out?'

The boy hung his head. He knew his reasons were unchanged, but all at once they seemed very foolish and unmanly to speak out.

'Only that we were on the keen jump for Injins,' continued the stranger, 'we wouldn't have seen you at all, and might hev shot you when we did. What possessed you to stay here?'

The boy was still silent. 'Kla'uns,' said a faint, sleepy voice from the mesquite, 'take me.' The rifle shot had awakened Susy.

The stranger turned quickly towards the sound. Clarence started and recalled himself.

'There,' he said bitterly, 'you've done it now, you've wakened her! *That's* why I stayed. I couldn't carry her over there to you! I couldn't let her walk, for she'd be frightened. I wouldn't wake her up, for she'd be frightened, and I mightn't find her again. There!' He had made up his mind to be abused, but he was reckless now that she was safe.

The men glanced at each other. 'Then,' said the spokesman quietly, 'you didn't strike out for us on account of your sister?'

'She ain't my sister,' said Clarence quickly. 'She's a little girl. She's Mrs. Silsbee's little girl. We were in the waggon and got down. It's my fault. I helped her down.'

The three men reined their horses closely round him, leaning forward from their saddles, with their hands on their knees, and their heads on one side. 'Then,' said the spokesman gravely, 'you just reckoned to stay here, old man, and take your chances *with her* rather than run the risk of frightening or leaving her — though it was your one chance of life!'

'Yes,' said the boy, a little weary of this feeble, grown-up repetition.

'Come here.'

The boy came doggedly forward. The man pushed back the well-worn straw hat from Clarence's forehead and looked into his lowering face. With his hand still on the boy's head he turned him round to the others, and said quietly,

'Suthin' of a pup, eh?'

'You bet,' they responded.

The voice was not unkindly, although the speaker had thrown his lower jaw forward as to pronounce the word 'pup' with a humorous suggestion of a mastiff. Before Clarence could make up his mind if the epithet was insulting or not, the man put out his stirruped foot, and, with a gesture of invitation, said, 'Jump up.'

'But Susy,' said Clarence, drawing back.

'Look; she's making up to Phil already.'

Clarence looked. Susy had crawled out of the mesquite, and with her sun-bonnet hanging down her back, her curls tossed around her face still flushed with sleep, and Clarence's jacket over her shoulders, was gazing up with grave satisfaction in the laughing eyes of one of the men who was, with outstretched hands, bending over her. Could he believe his senses? The terror-stricken, wilful, unmanageable Susy, whom he would have translated unconsciously to safety without this terrible ordeal of being awakened to the loss of her home and parents, at any sacrifice to himself — this ingenuous infant was absolutely throwing herself, with every appearance of forgetfulness, into the arms of the first newcomer! Yet his perception of this fact was accompanied by no sense of ingratitude. For her sake he felt relieved, and with a boyish smile of satisfaction and encouragement vaulted into the saddle before the stranger.

IV   The dash forward to the train, securely held in the saddle by the arms of their deliverers, was a secret joy to the children that seemed only too quickly over. The resistless gallop of the fiery mustangs, the rush of the night wind, the gathering darkness in which the distant waggons, now halted and facing them, looked like domed huts on the horizon — all then seemed but a delightful and fitting climax to the events of the day. In the sublime forgetfulness of youth, all they had gone through had left no embarrassing record behind it; they were willing to repeat their experiences on the morrow, confident of some equally happy end. And when Clarence, timidly reaching his hand towards the horse-hair reins lightly held by his companion, had them playfully yielded up to him by that bold and confident rider, the boy felt himself indeed a man.

But a greater surprise was in store for them. As they neared the waggons, now formed into a circle with a certain degree of military formality, they could see that the appointments of the strange party were larger and more liberal than their own, or, indeed, anything they had ever known of the kind. Forty or fifty horses were tethered within the circle, and the camp fires were already blazing. Before one of them a large tent was erected, and through the parted flaps could be seen a table actually spread with a white cloth. Was it a school-feast, or was this their ordinary household arrangements? Clarence and Susy thought of their own dinners usually laid on bare boards beneath the sky, or under the low hood of the waggon in rainy weather, and marvelled. And when they finally halted and were lifted from their horses, and passed one waggon fitted up as a bed-room and another as a kitchen, they could only nudge each other with silent appreciation. But here again the difference already noted in the quality of the sensations of the two children was observable. Both were equally and agreeably surprised. But Susy's wonder was merely the sense of novelty and inexperience, and a slight disbelief in the actual necessity of what she saw; while Clarence, whether from some previous general experience or peculiar temperament, had the conviction that what he saw here was the usual custom, and what he had known with the Silsbees was the novelty. The feeling was attended with a slight sense of wounded pride for Susy, as if her enthusiasm had exposed her to ridicule.

The man who had carried him, and seemed to be the head of the party, had already preceded them to the tent, and presently reappeared with a lady with whom he had exchanged a dozen hurried words. They seemed to refer to him and Susy; but Clarence was too much preoccupied with the fact that the lady was pretty, that her clothes were neat and thoroughly clean, that her hair was tidy and not rumpled, and that although she wore an apron it was as clean as her gown, and even had ribbons on it, to listen to what was said. And when she ran eagerly forward, and with a fascinating smile lifted the astonished Susy in her arms, Clarence, in his delight for his young charge, quite forgot that she had not noticed him. The bearded man, who seemed to be the lady's husband, evidently pointed out the omission, with some additions that Clarence could not catch, for after saying, with a pretty pout, 'Well, why shouldn't he?' she came forward with the same dazzling smile, and laid her small and clean white hand upon his shoulder.

'And so you took good care of the dear little thing? She's such an angel, isn't she? and you must love her very much.'

Clarence coloured with delight. It was true it had never occurred to him to look at Susy in the light of a celestial visitant, and I fear he was just then more struck with the fair complimenter than the compliment to his companion, but he was pleased for her sake. He was not yet old enough to be conscious of the sex's belief in its irresistible domination over mankind at all ages, — that 'Johnny' in his check apron would be always a hopeless conquest of 'Jeannette' in her pinafore, and that he ought to have been in love with Susy.

Howbeit, the lady suddenly whisked her away to the recesses of her own waggon, to reappear later, washed, curled, and beribboned like a new doll, and Clarence was left alone with the husband and another of the party.

'Well, my boy, you haven't told me your name yet.'

'Clarence, sir.'

'So Susy calls you — but what else?'

'Clarence Brant.'

'Any relation to Colonel Brant?' asked the second man carelessly.

'He was my father,' said the boy, brightening under this faint prospect of recognition in his loneliness.

The two men glanced at each other. The leader looked at the boy curiously, and said —

'Are you the son of Colonel Brant of Louisville?'

'Yes, sir,' said the boy, with a dim stirring of uneasiness in his heart. 'But he's dead now,' he added finally.

'Ah, when did he die?' said the man quickly.

'Oh, a long time ago. I don't remember him much. I was very little,' said the boy, half apologetically.

'Ah, you don't remember him?'

'No,' said Clarence, shortly. He was beginning to fall back upon that certain dogged repetition which in sensitive children arises from their hopeless inability to express their deeper feelings. He also had an instinctive consciousness that this want of a knowledge of his father was part of that vague wrong that had been done him. It did not help his uneasiness that he could see that one of the two men who turned away with a half-laugh misunderstood or did not believe him.

'How did you come with the Silsbees?' asked the first man.

Clarence repeated mechanically, with a child's distaste of practical details, how he had lived with an aunt of St. Jo, how his stepmother had procured his passage with the Silsbees to California, where he was to meet his cousin. All this with a lack of interest and abstraction that he was miserably conscious told against him, but he was yet helpless to resist.

The first man remained thoughtful, and then glanced at Clarence's sunburnt hands. Presently his large good-humoured smile returned.

'Well, I suppose you are hungry?'

'Yes,' said Clarence shyly. 'But—'

'But what?'

'I should like to wash myself a little,' he returned hesitatingly, thinking of the clean tent, the clean lady and Susy's ribbons.

'Certainly,' said his friend with a pleased look. 'Come with me.' Instead of leading Clarence to the battered tin basin and bar of yellow soap which had formed the toilet service of the Silsbee party, he brought the boy into one of the waggons, where there was a washstand, a china basin, and a cake of scented soap. Standing beside Clarence, he watched him perform his ablutions with an approving air which rather embarrassed his *protégé*. Presently he said, almost abruptly —

'Do you remember your father's house at Louisville?'

'Yes, sir; but it was a long time ago.'

Clarence remembered it as being very different from his home at St. Joseph's, but from some innate feeling of diffidence he would have shrunk from describing it in that way. He, however, said he thought it was a large house. Yet the modest answer only made his new friend look at him the more keenly.

'Your father was Colonel Hamilton Brant of Louisville, wasn't he?' he said, half-confidentially.

'Yes,' said Clarence hopelessly.

'Well,' said his friend cheerfully, as if dismissing an abstruse problem from his mind, 'let's go to supper.'

When they reached the tent again Clarence noticed that the supper was laid only for his host and wife and the second man — who was familiarly called 'Harry', but who spoke of the former always as 'Mr. and Mrs. Peyton' — while the remainder of the party, a dozen men, were at the second camp fire, and evidently enjoying themselves in a picturesque fashion. Had the boy been allowed to choose he would have joined them, partly because it seemed more 'manly', and partly that he dreaded a renewal of the questioning. But here Susy, sitting bolt upright on an extemporized high stool, happily diverted his attention by pointing to the empty chair beside her.

'Kla'uns,' she said suddenly, with her usual clear and appalling frankness, 'they is chickens and hamanaigs and hot biksquits, and lasses, and Mister Peyton says I kin have 'em all.'

Clarence, who had begun suddenly to feel that he was responsible for Susy's deportment, and was balefully conscious that she was holding her plated fork in her chubby fist by its middle, and, from his previous knowledge of her, was likely at any moment to plunge it into a dish before her, said softly —

'Hush!'

'Yes, you shall, dear,' says Mrs. Peyton, with tenderly beaming assurance to Susy, and a half-reproachful glance at the boy. 'Eat what you like, darling.'

'It's a fork,' whispered the still uneasy Clarence, as Susy now seemed inclined to stir her bowl of milk with it.

'Tain't now, Kla'uns, it's only a split spoon,' said Susy.

But Mrs. Peyton, in her rapt admiration, took small note of these irregularities, plying the child with food, forgetting her own meal, and only stopping at times to lift back the forward straying curls on Susy's shoulders.

Mr. Peyton looked on gravely and contentedly. Suddenly the eyes of husband and wife met.

'She'd have been nearly as old as this, John,' said Mrs. Peyton, in a faint voice.

John Peyton nodded without speaking, and turned his eyes away into the gathering darkness. The man 'Harry' also looked abstractedly at his plate as if he was saying grace. Clarence wondered who 'she' was, and why two little tears dropped from Mrs. Peyton's lashes into Susy's milk, and whether Susy might not violently object to it. He never knew until later that the Peytons had lost their only child, and Susy comfortably drained this mingled cup of a mother's grief and tenderness without suspicion.

'I suppose we'll come up with their train early to-morrow, if some of them don't find us to-night,' said Mrs. Peyton with a long sigh and a regretful glance at Susy. 'Perhaps we might travel together for a little while,' she added timidly. Harry laughed, and Mr. Peyton replied gravely, 'I am afraid we wouldn't travel with them, even for company's sake; and,' he added in a lower and graver voice, 'it's rather odd the search party hasn't come upon us yet, though I'm keeping Pete and Hank patrolling the trail to meet them.'

'It's heartless — so it is—' said Mrs. Peyton, with sudden indignation. 'It would be all very well if it was only this boy — who can take care of himself — but to be so careless of a mere baby like this, it's shameful!'

For the first time Clarence tasted the cruelty of discrimination. All the more keenly that he was beginning to worship — after his boyish fashion — this sweet-faced, clean, and tender-hearted woman. Perhaps Mr. Peyton noticed it, for he came quietly to his aid.

'Maybe they know better than we in what careful hands they had left her,' he said, with a cheerful nod towards Clarence. 'And, again, they may have been fooled as we were by Injin signs and left the straight road.'

This suggestion instantly recalled to Clarence his vision in the mesquite. Should he dare tell them? Would they believe him, or would they laugh at him before her? He hesitated, and at last resolved to tell it privately to the husband. When the meal was ended, and he was made happy by Mrs. Peyton's laughing acceptance of his offer to help her clear the table and wash the dishes, they all gathered comfortably in front of the tent before the large camp-fire. At the other fire the rest of the party were playing cards and laughing, but Clarence no longer cared to join them. He was quite tranquil in the maternal propinquity of his hostess, albeit a little uneasy as to his reticence about the Indian.

'Kla'uns,' said Susy, relieving a momentary pause, in her highest voice, 'knows how to speak. Speak, Kla'uns!'

It appearing from Clarence's blushing explanation that this gift was not the ordinary faculty of speech, but a capacity to recite verse, he was politely pressed by the company for a performance.

'Speak 'em, Kla'uns — the boy what stood unto the burnin' deck and said, "the boy, oh, where was he?"' said Susy, comfortably lying down on Mrs. Peyton's lap and contemplating her bare knees in the air. 'It's 'bout a boy,' she added confidently to Mrs. Peyton, 'whose father wouldn't never, never stay with him on a burnin' ship, though he said "Stay, father, stay", ever so much.'

With this clear, lucid, and perfectly satisfactory explanation of Mrs. Hemans's 'Casabianca', Clarence began. Unfortunately his actual rendering of this popular school performance was more an effort of memory than anything else, and was illustrated by those wooden gestures which a Western schoolmaster had taught him. He described the flames that 'roared around him', by indicating with his hand a perfect circle of which he was the axis: he adjured his father, the late Admiral Casabianca, by clasping his hands before his chin, as if wanting to be manacled in an attitude which he was miserably conscious was unlike anything to himself he had ever felt or seen before; he described that father 'faint in death below', and 'the flag on high', with one single motion. Yet something that the verses had kindled in his active imagination, rather perhaps than an illustration of the verses themselves, at times brightened his grey eyes, became tremulous in his youthful voice, and I fear occasionally incoherent on his lips. At times when not conscious of his affected art, the plain and all upon it seemed to him to slip away into the night, the blazing camp-fire at his feet to wrap him in a fateful glory, and a vague devotion to something — he knew not what — so possessed him that he communicated it, and probably some of his own youthful delight in extravagant voice, to his hearers, until when he ceased, whith a glowing face, he was surprised to find that the card-players had deserted their camp-fires and gathered round the tent.

V   'You didn't say "stay, father, stay", enough, Kla'uns,' said Susy critically. Then suddenly starting upright in Mrs. Peyton's lap, she continued rapidly: 'I kin dance. And sing. I kin dance High Jambooree.'

'What's High Jambooree, dear?' asked Mrs. Peyton.

'You'll see. Lemme down.' And Susie slipped to the ground.

The dance of High Jambooree, evidently of remote mystical African origin, appeared to consist of three small skips to the right and then to the left, accompanied by the holding up of very short skirts, incessant 'teetering' on the toes of small feet, the exhibition of much bare knee and stocking, and a gurgling accompaniment of childish laughter. Vehemently applauded, it left the little performer breathless, but invincible and ready for fresh conquest.

'I kin sing too,' she gasped hurriedly, as if unwilling that the applause should lapse. 'I kin sing. Oh dear! Kla'uns' (piteously), '*what* is it I sing?'

'"Ben Bolt",' suggested Clarence.

'Oh, yes. "Oh, don't you remember sweet Alers Ben Bolt?"' began Susy, in the same breath and the wrong key. '"Sweet Alers, with hair so brown, who wept with delight when you giv'd her a smile, and—"' with knitted brows and appealing recitative, 'what's er rest of it, Kla'uns?'

'"Who trembled with fear at your frown?"' prompted Clarence.

'"Who trembled with fear at my frown?"' shrilled Susy. 'I forget er rest. Wait! I kin sing—'

'"Praise God",' suggested Clarence.

'Yes.' Here Susy, a regular attendant in camp and prayer meetings, was on firmer ground.

Promptly lifting her high treble, yet with a certain acquired deliberation, she began, 'Praise God, from whom all blessings flow.' At the end of the second line the whispering and laughing ceased. A deep voice to the right, that of the champion poker-player, suddenly rose on the swell of the third line. He was instantly followed by a dozen ringing voices, and by the time the last line was reached it was given with a full chorus, in which the dull chant of teamsters and drivers mingled with the soprano of Mrs. Peyton and Susy's childish treble. Again and again it was repeated, with forgetful eyes and abstracted faces, rising and falling with the night wind and the leap and gleam of the camp-fires, and fading again like them in the immeasurable mystery of the darkened plain.

In the deep and embarrassing silence that followed at last the party hesitatingly broke up, Mrs. Peyton retiring with Susy after offering the child to Clarence for a perfunctory 'goodnight' kiss, an unusual proceeding, which somewhat astonished them both and Clarence found himself near Mr. Peyton.

'I think,' said Clarence, timidly, 'I saw an Injin to-day.'

Mr. Peyton bent down towards him. 'An Injin — where?' he asked quickly, with the same look of doubting interrogatory with which he had received Clarence's name and parentage.

The boy for a moment regretted having spoken. But with his old doggedness he particularized his statement. Fortunately, being gifted with a keen perception, he was able to describe the stranger accurately, and to impart with his description that contempt for its subject which he had felt, and which to his frontier auditor established its truthfulness. Peyton turned abruptly away, but presently returned with Harry and another man.

'You are sure of this?' said Peyton, half encouragingly.

'Yes, sir.'

'As sure as you are that your father is Colonel Brant and is dead?' said Harry, with a light laugh.

Tears sprang into the boy's lowering eyes. 'I don't lie,' he said doggedly.

'I believe you, Clarence,' said Peyton quietly. 'But why didn't you say it before?'

'I didn't like to say it before Susy and — her!' stammered the boy.

'Her?'

'Yes — sir — Mrs. Peyton — ' said Clarence, blushingly.

'Oh,' said Harry, sarcastically, 'how blessed polite we are!'

'That'll do. Let up on him, will you,' said Peyton, roughly, to his subordinate; 'the boy knows what he's about. But,' he continued, addressing Clarence, 'how was it the Injin didn't see you?'

'I was very still on account of not waking Susy,' said Clarence, 'and — ' he hesitated.

'And what?'

'He seemed more keen watching what *you* were doing,' said the boy, boldly.

'That's so,' broke in the second man, who happened to be experienced; 'and as he was to wind'ard o' the boy he was off *his* scent and bearings. He was one of their rear scouts; the rest o' them's ahead crossing our track to cut us off. Ye didn't see anything else?'

'I saw a coyote first,' said Clarence, greatly encouraged.

'Hold on!' said the expert, as Harry turned away with a sneer. 'That's a sign, too. Wolf don't go where wolf hez been, and coyote don't foller Injins — there's no pickins! How long afore did you see the coyote?'

'Just after we left the waggon,' said Clarence.

'That's it,' said the man, thoughtfully. 'He was driven on ahead, or hanging on their flanks. These Injins are betwixt us and that ar train, or following it.'

Peyton made a hurried gesture of warning, as if reminding the speaker of

Clarence's presence — a gesture which the boy noticed and wondered at. Then the conversation of the three men took a lower tone, although Clarence as distinctly heard the concluding opinion of the expert.

'It ain't no good now, Mr. Peyton, and you'd be only exposing yourself on their ground by breakin' camp agin to-night. And you don't know that it ain't *us* they're watchin'. You see, if we hand't turned off the straight road when we got that first scare from these yer lost children, we might hev gone on and walked plump into some cursed trap of those devils. To my mind, we're just in nigger luck, and with a good watch and my patrol we're all right to be fixed where we be till daylight.'

Mr. Peyton presently turned away, taking Clarence with him. 'As we'll be up early and on the track of your train to-morrow, my boy, you had better turn in now. I've put you up in my waggon, and as I expect to be in the saddle most of the night, I reckon I won't trouble you much.' He led the way to a second waggon — drawn up beside the one where Susy and Mrs. Peyton had retired — which Clarence was surprised to find fitted with a writing-table and desk, a chair, and even a bookshelf containing some volumes. A long locker, fitted like a lounge, had been made up as a couch for him, with the unwonted luxury of clean white sheets and pillow-cases. A soft matting covered the floor of the heavy waggon bed, which, Mr. Peyton explained, was hung on centre springs to prevent jarring. The sides and roof of the vehicle were of lightly panelled wood, instead of the usual hooked canvas frame of the ordinary emigrant waggon, and fitted with a glazed door and movable window for light and air. Clarence wondered why the big, powerful man, who seemed at home on horseback, should ever care to sit in this office like a merchant or a lawyer; and if this train sold things to the other trains, or took goods, like the pedlars, to towns on the route — but there seemed to be nothing to sell, and the other waggons were filled with only the goods required by the party. He would have liked to ask Mr. Peyton who *he* was, and have questioned *him* as freely as he himself had been questioned. But as the average adult man never takes into consideration the injustice of denying to the natural and even necessary curiosity of childhood that questioning which he himself is so apt to assume without right, and almost always without delicacy, Clarence had no recourse. Yet the boy, like all children, was conscious that if he had been afterwards questioned about *this*

203

inexplicable experience, he would have been blamed for his ignorance concerning it. Left to himself presently, and ensconced between the sheets, he lay for some moments staring about him. The unwonted comfort of his couch, so different from the stuffy blanket in the hard waggon bed which he had shared with one of the teamsters, and the novelty, order, and cleanliness of his surroundings, while they were grateful to his instincts, began in some vague way

to depress him. To his loyal nature it seemed a tacit infidelity to his former rough companions to be lying here; he had a dim idea that he had lost that independence which equal discomfort and equal pleasure among them had given him. There seemed a sense of servitude in accepting this luxury which was not his. This set him endeavouring to remember something of his father's house, of the large rooms, draughty staircases, and far-off ceilings, and the cold formality of a life that seemed made up of strange faces; some stranger — his parents; some kinder — the servants; particularly the black nurse who had him in charge. Why did Mr. Peyton ask him about it? Why, if it were so important to strangers, had not his mother told him more of it? And why was she not like this good woman with the gentle voice who was so kind to — to Susy? And what did they mean by making *him* so miserable? Something rose in his throat, but with an effort he choked it back, and, creeping from the lounge, went softly to the window, opened it to see if it 'would work', and looked out. The shrouded camp-fires, the stars that glittered but gave no light, the dim moving bulk of a patrol beyond the circle, all seemed to intensify the darkness, and changed the current of his thoughts. He remembered what Mr. Peyton had said of him when they first met. 'Suthin of a pup, ain't he?' Surely that meant something that was not bad! He crept back to the couch again.

Lying there, still awake, he reflected that he wouldn't be a scout when he grew up, but would be something like Mr. Peyton, and have a train like this, and invite the Silsbees and Susy to accompany him. For this purpose he and Susy, early to-morrow morning, would get permission to come in here and play at that game. This would familiarize him with the details, so that he would be able at any time to take charge of it. He was already an authority on the subject of Indians! He had once been fired at — as an Indian. He would always carry a rifle like that hanging from the hooks at the end of the waggon before him, and would eventually slay many Indians and keep an account of them in a big book like that on the desk. Susy would help him, having grown up a lady, and they would both together issue provisions and rations from the door of the waggon to the gathered crowds. He would be known as the 'White Chief', his Indian name being 'Suthin of a pup'. He would have a circus van attached to the train, in which he would occasionally perform. He would also have artillery for protection. There would be a terrific engagement, and he would rush into the waggon, heated and blackened with gunpowder, and Susy would put down an account of it in a book, and Mrs. Peyton — for she would be there in some vague capacity — would say, 'Really, now, I don't see but what we were very lucky in having such a boy as Clarence with us. I begin to understand him better.' And Harry, who, for purposes of vague poetical retaliation, would also drop in at that moment, would mutter and say, 'He is certainly the son of Colonel Brant; dear me!' and apologize. And his mother would come in also, in her coldest and most

205

indifferent manner, in a white ball dress, and start and say, 'Good gracious, how that boy has grown! I am sorry I did not see more of him when he was young.' Yet even in the midst of this came a confusing numbness, and then the side of the waggon seemed to melt away, and he drifted out again alone into the empty desolate plain from which even the sleeping Susy had vanished, and he was left deserted and forgotten. Then all was quiet in the waggon, and only the night wind moving round it. But lo! the lashes of the sleeping White Chief — the dauntless leader, the ruthless destroyer of Indians — were wet with glittering tears!

Yet it seemed only a moment afterwards that he awoke with a faint consciousness of some arrested motion. To his utter consternation, the sun, three hours high, was shining in the waggon, already hot and stifling in its beams. There was the familiar smell and taste of the dirty road in the air about him. There was a faint creaking of boards and springs, a slight oscillation, and beyond the audible rattle of harness as if the train had been under way, the waggon moving, and then there had been a sudden halt. They had probably come up with the Silsbee train; in a few moments the change would be effected and all of his strange experience would be over. He must get up now. Yet, with the morning laziness of the healthy young animal, he curled up a moment longer in his luxurious couch.

How quiet it was! There were far-off voices, but they seemed suppressed and hurried. Through the window he saw one of the teamsters run rapidly past him with a strange, breathless, preoccupied face, halt a moment at one of the following waggons, and then run back again to the front. Then two of the voices came nearer, with the dull beating of hoofs in the dust.

'Rout out the boy and ask him,' said a half-suppressed, impatient voice, which Clarence at once recognized as the man Harry's.

'Hold on till Peyton comes up,' said the second voice, in a low tone; 'leave it to him.'

'Better find out what they were like, at once,' grumbled Harry.

'Wait — stand back,' said Peyton's voice, joining the others; 'I'll ask him.'

Clarence looked wonderingly at the door. It opened on Mr. Peyton, dusty and dismounted, with a strange, abstracted look in his face.

'How many waggons are in your train, Clarence?'

'Three, sir.'

'Any marks on them?'

'Yes, sir,' said Clarence, eagerly; '"Off to California", and "Root, Hog, or Die".'

Mr. Peyton's eye seemed to leap up and hold Clarence's with a sudden, strange significance, and then looked down.

'How many were you in all?' he continued.

'Five, and there was Mrs. Silsbee.'

'No other woman?'

'No.'

'Get up and dress yourself,' he said gravely, 'and wait here till I come back. Keep cool and have your wits about you.' He dropped his voice slightly. 'Perhaps something's happened that you'll have to show yourself a little man again for, Clarence!'

The door closed, and the boy heard the same muffled hoofs and voices die away towards the front. He began to dress himself mechanically, almost vacantly, yet conscious always of a vague undercurrent of thrilling excitement. When he had finished he waited almost breathlessly, feeling the same beating of his heart that he had felt when he was following the vanished train the day before. At last he could stand the suspense no longer, and opened the door. Everything was still in the motionless caravan, except — it struck him oddly even then — the unconcerned prattling voice of Susy from one of the nearer waggons. Perhaps a sudden feeling that this was something that concerned *her*, perhaps an irresistible impulse overcame him, but the next moment he had leaped to the ground, faced about, and was running feverishly to the front.

The first thing that met his eyes was the helpless and desolate bulk of one of the Silsbee waggons a hundred rods away, bereft of oxen and pole, standing alone and motionless against the dazzling sky! Near it was the broken frame of another waggon, its fore-wheels and axles gone, pitched forward on its knees like an ox under the butcher's sledge. Not far away there were the burnt and blackened ruins of a third, around which the whole party on foot and horseback seemed to be gathered. As the boy ran violently on, the group opened to make way for two men carrying some helpless but awful object between them. A terrible instinct made Clarence swerve from it in his headlong course, but he

207

was at the same moment discovered by the others, and a cry arose of 'Go back!' 'Stop!' 'Keep him back.' Heeding it no more than the wind that whistled by him, Clarence made directly for the foremost waggon — the one in which he and Susy had played. A powerful hand caught his shoulder; it was Mr. Peyton's.

'Mrs. Silsbee's waggon,' said the boy, with white lips, pointing to it. 'Where is she?'

'She's missing,' said Peyton, 'and one other — the rest are dead.'

'She must be there,' said the boy, struggling, and pointing to the waggon, 'let me go.'

'Clarence,' said Peyton sternly, accenting his grasp upon the boy's arm, 'be a man! Look around you. Try and tell us who these are.'

There seemed to be one or two heaps of old clothes lying on the ground, and further on, where the men at a command from Peyton had laid down their burden, another. In those ragged dusty heaps of clothes, from which all the majesty of life seemed to have been ruthlessly stamped out, only what was ignoble and grotesque appeared to be left. There was nothing terrible in this! The boy moved slowly towards them; and, incredible even to himself, the overpowering fear of them that a moment before had overcome him left him as suddenly. He walked from the one to the other, recognizing them by certain marks and signs, and mentioning name after name. The groups gazed at him curiously; he was conscious that he scarcely understood himself, still less the same quiet purpose that now made him turn towards the furthest waggon.

'There's nothing there,' said Peyton; 'we've searched it.' But the boy, without replying, continued his way, and the crowd followed him.

The deserted waggon, more rude, disorderly, and slovenly than it had ever seemed to him before, was now heaped and tumbled with broken bones, cans, scattered provisions, pots, pans, blankets, and clothing in the foul confusion of a dust-heap. But in this heterogeneous mingling the boy's quick eye caught sight of a draggled edge of calico.

'That's Mrs. Silsbee's dress,' he cried, and leapt into the waggon.

At first the men stared at each other, but an instant later a dozen hands were helping him, nervously digging and clearing away the rubbish. Then one man uttered a sudden cry, and fell back with frantic but furious eyes uplifted against the pitiless, smiling sky above him.

208

'Great God! Look here!'

It was the yellowish, waxen face of Mrs. Silsbee that had been uncovered. But to the fancy of the boy it had changed; the old familiar lines of worry, care, and querulousness had given way to a look of remote peace and statue-like repose. He had often vexed her in her aggressive life; he was touched with remorse at her cold, passionless apathy now, and pressed timidly forward. Even as he did so, the man, with a quick but warning gesture, hurriedly threw his handkerchief over the matted locks, as if to shut out something awful from his view. Clarence felt himself drawn back; but not before the white lips of a bystander had whispered a single word —

'Scalped, too! by God!'

VI   Then followed days and weeks that seemed to Clarence as a dream. At first an interval of hushed and awed restraint, when he and Susy were kept apart — a strange and artificial interest taken little note of by him, but afterwards remembered when others had forgotten it; the burial of Mrs. Silsbee beneath a cairn of stones, with some ceremonies that, simple though they were, seemed to usurp the sacred rights of grief from him and Susy, and leave them cold and frightened; days of frequent and incoherent childish outbursts from Susy — growing fainter and rarer as time went on, until they ceased, he knew not when; the haunting by night of that morning vision of the three or four heaps of ragged clothes upon the ground, and a half regret that he had not examined them more closely; a recollection of the awful loneliness and desolation of the broken and abandoned waggon left behind on its knees as if praying mutely when the train went on and left it; the trundling behind of the fateful waggon in which Mrs. Silsbee's body had been found — superstitiously shunned by every one — and when at last turned over to the authorities at an outpost garrison, seeming to drop the last link from the dragging chain of the past. The revelation to the children of a new experience in that brief glimpse of the frontier garrison; the handsome officer in uniform and belted sword — an heroic, vengeful figure to be admired and imitated hereafter; the sudden importance and respect given to Susy and himself as 'survivors'; the sympathetic questioning and kindly exaggerations of their experiences — quickly accepted by Susy — all these, looking back upon them afterwards, seemed to have passed in a dream.

THE SANDS OF DESTRUCTION

KARL MAY

In the Caves of the Sahara

The sun was dipping westwards. Nevertheless, the heat was still oppressive, and I lay in the shade of my camel while the remaining members of the caravan sat down alongside the cloudy, evil-tasting water, and listened to the boasts of my servant, Kamil. I understood every word, and listened with secret pleasure as he tried to impress them with my countless merits.

'You are called Abram ben Sakir, and you are a wealthy man, are you not?' he asked a rich merchant from Murzuk, who was sitting next to him. 'How much a day are you paying your attendants?'

'Two hundred *kauris*,' replied the merchant, willingly. 'Is it not enough?'

'For a man of your riches, it is enough. But my *sidi* is far wealthier than you are. His name is Kara ben Nemsi, and in the oases of his father there graze a thousand horses, five thousand camels, ten thousand goats, and twenty thousand sheep with fat tails. He pays me one *abu nukat** a day, so that when I return home I shall be richer than you. Tell me, what are you compared to him?'

The braggart was modifying the truth a little: I was indeed paying him a thaler, but weekly, not daily, so that his daily wage was actually about fifty pfennig.

'Allah gives, Allah takes away; all men may not be equally rich,' shrugged the merchant.

'You are right,' Kamil assented. 'And since Allah favours my master, he has showered him with gifts. You have no idea how celebrated is the name of Kara ben Nemsi among all nations and in all lands! He speaks all the four thousand

---

* 'Father of Points' — a Theresian thaler

and fifty tongues of the earth, knows the names of all eighty thousand animals and plants, knows how to cure ten thousand ailments, and can kill a lion with a single shot. His mother was the most beautiful woman in the world, and his father's mother was called Embodiment of Virtue, and all thirty-six of his wives are obedient and charming, and scented with ambergris, like the flowers of Eden. Even the black panther trembles at the sound of his voice, and if we should be attacked by the Targi, for instance, for we are in their territory here, he would be able to drive them off with his small rifle. Look at him — do you see that he has two rifles, a big one and a small one? With the big one he can shoot a whole *kal'u*, a fortress, with one shot, and the small one he can shoot a hundred thousand times without reloading, so it is called *bundukijat 't takrar,* repeating rifle. I almost wish those scoundrels would come, just so that you might see...'

'Silence, by Allah!' he was quickly interrupted by the sheik *el jammalin,* leader of the caravan. 'Lest the sheitan hear you, or he will indeed bring them here, and we shall be lost.'

'Lost? With my effendi here, and me with him?'

Just then a rider came into view to the north. His *hejin,* or riding camel, was a fine runner. His weapons consisted of a long arab rifle and two knives, attached to his wrists with bracelets. It is a peculiarly lethal way of carrying them; in a fight all one has to do is embrace one's adversary and sink both blades into his back.

'*Salam!*' the rider greeted them, leaping from the saddle, without even bringing the animal to its knees. 'Allow me to water my *hejin,* and to warn you of an enemy!'

He wore a long white burnous, his black, heavily greased hair sticking out from under the hood. He was tall and strongly built. His face was full, flattened at the cheekbones, with a short, almost blunt nose, small eyes and a rounded chin. Were he wearing the *litham,* a veil which covers the face, leaving only the eyes unmasked, I should have sworn he was a Targi.

'You are welcome,' the sheik answered, as the stranger's camel ran to the water of its own accord. 'Of what enemy do you speak?'

'The Amahars,' was the reply. It is another name for the Targi, but is normally used only by the members of the tribe themselves.

'Do you mean the Targi?'

'Yes; they have occupied the oasis of Seghedem.'

'Allah! We wish to go there tonight!'

'Do not do it. Ours was a caravan of thirty men and eighty camels. We arrived from Bi'r Ishaj, and supposed we were safe. But as soon as we arrived at Seghedem, the Amahars attacked us, and only I escaped the massacre.'

'Allah!' the old man cried. 'The sheitan has sent the dogs! They will stay at Seghedem. What are we to do? Wait here at Bi'r Akbar, where the water is scarcely fit for man to drink, and does not suffice for the beasts?'

He glanced helplessly round the circle. Abram ben Sakir frowned.

'Is there no way round the oasis of Seghedem?'

'None,' said the sheik. 'We cannot go eastwards, for the nearest well is a full three days' journey hence, in the lands of the warrior Tibbu, and if we were to turn westwards, we should come to the hills of Maghajir es suchur, the rocky caves, where I do not know the way.'

'I do,' announced the stranger.

'You?' queried the sheik. 'Then you would be a more experienced *chabir*, leader, than I, and have I not twice your years?'

'I am a *chabir*. It is not a matter of age. I know that place, for I have been there several times. I was leader of the caravan the Amahars attacked, and I should never have been able to escape, did I not know my way in the desert. I am a warrior of the Rijah tribe, and am called Umar ibn Amara.'

The Rijah tribe did indeed live in Fezzan, but I could not believe that this *chabir* was an Arab, especially since he constantly referred to the Targi as Amahars. No Arab would ever do that. But the sheik did not seem to share my doubts, for he now said, 'I know that the men of the Rijah tribe know the route from Murzuk to Bilma well. Do you suppose we might avoid the Targi that way?'

'Indeed; it is not difficult. We shall travel in an arc to the right above Seghedem, and arrive safely at Bi'r Ishaj. I shall take you there, for I suppose it is the wish of you all.'

'It is our wish. Sit with us, and you shall be our guest.'

'I will gladly be your leader and guest, but first tell me, who are the men whose caravan you lead?'

'This is Abram ben Sakir, merchant of Murzuk, owner of all the drivers and

215

beasts of burden. I am to take him from Bilma to Murzuk. And over there are two strangers who have joined us — haji Kara ben Nemsi, a Frank, and his servant Kamil ibn Safaka.'

The *chabir* fixed us both with a piercing stare, and asked Kamil threateningly, 'What is your tribe?'

'I am a Jerar of the *firkat* Ashallu.'

'And you are not ashamed to serve a jaur? Fie!'

He spat in his face, and Kamil let him get away with it, since his courage was all in his words, and he was timid when it came to action. He managed only a reproachful question.

'*Sidi*, hero of all heroes, will you allow your faithful servant to be insulted?' he asked.

'Hero of heroes?' the *chabir* laughed insolently. 'I shall show him what it is to be a hero.'

He came within three paces of me and turned a pair of blazing eyes on me.

'You think I am going to take you to Murzuk?'

'No! You are not going to take anyone to Murzuk!'

'What do you mean?' he retorted, involuntarily.

'You are *jasus*, a spy, and you wish to deliver the caravan up to the Targi.'

'*Ma sha'allah!* Me, a *jasus!* You shall pay for such an insult!'

'First tell me why you wish to return to Murzuk: why do you not travel on to Bilma? Why did you not return direct from Seghedem, since you were able to escape? Why did you travel on for a whole day?'

My questions seemed to take him off guard. He even stopped threatening me.

'The Amahars had me cut off.'

'That does not explain why you rode on for a whole day. I don't believe a word you say. The Targi are lying in wait for us, but not at Seghedem. They are more likely to ambush us among the rocks where you would lead us.'

Instead of answering, he leapt at me with outstretched arms, about to sink his knives into my back. But my fist struck first: I punched him under the chin with all my might, so that he was lifted off the ground and fell senseless in the sand.

'What have you done!' cried the sheik. 'Is this how you reward us for taking you among us? This man wished to save us, and you have slain him.'

'He wishes to destroy us, not to save us. And he is not dead, only stunned!'

This failed to lessen the sheik's anger.

'You have insulted him. According to the law of the desert that requires blood. We shall have to pass judgement on you.'

'Save your judgement for him. I say he is a Targi, and he wants to destroy us. If you do not believe me now, you will soon discover the truth of my words, to your undoing. I have no fear for myself. I have weapons, and I know how to defend myself.'

The sheik looked as if he had not heard, and had the unconscious man carried to the water in order to bring him round. While the *chabir* was coming to his senses, and the others pressed about him, Kamil took the rich merchant to one side and began to speak to him, quickly and quietly. After a while Abram came over to me.

'*Sidi*, your servant tells me I should put my faith in you, instead of in the sheik *el jammalin*. Do you really think this fellow is a spy of the robbers?'

'I do. I have been to the Sahara before, and I know his type. I haven't the least inclination to ride to the hills and fall into the hands of the Targi.'

'*Allah, vallah, tallah!* What am I to do? I have promised to take the orders of the sheik *el jammalin* in all things. My people put more faith in him than in your words. I would ask one thing of you, *sidi*. Do not desert me, if I have to enter the rocky lands.'

'There is no need for you to ask my help; you need only say that you wish to ride to Seghedem at all costs.'

'I am outvoted. You surely know that it is the custom in the desert that the voice of the servant is of equal value to that of the master. Do not desert me!'

'I shall consider the matter.'

'Then consider; anyway, who knows, you may be mistaken. I find it difficult to believe that anyone could stoop so low!'

'And yet it is so. See, he shows no sign of having defended his caravan. See how he now sits calmly by the well, without thought of vengeance. A moment ago he leapt upon me in rage, but now he is not impatient to take his revenge, for he knows he may take it without danger when we ride with him among the rocks.'

'*Sidi*, when I hear you speak, it seems to me that you are quite right. Therefore I beg you a third time: take me under your protection.'

'If I do so, then I shall very soon require protection myself. Because of you...'

At that moment the sonorous voice of the sheik *el jammalin* gave the order. 'Rise up, ye faithful; make your evening prayers, for darkness is come, and the last rays of the sun have sunk beneath the horizon!'

The men knelt down, facing Mecca, wet their hands, chest and forehead with water, and said their prayers. Then the sheik rose and ordered the camels to be loaded. 'We shall leave.'

'Whither?' asked the merchant.

'To the hills, of course,' came the reply.

'Would it not be wiser to ride to the oasis of Seghedem?'

'Do you speak so because Kara ben Nemsi would have it so?'

'It is so.'

'If you place more trust in the opinion of a foolish jaur, then you may ride where you will — no one will stop you. As for the rest of us, we shall make a detour through the rocky caves.'

'My servants must go with me!'

'Must? They are free men, and you have promised to obey my orders. We shall take a vote, and you will see whether they follow you, or their own prudence.'

A vote was taken, and all except the merchant, myself and my servant were willing to go with the *chabir*. Abram ben Sakir took me aside, apologized, and begged me a fourth time not to desert him.

As our group was breaking up, we heard some kind of noise to the west. In a little while we could make out the tramp of camels, and a cluster of riders emerged from the darkness. They must have seen us, too, for a loud voice called out, '*Vakkif!* Halt! There is someone at the well. To arms!'

Our old sheik *el jammalin* replied. 'Peace! We are neither warriors nor robbers. Come closer, and take water for yourselves and your beasts!'

'You are a *kafila*?'

'We are.'

'Whence, and whither?'

'From Bilma to Murzuk.'

'How many?'

'Fourteen men.'

'Stand back! But if you lie it shall cost you your head!'

They approached cautiously. Their spokesman rode a few camel lengths ahead, surveyed the ground, and then nodded to the others.

'He speaks the truth. They are fourteen. We need not fear. Come hither!'

He spoke Arabic, but in a dialect which revealed him to be a Tibbu. As the riders dismounted, I counted them. There were exactly twenty. It seemed they had a woman or a girl with them, for a *tahtaruvan*, or light bamboo litter, hung from one of the camels, its curtains and long poles making a ghostly sight in the darkness.

The leader of the new caravan ordered his men to take up positions which would put them at an advantage in case of sudden attack. His warlike disposition was confirmed by the many weapons he carried. He had a long rifle, two spears, a sabre, and probably also knives and a pistol. The sheik *el jammalin* greeted him with a courteous *salam*.

'As you see, you have nothing to fear. And you will surely forgive our asking who you are.'

'We are Tibbu of the Reshad tribe, and we are travelling to Aba,' the man replied proudly.

'You are of the Reshad tribe? Then you are the sworn enemies of the Assaben Targi.'

'Indeed we are — may Allah's curse be upon them.'

'But you come from the west, from their territory.'

'It is so.'

'Then you are bold men. For such a small band of warriors to venture into the lands of their sworn enemies...'

He was interrupted by a cry from the *tahtaruvan*. I heard three or four words which I did not understand. The tongue seemed to me to be Berber. I knew only the dialect of the Mesah-Berbers, so I guessed this must be the language of the Targi. And, stranger still, as soon as the words were spoken, the *chabir* rose, hurried over to the litter, and asked something, again in a language I did not know. From under the curtains he received some sort of answer in a soprano voice: a woman? It might also have been the voice of a boy.

The leader of the Tibbu leapt up, took the *chabir* by the shoulders, shook him, and began to rebuke him angrily,

'What are you doing near the litter of my *umm bint?* Do you not know it is forbidden?'

Umm bint means daughter's mother. The Arabs use this form of words to describe their wives, a word they consider indecent.

For a moment the *chabir* stood motionless, as though trying to control his feelings. Then he replied in a voice of studied indifference. '*Umm bint?* The voice sounded like that of a boy.'

'It is no boy. And even if it were, he would scarcely call to you. Who are you?'

'My name is Umar ibn Amara, and I am the *chabir* of this caravan.'

'When are you leaving?'

'We were just setting out.'

'We too shall not stay long, for we are in a hurry to get to Aba. If you are peaceful men, we might travel to the oasis together.'

'We do not ride for Seghedem: the Targi have occupied the oasis and all the land about it.'

The Tibbu drew back, as if shocked by the news.

'The Targi — those dogs? Are you sure?'

'Indeed, for I am come from Seghedem. I am *chabir* of the *kafila* which they attacked and massacred. Only I escaped. We shall avoid Seghedem, and ride in a westward arc to the well at Ishaja. We cannot turn eastwards, for the Amahars are still prowling there.'

Once again he said Amahars instead of Targi.

I noted that he spoke the last sentence with special emphasis. Why? This score of warriors might turn out to be quite a nuisance to the Targi's plans. Could it be that he had understood the cry from the litter? Then he was certainly a Targi.

The Tibbu questioned him further for some moments, then called his warriors to him and quietly held a short council.

'Do you know from which tribe were the Targi of whom you speak?' he asked the *chabir.*

'No. I do not understand a word in the tongue of these Amahars. But when they attacked us, they shouted the same two words over and over again, and I have heard that when they attack, they always call the names of the tribe and of their leader. The words were Kelovi and Rhagata.'

'Allah, Allah, it may be so! Rhagata is the name of the *amghar,* the leader of the eastern Kelovi-Targi, and I know he has led his warriors out on an expedition of robbery. What good fortune it is that I have met you. So you wish to travel through Maghajir es suchur? It is a hard road! Do you think we may reach the well of Ishaja in safety by this route?'

'We certainly shall not meet any Targi.'

'At Ishaja I should turn eastwards, and we should thus avoid danger. But before I decide to ride with you, I must know who you are.'

'You know me already. Our *kafila* belongs to this merchant from Murzuk; Abram ben Sakir is his name. The rest are peaceable camel drivers. Over there sits a man who joined them yesterday, with his servant. He is called Kara ben Nemsi, and he is a Frank and a jaur.'

'A jaur! And I am to travel with you?'

He came up close to me, and his eyes bored into my face. I sat on, motionless. He walked away, and spat on the ground.

'He has the face of a man, but his spirit is that of a woman, or he would not bear the glance of scorn. The lion allows the jackal to follow in his footsteps, for he is too proud even to turn his head. Let the stranger ride with us, but at the back, or I shall tear him apart like some annoying insect.'

I put up with his insults, not considering it a fit moment to prove him wrong.

Abram ben Sakir had his camels loaded. As this was being done, he spoke to the *chabir.* Then he came over to me.

'*Sidi,* he knows the tongue of the Hausa. He answered me correctly when I addressed him in that speech.'

'Then he is a Targi.'

'And yet I still cannot believe it. The leader of the Tibbu would see through him. It is clear that he is a great warrior.'

'You may be mistaken. The Tibbu is himself glad that no one has seen through him.'

'What do you mean?'

'Robber hates robber, but one is like another.'

'You speak in riddles.'

'You will soon solve them.'

'But will you ride with us, even if you must ride behind?'

'Who says so?'

'The Tibbu.'

'He has no right to give me orders. I am a free man, and I shall ride where I wish.'

He merely shook his head.

I took my *hejin* to the water to let it have a good drink.

The loading went on, accompanied by the unpleasant braying of the beasts of burden; then the riders mounted, and the procession set off. The loaded camels were joined together, the tail of one being attached to the bridle of another.

The *chabir* rode at the head. Behind him was the sheik *el jammalin*, followed by the Tibbu, accompanied by his *tahtaruvan*. Behind him rode his warriors, and behind them Abram ben Sakir with his long *kafila*. I waited for them to ride on a while before following slowly with Kamil. The stars shone so clearly that there was no danger of my losing sight of the caravan.

'So now we must ride behind them!' my bold servant complained. 'Why do you obey him, *sidi*? Am I not a Jerar of the Ashallu *firkat*, and should I not ride proudly in front of them all?'

'No one is preventing you. Ride forward if you wish!'

'Not without you! You know that you are close to my heart, and I will not leave you alone in shame and disdain. But tell me, do you really think we shall fight with these people?'

'Yes, and soon — first of all with the *chabir*.'

'You believe him to be a Targi?'

'I do. He wants to destroy the caravan. The Targi are waiting for us at Maghajir es suchur, and the sheik in his blindness is leading these people to their deaths; but I still hope that he will heed my warning at the last moment.'

'And if he does not?'

'Then I shall try to save the merchant at least. The Tibbu will help us do that.'

'How? You are relying on the Tibbu? They will be ambushed along with the others, will they not?'

'Certainly; but they have something with them which may help us out of our peril — the *tahtaruvan*.'

'How can the litter help us?'

'Not the litter, but its contents. There is probably a boy inside.'

'Why should there be a boy there, *sidi?*'

'They kidnapped him from the Targi.'

Kamil was speechless with surprise. But after a while he said:

'A Targi boy! *Sidi,* you are *sha'ir,* a poet; it is impossible.'

'It is quite possible. The Tibbu are sworn enemies of the Targi. When a score of warriors secretly ventures into enemy territory and returns with such a *tahtaruvan,* tightly shut, we know how to explain it. Or do you suppose the Tibbu really took his *umm bint* with him on such a dangerous journey?'

'No, of course!'

'They have kidnapped the son of some Targi sheik. It is the worst thing one can possibly do to one's enemy. The *chabir* has also discovered it.'

'You want to free the boy?'

'I don't quite know what I shall do yet. I shall decide according to the situation. If you are afraid, you may leave me and ride to Seghedem.'

'Afraid? What do you think of me, *sidi!* Even if there were no Targi or Tibbu here, you must admit that I should not hesitate to risk my life for you. Why, there is no more perilous part of the desert than the rocky caves. In the midst of the cliffs lies Raml el halak, the Sands of Destruction — a lake without water, only feather-light sand, in which all living creatures must drown mercilessly.'

'Indeed?' I asked, surprised.

With great relish and in great detail Kamil told me of the men and camels which had been swallowed up in Raml el halak, and of their ghosts, which were said to haunt Maghajir es suchur. As he did so, time passed quickly, and it was midnight by the time I decided we should show ourselves to the caravan. We spurred our camels on, and soon caught up with the last of the beasts of burden. First we sped past their long line, then past the Tibbu, who cast angry glances in our direction. Their leader heard the thundering hooves of our camels and turned around.

'Get back!' he shouted.

We ignored him.

'Get back, or there will be trouble!'

We passed him without taking any notice, and soon overtook the sheik and the *chabir* as well. Just then a shot rang out behind us, and a bullet whistled past my head. I pulled up my *hejin* at once, and Kamil did the same. We waited until the leaders of the caravan came up on us.

'Who shot at me?' I asked.

'I did,' said the Tibbu. 'And if you don't get back where you belong, I shall shoot again.'

'I am afraid you will shoot no better than the first time. Allow me to show you how. Kamil, get off your camel.'

He jumped down. Meanwhile, the Tibbu had halted a pace away from me. I took the two spears which hung from his saddle-horn.

'Give back those spears, dog!' he shouted.

'I shall show you how to shoot. Watch carefully!'

I handed Kamil one of the spears, ordering him to ride away until I told him to stop. Then he had to hold the spear up above his head. I drew my revolvers and fired off both magazines, each containing six rounds. Then I called Kamil back again.

'Look!' I invited the Tibbu. 'Twelve shots, twelve hits.'

He examined the shaft of the spear, speechless with wonder. The caravan stood still. Then I sent Kamil to drive the second spear into the sand at a distance where I could just make it out in the starlight. My camel was used to gunfire, and never flinched at the shots, so I did not have to dismount.

'Count the shots!' I told the Arab, and put my Henry to my shoulder. I took careful aim, and fired off one shot after another, each a little higher than the last.

'How many?' I asked.

'Fifteen,' replied the Tibbu, unable to comprehend how someone could fire so many shots without reloading.

'Look at the spear!'

They brought it to him. He felt the holes with his fingers and counted them.

'*Ma sha'allah!* Fifteen holes!' he cried in consternation. 'He is *sahir,* a magician, and his rifle is *bundukija mu'jiza*. The barrel contains countless bullets.'

'You see that you were too hasty,' I told him. 'I am no coward, and when necessary I can shoot well. Do not forget it.'

He did not say a word, and the others, too, seemed struck dumb. On my orders Kamil remounted his camel, and we rode out front; this time no one tried to prevent us. Naturally, the first thing I did was to reload my revolvers and replace the spent cartridges in my rifle.

From then on we rode as we wished — sometimes in front, sometimes on the flank or at the rear, but always in such a way that no treacherous bullet might find us.

We rode across the desert sands until dawn, then halted. After two hours' rest we continued our journey. The landscape changed suddenly. To the left there was still flat, sandy desert, but to the right there appeared ever taller rocks of such strange shape that from a distance we were unsure whether they were the work of nature or of human hands. We thought we saw walls, columns, battlements, bays, windows and tall, arched gateways. I should have liked to ride up to them, but I was reluctant to leave the caravan for any length of time, feeling that we should soon be where the *chabir* wanted us.

On and on the picturesque rocks lined our right flank, as if there were no end to them. The hour before noon was so hot that both men and beasts longed for a respite. In front of us the rocks opened out like a sort of horseshoe. The place seemed to everyone to be an ideal spot to rest. Only I felt unhappy about it, since it was enough to cut off the open end of the horseshoe, and we were trapped. But since the rest were already dismounting, I kept my misgivings to myself. No one would have listened to me anyway.

When they had made camp, caution drove me to ride out to a knoll in the desert, from which I had a good view of the surroundings. Something struck me immediately. To the north, perhaps a quarter hour's ride from us, a number of *nusur as sahra*, vultures, were circling above the rocks. They flew alternately up and down.

Quickly, I returned to the camp and went to the *chabir*, beside whom the Tibbu was standing.

'We must leave,' I said. 'The Targi are encamped ahead of us, and are preparing to ambush us.'

'Who told you this?'

'The vultures which are flying above them.'

'Since when have vultures spoken?' asked the *chabir*, mockingly.

'I understand their speech.'

227

'Calm yourself. I am the *chabir*, and the safety of the *kafila* is my responsibility. I shall go to take a look whether this enemy is a figment of your imagination. Come with me!'

It was a clever move. If I went with him, I should be the first to fall into the hands of the Targi. I matched cunning with cunning.

'This is a matter for the leaders. Let the Tibbu go with you. He is a renowned desert warrior, while I am a stranger. His hawk's eyes may be relied upon. When you return, he shall tell me whether or not I was mistaken.'

It did the trick. The Tibbu was willing to go, and it did not seem to matter to the *chabir* who was the first to fall into the Targi's hands. So they went off together on a scouting expedition, the outcome of which was already clear to me.

I went to warn Abram ben Sakir, but he laughed at my fears, and at this late hour he refused to leave with me. So I stayed, too; only one means of salvation remained, and that was the secret occupant of the litter.

The Scourge of the Desert

The Tibbu took the *tahtaruvan* from the camel and set it down by the cliff face, in which there happened to be a deep cleft, reaching right down to the ground. I noted at once that there were animal tracks leading to it, and concluded that the cleft was passable.

I skirted the cliff, and on the other side soon found a fissure, through which I was able to slip quite easily, since it was fairly wide and straight. I soon saw light at the other end, and in a while the horseshoe where the camp lay came into sight, with the *tahtaruvan* propped close by.

I returned to the camp and led Kamil and our mounts off into the rocks to hide them from the attackers. We tied the camels' front legs together, but only loosely, so that we might quickly untie them in case of need.

'What do you want to do, *sidi*?' Kamil asked.

'We shall escape,' I replied. 'But we shall take the boy with us. Listen carefully. When the Targi attack, all will be thrown into confusion, and before anyone notices, I shall carry the boy off through that cleft — do you see it? Over there! I shall hide there now, but you go out into the desert in front of the camp, and keep watch. As soon as you see the Targi, run into the camp and raise the alarm. I shall take the child from the litter and disappear. You shall wait for me with both *hejin,* ready to ride; you will hold the boy for me until I mount, then you will jump into the saddle, and we shall ride away. If anyone asks you, don't say ...'

'Don't worry, *sidi,*' Kamil interrupted. 'Leave the rest to me.'

I crawled into the cleft and squeezed along almost to the far end, so that I could see not only the *tahtaruvan,* but Kamil also. I saw him stroll slowly out of the camp, as if he simply had nothing better to do; then he gazed northwards for a while, and yawned. I was just wondering how long we were going to have to wait, when he turned about and, with long strides, ran to the camp.

'Riders, many riders! Go, quickly, and see who it is! Could it not be the Targi, of whom my *sidi* warned you?' he shouted.

They all ran from the camp, and the *tahtaruvan* was left unguarded. In a leap I was beside it, and pulled aside the curtains. I saw a dark-eyed little boy of about five. He was bound. I quickly cut the cords, took him in my arms, and ran into the cleft in the rocks. Cries of alarm went up behind me, 'Targi! Targi! To the camels!'

'Keep quiet, and do not be afraid, I shall rescue you!' I whispered to the boy in Arabic, not knowing the language of the Targi. Either he understood, or he was afraid, but he did not make a sound.

I slipped through the fissure as fast as I could. Kamil was waiting outside with the camels. I handed him the boy, and climbed into the saddle. The first shots could be heard. Kamil sat the boy in front of me, and leapt on his animal. Off we rode. In the heat of the battle whose din could be heard behind our backs, no one noticed our escape.

We rode along the cliffs, deep into the hills, and sped across their slopes for a good two hours, before we found a suitable place to stop. A narrow track led gently upwards to a knoll surrounded by steep cliffs, rising abruptly from the surrounding countryside. We were safe. Here we could hold off a large number of attackers — apart from the fact that the boy was a very effective hostage.

It was only now that we got a good look at our captive. The child sat on a rock and looked at me, half anxiously, half trustfully. He was a handsome, brown-skinned boy, with large black eyes, which thirst, hunger, fear and distress had deprived of their sheen.

'Do you speak Arabic?' I asked him.

'Yes,' he replied, to my delight.

'What is your name?' I asked.

'Chaloba.'

'Who is your father?'

'Rhagata, head sheik of the Kelovi.'

Then I had guessed correctly. He was the son of a Targi chief, leader of the very tribesmen who had attacked us. I learned how he had fallen into the hands of the Tibbu. When his father had ridden off with the warriors, a Hausa had come to their tents asking for hospitality. In the night, when all were asleep, he seized the boy and carried him off to a place where nineteen men were waiting with a *tahtaruvan*. The kidnapper was a Tibbu chieftain, but he also had a blood feud with the chief of the Kelovi. Thus he had taken the most extreme form of revenge — he had kidnapped his mortal enemy's only son. The boy asked me if I would return him to his father, and I assured him I would. I intended to ride back to our camp the same evening, since I assumed the Targi would spend the night there, and to inform their chief that his son was in my power, and that I was willing to exchange him for the merchant Abram ben Sakir, his men and all his goods. In the meantime Kamil would guard the boy, and I should come for him only when I was sure that the Targi would meet my demands and accept myself and Kamil as friends of their tribe.

After a simple lunch, I went to sleep. Kamil kept watch, and woke me up when twilight came. I got on my camel and rode off.

I reached my goal without obstacle. The victors, about eighty Targi, were sitting around a fire, while their captives lay bound hand and foot some distance away; among them was the merchant from Murzuk. Without fear I went up to the fire, ignoring the excitement my unexpected arrival caused.

'It is Kara ben Nemsi! He struck me to the ground. Seize him and bind him!' someone called, leaping to his feet.

It was the *chabir*. But, frozen with amazement at my audacity, they somehow failed to respond. So he took hold of me himself. I pushed him aside so firmly that he fell to the ground.

'Where is Rhagata, your chief?' I demanded.

'I am he,' replied a man with a bold and surly face, who had been sitting beside the *chabir* at the fire. 'If you are indeed the stranger who slighted our spy, then it was madness for you to return here. He who was insulted will take his revenge, and you shall die a cruel death.'

'Do not be hasty in judgement, O sheik!' I said, softly. 'First hear what I have to say. Have you a son named Chaloba?'

'Indeed,' he replied, in wonder.

'He was kidnapped, and only I know where he is. If you agree to my terms, he shall be returned to you.'

I sat calmly down beside him at the fireside. All were amazed, believing me only when I showed them the copper bracelet which I had taken from the boy and brought with me to prove the truth of my words. Long negotiations followed, but in the end I achieved the bargain I was seeking. The persons of Kamil and myself were to be inviolable, as was our property. Abram ben Sakir was to have his freedom, his servants and his animals and goods. Only the Tibbu received no concession.

The Targi sealed the bargain with great oaths, so that, in view of their reputed religiousness, I felt I might believe them. Only the unexpectedly conciliatory manner of the *chabir* caused me some concern. A moment ago he was smouldering with hatred, and now he was the first to persuade the obdurate ones to shake hands with me.

Accompanied by a small group of Targi I rode to fetch the boy. Naturally, Kamil returned with us. Rhagata embraced his son with such evident joy that my last doubts as to the efficacy of our agreement slipped away. Everyone thanked me, and everywhere I turned the faces bore friendly expressions. On the Tibbu, however, they swore to take bloody revenge.

Suddenly, I was struck a sharp blow on the back of the head with a rifle butt. A burst of stars appeared before my eyes, and I dropped unconscious to the ground.

When I came round, Kamil and I were lying bound and robbed among the other prisoners. Beside me stood the *chabir*.

'Now you are in my power, o proud one! You shall die, but not easily. For you I shall devise a death which hell itself will envy me!' he said with a grin.

I pretended not to hear. My ears were buzzing, my eyes clouded. I ignored both the kicks and the threats which the scoundrel showered upon me. At last he went away. For a long time I lay there motionless with my eyes closed, until I felt a gentle touch to my face.

'En-ta tajjib — you are good!' a soft voice whispered in my ear, in uncertain Arabic.

I opened my eyes and saw the boy kneeling there. He stroked my cheek. There was the sound of footsteps, and he ran off quickly. En-ta tajjib; my anxiety had left me.

Beside me Kamil lamented with remarkable eloquence. But in the end even he was silent, and we both slept until dawn. When we awoke, we saw that the Targi were preparing to set out again. They lifted us onto camels and tied us on securely, and the caravan moved slowly off.

We travelled south-west, straight into the desert. There was not a breeze in the air; the sky was clear, and it seemed to be a day like any other. Not even at noon was there any sign of the danger which awaited us.

We were resting through the worst of the day's heat, when the loathsome chabir came up to me again. This time the sheik himself was with him.

'You are insolent. Twice you have struck my warrior. You are arrogant. You always know better. You know the answer to everything. Let us see how you deal with a sea of sand. We shall throw you into Raml el halak. It will surely be a simple matter for you to get out.'

Did he mean it? Or was he simply trying to frighten me? I did not say a word. Disappointed, they went away again.

When the sun began to sink westwards, we set off again. We had scarcely been travelling half an hour, when I noted that the camels had of their own accord begun to quicken their pace. Since it was my habit to notice everything, I also saw that the beasts were all trying to turn in a more southerly direction. To the north, behind our backs, was something that was not to their liking. I turned round, as best I could in view of the bonds, and saw in the distance a small cloud like a spider's web. I knew at once the danger that threatened us.

'Quickly!' I cried. 'Hurry for shelter — there is a sandstorm on the way!'

At first they laughed at me, but in two or three minutes' time their faces turned grim. The cloud had grown and darkened. They grabbed their goads, and now the caravan moved forward as fast as the camels could run. Soon the cloud had covered the whole sky. What would happen to us when the camels threw themselves to the ground? We should be crushed.

'Untie us! Untie us!' I yelled at the top of my voice.

'No, leave them!' came the voice of the sheik. 'Let them die in the sand — they deserve no better!'

My anger gave me strength. I summoned all the power that was left in my muscles, and thrust my bound hands away from my body. The cord snapped at the first attempt. It must have been rotten. As soon as my hands were free, I urged the camel on to full speed with my knees. In front of me was the unsuspecting *chabir*. I caught up with him, our mounts almost touching, threw my left arm around his waist, and drew him towards me. When I had taken the knife from his girdle, I thrust him to the ground.

In a moment I was at Kamil's side, and at full tilt I cut his bonds. Then I hurried over to Abram, and in two strokes cut through the cords that bound the merchant. The rest would have to take their chance, for I could already hear a thunderous roar behind our backs, and when I looked round I saw, hurtling towards us, a dark wall reaching from earth to sky. It was sand, caught up in the fury of the wind.

It was beginning to get dark in front of us, too. The storm was upon us. A wild gust of wind almost flung me from the saddle. I held on tight to the saddle-horn. The storm drove the beasts forward as if carrying them along. So far this was only the wind. We might still escape. Then I saw the riders in front of me spreading out. We had reached the edge of the *var*, the stony desert. Scattered round about were boulders and rocks, behind which it was possible to take shelter. There was no need to direct my camel. Of its own accord it turned towards one such rock and fell to the ground on its leeward side so quickly that I scarcely had time to jump. I slipped in between the boulder and the camel, thrust a corner of my kazajka into my mouth, and wound the scarf of my turban round my head. Hardly had I done this, when the wall of sand struck, and, caught in its overwhelming pressure, I became oblivious to all save a craving for air.

How long it went on, I cannot tell. But when I came to, there was an unearthly silence all around, and my camel began to move. I tried to stand, but first I had to dig my way out of the sand. Only when I had finally got to my feet did I realize what a great pile of sand had been lying on top of me. Sand as fine as flour had got into every opening in my body — nose, ears, even into my mouth, in spite of the scarf. My eyes had been closed tight, but still I had sand under my lids. It was no easy task to shake even the worst of it off myself. Then I looked around.

There were stones everywhere, and behind them men and animals struggling with the sand. My own beast was now standing, too. The worst off were the prisoners who were still tied up. The camels had thrown themselves to the ground with these still bound to them, and now, as the beasts stood up again, the poor fellows were hanging from them in the most precarious of attitudes.

I waded through the sand towards them and cut their bonds. The Targi did not protest. They had other worries. They would have found it difficult to prevent me anyway; I was untied, and I had a knife in my hand. But if I had had my rifles, that would have been a different matter... Ah! My rifles! Where could they be? The chieftain had had them. Where was he? Searching around, I spotted him behind one of the rocks. He was unarmed, having just dug himself out of the sand. He walked from one to another of his men. He must have been asking about his son, for the latter was nowhere to be seen. I made use of the opportunity. The further the sheik moved away from his camel, the closer I drew to it myself. In a few moments I had seized my things and disappeared.

Fortunately, the storm had not been dangerous, and was soon over. No one had come to any harm, and soon we even saw a straggling line of figures approaching from the north-east. It was the beasts of burden with their drivers, who had also come through the storm safely.

Only one man was beside himself with fear and anxiety, and that was the sheik, for there was still no sign of his son. He asked about him everywhere, but to no avail, even though the *tahtaruvan* with its tall poles could scarcely have been buried in the sand.

We sat down together with Abram and his men. Each recounted his experiences, but in spite of the horror we were grateful to the storm for having set us free. Though I was the only one who was armed, I was resolved that we should not allow ourselves to become captives again.

The beasts of burden had just reached us, when the sheik came over.

235

'What is this? You are free, and you have your rifles!' he cried, aghast. 'I shall have you tied up again at once!'

He turned to summon his Targi, but I leapt upon him, hurled him to the ground, knelt on his stomach, and placed my knife to his chest.

'Silence! If you so much as make a sound, I shall sink the knife into your heart!' I threatened.

He was so startled that he neither spoke nor moved.

'Bind his hands and feet!' I ordered the merchant's men.

'Did your spy tell you that I have magic rifles?' I then asked the sheik.

'Yes,' he snarled, angrily, but with some anxiety nonetheless.

'Then you know it is useless to resist. I want nothing more than for you to keep your promise, which you have so faithlessly broken. If you do so, I shall release you, and I shall not harm a hair of your Targi's heads. If you refuse, you shall not escape the knife, and I shall shoot any Targi who come within five hundred paces of us. You have until I count to ten.'

I bared his chest, laid the point of the knife on his skin, placed my left hand on his throat, and began to count.

'*Vahid... itnen... talata... arba... chamsa...*'

'Enough!' he cried. 'It shall be as you ask.'

'Do not imagine that you will trick us again! Now order your men to withdraw to at least a thousand paces from us. Ten of them will bring us our camels and our goods. Then I shall release you, and you will continue southwards while we travel north. Do you agree? I have only counted to five. I shall continue.'

'Take away the knife! I shall do all you ask.'

'I shall take the knife from your chest when I see that my conditions have been fulfilled.'

Most of the Targi had gathered around the beasts of burden. One of them came running up to us. 'Where is the sheik? Has something...' he called.

He broke off in the middle of the sentence and stood still in amazement, for on my command those around me had stepped back, and he saw his sheik lying bound on the sand, and me kneeling on him with the knife in my hand.

'*Allah kerim!*' he gasped. 'You are untied, and there lies...'

'Your sheik, as you can see,' I interrupted him. 'If you wish to save his and all your lives, come here and listen to what he tells you.'

He came up to us, and it was marvellous to see how the one, pale with anger, gave his orders, and the other, equally bloodless, listened to them and left to see them carried out.

We could see the Targi gathering round and consulting noisily. Then ten of them came up to us with our camels and property, while the rest withdrew the required thousand paces.

'Your conditions are fulfilled,' said the sheik. 'Now I shall see whether you know how to keep your word. Let me go!'

'A man is as good as his word. I have heard that the Targi have such a proverb. Though some pay less attention to their honour than did their grandfathers. Go, and get out of my sight quickly!'

'We must remain here, for my son is lost.'

'Then find him quickly, for we shall not leave until we are sure you are on your way.'

I untied him. He rose, and walked away a few paces, but then turned and, holding up his right hand as if swearing an oath, said to me in a voice full of hatred:

'You have shamed me. Flee this country, jaur. For if we ever meet again, you shall die.'

The Targi appeared to greet him with reproaches. Then they spread out in search of the child. We were delighted with the fortunate outcome of our adventure, and watched as the Targi searched in vain for little Chaloba. I should have liked to help them, for I could still hear the boy's words — *En-ta tajjib*. But I dared not go among these enraged men. At last they must have found some tracks, because they ran to their camels and galloped off southwards.

We waited half an hour, and when they did not return, we said to ourselves that they would not come now, and made ready to move off. I was about to mount my camel, when Kamil pointed southwards. 'Wait, *sidi!* Over there — riders!' he called.

He was right. We could see eight or ten men on camels riding towards us at full speed. They were our Targi, with the sheik at their head. What could they want? Was this some new trap? I picked up my rifle, determined not to let them get near us.

'Do not shoot! Peace! Peace!' called the sheik.

His companions halted, and he came on alone. I lowered the barrel of my rifle. Fifteen paces away he halted his camel and said, *'Sidi,* I come not as a foe, but as a suppliant. You are the only one who can help us!'

He came right up to us, but remained in the saddle. Distress was written across his face, and he was breathing heavily. I was curious to know what he wanted.

'Take saddle and come with me quickly!' he requested. 'We do not know what to do. Only you can save my Chaloba!'

'What is the matter? What has happened to him?'

'The storm has driven him into Raml el halak.'

'And how am I to save him?'

'If you do not save him, no one will.'

Was it a trap? No, the deadly fear mirrored in his face did not lie. I did not hesitate. I climbed on my camel. *En-ta tajjib* — I could hear the boy's voice as we sped off towards the sands of destruction. The rocks opened out. At their foot the Targi were encamped. Their camels lay in the sand, turning their heads towards us as we arrived. At a glance I took in the situation.

I was standing on the brink of an immense rocky basin some two kilometres in diameter. I could not guess how deep it was, but it must have been deep enough, judging by the steep, almost vertical walls of the perimeter. It was impossible to say what exactly the basin was filled with. It seemed to contain wet, fine, light sand, unable to support an object of any weight. This giant bowl had probably originally contained water, or some other liquid. Then the wind had filled it with desert sand. The heavier particles of sand at the base of a moving wall such as the one we had encountered that afternoon would be trapped by the surrounding rocks, and only the light dust dispersed in the air would fall into the lake, where it would not sink to the bottom, being lighter than water. At least, that was how I assumed this sea of sand to have come about, and I do not suppose I was far wrong.

In this sea of destruction, a good twenty-five metres from the bank, lay the *tahtaruvan.* The thin material and long poles had kept it afloat. In it sat Chaloba. He was sensible enough not to move about, but he called incessantly for help.

'Ta'al, ta'al, ja sidi! Challisni min il maut, nagdaa, nagdaa! Come, come, *sidi!* Save me from death! Help, help!' he begged tearfully as soon as he saw me.

'I am coming!' I replied. 'Sit still, so as not to fall into the sand!'

The Targi were silent. They surveyed me grimly, but without hatred — more in hope. When I had spoken the sheik took both my hands in his.

'Will you really go to him? Do you think he can be saved?'

'I shall try. Either I save the boy, or I die with him.'

'You are a noble man. But how do you intend to do it, *sidi?*'

'I shall make a raft.'

'A *kelek?* From what?'

'It must be light, broad and long. The frame will be of tent poles, and we shall attach tent linen to it. But first I must find out how deep the sand is, and how much weight it will carry.'

I took a tent pole and went cautiously to the edge of the sand lake. It was impossible to tell exactly where the quicksand began, since it was indistinguishable from the rest of the sand, so every step might well have been my last. I soon felt the ground sinking beneath my feet. I knelt down and thrust the pole into the sandy morass. It did not touch the bottom. The Targi tied a number of lengths of rope together and attached a stone to the end. I dropped it in the sand. The rope was at least twenty metres long; it uncoiled, but the stone did not fall to the bottom. The sand lake was very deep right from the edge. It was a disturbing thought, that if the raft was a failure, this sandy quagmire would mercilessly close over me for ever.

We set to building the raft. I had to think hard to decide how best to put this vessel together, and how to make a suitable oar. In the end I used a short pole with a piece of linen attached to it at right angles. I should need it only for the trip out, since the Targi were to haul us back with a rope.

The construction of the raft and oar took a long time, and we had constantly to cheer the lad up, so that he would not lose his patience or courage. At last all was ready. Now came the most difficult part: getting aboard. The linen raft was naturally very flexible, and it bent and swayed in all directions. I had literally to crawl onto it on my stomach. Then the Targi pushed it off using poles, and I took up the oar. So far, so good. But twenty-five metres!

In water it would have been a simple matter, but in this hellish sludge it took all of half an hour. I had often been in danger before, but I had never had such an acute sense of my predicament as I did now. The squishing, squelching, bubbling and gurgling of the slimy substance across which I was creeping made my hair stand on end. The Targi watched my progress with bated breath, and once, when my vessel almost capsized, there was unfeigned despair in their cries.

Finally, I got so close to the *tahtaruvan* that I almost collided with it.

'Save me, *sidi!*' cried the boy.

'Do not be afraid!' I reassured him. 'Sit still, so as not to upset the litter, and I shall take you safely back to your father. If the *tahtaruvan* should start rocking, lean quickly where I tell you to.'

I tied one end of a slender rope to the front of the raft frame, made a loop at the other, and threw it over the lower crosspiece of the *tahtaruvan*. It caught first time.

'Pull, you men, but very slowly!' I called to the bank.

The rope drew taut, my raft moved off backwards, and the *tahtaruvan* was taken in tow. The litter was light enough to stay afloat, but it made a very poor sledge. It bobbed and swayed, and would certainly have toppled over, if I had not had ready two more ropes with loops on the end. Throwing one over each of the two ends of the top crosspiece, I was able to tug at them alternately, and so control the perilous swaying. A further great help was that Chaloba obeyed my orders to lean to and fro skilfully and courageously.

Nevertheless, the return trip took much longer. It took us a full three quarters of an hour to reach the bank. The father picked up his son and pressed him to his breast, and the Targi cheered. The sheik then came up to me, embraced me, and kissed me.

'*Sidi*, I have wronged you. Tell me how I may make amends. Ask for my finest mare, my ten best camels; ask what you will, I shall give you all you desire!'

To offer his finest mare was indeed a sign of great gratitude. All listened to hear what I should ask for.

'I should indeed like to ask something of you,' I replied, 'nor will it be a small thing.'

'Speak!'

'The next time, do not despise a stranger simply because he is a stranger. A good man is your brother, even if he is not of your tribe. And an evil man and a traitor is still evil and treacherous, even if he was born beneath your own tent.

241

In future, judge men by their deeds, and keep the same faith for all men, whether Targi, Arabs or Franks. Only then will you truly be a great sheik.'

For a long time he gazed silently at the ground; then he put out his hand.

'Your words are like precious pearls; I shall keep them by my heart. Will you be my brother, a man honoured by the people of my tribe, and a welcome guest in our huts and tents?'

'I will.'

'Then we shall leave this place of doom and return to Abram the merchant. There we shall pitch camp and swear friendship according to the law of the desert. You have saved my son's life. Your friend is my friend, and your enemy shall be my enemy. My heart belongs to you, and you shall give me yours. May love endure between us for ever.'

THE SPRING RUNNING

RUDYARD KIPLING
(from THE SECOND JUNGLE BOOK)

Man goes to Man! Cry the challenge through the Jungle!
He that was Brother goes away.
Hear, now, and judge, O ye People of the Jungle, —
Answer, who shall turn him — who shall stay?
Man goes to Man! He is weeping in the Jungle:
He that was our Brother sorrows sore!
Man goes to Man! (Oh, we loved him in the Jungle!)
To the Man-Trail where we may not follow more.

The second year after the great fight with Red Dog and the death of Akela, Mowgli must have been nearly seventeen years old. He looked older, for hard exercise, the best of good eating, and baths whenever he felt in the least hot or dusty, had given him strength and growth far beyond his age. He could swing by one hand from a top branch for half an hour at a time, when he had occasion to look along the tree-roads. He could stop a young buck in mid-gallop and throw him sideways by the head. He could even jerk over the big, blue wild boars that lived in the Marshes of the North. The Jungle People who used to fear him for his wits feared him now for his strength, and when he moved quietly on his own affairs the mere whisper of his coming cleared the wood-paths. And yet the look in his eyes was always gentle. Even when he fought, his eyes never blazed as Bagheera's did. They only grew more and more interested and excited; and that was one of the things that Bagheera himself did not understand.

He asked Mowgli about it, and the boy laughed and said, 'When I miss the kill

I am angry. When I must go empty for two days I am very angry. Do not my eyes talk then?'

'The mouth is hungry,' said Bagheera, 'but the eyes say nothing. Hunting, eating, or swimming, it is all one — like a stone in wet or dry weather.' Mowgli looked at him lazily from under his long eyelashes, and, as usual, the panther's head dropped. Bagheera knew his master.

They were lying out far up the side of a hill overlooking the Waingunga, and the morning mists hung below them in bands of white and green. As the sun rose it changed into bubbling seas of red gold, churned off, and let the low rays stripe the dried grass on which Mowgli and Bagheera were resting. It was the end of the cold weather, the leaves and the trees looked worn and faded, and there was a dry, ticking rustle everywhere when the wind blew. A little leaf tap-tap-tapped furiously against a twig, as a single leaf caught in a current will. It roused Bagheera, for he snuffed the morning air with a deep, hollow cough, threw himself on his back, and struck with his fore-paws at the nodding leaf above.

'The year turns,' he said. 'The Jungle goes forward. The Time of New Talk is near. That leaf knows. It is very good.'

'The grass is dry,' Mowgli answered, pulling up a tuft. 'Even Eye-of-the-Spring (that is a little trumpet-shaped, waxy red flower that runs in and out among the grasses) — even Eye-of-the-Spring is shut, and... Bagheera, *is* it well for the Black Panther so to lie on his back and beat with his paws in the air, as though he were the tree-cat?'

'Aowh?' said Bagheera. He seemed to be thinking of other things.

'I say, *is* it well for the Black Panther so to mouth and cough, and howl and roll? Remember, we be the Masters of the Jungle, thou and I.'

'Indeed, yes; I hear, Man-cub.' Bagheera rolled over hurriedly and sat up, the dust on his ragged black flanks. (He was just casting his winter coat.) 'We be surely the Masters of the Jungle! Who is so strong as Mowgli? Who so wise?' There was a curious drawl in the voice that made Mowgli turn to see whether by any chance the Back Panther were making fun of him, for the Jungle is full of words that sound like one thing, but mean another. 'I said we be beyond question the Masters of the Jungle,' Bagheera repeated. 'Have I done wrong? I did not know that the Man-cub no longer lay upon the ground. Does he fly, then?'

Mowgli sat with his elbows on his knees, looking out across the valley at the daylight. Somewhere down in the woods below a bird was trying over in a husky, reedy voice the first few notes of his spring song. It was no more than a shadow of the liquid, tumbling call he would be pouring later, but Bagheera heard it.

'I said the Time of New Talk is near,' growled the panther, switching his tail.

'I hear,' Mowgli answered. 'Bagheera, why dost thou shake all over? The sun is warm.'

'That is Ferao, the scarlet woodpecker,' said Bagheera. '*He* has not forgotten. Now I, too, must remember my song,' and he began purring and crooning to himself, harking back dissatisfied again and again.

'There is no game afoot,' said Mowgli.

'Little Brother, are *both* thine ears stopped? That is no killing word, but my song that I make ready against the need.'

'I had forgotten. I shall know when the Time of New Talk is here, because then thou and the others all run away and leave me alone.' Mowgli spoke rather savagely.

'But, indeed, Little Brother,' Bagheera began, 'we do not always —'

'I say ye do,' said Mowgli, shooting out his forefinger angrily. 'Ye *do* run away, and I, who am the Master of the Jungle, must needs walk alone. How was it last season, when I would gather sugar-cane from the fields of a Man-Pack? I sent a runner — I sent thee! — to Hathi, bidding him to come upon such a night and pluck the sweet grass for me with his trunk.'

'He came only two nights later,' said Bagheera, cowering a little; 'and of that long, sweet grass that pleased thee so he gathered more than any Man-cub could eat in all the nights of the Rains. That was no fault of mine.'

'He did not come upon the night when I sent him the word. No, he was trumpeting and running and roaring through the valleys in the moonlight. His trail was like the trail of three elephants, for he would not hide among the trees. He danced in the moonlight before the houses of the Man-Pack. I saw him, and yet he would not come to me; and *I* am the Master of the Jungle!'

'It was the Time of New Talk,' said the panther, always very humble. 'Perhaps, Little Brother, thou didst not that time call him by a Master-word? Listen to Ferao, and be glad!'

Mowgli's bad temper seemed to have boiled itself away. He lay back with his head on his arms, his eyes shut. 'I do not know — nor do I care,' he said sleepily. 'Let us sleep, Bagheera. My stomach is heavy in me. Make me a rest for my head.'

The panther lay down again with a sigh, because he could hear Ferao practising and repractising his song against the Springtime of New Talk, as they say.

In an Indian Jungle the seasons slide one into the other almost without division. There seem to be only two — the wet and the dry; but if you look closely below the torrents of rain and the clouds of char and dust you will find all four going round in their regular ring. Spring is the most wonderful, because she has not to cover a clean, bare field with new leaves and flowers, but to drive before her and to put away the hanging-on, over-surviving raffle of halfgreen things which the gentle winter has suffered to live, and to make the partly-dressed stale earth feel new and young once more. And this she does so well that there is no spring in the world like the Jungle spring.

There is one day when all things are tired, and the very smells, as they drift on the heavy air, are old and used. One cannot explain this, but it feels so. Then there is another day — to the eye nothing whatever has changed — when all the smells are new and delightful, and the whiskers of the Jungle-People quiver to their roots, and the winter hair comes away from their sides in long, draggled locks. Then, perhaps, a little rain falls, and all the trees and the bushes and the bamboos and the mosses and the juicy-leaved plants wake with a noise of growing that you can almost hear, and under this noise runs, day and night, a deep hum. *That* is the noise of the spring — a vibrating boom which is neither bees, nor falling water, nor the wind in tree-tops, but the purring of the warm, happy world.

Up to this year Mowgli had always delighted in the turn of the seasons. It was he who generally saw the first Eye-of-the-Spring deep down among the grasses, and the first bank of spring clouds, which are like nothing else in the Jungle. His voice could be heard in all sorts of wet, star-lighted, blossoming places, helping the big frogs through their choruses, or mocking the little upside-down owls that hoot through the white nights. Like all his people, spring was the season he chose for his flittings — moving, for the mere joy of rushing through the warm air, thirty, forty, or fifty miles between twilight and the morning star, and coming back panting and laughing and wreathed with strange flowers. The Four did not follow him on these wild ringings of the Jungle, but went off to sing songs with other wolves. The Jungle-People are very busy in the spring, and Mowgli could hear them grunting and screaming and whistling according to their kind. Their voices then are different from their voices at other times of the year, and that is one of the reasons why spring in the Jungle is called the Time of New Talk.

But that spring, as he told Bagheera, his stomach was changed in him. Ever since the bamboo shoots turned spotty-brown he had been looking forward to the morning when the smells should change. But when the morning came, and Mor the Peacock, blazing in bronze and blue and gold, cried it aloud all along the misty woods, and Mowgli opened his mouth to send on the cry, the words choked between his teeth, and a feeling came over him that began at his toes and ended in his hair — a feeling of pure unhappiness, so that he looked himself over to be sure that he had not trod on a thorn. Mor cried the new smells, the other birds took it over, and from the rocks by the Waingunga he heard Bagheera's hoarse scream — something between the scream of an eagle and the neighing of a horse. There was a yelling and scattering of *Bandar-log* in the new budding branches above, and there stood Mowgli, his chest, filled to answer Mor, sinking in little gasps as the breath was driven out of it by this unhappiness.

He stared all round him, but he could see no more than the mocking *Bandar-log* scudding through the trees, and Mor, his tail spread in full splendour, dancing on the slopes below.

'The smells have changed,' screamed Mor. 'Good hunting, Little Brother! Where is thy answer?'

'Little Brother, good hunting!' whistled Chil the Kite and his mate, swooping down together. The two baffed under Mowgli's nose so close that a pinch of downy white feathers brushed away.

A light spring rain — elephant-rain they call it — drove across the Jungle in a belt half a mile wide, left the new leaves wet and nodding behind, and died out in a double rainbow and a light roll of thunder. The spring hum broke out for a minute, and was silent, but all the Jungle-Folk seemed to be giving tongue at once. All except Mowgli.

'I have eaten good food,' he said to himself. 'I have drunk good water. Nor does my throat burn and grow small, as it did when I bit the blue-spotted root that Oo the Turtle said was clean food. But my stomach is heavy, and I have given very bad talk to Bagheera and others, people of the Jungle and my people. Now, too, I am hot and now I am cold, and now I am neither hot nor cold, but angry with that which I cannot see. Huhu! It is time to make a running! To-night I will cross the ranges; yes, I will make a spring running to the Marshes of the North, and back again. I have hunted too easily too long. The Four shall come with me, for they grow as fat as white grubs.'

He called, but never one of the Four answered. They were far beyond earshot, singing over the spring songs — the Moon and Sambhur Songs — with the wolves of the Pack; for in the springtime the Jungle-People make very little difference between the day and the night. He gave the sharp, barking note, but his only answer was the mocking *maiou* of the little spotted tree-cat winding in and out among the branches for early birds' nests. At this he shook all over with rage, and half drew his knife. Then he became haughty, though there was no one to see him, and stalked severely down the hillside, chin up and eyebrows down.

But never a single one of his people asked him a question, for they were all too busy with their own affairs.

'Yes,' said Mowgli to himself, though in his heart he knew that he had no reason. 'Let the Red Dhole come from the Dekkan, or the Red Flower dance among the bamboos, and all the Jungle runs whining to Mowgli, calling him great elephant-names. But now, because Eye-of-the-Spring is red, and Mor, forsooth, must show his naked legs in some spring dance, the Jungle goes mad as Tabaqui... By the Bull that bought me! am I the Master of the Jungle, or am I not? Be silent! What do ye here?'

A couple of young wolves of the Pack were cantering down a path, looking for open ground in which to fight. (You will remember that the Law of the Jungle forbids fighting where the Pack can see.) Their neck-bristles were as stiff as wire, and they bayed furiously, crouching for the first grapple. Mowgli leaped forward, caught one outstretched throat in either hand, expecting to fling the creatures backward as he had often done in games or Pack hunts. But he had never before interfered with a spring fight. The two leaped forward and dashed him aside, and without word to waste rolled over and over close locked.

Mowgli was on his feet almost before he fell, his knife and his white teeth were bared, and at that minute he would have killed both for no reason but that they were fighting when he wished them to be quiet, although every wolf has full right under the Law to fight. He danced round them with lowered shoulders and quivering hand, ready to send in a double blow when the first flurry of the scuffle should be over; but while he waited the strength seemed to ebb from his body, the knife-point lowered, and he sheathed the knife and watched.

'I have surely eaten poison,' he sighed at last. 'Since I broke up the Council with the Red Flower — since I killed Shere Khan — none of the Pack could fling me aside. And these be only tailwolves in the Pack, little hunters! My strength is gone from me, and presently I shall die. Oh, Mowgli, why dost thou not kill them both?'

The fight went on till one wolf ran away, and Mowgli was left alone on the torn and bloody ground, looking now at his knife, and now at his legs and arms, while the feeling of unhappiness he had never known before covered him as water covers a log.

He killed early that evening and ate but little, so as to be in good fettle for his

spring running, and he ate alone because all the Jungle-People were away singing or fighting.

It was a perfect white night, as they call it. All green things seemed to have made a month's growth since the morning. The branch that was yellow-leaved the day before dripped sap when Mowgli broke it. The mosses curled deep and warm over his feet, the young grass had no cutting edges, and all the voices of the Jungle boomed like one deep harp-string touched by the moon — the Moon of New Talk, who splashed her light full on rock and pool, slipped it between trunk and creeper, and sifted it through a million leaves. Forgetting his unhappiness, Mowgli sang aloud with pure delight as he settled into his stride. It was more like flying than anything else, for he had chosen the long downward slope that leads to the Northern Marshes through the heart of the main Jungle, where the springy ground deadened the fall of his feet. A man-taught man would have picked his way with many stumbles through the cheating moonlight, but Mowgli's muscles, trained by years of experience, bore him up as though he were a feather. When a rotten log or a hidden stone turned under his foot he saved himself, never checking his pace, without effort and without thought. When he tired of ground-going he threw up his hands monkey-fashion to the nearest creeper, and seemed to float rather than to climb up into the thin branches, whence he would follow a tree-road till his mood changed, and he shot downward in a long, leafy curve to the levels again. There were still, hot hollows surrounded by wet rocks where he could hardly breathe for the heavy scents of the night flowers and the bloom along the creeper buds; dark avenues where the moonlight lay in belts as regular as checkered marbles in a church aisle; thickets where the wet young growth stood breast-high about him and threw its arms round his waist; and hilltops crowned with broken rock, where he leaped from stone to stone above the lairs of the frightened little foxes. He would hear, very faint and far off, the *chug-drug* of a boar sharpening his tusks on a bole; and would come across the great grey brute all alone, scribing and rending the bark of a tall tree, his mouth dripping with foam, and his eyes blazing like fire. Or he would turn aside to the sound of clashing horns and hissing grunts, and dash past a couple of furious sambhur, staggering to and fro with lowered heads, striped with blood that showed black in the moonlight. Or at some rushing ford he would hear Jacala the Crocodile bellowing like a bull, or disturb a twined knot of the Poison People, but before they could strike he would be away and across the glistening shingle, and deep in the Jungle again.

So he ran, sometimes shouting, sometimes singing to himself, the happiest thing in all the Jungle that night, till the smell of the flowers warned him that he was near the marshes, and those lay far beyond his farthest hunting-grounds.

Here, again, a man-trained man would have sunk overhead in three strides, but Mowgli's feet had eyes in them, and they passed him from tussock to tussock and clump to quaking clump without asking help from the eyes in his head. He ran out to the middle of the swamp, disturbing the duck as he ran, and sat down on a moss-coated tree-trunk lapped in the black water. The marsh was awake all round him, for in the spring the Bird-People sleep very lightly, and companies of them were coming or going the night through. But no one took any notice of Mowgli sitting among the tall reeds humming songs without words, and looking at the soles of his hard brown feet in case of neglected thorns. All his unhappiness seemed to have been left behind in his own Jungle, and he was just beginning a full-throat song when it came back again — ten times worse than before.

This time Mowgli was frightened. 'It is here also!' he said half aloud. 'It has followed me,' and he looked over his shoulder to see whether the It were not standing behind him. 'There is no one here.' The night noises of the marsh went on, but never a bird or beast spoke to him, and the new feeling of misery grew.

'I have surely eaten poison,' he said in an awe-stricken voice. 'It must be that carelessly I have eaten poison, and my strength is going from me. I was afraid — and yet it was not *I* that was afraid — Mowgli was afraid when the two wolves fought. Akela, or even Phao, would have silenced them; yet Mowgli was afraid. That is true sign I have eaten poison... But what do they care in the Jungle? They sing and howl and fight, and run in companies under the moon, and I — *Hai-mai!* — I am dying in the marshes, of that poison which I have eaten.' He was so sorry for himself that he nearly wept. 'And after,' he went on, 'they will find me lying in the black water. Nay, I will go back to my own Jungle, and I will die upon the Council Rock, and Bagheera, whom I love, if he is not screaming in the valley — Bagheera, perhaps, may watch by what is left for a little, lest Chil use me as he used Akela.'

A large, warm tear splashed down on his knee, and, miserable as he was, Mowgli felt happy that he was so miserable, if you can understand that upside-down sort of happiness. 'As Chil the Kite used Akela,' he repeated, 'on the night I saved the Pack from Red Dog.' He was quiet for a little, thinking of the last words of the Lone Wolf, which you, of course, remember. 'Now Akela said to me many foolish things before he died, for when we die our stomachs change. He said... None the less, I *am* of the Jungle!'

In his excitement, as he remembered the fight on Waingunga bank, he shouted the last words aloud, and a wild buffalo-cow among the reeds sprang to her knees, snorting, 'Man!'

'Uhh!' said Mysa, the Wild Buffalo (Mowgli could hear him turn in his wallow), '*that* is no man. It is only the hairless wolf of the Seeonee Pack. On such nights he runs to and fro.'

'Uhh!' said the cow, dropping her head again to graze, 'I thought it was Man.'

'I say no. Oh, Mowgli, is it danger?' lowed Mysa.

'Oh, Mowgli, is it danger?' the boy called back mockingly. 'That is all Mysa thinks for: Is it danger? But for Mowgli, who goes to and fro in the Jungle by night, watching, what do ye care?'

'How loud he cries!' said the cow.

'Thus do they cry,' Mysa answered contemptuously, 'who, having torn up the grass, know not how to eat it.'

'For less than this,' Mowgli groaned to himself, — 'for less than this even last Rains I had pricked Mysa out of his wallow, and ridden him through the swamp on a rush halter.' He stretched a hand to break one of the feathery reeds, but drew it back with a sigh. Mysa went on steadily chewing the cud, and the long grass ripped where the cow grazed. 'I will not die *here,*' he said angrily. 'Mysa, who is of one blood with Jacala and the pig, would see me. Let us go beyond the swamp and see what comes. Never have I run such a spring running — hot and cold together. Up, Mowgli!'

He could not resist the temptation of stealing across the reeds to Mysa and pricking him with the point of his knife. The great dripping bull broke out of his wallow like a shell exploding, while Mowgli laughed till he sat down.

'Say now that the hairless wolf of the Seeonee Pack once herded thee, Mysa,' he called.

'Wolf! *Thou?*' the bull snorted, stamping in the mud. 'All the Jungle knows thou wast a herder of tame cattle — such a man's brat as shouts in the dust by the crops yonder. *Thou* of the Jungle! What hunter would have crawled like a snake among the leeches, and for a muddy jest — a jackal's jest — have shamed me before my cow? Come to firm ground, and I will — I will...' Mysa frothed at the mouth, for Mysa has nearly the worst temper of any one in the Jungle.

Mowgli watched him puff and blow with eyes that never changed. When he could make himself heard through the spattering mud, he said: 'What Man-Pack lair here by the marshes, Mysa? This is new Jungle to me.'

'Go north, then,' roared the angry bull, for Mowgli had pricked him rather sharply. 'It was a naked cow-herd's jest. Go and tell them at the village at the foot of the marsh.'

'The Man-Pack do not love jungle-tales, nor do I think, Mysa, that a scratch more or less on thy hide is any matter for a council. But I will go and look at this village. Yes, I will go. Softly now. It is not every night that the Master of the Jungle comes to herd thee.'

He stepped out to the shivering ground on the edge of the marsh, well knowing that Mysa would never charge over it, and laughed, as he ran, to think of the bull's anger.

'My strength is not altogether gone,' he said. 'It may be that the poison is not to the bone. There is a star sitting low yonder.' He looked at it between his half-shut hands. 'By the Bull that bought me, it is the Red Flower — the Red Flower that I lay beside before — before I came even to the first Seeonee Pack! Now that I have seen, I will finish the running.'

The marsh ended in a broad plain where a light twinkled. It was a long time since Mowgli had concerned himself with the doings of men, but this night the glimmer of the Red Flower drew him forward.

'I will look,' said he, 'as I did in the old days, and I will see how far the Man-Pack has changed.'

Forgetting that he was no longer in his own Jungle, where he could do what he pleased, he trod carelessly through the dew-loaded grasses till he came to the hut where the light stood. Three or four yelping dogs gave tongue, for he was on the outskirts of a village.

'Ho!' said Mowgli, sitting down noiselessly, after sending back a deep wolf-growl that silenced the curs. 'What comes will come. Mowgli, what hast thou to do any more with the lairs of the Man-Pack?' He rubbed his mouth, remembering where a stone had struck it years ago when the other Man-Pack had cast him out.

The door of the hut opened, and a woman stood peering out into the darkness. A child cried, and the woman said over her shoulder, 'Sleep. It was but a jackal that waked the dogs. In a little time morning comes.'

Mowgli in the grass began to shake as though he had fever. He knew that voice well, but to make sure he cried softly, surprised to find how man's talk came back, 'Messua! O Messua!'

'Who calls?' said the woman, a quiver in her voice.

'Hast thou forgotten?' said Mowgli. His throat was dry as he spoke.

'If it be *thou,* what name did I give thee? Say!' She had half shut the door, and her hand was clutching at her breast.

'Nathoo! Ohé Nathoo!' said Mowgli, for, as you remember, that was the name Messua gave him when he first came to the Man-Pack.

'Come, my son,' she called, and Mowgli stepped into the light, and looked full at Messua, the woman who had been good to him, and whose life he had saved from the Man-Pack so long before. She was older, and her hair was grey, but her eyes and her voice had not changed. Woman-like, she expected to find Mowgli where she had left him, and her eyes travelled upward in a puzzled way from his chest to his head, that touched the top of the door.

'My son,' she stammered; and then, sinking to his feet: 'But it is no longer my son. It is a Godling of the Woods! Ahai!'

As he stood in the red light of the oil-lamp, strong, tall, and beautiful, his long black hair sweeping over his shoulders, the knife swinging at his neck, and his head crowned with a wreath of white jasmine, he might easily have been mistaken for some wild god of a Jungle legend. The child half asleep on a cot sprang up and shrieked aloud with terror. Messua turned to soothe him, while Mowgli stood still, looking in at the water-jars and the cooking-pots, the grain-bin, and all the other human belongings that he found himself remembering so well.

'What wilt thou eat or drink?' Messua murmured. 'This is all thine. We owe our lives to thee. But art thou him I called Nathoo, or a Godling, indeed?'

'I am Nathoo,' said Mowgli. 'I am very far from my own place. I saw this light, and came hither. I did not know thou wast here.'

'After we came to Khanhiwara,' Messua said timidly, 'the English would have helped us against those villagers that sought to burn us. Rememberest thou?'

'Indeed, I have not forgotten.'

'But when the English Law was made ready, we went to the village of those evil people, and it was no more to be found.'

'That also I remember,' said Mowgli, with a quiver of his nostril.

'My man, therefore, took service in the fields, and at last — for, inded, he was a strong man, — we held a little land here. It is not so rich as the old village, but we do not need much — we two.'

'Where is he — the man that dug in the dirt when he was afraid on that night?'

'He is dead — a year.'

'And he?' Mowgli pointed to the child.

'My son that was born two Rains ago. If thou art a Godling, give him the Favour of the Jungle, that he may be safe among thy — thy people, as we were safe on that night.'

She lifted up the child, who, forgetting his fright, reached out to play with the knife that hung on Mowgli's chest, and Mowgli put the little fingers aside very carefully.

'And if thou art Nathoo whom the tiger carried away,' Messua went on, choking, 'he is then thy younger brother. Give him an elder brother's blessing.'

'*Hai-mai!* What do I know of the thing called a blessing? I am neither a Godling nor his brother, and — O mother, mother, my heart is heavy in me.' He shivered as he set down the child.

'Like enough,' said Messua, bustling among the cooking-pots. 'This comes of running about the marshes by night. Beyond question, the fever has soaked thee to the marrow.' Mowgli smiled a little at the idea of anything in the Jungle hurting him. 'I will make a fire, and thou shalt drink warm milk. Put away the jasmine wreath: the smell is heavy in so small a place.'

Mowgli sat down, muttering, with his face in his hands. All manner of strange feelings that he had never felt before were running over him, exactly as though he had been poisoned, and he felt dizzy and a little sick. He drank the warm milk in long gulps, Messua patting him on the shoulder from time to time, not quite sure whether he were her son Nathoo of the long-ago days, or some wonderful Jungle being, but glad to feel that he was at least flesh and blood.

'Son,' she said at last — her eyes were full of pride, — 'have any told thee that thou art beautiful beyond all men?'

'Hah?' said Mowgli, for naturally he had never heard anything of the kind. Messua laughed softly and happily. The look in his face was enough for her.

'I am the first, then? It is right, though it comes seldom, that a mother should tell her son these good things. Thou art very beautiful. Never have I looked upon such a man.'

Mowgli twisted his head and tried to see over his own hard shoulder, and Messua laughed again so long that Mowgli, not knowing why, was forced to laugh with her, and the child ran from one to the other, laughing too.

'Nay, thou must not mock thy brother,' said Messua, catching him to her breast. 'When thou art one-half as fair we will marry thee to the youngest daughter of a king, and thou shalt ride great elephants.'

Mowgli could not understand one word in three of the talk here; the warm milk was taking effect on him after his long run, so he curled up and in a minute was deep asleep, and Messua put the hair back from his eyes, threw a cloth over him, and was happy. Jungle-fashion, he slept out the rest of that night and all the next day; for his instincts, which never wholly slept, warned him there was nothing to fear. He waked at last with a bound that shook the hut, for the cloth over his face made him dream of traps; and there he stood, his hand on his knife, the sleep all heavy in his rolling eyes, ready for any fight.

Messua laughed, and set the evening meal before him. There were only a few coarse cakes baked over the smoky fire, some rice, and a lump of sour preserved tamarinds — just enough to go on with till he could get to his evening kill. The smell of the dew in the marshes made him hungry and restless. He wanted to finish his spring running, but the child insisted on sitting in his arms, and Messua would have it that his long, blue-black hair must be combed out. So she sang, as she combed, foolish little baby-songs, now calling Mowgli her son, and now begging him to give some of his Jungle power to the child. The hut door was closed, but Mowgli heard a sound he knew well, and saw Messua's jaw drop with horror as a great grey paw came under the bottom of the door, and Grey Brother outside whined a muffled and penitent whine of anxiety and fear.

'Out and wait! Ye would not come when I called,' said Mowgli in Jungle-talk, without turning his head, and the great grey paw disappeared.

'Do not — do not bring thy — thy servants with thee,' said Messua. 'I — we have always lived at peace with the Jungle.'

'It is peace,' said Mowgli, rising. 'Think of that night on the road to Khanhiwara. There were scores of such folk before thee and behind thee. But I see that even in springtime the Jungle-People do not always forget. Mother, I go.'

Messua drew aside humbly — he was indeed a wood-god, she thought; but as his hand was on the door the mother in her made her throw her arms round Mowgli's neck again and again.

'Come back!' she whispered. 'Son or no son, come back, for I love thee — Look, he too grieves.'

The child was crying because the man with the shiny knife was going away.

'Come back again,' Messua repeated. 'By night or by day this door is never shut to thee.'

Mowgli's throat worked as though the cords in it were being pulled, and his voice seemed to be dragged from it as he answered, 'I will surely come back.'

'And now,' he said, as he put by the head of the fawning wolf on the threshold,

'I have a little cry against thee, Grey Brother. Why came ye not all four when I called so long ago?'

'So long ago? It was but last night. I—we—were singing in the Jungle the new songs, for this is the Time of New Talk. Rememberest thou?'

'Truly, truly.'

'And as soon as the songs were sung,' Grey Brother went on earnestly, 'I followed thy trail. I ran from all the others and followed hot-foot. But, O Little Brother, what *hast* thou done, eating and sleeping with the Man-Pack?'

'If ye had come when I called, this had never been,' said Mowgli, running much faster.

'And now what is to be?' said Grey Brother.

Mowgli was going to answer when a girl in a white cloth came down some path that led from the outskirts of the village. Grey Brother dropped out of sight at once, and Mowgli backed noiselessly into a field of high-springing crops. He could almost have touched her with his hand when the warm, green stalks closed before his face and he disappeared like a ghost. The girl screamed, for she thought she had seen a spirit, and then she gave a deep sigh. Mowgli parted the stalks with his hands and watched her till she was out of sight.

'And now I do not know,' he said, sighing in his turn. '*Why* did ye not come when I called?'

'We follow thee — we follow thee,' Grey Brother mumbled, licking at Mowgli's heel. 'We follow thee always, except in the Time of New Talk.'

'And would ye follow me to the Man-Pack?' Mowgli whispered.

'Did I not follow thee on the night our old Pack cast thee out? Who waked thee lying among the crops?'

'Ay, but again?'

'Have I not followed thee to-night?'

'Ay, but again and again, and it may be again, Grey Brother?'

Grey Brother was silent. When he spoke he growled to himself, 'The Black One spoke truth.'

'And he said?'

'Man goes to Man at the last. Raksha, our mother, said—'

'So also said Akela on the night of Red Dog,' Mowgli muttered.

'So also says Kaa, who is wiser than us all.'

'What dost thou say, Grey Brother?'

'They cast thee out once, with bad talk. They cut thy mouth with stones. They sent Buldeo to slay thee. They would have thrown thee into the Red Flower. Thou, and not I, hast said that they are evil and senseless. Thou, and not I—I follow my own people — didst let in the Jungle upon them. Thou, and not I, didst make song against them more bitter even than our song against Red Dog.'

'I ask thee what *thou* sayest?'

They were talking as they ran. Grey Brother cantered on a while without replying, and then he said, — between bound and bound as it were, — 'Man-cub — Master of the Jungle — Son of Raksha, Lair-brother to me — though I forget for a little while in the spring, thy trail is my trail, thy lair is my lair, thy kill is my kill, and thy death-fight is my death-fight. I speak for the Three. But what wilt thou say to the Jungle?'

'That is well thought. Between the sight and the kill it is not good to wait. Go before and cry them all to the Council Rock, and I will tell them what is in my stomach. But they may not come — in the Time of New Talk they may forget me.'

'Hast thou, then, forgotten nothing?' snapped Grey Brother over his shoulder, as he laid himself down to gallop, and Mowgli followed, thinking.

At any other season the news would have called all the Jungle together with bristling necks, but now they were busy hunting and fighting and killing and singing. From one to another Grey Brother ran, crying, 'The Master of the Jungle goes back to Man! Come to the Council Rock.' And the happy, eager People only answered, 'He will return in the summer heats. The Rains will drive him to lair. Run and sing with us, Grey Brother.'

'But the Master of the Jungle goes back to Man,' Grey Brother would repeat.

'*Eee-Yoawa?* Is the Time of New Talk any less sweet for that?' they would reply. So when Mowgli, heavy-hearted, came up through the well-remembered rocks to the place where he had been brought into the Council, he found only the Four, Baloo, who was nearly blind with age, and the heavy, cold-blooded Kaa coiled around Akela's empty seat.

'Thy trail ends here, then, Manling?' said Kaa, as Mowgli threw himself down, his face in his hands. 'Cry thy cry. We be of one blood, thou and I — man and snake together.'

'Why did I not die under Red Dog?' the boy moaned. 'My strength is gone from me, and it is not any poison. By night and by day I hear a double step upon my trail. When I turn my head it is as though one had hidden himself from me that instant. I go to look behind the trees and he is not there. I call and none cry again; but it is as though one listened and kept back the answer. I lie down, but I do not rest. I run the spring running, but I am not made still. I bathe, but I am not made cool. The kill sickens me, but I have not heart to fight except I kill. The Red Flower is in my body, my bones are water — and — I know not what I know.'

'What need of talk?' said Baloo slowly, turning his head to where Mowgli lay. 'Akela by the river said it, that Mowgli should drive Mowgli back to the Man-Pack. I said it. But who listens now to Baloo? Bagheera — where is

Bagheera this night? — he knows also. It is the Law.'

'When we met at Cold Lairs, Manling, I knew it,' said Kaa, turning a little in his mighty coils. 'Man goes to Man at the last, though the Jungle does not cast him out.'

The Four looked at one another and at Mowgli, puzzled but obedient.

'The Jungle does not cast me out, then?' Mowgli stammered.

Grey Brother and the Three growled furiously, beginning, 'So long as we live none shall dare —' But Baloo checked them.

'I taught thee the Law. It is for me to speak,' he said; 'and, though I cannot now see the rocks before me, I see far. Little Frog, take thine own trail; make thy lair with thine own blood and pack and people; but when there is need of foot or tooth or eye, or a word carried swiftly by night, remember, Master of the Jungle, the Jungle is thine at call.'

'The Middle Jungle is thine also,' said Kaa. 'I speak for no small people.'

'*Hai-mai,* my brothers,' cried Mowgli, throwing up his arms with a sob. 'I know not what I know! I would not go; but I am drawn by both feet. How shall I leave these nights?'

'Nay, look up, Little Brother,' Baloo repeated. 'There is no shame in this hunting. When the honey is eaten we leave the empty hive.'

'Having cast the skin,' said Kaa, 'we may not creep into it afresh. It is the Law.'

'Listen, dearest of all to me,' said Baloo. 'There is neither word nor will here to hold thee back. Look up! Who may question the Master of the Jungle? I saw thee playing among the white pebbles yonder when thou wast a little frog; and Bagheera that bought thee for the price of a young bull newly killed, saw thee also. Of that Looking-over we two only remain; for Raksha, thy lair-mother, is dead with thy lair-father; the old Wolf-Pack is long since dead; thou knowest whither Shere Khan went, and Akela died among the dholes, where, but for thy wisdom and strength, the second Seeonee Pack would also have died. There remains nothing but old bones. It is no longer the Man-cub that asks leave of his Pack, but the Master of the Jungle that changes his trail. Who shall question Man in his ways?'

'But Bagheera and the Bull that bought me,' said Mowgli. 'I would not—'

His words were cut short by a roar and a crash in the thicket below, and

Bagheera, light, strong, and terrible as always, stood before him.

'*Therefore,*' he said, stretching out a dripping right paw, 'I did·not come. It was a long hunt, but he lies dead in the bushes now — a bull in his second year — the Bull that frees thee, Little Brother. All debts are paid now. For the rest, my word is Baloo's word.' He licked Mowgli's foot. 'Remember, Bagheera loved thee,' he cried, and bounded away. At the foot of the hill he cried again long and loud, 'Good hunting on a new trail, Master of the Jungle! Remember, Bagheera loved thee.'

'Thou hast heard,' said Baloo. 'There is no more. Go now; but first come to me. O wise Little Frog, come to me!'

'It is hard to cast the skin,' said Kaa as Mowgli sobbed and sobbed, with his head on the blind bear's side and his arms round his neck, while Baloo tried feebly to lick his feet.

'The stars are thin,' said Grey Brother, snuffing at the dawn wind. 'Where shall we lair to-day? for, from now, we follow new trails.'

AN
OBJECT
OF
BEAUTY

Also by Steve Martin

NOVELS
The Pleasure of My Company
Shopgirl

PLAYS
Picasso at the Lapin Agile
WASP

NON-FICTION
Born Standing Up
Pure Drivel
Cruel Shoes

SCREENPLAYS
Shopgirl
Bowfinger
L.A. Story
Roxanne
The Jerk (co-author)

AN
OBJECT
OF
BEAUTY

STEVE MARTIN

Weidenfeld & Nicolson
LONDON

First published in Great Britain in 2010 by Weidenfeld & Nicolson
An imprint of the Orion Publishing Group Ltd
Orion House, 5 Upper St Martin's Lane
London WC2H 9EA

An Hachette UK Company

1 3 5 7 9 10 8 6 4 2

Sizes and dates of the works of art that appear in this book were provided
by reputable sources and are accurate to the best of the author's knowledge.

For all photo credits and copyright information, see page 293.

This book is a work of fiction. Any use of real names or places is done in a wholly
fictitious manner and is not to be taken literally. There was a young girl who modelled for Maxfield
Parrish named Kitty Owen – incidentally, the granddaughter of William Jennings Bryan – but
all references in this novel to Kitty Owen and her family, and all other characters in the book, are
completely imaginary and not to be ascribed to any real people, living or deceased.
Any resemblances to real people or events are a matter of coincidence.

A CIP catalogue record for this book is available from the British Library.

ISBN 978 0 297 86329 8 (cased)
ISBN 978 0 297 86330 4 (trade paperback)

Printed by R. R. Donnelly, Crawfordsville, Indiana, USA.

The Orion Publishing Group's policy is to use papers that are natural,
renewable and recyclable products and made from wood grown in sustainable
forests. The logging and manufacturing processes are expected to conform to
the environmental regulations of the country of origin.

www.orionbooks.co.uk

AN
OBJECT
OF
BEAUTY

PART

1.

I AM TIRED, so very tired of thinking about Lacey Yeager, yet I worry that unless I write her story down, and see it bound and tidy on my bookshelf, I will be unable to ever write about anything else.

My last name is Franks. Once, in college, Lacey grabbed my wallet and read my driver's license aloud, discovering that my forenames are Daniel Chester French, after the sculptor who created the Abraham Lincoln memorial. I am from Stockbridge, Massachusetts, where Daniel Chester French lived and worked, and my parents, being parochial Americans, didn't realize that the name Daniel Chester French Franks read funny. Lacey told me she was related to the arts by blood, too, but declined to tell me the full story, saying, "Too long. Later I'll tell you, French Fries." We were twenty.

I left Stockbridge, a town set under the glow of its even more famous citizen, the painter of glad America, Norman Rockwell. It is a town that is comfortable with art, although uncomplicated art, not the kind that is taught in educational institutions after high school. My goal, once I discovered that my artistic aspirations were not accompanied by artistic talent, was to learn to write about art with effortless clarity. This is not as easy as it sounds: whenever I attempted it, I found myself in a convoluted rhetorical tangle from which there was no exit.

After high school, I went south to Davidson College in North

Carolina, while Lacey drove north from Atlanta, and there, Lacey and I studied art history and had sex together exactly once.

Even at the age of twenty, Lacey's entry into the classroom had the pizzazz of a Broadway star. Our eyes followed her down the aisle, where she would settle into her seat with a practiced hair-flip. When she left a room, there was a moment of deflation while we all returned to normal life. It was apparent to everyone that Lacey was headed somewhere, though her path often left blood in the water.

If one of her girlfriends was in a crisis, Lacey would rush in, offering tidal waves of concern. She could soothe or incite in the name of support: "Honey, get over it," or, conversely, "Honey, get even." Either bit of advice was inspiring. The emotions of men, however, were of a different order. They were pesky annoyances, small dust devils at her feet. Her knack for causing heartbreak was innate, but her vitality often made people forgive her romantic misdeeds. Now, however, she is nearing forty and not so easily forgiven as when her skin bloomed like roses.

I slept with her in our second year. I was on the rebound and managed to avoid devastation by reconnecting with my girlfriend days—or was it hours—later, and Lacey's tentacles never had time to attach. But her sense of fun enchanted me, and once I had sufficiently armored myself against her allure by viewing her as a science project, I was able to enjoy the best parts of her without becoming ensnared.

I will tell you her story from my own recollections, from conversations I conducted with those around her, and, alas, from gossip: thank God the page is not a courtroom. If you occasionally wonder how I know about some of the events I describe in this book, I don't. I have found that—just as in real life—imagination sometimes has to stand in for experience.

2.

LACEY'S LIFE AND MINE have paralleled each other for a long while. When we were twenty-three, our interest in art as a profession landed us both in New York City at a time when the art world was building offshore like a developing hurricane. Our periodic lunches caught me up with her exploits. Sometimes she showed up at a Manhattan café with a new boyfriend who was required to tolerate my unexplained presence, and when she excused herself to the restroom, the boyfriend and I would struggle for conversation while he tried to discover if I was an ex-lover, as he soon would be.

In August 1993, she showed up at one of these lunches in a summer dress so transparent that when she passed between me and a bay window hot with sunlight, the dress seemed to incinerate like flash paper. Her hair was clipped back with a polka-dot plastic barrette, which knocked about five years off her age.

"Ask me where I was," she said.

"And if I don't?"

She made a small fist and held it near my face. "Then socko."

"Okay," I said. "Where were you?"

"At the Guggenheim. A furniture show."

The Guggenheim Museum is Frank Lloyd Wright's questionable masterpiece that corkscrews into Fifth Avenue. Questionable because it forces every viewer to stand at a slant.

"'The Italian Metamorphosis,'" I said. "I wrote about it. Too late to get into a magazine. What did you think?"

"I'd rather fuck an Italian than sit on his furniture," she said.

"You didn't like it?"

"I guess I was unclear. No."

"How come?"

"Taste?" she said, then added, "Only one thing could have made it better."

"What's that?"

"Roller skates."

Lacey talked on, oblivious to the salivations that her dress was causing. She had to know of its effect, but it was as though she'd put it on in the morning, calculated what it would do, then forgot about it as it cast its spell. Her eyes and attention never strayed from me, which was part of her style.

Lacey made men feel that she was interested only in that special, unique conflation of DNA that was *you*, and that at any moment she was, just because *you* were so fascinating, going to sleep with *you*. She would even take time to let one of your jokes sweep over her, as though she needed a moment to absorb its brilliance, then laugh with her face falling forward and give you a look of quizzical admiration, as if to say, "You are much more complicated and interesting than I ever supposed."

"Come with me," she said after coffee.

"Where to?"

"I'm buying a dress. I'm interviewing at Sotheby's tomorrow and I have to look like a class act."

The New York heat baked us till we found the inside of a moderately cooler downtown dress shop that featured recycled class-act clothing. Music blared as Lacey zeroed in on a dark blue tight skirt and matching jacket. She winced at the price, but it did not deter her. She pulled the curtain of the changing room, and I could hear the rustle of clothes. I pictured the skirt being pulled on and zipped up. She emerged wearing the jacket loosely opened, with nothing on underneath—which created a sideways cleavage—and started buttoning it up in front of the mirror, surveying herself. "I've got a blouse at home I can wear with this," she muttered to me. She straightened up and pulled the barrette from her hair, causing the blond mix of yellows and browns to fall to her shoulders, and she instantly matured.

"They're going to love you," I said.

"They goddamn better because I'm broke. I'm down to seven thousand."

"Last week you said you had three thousand."

"Well, if I've got three, I'm fucked. So let's call it seven."

Lacey turned from the mirror for the first time and struck a pose in the preowned Donna Karan.

"You look great. A lot of people our age don't know how to go in and apply for a job," I said.

Lacey stared at me and said, "I don't go in and apply for a job. I go in and *get* a job."

And so Lacey joined the spice rack of girls at Sotheby's.

Sotheby's and Christie's, the two premier auction houses in New York, drew young, crisp talent from Harvard and its look-alikes. Majors in art history were welcomed over majors in art making, and pretty was preferred in either sex. The houses wanted the staff to look swell as they crisscrossed the busy galleries on exhibition days, holding in their arms files, faxes, and transparencies. Because the pay was low, the young staff was generally financed from home. Parents thought well of it because their children were at respectable firms, working in a glamorous business, with money of all nations charging the atmosphere. The auction houses seemed not as dull as their financial counterparts on Wall Street, where parents of daughters imagined glass ceilings and bottom patting.

Sotheby's was an institution that implied European accents and grand thoughts about art and aesthetics coexisting with old and new money in sharp suits and silk ties. This was a fresh and clean New York, where you dressed nicely every day and worked in a soaring, smoke-free, drugless architectural building filled with busts, bronzes, and billionaires. What the parents forgot about were the weekends and evenings when their children left the Cézannes and Matisses and crept underground, traveling back to shared downtown spaces where they did exactly the same things they would have done if they had joined a rock band.

Lacey's first assignment was in the bins, cataloging and measuring nineteenth-century pictures in a dim basement that was largely unpopulated. Her Donna Karan was wasted on the shippers and craters, but she kept her wardrobe keen for her occasional pop-ups to the fourth-floor offices. An ivy-embraced college may have been her education in the high ground of art, but Sotheby's basement was her education in the fundamentals. She hoisted pictures onto a carpet-covered table, stretched her tape measure over their backs, and wrote down everything she could. She flipped them over and noted signatures and monograms, trying to decipher artists' illegible scrawls, and she scratched around in the cumbersome reference dictionaries, Myers and Benezit, to find listings of obscure artists so she could report a successful attribution to her superiors. During her first year, she saw the fronts and backs of thousands of paintings. She learned to precisely tap a painting with the back of her finger: a hard, stiff canvas indicated the picture had been relined, usually a warning sign about a painting's poor condition. She was taught to identify varnished prints that were trying to pass themselves off as paintings—a magnifying glass would reveal printer's dots (to the disappointment of excited sellers who believed they owned an original). She learned to distinguish etchings from lithographs by raking the print in a hard light, looking for telling shadows in the groove of the etched line.

The paintings in the basement were generally dogs; the finer works remained upstairs, hung over a director's desk or in a private room until their grand display in one of the large galleries. The masterpieces were examined by conservators bearing loupes and black lights, while Lacey toiled downstairs in the antique dust like Sneezy the Dwarf. The subject matter she faced every day was not the apples of Cézanne, but the kitsch of the nineteenth century: monks tippling, waifs selling flowers, cardinals laughing, cows in landscapes, Venetian gondoliers, baby chicks in farmyards, mischievous shoeshine boys, and still lifes painted so badly that objects seemed to levitate over the tabletop on which they were supposed to be gravitationally attached. On her rare visits upstairs, she found serenity in the sight of the occasional Seurat or Monet and, sometimes, Rembrandt. However, through the drudgery downstairs, Lacey was developing an instinct that would burrow inside her and stay forever: a capacity to know a good painting from a bad one.

Her walk-on role at Sotheby's stood in contrast with her starring role in the East Village bars and cafés. After her practiced and perfected subway ride home, which was timed like a ballet—her foot forward, the subway car doors opening just in time to catch her—she knew the bar lights were coming on, voices were raised, music edging out onto the sidewalks. She felt like the one bright light, the spotlit girl scattering fairy dust, as she walked the few blocks to her walk-up. Once inside, she slumped sideways on her bed, cocked the phone against her head, and sipped Scotch while she phoned Angela or Sharon, or sometimes, me.

"Hey...God, I miss you! Where are you? Meet me at Raku for sushi. Goddamn it! Sorry, I sloshed Scotch on me. Meet me now... No, *now*."

Raku was the mystery restaurant of the Lower East Side. Large portions, low prices, and never more than four customers no matter what time of the day it was. Tables waited for Lacey like kennel puppies hoping to be picked. She rolled in at seven p.m. and sat down in solitude.

Lacey was just as happy alone as with company. When she was alone, she was potential; with others she was realized. Alone, she was self-contained, her tightly spinning magnetic energy oscillating around her. When in company, she had invisible tethers to everyone in the room: as they moved away, she pulled them in. She knew who was doing better than she was, what man she would care to seduce just to prove she could. She was a naval commander knowing the location of all her boats.

The East Village mixed the fast life with the slow life, and the two were sometimes indistinguishable. Actors huddled and chatted in crappy bars, while old-timers to whom the neon beer sign was not a kitschy collectible but simply a neon beer sign sat on stools and remained unaware that they would be, this year or next, pushed out of the increasingly younger neighborhood. Sometimes the newer crowd would clumsily light up cigarettes, and Lacey occasionally joined them.

The contemporary art scene was the left bank suburb to Lacey's right bank, uptown art world. Her connection to it was the numerous young hyphenates that would drift across the barroom floors: artist–house painter, artist–art mover, artist-musician. One of her favorites, Jonah Marsh, had a rarer label, artist-deejay. He could be a good artist but made paintings that no matter how much he changed them or developed them still looked derivative of someone better. However, as a deejay, he was very, very cute. One night at a bar, he was circling around Lacey, trying to appear smart, funny, impetuous, raucous, pathetic, anything to get her in bed, that night, now. Lacey, giving in, said to him, "Look, I just want to get off." They went to her place and afterward he conveniently said, "I have to get up early," and left, to Lacey's relief.

3.

ONE TUESDAY, near starvation caused Lacey to finally splurge in the Sotheby's lunchroom, a smartly done, packaged-sandwich place with Formica tables and uptown prices. Here, the staff mingled with the department heads and Lacey could easily discern one class from the other based on thread count. The department heads were usually less alluring than the staff, since they were hired on expertise, not glamour, and they were usually less haggard than the tireless employees who were sent running from floor to floor. At one table was Cherry Finch, head of American Paintings, while at another was Heath Acosta, head of European Paintings and natty in a gray suit and tie, sitting with an obvious client. Obvious because of his black hair that hung in short ringlets and was laden with *product*. His Mediterranean skin and open silk shirt said clearly that he was not an employee. He was mid-thirties, foreign, and handsome enough that Lacey's inner critic did not object to his playboy rags.

With regularity, the client's eyes strayed to Lacey. Lacey ate more and more slowly, trying to stop the clock before she had no further excuse to stay. Eventually, when their check was paid, Acosta and the client made a deliberate move to her table.

"Hello, I've seen you, but we haven't met. I'm Heath Acosta, from European Paintings."

"Well then, you're like everyone in the company: my superior. I'm Lacey Yeager. I work down in Hades."

"Ah, the bins."

"Hence my lack of tan."

The client lurched in: "Better than leather skin at forty. Hello, I'm Patrice Claire." His face was a bottle bronze, and his French accent surprised Lacey; she was expecting Middle Eastern. "Do you enjoy European painting?"

"I'm sure I will one day," Lacey said.

"Maybe you haven't seen the right ones," said Patrice. Then to Acosta, "It's unfair that you separate the Impressionists into their own group. Aren't they Europeans?"

Acosta replied, "Impressionists aren't tidy enough for our European collectors."

"Well then, they wouldn't like me, either," said Lacey. Patrice's face signaled the opposite.

"Have you been to an auction yet?" said Acosta.

"I didn't know if I was allowed..."

"Come to the European sale next week," he said. "Ten a.m. Thursday. We can excuse you from Hades that day."

"Do I need to get there early for a seat?" said Lacey.

"Heavens, no, not for European. The recession has seen to that."

Acosta turned to go, and Patrice added, "Be sure not to cough, sneeze, or scratch."

She had no doubt that the visit to the table was at Patrice's request, to make contact and take a closer look. Lacey gave him a look back that said she was fuckable, but not without a bit of work.

4.

THURSDAY MORNING, Lacey slipped into one of the folding chairs at the European sale. The hall was half-full, and the rumored excitement of a live auction was belied with every tired raise of a paddle, followed by bidders' early exits. The art market had collapsed a few years ago and was still sputtering. By 1990 the boom had withered, but before that date, carloads of inferior French paintings had been sold to the Japanese and then hurriedly crated and shipped overseas before the buyers realized that perhaps their eye for Impressionism had not been fully developed. Sotheby's, Christie's, and dealers along Madison Avenue had found a repository for their second- and third-best pictures, and they all feared the moment when the Japanese would decide to sell the gray Pissarros and the fluffy, puffy Renoirs—proudly hung in Japanese department stores to impress their customers—and recognize that they had been had. Thankfully, an art market crash gave the dealers an excuse to avoid urgent pleas for buybacks when the Japanese would discover just how bad were the pictures they had been sold: "Oh, the economy has just collapsed!"

Lacey watched the auction unfold and wondered how people could afford twenty thousand dollars to buy a sketch by an unfamiliar Spaniard with three names. She watched Heath Acosta on the sideline, beaming, but she couldn't figure out what he was beaming about. Every other picture remained unsold. He was probably trying to put a brave face on the crashing sale. She watched as pictures she had grown fond of downstairs stiffed in front of the sullen crowd, meaning they would be returned downstairs, where they would wait for their disappointed owners to claim them.

Next up was James Jacques Joseph Tissot's picture of a theater lobby filling up just after the curtain call. Men in opera hats steer their young femmes toward the exit; the women wear lavish dresses, sport hats that cost as much as carriages, and swim under billows of fur. Tissot was the master of a small subject—the rich—and he swathed the women in yards of fabric and painted them midflounce as they

La Mondaine, James Tissot, 1883–1885
58.3 × 40.5 in.

disembarked from boats, lounged in parks, or sat on window seats overlooking the sea.

The estimate on the Tissot was five hundred thousand to seven hundred thousand. There was a small stir when the rotating display brought it into view; it looked good. If it stalled, it would be hard for Acosta to maintain his plastered beam. The picture started off at three hundred fifty thousand, and no paddles were raised. Acosta seemed unfazed. He scanned the room, then nodded, and the auctioneer called out, "I have three hundred fifty thousand." Soon, four hundred thousand. Then, four hundred fifty thousand. Then the auctioneer took a leap: no more fifty-thousand-dollar increments. Six hundred thousand. Seven hundred thousand. The picture crossed a million, then a million five, and then once again in fifty-thousand-dollar increments, finally selling at two million dollars.

Was this a one-off, or was the art recession loosening? Was Acosta smiling because he had known of secret bids aimed at the Tissot? Auctioneers often knew in advance what someone was willing to bid. Lacey noticed that as the pace of the bids picked up, she felt a concomitant quickening of her pulse, as though she had been incised by an aphrodisiacal ray.

That evening she called Jonah Marsh, the cute deejay, and met him late night at MoMA. They walked around and looked at paintings until she had recharged the morning's ardor, finally taking him home with her. After sexual due process—an outbreak of inhibition, contortion, flying words, and sweat with fair exchanges on both sides—Jonah groggily left, again relieving Lacey of the burden of postcoital chat. She sipped port and stared out her window, a window still grimy with the residue of winter, and relived the auction earlier that day. One million, one million five...two million. Someone had just cashed in grandly, unexpectedly. It made her wonder: Could she make money in art, Tissot money?

15

At Sotheby's, she started to look at paintings differently. She became an efficient computer of values. The endless stream of pictures that passed through the auction house helped her develop a calculus of worth. Auction records were available in the Sotheby's library, and when a picture of note came in, she diligently searched the Art Price Index to see if it had auction history. She factored in condition, size, and subject matter. A Renoir of a young girl, she had witnessed, was worth more than one of an old woman. An American western picture with five tepees was worth more than a painting with one tepee. If a picture had been on the market recently without a sale, she knew it would be less desirable. A deserted painting scared buyers. Why did no one want it? In the trade, it was known as being "burned." Once a picture was burned, the owner had to either drastically reduce the price or sit on it for another seven years until it faded from memory. When Lacey began these computations, her toe crossed ground from which it is difficult to return: she started converting objects of beauty into objects of value.

5.

LACEY KNEW I was coming uptown and insisted I stop by Sotheby's for lunch. She had something to show me, she said. I met her at the Sotheby's sandwich bar, and we snagged a sunny corner table.

"Do you want to see a picture of my grandmother?" asked Lacey.

"Is this a trick question?" I said.

She reached into her wide-mouth purse and withdrew a very used art book covered with library acetate and bearing a small, rectangular label with what looked like a Dewey Decimal System number and a second label that clearly, seriously said, "Property of Sotheby's." She handled the book so freely in the lunchroom that I knew it had been legitimately checked out of the library and did not represent a heist.

"Remember when I told you I was related to the arts?"

"Well, no, but go on."

"My grandmother is Kitty Owen."

Lacey laid the book on the table and spun its face toward me. On the cover was a painting by Maxfield Parrish. I knew a bit about him. In the twenties, he was America's most famous artist. His pictures featured young girls lounging by lakes or sitting naked on tree swings in fanciful arcadias. These delicately painted pictures also sold tires and magazines. Logos were emblazoned across reproductions on calendars and posters, sometimes painted into the work itself. Parrish hovered between being an illustrator and an artist.

17

Daybreak, Maxfield Parrish, 1922
26.5 × 45.5 in.

Lacey poked her finger down on the cover.

"That's my grandmother," she said. "She was eighteen when she took off all her clothes for him and posed. See, you're not the only one with wise-ass art credentials."

"Is she…" Alive, I was going to say.

"She's ninety-two. She still has that skin, but the red hair is phfft." I looked at the slender, pale girl on the cover of the book, who looked like a faun standing over an idyllic pool trimmed in iridescent tiles.

"She owns a print with her in it. He gave it to her. I checked the Sotheby's records to see how much it was worth. Not much. Two hundred bucks. It's our only artistic heirloom. It's got a nice story with it.

"Kitty, Gram, had posed for a painting. She was nude, lying on a rock. Parrish had prints made. There was a stack of them on a table, and he told Kitty he wanted to give her something. Then he reached from behind the table and gave her one in a very expensive frame and under glass. Very special."

"You think there was…involvement?" I said.

18

"No, Parrish went for another model. He and his wife and the model lived happily/horribly ever after. The picture has hung in our house for as long as I can remember, and sometimes, when the house was empty, I would take off all my clothes and lie on the floor and look up at the picture, dreaming that I was like her, in the most beautiful forest, stretched long, arching up, and facing the twilight. I pretended that I was in heaven."

6.

A YEAR AND A HALF passed well. I had reviewed a small show for the *Village Voice* and received a complimentary note from Peter Schjeldahl, who was the main critic there at the time. Lacey was moving up at Sotheby's, literally. Frequent paperwork kept her upstairs, and she found that newcomers, mostly young white girls just off a collegiate slave boat, were being sent down the mine shaft to replace her, staggering out of the elevator hours later with dilated eyes, happy once again to see the sun. She was kept from a significant raise on the premise that new employees were really interns learning the business, and during one of our increasingly rare lunches, she told me this: "Guess what I figured out: Sotheby's is my yacht. *It's a money pit.* I'm losing money just to work there. I can last another year and then I'm headed for whore town, which could be kind of good, depending on the outfits."

Upstairs, information passed more freely. It came in overheard slices and tidbits, and in facial expressions, too. A sneer or sigh directed at a Picasso by one of the experts meant something, and she started to grasp why one Picasso warranted a snub while another one elicited awe. Her clothes meant more, too. Like a teen at Catholic school, she knew how to tweak the prescribed outfit with sultry modifications, the outline of her black bra under white silk, an embroidered cuff, an offbeat shoe. So, while fitting in, she was like a wicked detail standing out against a placid background.

In the glamorous world of the fourth floor, the artworks she had cataloged downstairs—the minor works of art by well-known names and the major works by unknown names—became like old high school friends: she had moved on, but they hadn't. Oh yes, she still liked them, but when two handlers with white gloves brought in a 1914 Schiele drawing of a nude and handled it like something precious and valuable, it made the basement seem like playschool. The special treatment it received made her look closer, too. After the conservative, unimaginative dabs downstairs, Schiele's daring teen nudes, contorted and imaginatively foreshortened, were shocking. These were not cows in a landscape. She imagined his boudoir in Vienna with its swinging door of stoned young girls spreading their legs while Schiele drew them in.

The fourth floor brought an annoyance into Lacey's life. Tanya Ross was one year older than Lacey, had been at her job a year longer than Lacey, and had already steamed ahead in her career at Sotheby's. She bustled around with confidence, and she always seemed to be in Lacey's view no matter how often Lacey twisted in her chair. She was taller than Lacey; she was prettier than Lacey: a deep brunette whose trademark was efficiency. This last quality made her perfect for dealing with serious clients who expected no nonsense. Certain dour customers asked for her by name, which gave Tanya a splendid position as an up-and-comer in the company.

Lacey had a keen eye for rivals, and at one of our lunches only a week after the elevator promotion, she pronounced Tanya an "up-talking Canadian. She touts Art History 101 like it's a PhD, but she also knows that cleavage works." I checkmarked this comment, since Lacey was capable of an equally manipulative display of cleavage at the right time, for the right person, for the right ends.

"Maybe you have to get to know her," I mistakenly said.

"There's nothing there to know," she rasped, and held up her fist as if to punch me. "They brought up a Picasso the other day, and I saw her look at the label on the back to find out who painted it. *She had to look at the label.* Plus she's financed. I think her last name is Wham-o or something. Tanya Wham-o. When someone less capable is ahead of me, I am *not pleased.* It makes me insane."

"Makes you insane? You already are," I said. Then, "What if someone more capable is ahead of you?"

"That's even worse," she said.

This being a cool spring, Lacey's clothes were less revealing than in the torrid summer, and she relied on fashion quirks to make up for the lost power. She buttoned up her blouse neck high, over which she had donned a child's sweater, a size large but still too small, which clung to her and rode up three inches above her waist. The food came.

"I'm thinking of getting a dog," she said.

"What kind?" I asked.

"One that's near death."

"Why?"

"Less of a commitment," she answered.

This was Saturday. Lacey would return to work and process a few midrange pictures that were being delivered. She liked the Saturday deliveries because they were special arrangements always brought in by clients, since the art handlers only worked weekdays. Sotheby's wasn't a pawnshop, so the sellers usually weren't desperate; they were just sellers. They might be a New Jersey couple who had heard about a successful sale of an artist they owned, or people with inherited pictures, or a young man helping his elderly relatives through the hoops of a Sotheby's contract. Pictures from Connecticut were generally overframed decorator concoctions surrounding dubiously attributed horse paintings. But pictures from New Jersey were usually the genuine article, purchased years ago from galleries or even from the artists themselves. The pictures typically bore ugly frames created by local framers who used gold paint rather than gold leaf or slathered them in a dull green or off-white substance reminiscent of caulk. One elderly couple hobbled in carting a small but sensational Milton Avery in a frame so ghastly that Cherry Finch looked at the painting with her fingers squared so as to screen it out. When Cherry told the couple the picture would be estimated at sixty to eighty thousand, the gentleman's phantom suspenders almost popped. They had paid three hundred dollars for it in 1946, the year it was painted, and the price was still stuck to the back.

Milton Avery was an isolated figure in American painting, not falling neatly into any category. He would reduce figures and landscapes to a few broad patches of color: a big swath of black would be the sea, a big swath of yellow would be the sand, a big swath of blue would be the sky, and that would be it. His pictures were always polite, but they were polite in the way that a man with a gun might be polite: there was plenty to back up his request for attention. Though his style changed only slightly during his career, he was not formulaic, indicated by the

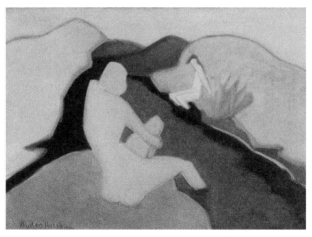

Nude Bathers, Milton Avery, 1946
25.5 × 35.5 in.

existence of as many paintings that worked as ones that didn't. The painting that Cherry was looking at was one that did.

When the couple left, Cherry turned to Lacey and asked her what she thought the picture would bring. Lacey knew this was a test and decided to make a calculated but extravagant guess. She thought it might be better to have her guess remembered than forgotten. She considered the picture to be a small gem that could easily snare a strong bid, so she said, "Probably one hundred seventy thousand." Cherry smiled at the poor, innocent child.

Lacey ran down the interior escalators. The Avery couple were on their way out of the building when Lacey caught up with them. "Do you mind if we reframe the picture?" she asked. "It might help."

Not quite understanding why—it had been framed the same way for fifty years—they consented at Lacey's professional urgency.

She took the picture downstairs and measured it, knocked off early, and dropped by Lowy, the Upper East Side framer to the magnificent. She approached the woman at the desk: "Hello, I'm Lacey Yeager, I'm with Sotheby's. I'd like to talk about a frame for a Milton Avery."

Lacey's voice carried past the desk to the racks of luxurious samples, where velvet easels held pictures while corners of frames were laid over them. Customers stood back and imagined the other three-fourths of the frame. A man walked over to her. "Hello, I'm Larry Shar. How can I help you?"

"We have a Milton Avery that needs a frame. It's being auctioned in the next sale. Could something be done in that time?"

"Sure. Where's the picture?"

"Well, here's the situation. The couple who's selling it can't really afford a frame, so I was wondering if you could make a frame on spec. We could auction the picture stating that the frame is on loan from you. Whoever buys the picture would certainly want to purchase the frame. Your work is so good."

"We usually—"

"And if they don't buy the frame," Lacey added, "I will."

Larry said curiously, "What is your name?"

With that, Lacey knew he had consented.

7.

LACEY LIKED THE GAMBLE, and she flew home with other thoughts of how to ratchet up the picture's appeal. She had noticed after it had been pulled from the frame that the picture was brighter where it had been hidden under the liner. Maybe the owners were smokers or had hung the picture over a fireplace, where it had been layered with grime. Certainly the picture could be freshened. She had an idea that she could corner Tony, the conservator from downstairs, and persuade him to give it a light cleaning.

When she got home there was a message on her machine from Jonah Marsh: "Hey, want to do X tonight? I've got some."

Sure, Lacey thought, let's do X.

Jonah Marsh arrived at six p.m., minutes before dark. Lacey threw a maroon scarf over a lamp, reddening the room. Outside, the streets were wet from a sudden, cooling rain. Lights were coming on in windows across the street. Jonah produced the pills, displaying them in his hand like buttons. "Supposed to be excellent and very clean," he said.

Lacey poured two glasses of tap water and momentously swallowed a pill, then laid the other pill on Jonah's tongue, gave him the water, and kissed him as the pill was going down.

"You've done it before?" asked Jonah.

"Yes, once."

"What was it like?"

"I saw my goddess."

Huh? thought Jonah.

Minutes passed. He lay on her bed, and Lacey lay down next to him, not with romantic proximity, but at the polite distance of two travelers sharing a bed. The sex that Jonah had anticipated now seemed very distant to him. Lacey breathed deeply, and an eerie wave shimmied up her body. She gripped the bedspread beneath her and hung on until the unpleasantness passed. She comforted herself and had closed her eyes again, when, unexpectedly, a stronger, final flood of chemistry saturated her body from head to toe, placing her in its ecstatic grip. In this dream state, she saw her mother extending her hand toward her. Her mother led her through her childhood home, swung her on the backyard swing, held her close. She led her to the Maxfield Parrish, where she saw the silken girl that was her grandmother, whose luminosity Lacey had inherited, who was now in Atlanta, lying so ill in her bed. Lacey wondered whether her grandmother was looking backward over her life, finding her face reflected in one of Parrish's pools, or if she was in the present, staring into the face of death.

One hour had gone by. Jonah and Lacey were now suspended in an artificial nirvana. They loved their friends and understood their enemies. They loved their mothers and fathers, they loved the bed they were in and the street noise outside, they loved the person next to them. Jonah, in a low mutter addressed to himself, whispered, "Wow, wow," as though a revelation had just transformed him, a thought that he brought to himself in cupped hands after holding them under a fountain.

Nighttime had fully arrived, and Jonah slid the covers lower, to Lacey's waist, and looked at her without the cloud of sexual desire. She was a ceramic, her skin reflecting light, the ribs highlighted, the slope of her stomach shading into desert tan. His palm glided over her upper body, hovering like a hydroplane, a few fingers occasionally touching down. Lacey then sat up like a yogi, and Jonah did the same. Lacey pulled the curtains shut.

The drug made Jonah a perfect lover. Time was slower, making his normal masculine drive turn feminine, while Lacey's normal masculine overdrive downshifted into the pace of a luxurious Sunday outing.

"I love you," said Lacey. "I love you so much."

In the morning they stirred, relapsed into sleep, and were at last out of bed at eleven a.m. They moved like slugs around the apartment until Jonah pulled on his socks, his pants, and the fancy shirt that he'd thought he was going to need last night. He looked out the window and said, "Thank God it's gray. No sunglasses."

He told Lacey, "Last night, I saw a painting. Now I'm going to go home and paint it." It was a momentous night for each of them. The only problem was that when Lacey told Jonah she loved him, he believed her.

8.

I MET LACEY at the Cranberry Café near 10th Street on an unexpectedly blessed spring day, which appeared after a string of cold weekdays that blossomed into sudden glory on Saturday. Her conversation was full of spit and vinegar, and her complaints about one person would effortlessly weave themselves into praise for another person, so it wasn't as though she hated everybody. She gave me every detail of the Ecstasy trip, recounted all the complexities of her work life at Sotheby's, and even managed to inquire how I was doing. Having my torpid accounting of my last few months spill out in such proximity to Lacey's salacious and determined adventures made me feel all the more dull. I had just had a two-year relationship end because of boredom on both sides. Even the breakup was boring.

Lacey was anticipating the sale of the Milton Avery in a few weeks. She had focused on pumping it up to the exclusion of all other interests, including returning Jonah Marsh's forlorn phone calls. Lacey, I believe, liked to know that he was hanging on, that he was hers when she wanted him. She would occasionally leave him an affectionate message—crafted to be both enticing and distancing—when she guessed he wasn't home, just to keep the pot stirred.

Then Lacey leaned in, as though she were going to tell me a secret.

"I was in Atlanta last Sunday. It was so vivid when I saw my grandmother dying, I went."

"Is she lucid?" I asked.

"More than you, not as much as me," she said. "The Parrish print I told you about? It was across from her, and its presence was almost cruel. She's so withered, but the print is bright. I took it closer to Gram; she wanted to look at it. I looked at it, too." Then Lacey started to talk more excitedly. "Daniel, I've known that print all my life, but I..."

She paused, strangely, as though she were distracted by the implications of the next sentence. I could almost see her head bobbing along to the words like a bouncing-ball sing-along.

"But what?" I said.

She was silent. It was as though she were trying to retract what she had told me. Her mind was turning something over, then she looked up at me and stammered through the rest of the meal, as though she had an idea she needed to hang on to.

Outside, as we rambled around the East Village, Lacey would throw exaggerated looks to me as we passed the overweight, the underclothed, and a wandering family of tourists who looked as if they were at least forty blocks away from where they wanted to be. I laughed shamefully every time as Lacey parodied each sorrowful personality with a quick, exact facial expression.

Then I found myself participating in an unpleasant coincidence. We rounded a corner and Jonah Marsh was walking toward us. Spotting him, Lacey did an awful thing: she took my arm. Guessing that Jonah was probably dumped by Lacey, I instantly tried to look as nonthreatening, as nonromantic, as I could. But Lacey's bearing didn't change; she clung to my arm as though we had just gotten engaged.

Then, "Oh, Jonah! I've missed you!" she cried, and hugged him like a returning army husband. "How was your birthday? I'm sorry I couldn't come...This is my friend Daniel. Daniel is a great art writer. He should see your pictures."

"Hi," I said.

Jonah tried to let nothing show, though he may have lightened in color. He knew that Lacey was up for anything and that my hip-nerd look was something that she might go for.

"Jonah, are you doing anything now?" she asked.

I guessed that whatever Jonah might have been doing would be thrown aside if Lacey was implying anything from a tryst to a walk around the block.

"Not right now," he said.

Then Lacey turned to me. "Were you headed midtown?"

"Yes," I said.

"I think I'll stick around here, okay?"

"Sure," I said, and after one of those intense, show-off hugs from Lacey, I headed for the subway. I don't know what happened after that.

9.

BY MAY 1995, Lacey had become conversant with American painting up to 1945 (because that was where the auction catalogs stopped) and it was becoming her default specialty. Default because although she had a collegiate overview of art history, her heavy lifting had taken place in the Sotheby's sales department. She had learned to differentiate good pictures from bad ones, but because prices usually followed quality she was now learning the difference between good pictures and desirable pictures. What lifted a picture into the desirable category was a murky but parsable combination of factors. Paintings were collected not because they were pretty, but because of a winding path that leads a collector to his prey. Provenance, subject matter, rarity, and perfection made a painting not just a painting, but a prize. Lacey had seen the looks on the collectors' faces as they pondered various pictures. These objects, with cooperating input from the collector's mind, were transformed into things that healed. Collectors thought *this one artwork* would make everything right, would complete the jigsaw of their lives, would satisfy eternally. She understood that while a collector's courtship of a picture was ostensibly romantic, at its root was raw lust.

From her experience with men, she knew that lust made them controllable, and she wondered if this principle could be applied to the art business.

Unfortunately, the Avery was not a picture that would arouse lust.

It was a respectable girlfriend you would take home to Mom, without stopping first to have sex in the car. After Lacey had tweaked the picture in every way it could be tweaked, it hung in the galleries during the Sotheby's previews, wearing its new frame like a bridal gown. Lacey explained this change to Cherry Finch by simply saying, "I reframed it," as though this were the most natural thing in the world. Because this strategy had been used at Sotheby's before, Cherry assumed Lacey was implementing a standard practice, not, as Lacey believed, creating one. Lacey had connived to have the picture hung in the main gallery, near the star lot, a nearly perfect Homer watercolor of a trout squirming on a fishing line. She would pass by the picture during viewing hours to see who paused, who commented, who nodded. A particular couple, the Nathansons, had swung by the picture a few times and, quickly sizing her up as an employee, turned to Lacey, who had been eavesdropping.

"Do you know the condition of this picture?" they asked.

She was not supposed to answer floor questions, but she couldn't resist. "It's perfect," she said. "We gave it a light cleaning, that was all."

"Could we see it under a black light?"

"Certainly," dared Lacey. "Just a moment."

She dashed to the in-house phone and explained the situation to Cherry, overstating the haphazardness with which she happened to be gliding by. Because time spent with a painting created an interested buyer, Cherry was eager to have pictures flipped over, hefted, and examined. She told Lacey to bring the Avery to room 272, where a black light would be produced and Cherry, too, if she could make it.

Saul Nathanson—his suit was dapper, but his tie wasn't—leaned back and looked at the picture as it hung on a universal nail in the cramped viewing room. His wife, Estelle, her hair a bit too orange but otherwise just as turned out as Saul, stood by, commenting.

"We knew Milton," she said.

"Lovely guy," said Saul. "Do you mind?" he said, indicating he would like to take the picture off the wall. He held up the picture and looked closely at it.

"He likes to hold pictures. I say why do you have to hold them?"

"She's right," Saul said amiably, "I don't know what it means, but I do it."

"You do it a lot," said Estelle.

Saul grinned at Lacey. "See what I go through?" Then he turned his attention back to the painting. "Avery knew Rothko and Gottlieb. He may have influenced Rothko with his flat planes of color."

Cherry Finch, slightly harried, opened the door. Cherry knew the Nathansons, so Lacey figured they must be regular customers. Everyone milled around the picture, and Cherry explained that it had never been on the market, which made Saul nod, pleased.

"When's the sale?" asked Saul.

"Next Tuesday," Cherry said as they began to exit the room.

Lacey, reminding them of her presence, said, "It's a very beautiful picture, and a great year, 1946." Cherry glanced at Lacey.

After the Nathansons left, Cherry turned to Lacey. "Lacey, some advice: You don't have to sell paintings. All you have to do is put a good picture in front of a knowledgeable collector and stand back."

10.

AS THE WEEK WENT ON, the public viewing of the American pictures drew only light crowds. Tanya Ross was officially on the floor, but Lacey made detours across the gallery, whenever possible, to promote the Avery when Tanya might lapse. Tanya—her back turned—was on the far side of the floor when Lacey came upon an unlikely customer, a young man, Jamaican, perhaps, his head circled in a scarf with sun-bleached dreadlocks piled on top, looking like a plate of soft-shell crabs. He was paused in front of the Avery.

"If you have any questions...," Lacey began.

The young man turned. "Who's this?"

Sensing this was not a knowledgeable collector, Lacey went through her pitch: "American Modernist...America's Matisse," she spouted, and then threw in her latest slogan: "Deeply influenced Rothko." Through Lacey's compromised history, Avery now "had deeply" influenced Rothko rather than "may have." The man didn't have the savvy of the Nathansons, but there was still an aura of money about him.

"Do you have a card?" he asked.

Lacey said she was out but told him: "You can reach me here, I'm Lacey Yeager."

The man wandered away, looking puzzled as he surveyed other pictures in the gallery. It was then that Lacey realized he was not a customer, and she had a dim visual recall: he had followed her in from the subway and had just wangled her name and phone number.

When she arrived at the office floor, there was a phone call already waiting for her, but she backed away from the friendly secretary and waved it off, miming, "Take the number."

Over the next few days, several people inquired about the Avery, but Lacey didn't know who they were, and Tanya wouldn't tell her.

Lacey took one extra gamble. She manipulated Tanya into predicting the outcome of the Avery in front of Cherry Finch. Assuming an air of indifference, Lacey said in her most casual voice, "What dya think that Avery's going to bring?"

"High estimate at most," said Tanya.

"So seventy-five?" Lacey said, making sure the number registered in everyone's brain.

American sales started at ten a.m. Unlike the flashier Impressionist and contemporary sales that began at a glamorous seven p.m., where people dressed in their showcase clothes, the day sales attracted attendees who wore brown pants with blue blazers and shirt collars that lay crushed under their lapels. Lacey had improved her single invitation from Heath Acosta to attend one sale into a standing invitation to attend any sale, and nobody seemed to notice.

The auction started off with a few alarming bumps. An uncharacteristic John Singer Sargent oil, decent enough, died a lonely death without a single bid. The failure was made even more visible because the auctioneer quickly escalated false bids against the reserve to give the illusion of furious bidding, only to promptly sputter out upon reaching the reserve, where he was forced to dwell in a few lingering seconds of ringing silence. It felt as though a shroud of death had fallen over the room. This was especially alarming as last year a Sargent had stunned the crowd, topping out at seven million dollars. Sargent was desirable, more desirable than Milton Avery, and Lacey felt a nervous chill as she acknowledged to herself that the sale could have a disappointing outcome. One would think that the seven-million-dollar figure would motivate at least one buyer to pop for a hundred grand, even for a not-so-great Sargent, if only for the signature, but the auctioneer had to muffle his obligatory announcement, "Passed," by saying the word exactly as his gavel struck the lectern.

The Avery now seemed like an outside shot to reach even the reserve. There was a sign of life as a Whistler watercolor, expected to bring between sixty and eighty thousand, sparkled enough to double the estimate, and Lacey's emotions began flip-flopping like one of Winslow Homer's just-landed trout.

The carousel turned and the Avery swung into view. Now she worried about the frame. Sotheby's tarted-up lighting reflected harshly off its expensive silver leaf. Thankfully, an art handler, who rode in with each picture, tilted it forward to diminish the glare, and the picture looked better than ever.

"Let's start with thirty thousand..." Then the auctioneer quickly manufactured a frenzy with an ersatz bidding war: "Thirty-five, forty, forty-five thousand, fifty thousand..." One would have thought there were a hundred bidders in pursuit of this bashful Avery, but really there were none. Then there was that ugly pause. The next bid, fifty-five thousand, would mean that the picture had sold to an actual, existing buyer. A savvy collector might read this pause, if no bids followed, as an opportunity to buy the picture after the sale at a discount and would sit on his hands instead of bidding against the reserve. Lacey looked around to the few recruits, including Tanya Ross, who were manning the phones, hoping for movement. Tanya stood poised, listening, when her heel slipped off the dais, and she clumsily fumbled the phone, dropping it over her counter, where it swung by its cord. Tanya held up her hand to the auctioneer, as if asking for a time-out. This produced the kind of laugh one hears in a restaurant when a waiter drops a stack of plates. She pulled up the phone and stuck it to her ear. Then, raising her finger as if to make a point, Tanya said meekly, "Fifty-five."

A paddle was raised in the center of the room: "Sixty." Then, the pall broken, there were raises and reraises, taking the picture to eighty-five thousand, after which there was again, in the room, stillness. But this time the auctioneer didn't show a detectable squirm. Rather, he turned his body fully toward the phone and waited patiently. "Ninety," relayed Tanya. Then, turning his body back to the floor as if he were on a spindle, he stared into the face of the floor bidder, whom Lacey could not see. "Will you make it ninety-five?" The ninety-five came and went, the picture crossing a hundred, edging further from Tanya's prediction and more toward Lacey's. The auctioneer brought the price up and up and finally, when he felt there was no more, said, "Last chance...selling, then, at one hundred fifty thousand dollars." Smash. He looked over at the phone. "Paddle number?"

And Tanya replied, "Five oh one."

Lacey was elated and disappointed. She had won her self-imposed contest, one in which she had enrolled, without her knowledge, only one other contestant, but she had hoped the picture would land on her magic number, one hundred seventy thousand, making her victory more memorable.

After the sale, she blitzed back to the office, trying to make her absence less conspicuous, and she was already in place when Cherry came out of the elevator. Cherry saw Lacey, an armload of superfluous papers held against her stomach, and said, "Good one, Lacey, you hit it." Lacey was thrilled that her guess had even been remembered, that her plan for professional notice had succeeded, and especially pleased that Tanya Ross had to witness her win.

"I was a bit over, but I thought it was a good picture," said Lacey, feigning modesty.

"What do you mean?" said Cherry. "You hit it within a few thousand."

"How?" said Lacey.

"The buyer's premium, twelve percent added on," said Cherry.

The addition of the buyer's premium streaked in like a come-from-behind win at a horse race. Lacey felt like a prom queen, even if no one else in the office felt it was that much of a triumph, as numbers routinely bounced around the staff for weeks prior to an auction. But Lacey knew that she was firmly impressed on Cherry's cortex and that above the name "Lacey," whenever it slipped across her consciousness, was a shining gold star.

11.

LACEY'S BANK ACCOUNT—A parental send-off for her life in New York—had halved in the two years she had worked at Sotheby's. New York was cruel to cash reserves, and her Sotheby's check, even with the routine raises, failed to replenish the pot at the same rate of depletion. Lacey always had magic happen to her at moments of financial crisis, but New York now seemed to vex her. She didn't believe in guardian angels, except for the guardian angel of her own self, and usually she laid the groundwork for financial salvation way in advance, and often in such unconscious ways that she didn't even know she was doing it. Her independence kept her from friends offering money, but her cleverness kept it sputtering in. But the past few years were unusually fallow.

My own life was on a gentle gradient moving quietly upward. My contributions to art magazines—I wrote the capsule reviews, usually unsigned—gave me a life and got me out of my apartment, and I found myself with continuing work. There were also relationships, almost romantic, that seemed to lack ignition. My style is courtly, which fails to excite those who anticipate drama. I had to introduce myself to gallery owners a half dozen times before my face started to become familiar.

12.

LACEY HAD, in the course of her work, come to know the Upper East Side. After lunch at 3 Guys, a coffee shop gone crazy with a menu as expansive as a Nebraska plain, she made routine stops at various nineteenth-century galleries along Madison Avenue. Hirschl & Adler, an elegantly staid establishment on 70th Street, held sway in the world of American paintings; they had a knack for polishing and framing a picture so it glowed, and they knew the location of just about every American picture of quality. Next, on 57th Street, was Kennedy Galleries, which had hoarded enough masterpieces to keep it active in the American market but was being sapped of its pictures through the attrition of time. All great pictures flow toward museums. They are plucked off the market by hungry institutions snaring them one by one as the decades march forward. (There are dozens of masterpieces in high apartments along Fifth Avenue, in sight of the Met, longing to make the leap into its comforting arms.)

Lacey had made herself known to the dealers, inquiring about prices and even occasionally helping them out by researching a provenance question about a picture that had passed through Sotheby's, and her name started to come up irregularly when I traveled above 57th Street.

On one of these afternoons, as summer approached and also the end of the art season—leaving the galleries' air-conditioning blazing and floors unpopulated—she wandered into the Kenneth Lux Gallery, which

Mug, Pipe and Book, John Frederick Peto, circa 1880
Size unknown.

specialized in more moderately priced American paintings. On the wall
was a small picture by John Peto. Peto was a nineteenth-century still life
painter who presented books, pipes, and mugs arrayed on a tabletop. The
still lifes were rendered in dark greens and browns, the books ragged at
the edges, close-ups of a tenement dweller's humble routine. Peto was forgotten until the early 1950s, when a scholar, Alfred Frankenstein, noticed
that the most popular of the nineteenth-century still life painters, W. M.
Harnett, whose pictures were quite valuable, appeared to have two distinct styles. One was photographic; every object in those pictures was
vivid and defined. The other was looser; the edges of the books and tabletop objects seemed to evaporate and blend softly into the surrounding air.
Frankenstein discovered that the second version of Harnett's work was

Herald, William Michael Harnett, circa 1878
Size unknown.

actually by Peto. Fakers, wanting to cash in on the more valuable Harnett, erased poor Peto's signature on any of his pictures they could find and added crude monograms of Harnett. When the decades-old fraud was revealed, Peto's prices shot up, nearly matching Harnett's.

Lacey, trying to determine a price for a Peto that was coming up at Sotheby's, asked Ken Lux what the cost of the small picture was. "Thirty-five thousand dollars," he said. Lacey thought the picture was fine and asked for a photo for comparison to Sotheby's picture. "Sure," he said, and gave her a small transparency. Then, continuing her walk, Lacey went around the corner to Hirschl & Adler, where, coincidentally, another small, comparable Peto was hanging. She inquired about the price. "Sixty-five thousand," was the reply. Lacey, stuffed from a deli sandwich she had devoured at 3 Guys, hiccuped. The two pictures were so close in subject matter, they could be a pair.

"Oh," she said, and she walked outside and scraped Ken Lux's label from the transparency. Lacey had heard that art dealers don't communicate with one another, trying to keep their offerings private so rival dealers can't bad-mouth them. This would be a test.

She walked back into H & A, transparency in hand. "Is there someone I could talk to about a Peto I have for sale?"

"Certainly." The secretary asked her name, then buzzed upstairs. "You can go on up to the third floor." And she pointed to an elevator just big enough for two.

She was greeted by Stuart Feld, the powerhouse American dealer with a critical eye for pictures that could make a boastful collector wither. Feld not only sold nineteenth-century pictures, he *felt* nineteenth century. He looked perfectly suited—his suit was perfect—for sitting in his favored neoclassical American furniture. She pulled the photo from her purse. Feld held it up to a light box.

"How big is it?" he asked.

"Eight by twelve inches," she said.

Silence was his response until, "Where is it?" he asked.

Lacey's first real dealing in the art world incorporated tiny lies into its construct. "It's at another dealer's, but he's deliberating. The owner is looking for the money now." It was the perfect response. There was enough truth in the statement for it to be convincing, and it inadvertently sparked Feld's competitive spirit.

"We don't make offers," said Feld. "Tell us what you want."

Lacey calculated the asking price on Feld's Peto, discounting it appropriately.

"Forty thousand," she said.

"That's a bit rich, but perhaps, providing it's in good shape," he said.

Lacey went around the corner to Ken Lux but could only get him down to thirty-three thousand. Still, seven thousand dollars was not bad for a walk around the corner. Ken was a dealer who began in the 1960s, when pictures were hard to sell and were easily let out of the gallery to hang in a collector's house for a few days' trial or even shipped out of state with only a promise by phone to secure the painting. The deals were conducted on handshakes alone and often without even that. It wasn't until the prices started jumping in the mid-1980s—and a few dealers went to jail for selling the same picture twice—that paperwork became necessary. Ken knew Lacey well enough from the floor at Sotheby's, and relying on old-fashioned instinct, he let the picture out of the gallery with just a one-page contract and a promise to pay in two weeks. (Once he had put a painting out for approval to a motorcycle gang, who for some reason wanted a picture of bears frolicking in human clothes. He got paid the next day, in cash pulled in wads from the gang's pockets.)

With the picture under her arm, she rounded the corner once again to H & A, got a check, and pocketed seven grand. Lacey hadn't really lied, she had only been crafty, but she had tasted honey in the art market, and she momentarily felt smarter than Stuart Feld, Ken Lux, and the rest of the dealers who were burrowed in the brownstones stippling Madison Avenue.

13.

THE NATHANSONS had called Sotheby's—yes, they had bought the Avery. Could it be delivered to D.C. today? It would be an object of conversation at their dressy dinner party tonight. Was there a walker who could escort the picture and deliver it? It's only a four-hour train ride. Sometimes the lowliest employees get the best jobs, and Lacey was on a train by ten a.m., with the Avery wrapped in cardboard, bound with a splintery sisal string affixed to a wooden handle, and fully insured. This seemed like a snow day to Lacey, although there was no snow in sight for six months.

The wide train windows looked onto verdant pastures, soot-smudged buildings, and shuttered storefronts like a rapidly unscrolling panorama as the train whizzed past them. Her wrinkle-proof dress clung statically to her legs, and each move of her arm pulled it this way or that above a knee, which was noted by a slouching youth facing backward and adjacent to her.

Lacey had picked D.C. highlights from her mental guidebook of sights to see. The National Gallery and the Hirshhorn Museum had moved up the wish list every time they were cited in illustrations as being the home of her favorite paintings. All she had to do was crib some time from the Nathansons to devote to holiday sightseeing in D.C.

The Avery, stowed overhead in the steel-pipe luggage rack, was projecting out just enough to thwack a man on the forehead. Lacey's rifle response, said before she even turned her head—"You can sue me, but I've got nothing"—charmed the man enough that he said, "Is this seat taken?"

"Sit down, father figure."

He was older, professorial. Wearing a suit and tie and crowned with a muss of gray hair. He muttered his name, but Lacey didn't catch it.

"Who's the artist who clobbered me?"

"Milton Avery," she said.

"Milton Avery? That's a big name for such a slow train. Shouldn't he be on the express?"

"I would have preferred it. I don't think the painting cares," Lacey said.

I should tell you now about Lacey and strangers. She loved codgers and coots, truck drivers and working folk, any sort of type that she wasn't familiar with. She would engage them in bars and parks, focusing on their accents and slang, probing them for stories, and the slightest accomplishments, including whittling, elevated them to heroes. The man next to her didn't qualify as a folk hero, he was too well dressed for that, but Lacey liked the opportunity for repartee and felt she could keep pace with anybody.

"How do you know about Milton Avery?"

"I try to be a gentleman of taste, even when it comes to getting clocked in the head." He glanced up and down, taking her in. "What do you do?" he said.

"What do *you* do?" she said.

"What do *you* do?" he said.

"Okay. You outmaneuvered me. I work at Sotheby's and I'm delivering a painting to Washington."

"Oh, Sotheby's. Then perhaps you can answer a question I've been mulling over. Or maybe you're too young."

"Just give me the question."

"How is it that rich people know about good paintings?" he said.

Lacey said nothing but implied that he should continue.

"Well, think about it. How do they have the eye for it? Why is a five-million-dollar picture always a Velásquez or some other fancy name, and not a Bernard Buffet?"

"Maybe you just explained it to yourself," said Lacey.

"How?"

"You said 'fancy name.' Maybe they're just buying fancy names."

"But then a lousy Velásquez would bring as much as a good one. They actually seem to know which one is better. How does a steel magnate or a car dealer or oil baron learn what scholars take years to learn?"

"I'm going to need some train wine," she said.

"I'll get it," he volunteered, loosening his tie. Minutes later, he reappeared holding two plastic cups that didn't bother to imitate wineglasses. Lacey took a sip, "Acheson, Topeka, 1994."

After he had settled in, now using his briefcase as a table, he relaxed deep into his seat's leatherette cushion.

"I see it this way. Paintings," he said, "are Darwinian. They drift toward money for the same reason that toads drifted toward stereoscopic vision. Survival. If the masterpieces weren't coveted, they would rot in basements and garbage heaps. So they make themselves necessary."

She laughed and stared at him with a pixie face. "I must be drunk, because I think I understood you," she said, and cranked her body sideways to better see his pleased response.

The noontime wine wore off just as the train pulled into the station. The gentleman stood, saying, "Lacey, have a great day. You shortened the trip for me."

Lacey, responding with warmth, said, "You too; you have a great trip, too."

Lacey never knew the man's name until a month later when she saw his photo on the inside of the book's dust jacket. It was John Updike.

14.

LACEY ANGLED THE PICTURE into the backseat of a taxi, its corner sticking into her knees because of the drivetrain hump on the floor. She braced it with her palm for self-protection as well as for its own good as the taxi bounced and rattled from one stoplight to the next. The taxi pulled up to a Georgian brownstone with gardens neat and trimmed and a crisp white door with a brass knocker. On the street were laborers unloading party chairs and caravanning them into a side door. She got out of the taxi, and the driver, a vociferous cabbie with a resonant voice who had entertained her by singing the songs of John Lee Hooker, pulled the picture from the backseat. The white door of the brownstone swung open with a faint jingle-bell tinkle, and Saul Nathanson waved with full panic, shouting, "Don't come up the steps!"

So many interpretations. Was he shouting at Lacey, the painting, or the taxi driver? "Don't step on the walkway!" Was the concrete wet? But Saul ran toward them more sheepish than commanding, and they all stayed put.

"I thought by having you bring the picture," Saul said, panting, "that we were taking delivery of the picture in Washington. But it seems to be disputable that this might constitute taking delivery in New York."

Lacey looked at Saul, then at the taxi driver. He pulled his cap back and scratched his head. "Oh yeah, sales tax," he said.

"What?" said Lacey.

"My wife sells jewelry. There's always a sales tax issue."

Saul pointed at the driver with a silent "bingo." "We've got to have it shipped to us from New York by a reputable carrier."

Lacey muttered, "I'm reputable."

"But unlicensed. We've got a questionable situation here. You've got to take it back. It's a difference of almost ten thousand dollars," said Saul.

The statement hung in the air, until the taxi driver said, "You mean that box is worth a hundred and fifty thousand dollars?"

Lacey turned to him. "Who are you, Rain Man?"

Saul was balanced on his toes. "I'm so sorry, Lacey, we tried to turn you around, but we just learned it an hour ago. Here's something for you"—he handed her a folded hundred-dollar bill—"and don't let the painting touch the walkway."

"I'll be a witness," said the grinning taxi driver, implying there could be another tip due.

"I can't even invite you in," said Saul. Then he turned to the half-opened door. "Estelle! Wave hello to Lacey!"

Estelle poked her head out of an upstairs window. "Hello, Lacey. Saul's insane!"

Saul, standing away from them as though the state boundary line ran right down the middle of his sidewalk, pressed the driver. "Could you put it back in the taxi, please?"

"I'm not touching it," said the driver. "It could be an insurance nightmare."

"Well, I can't touch it," said Saul.

"I got it in once; I can get it in again," said Lacey, hefting it toward the still open cab door, as Saul stuck to his side of the imaginary line that separated him from a ten-thousand-dollar tax bill.

The driver was now gliding the taxi around potholes and speed bumps and slowing the car with the gentle braking that he reserved for fares involving infants and the elderly. "Rats," said Lacey. "I wanted to go to the museums, but now I'm stuck with Pricey."

"You can go," the driver said.

"What do I do with Pricey?"

"Check it at the museum, in the cloakroom. There's nothing but guards around there. Safe as a bank."

"Hell, I had it on a train. You're the one who spooked me about how much it's worth. Okay. Let's go to the National Gallery."

The taxi arrived, and Lacey pulled her burden from the cab. She gave the driver a healthy tip, all to go on Sotheby's expense tab. "Thank you so much, O kindly taxi driver."

"Adios, amigo. By the way, my name's Truman," he said. "What time you coming out?"

"An hour?" she answered.

Lacey went to the cloakroom, deposited the Avery, then passed through a security check so lax that she instinctively swung her head back to the cloakroom to see if the Avery was still there.

She wound down the vast interior stairs of the National Gallery. The cavernous entrance had little art to be seen. Only a gigantic, though airy, Calder mobile, swaying from above, indicated that this was an art museum and not an intergalactic headquarters.

With little interest in contemporary art, she headed underground to the west wing, where she speed-walked past neglected masterpieces in the near empty galleries of American art. There was a surprise around every corner: she had only seen John Singleton Copley's 1778 painting *Watson and the Shark* in two-by-three-inch reproductions in books, and the picture, a dramatic tableau of a rowboat staffed with sailors, in waters turned hellish by a circling shark that has just bitten off the leg of a thirteen-year-old boy, stunned her with its monumental size and perverse beauty. *Jaws,* the beginning, she thought.

Lacey later told me that while she was steaming past the pictures,

Watson and the Shark, John Singleton Copley, 1778
71.75 × 90.5 in.

she had a sudden, comic overview of herself in motion. She saw her head leaning forward as she entered a picture's sight lines, her feet trailing. Then her head would slow down while her feet caught up and advanced, so her eyeballs could spend as much time with a picture as possible without retarding her forward motion. Her upper body remained slow and steady, with her feet a futurist blur below.

After twenty minutes in the downstairs picture gallery, Lacey found that her time at Sotheby's had instilled in her a new way to experience a museum. In addition to her normal inquisitiveness about a work, who painted it and when, and a collegiate hangover necessitating a formulaic, internal monologue about what the painting meant—which always left her mind crackling with static—she now found she had added another task: she tried to estimate a painting's worth. Lacey's internal wiring had been altered by her work in Manhattan.

Her acceleration in the west wing meant that she had time to do the same sprint in the east wing. Here, the giant modern pictures loomed over her. Even the Copley was small compared with the antic Jackson Pollock. At first, she didn't catch the phallic silhouettes of Robert Motherwell's *Elegy*, but on instinct her head turned back, confirming, "Oh yeah, a dick and balls." A Rothko offered just two colors, more or less, but it made Lacey downshift a gear to take it in, and an Andy Warhol silk screen of a newspaper headline, which seemed so haphazard after the persnickety detail of the nineteenth-century flower pictures and desktop still lifes she had just seen, left her suspicious and not impressed.

There was a special exhibition of works by Willem de Kooning, and she stopped in front of one showing a female figure as grotesque totem. In the 1950s, de Kooning had aggressively painted women, and in the 1970s, these pictures endured the wrath of feminism. They were regarded as angry, misogynistic depictions of the female as beast: once again, it was claimed, a male artist was on the attack, reducing women to animals.

But Lacey, staring at de Kooning, taking in the roiling flesh and teeth, recognized herself. This painting was not an attack; this was an acknowledgment of her strength. de Kooning painted women not as horrific monster but as powerful goddess. Lacey felt this way about herself every day. Yes, she had a ghoul's teeth; yes, she had seductive breasts, long, pink legs, and a ferocious sway. She knew she had sexual resources that remained sheathed. But one day, when she used them, she knew her true face would resemble de Kooning's painted woman.

She went down the stairs of the National Gallery, heading toward the coat check. There was no line, but there were three security guards

Woman I, Willem de Kooning, 1950–1952
6 ft. 3.875 × 58 in.

talking into shoulder mikes and a smartly dressed woman in glasses, standing next to Lacey's cardboard box, which had been leaned against the marble wall of the foyer. Lacey instantly read the situation. Her first thought was, Oh shit, and her second was, What fun. She then put on her toughest face, graveled her voice, and said, "I think I'm the one you're lookin' for." She turned backward and put her wrists in handcuff position. So far, no one had changed expression, which meant that her comedy routine had bombed.

"Oh, I'm sorry," she said, turning back, "I'm with Sotheby's and I'm delivering that picture. It's a Milton Avery. Here's my card."

The smartly dressed woman spoke: "Do you mind if we open it?"

"Not at all."

Lacey felt a shiver at her fleeting thought that the Avery had been mysteriously replaced with the National Gallery's Watteau and that she would be sent up the river, unable to explain it even to herself. But the guard sliced open the tape, revealing the still pristine picture, while the woman radioed to someone, giving them the date and title and size of the painting. After a moment, the woman said, "Not one of ours. I'm so sorry, Miss... Yeager. I'm sure you understand."

As a guard with paper tape sealed the cardboard back up, he turned to Lacey and said, "Nice Avery."

Lacey stepped into the street, and before she could raise her hand, Truman's taxi sped into view. The window rolled down. "I waited for you... slow day."

"Okay, let's go, Truman. My last tip includes this. The Hirshhorn, please."

Lacey did the same routine at the Hirshhorn. She almost left the Avery in the taxi because she now trusted that Truman was a good fellow and a working-class hero. But a preview unspooled in her head of how she would feel if she came out and there was no taxi and no Truman; so she hauled the picture inside and got an institutionally authorized claim check.

In the Hirshhorn, she sped along with the same gallop as at the National Gallery, racing by masterpieces with her head swiveling. One picture, however, stuck her feet in cement. Painted in 1967, Ed Ruscha's large canvas depicted the Los Angeles County Museum on fire. Devoid of people on the grounds, the museum was shown in cool tones and sharp outline, while flames blew out from behind the building. The picture was so unlike the slash-and-burn canvases of the abstract pictures she had just seen. Those pictures asked for an emotional response. This one asked for an intellectual response. Was this a tragic image or a surreal one? The horror going on inside was unrevealed and only imagined. And where were the people? Then, as she waited in front of the picture for a thought to congeal, Lacey's mental gears cranked down,

Los Angeles County Museum on Fire, Ed Ruscha, 1968
53.5 × 133.5 in.

the questions stopped, and for a moment, her brain stopped churning and she just stared at it.

Lacey glanced at her watch as she headed toward the Hirshhorn's coat check, worried that a kerfuffle over the Avery would slow down her schedule, which now demanded precision. But nothing happened, the picture was retrieved and Truman sped her to the depot for the long ride home.

Lacey crawled into her apartment at ten p.m., still lugging the picture. Her tired body longed for a Scotch, which she poured over ice. She lay back on her bed. Light from the street lamps, diffused by summer leaves, gave her room movement. The idea of the Scotch hit her even before the alcohol did, so she was relaxed at just the taste. Her window was cracked open enough to let in the light summer breeze, and her eyes meandered around the dim room, moving slowly, high and low, from a vase of flowers, across her half kitchen, to a photograph, to a lamp. Her eyes drifted toward a closet door and the Avery that leaned against it. It's here, she thought. Why not hang it?

She unwrapped the Avery with care, more care, she felt, than was given it at the National Gallery, and hung it on the wall. She took a lamp off her chest of drawers and put it on a low stool in front of the

Avery, so that light was thrown upward on the picture from below. Then she lay back again. Without looking, she reached out and her hand landed perfectly on the glass of Scotch.

Would Leonardo's *Annunciation* be as beautiful hanging crooked in a messy college dorm at a party school in Florida? No, not as beautiful as it is in the Uffizi, framed, lit, and protected as the prize it is, while two thousand years of history flow by in the Arno outside. Context matters, but in Lacey's apartment, where nothing exquisite had ever been, where just the two of them looked back at each other, the Avery was the most beautiful thing she had ever seen. This moment was a secret among the Avery, the Scotch, and Lacey, and she saw clearly something that had eluded her in her two years in the art business. In a few minutes of unexpected communion, she understood why people wanted to own these things.

She rescanned the room. Where before she saw a photograph, a kitchen, a vase, she now added an adjective: she saw a *student's* photograph, a *student's* kitchen, a *student's* vase. The painting was an adult object, by and for people with grown-up eyes. This apartment, these things, were instantly in Lacey's past. They were on the way out, ready to be sold or boxed. The Avery had dipped her in an elixir. She wanted fine things, beautiful things, like the Avery. She wanted to grow up, no longer to live like a student. Lacey knew that what she needed was an amount of money that could support her rapidly evolving taste. This need repainted moral issues that were formerly black-and-white into a vague gray, and a dark idea that she had formed in her head as hypothesis now had to become actual.

Lacey called me late that evening. "Oh Daniel. I need you to do me a favor," she said. I agreed because her incomplete explanation made it seem like an adventuresome art world lark. I did not know that, if its nature were ever revealed, this favor would jeopardize my budding career as an art writer.

PART

II

15.

BY 1997, the art market, becalmed over the previous seven years, was beginning to catch wind. A day spent trekking from Sotheby's to Christie's with a lunch stop at Sant Ambroeus on Madison Avenue was a collector's version of the Grand Tour. Increased foot traffic at galleries and auction houses indicated a widening public interest. Prices were now reported in *The New York Times*, and even though I was somewhat acclimated to the art world while writing my fledgling reviews for *ARTnews* or *Artforum*, I was still surprised that no belligerent letters appeared in the paper condemning huge sums spent on art that could be better spent on children's hospitals. The public seemed to accept these sudden escalations with either resignation or glee, I couldn't tell which. I can't imagine that art prices reported around the water cooler were ever responded to with a "That's fantastic"—except the water cooler at the auction houses—and more than likely they were met with a dismissive sniff or complaint.

In the spring of 1997, Lacey sat at her desk, which had not, as yet, a cubicle around it, and saw, through an open doorway to the executive office, a picture leaning on an upholstered easel. It was covered with dark green velour, weighted at the bottom by a brass rod. A hand lifted the velour to reveal a Van Gogh drawing so fine that the only improvement it could make would be to turn itself into a painting. It showed Van Gogh's finest landscape subject, wheat fields being harvested by workers loading wheat into a hay wain. The velour, in place to keep sunlight off the drawing, was lifted only on occasions of aesthetic contemplation or for reasons of commerce. The person doing the lifting was Tanya Ross, and the person doing the viewing, Lacey later learned, was Barton Talley, whose cup was full with equal amounts of notoriety and respect.

Barton Talley's history was part glorious résumé and part rap sheet. He wore pale blue suits and expensive shoes, which were a sartorial trademark. He had a PhD in art history from Yale and had vaulted into fame and position with essays, art scholarship, and charm. After a decade in a curatorial position at the Boston Museum of Fine Arts, he had been let go for using his known and respected expertise to advise collectors on purchases and then receiving gifts of appreciation with dollar signs in front of them. Among the legacy trustees, he was still thought of as sullied.

He then formed a gallery in New York City, Talley, with funding that seemed bottomless, and he specialized in Very Expensive Paintings. He was a rare entity in the art world: a dealer with the credentials of a scholar. Most dealers knew only their own area, and it seemed that dealers in contemporary art knew nothing that happened before 1965. But Talley knew it all, except for the very latest. His familiarity with the ways of the rich, learned during his malfeasant tenure at the Boston Museum, as well as his own financial ease, gave him the clout of equality with international collectors. He never pushed to close a sale, making him the chased rather than the chaser.

Talley didn't like the artificial light in the small display room, so he brought the Van Gogh out to the offices, where ambient sunlight would make any flaws in the drawing more visible. He hovered around Lacey's desk, tilting it this way and that, looking for fading, looking for foxing. Lacey presumed he didn't notice her, but when he said, "A beautiful thing…a beautiful thing," Lacey, at her desk, said, "I do my best."

Talley looked at her, gave her an approving smile for her chutzpah—though neither of them could claim ethnic rights to the word—and then angled the drawing so he could see it under the raking light. Without moving his eyes from the drawing, he said, "Is there a lot of interest in it?"

Looking down at her desk, Lacey said, "There have been three or four people in to look at it, but let's keep that between us friends." Tanya Ross peered across the room at them from behind her doorway but sensed nothing unusual. They were like two spies looking at a sunset while they exchanged top-level information.

That spring, in London, the drawing achieved an exhilarating fourteen million dollars, and the auction room froze for a few seconds of unusual silence after such a spectacular price, before ripping into applause reserved for Derby winners and sports matches. Reports of cheering in the auction room when a painting soared past its reasonable limit and into the unreasonable stratosphere sound like a crass symptom of our age, but auction applause dates back centuries. Auctions were, and still are, spectator sports, where the contestants are money. In the nineteenth century, pictures were wheeled out to hoots and clapping, like boxers entering the ring, and the spectators responded to escalating bids as if they were hard lefts and roundhouse rights.

The Van Gogh represented one of a few stunning prices that had perked up the market in the last few years. Gossip and awe reverberated around Manhattan when rumors of fifty-million-dollar private sales began to circulate. Those overachieving paintings had great names attached to them: Picasso, Renoir, Degas. Prices were beginning to recall the glory days of the previous decade, and Lacey found herself rubbing elbows not only with these mighty names from the past, but with the well-funded dealers and collectors of the present. Sotheby's Impressionist and Modern Art divisions, however, were fully staffed and immutable. No one in this upturning market was going anywhere, and there was no nook that Lacey could be wedged into without popping someone else out from the other side.

Cherry Finch liked Lacey, which also inhibited her transfer from American to Modern Art. Tanya Ross, Lacey's slight superior, did not like her. She perceived that Lacey's genie bottle of charm was uncorked when the Sotheby's elite were on parade and recorked after they passed by. Although she saw this habit as good business sense rather than manipulative evil, Tanya correctly understood that she was the next person up the ladder whom Lacey could displace. So Tanya was attentive when Lacey was called into Cherry's office, and she watched Lacey cross the room, the door closing behind her.

"Do you know who Rockwell Kent is?" asked Cherry.

"Somewhat," said Lacey. "Illustrated *Moby-Dick*, right? Painter too."

"Painter, mainly," replied Cherry. "Not one of the top Americans, but rare. Plus, he had ties to Robert Henri, and the Canadians, Lawren Harris, Group of Seven. Landscape painter, mostly. Greenland was his big subject. Icy fjords with Eskimo dogs in tiny perspective standing by their masters. During his lifetime everyone admired them but nobody bought them. Communist sympathizer, 'man for the people' type. He ended up owning most of his own major works. Then in the fifties, at the worst time for a citizen to be sympathetic to Russia, he snubbed America and donated most of his work to 'the Russian people.' What already looked bad became actually bad.

"Now forty years have gone by and nobody remembers his Communist bent, and people who want a Rockwell Kent *of size* can't get one, and there are about eighty large paintings sitting in Russia, and Russia couldn't care less."

Cherry shuffled some papers, as though she were waiting for Lacey to figure it all out. Finally, Lacey said the only thing she could think of:

"What are they worth?"

November in Greenland, Rockwell Kent, 1932
34.25 × 44.5 in.

"A top, top Kent would bring about four hundred to six hundred thousand dollars."

"Times eighty," said Lacey.

"Not really," said Cherry, "because you couldn't put them on the market all at once, and some are better than others. But placing a few pictures in conspicuous museums, and releasing one or two a year onto the market could be a nice annuity for someone."

Lacey wondered for whom. "But you can't get them out of Russia?"

"That's what we're going to try and find out. Could you meet Barton Talley at his gallery on Monday, around eleven a.m.?"

The weekend was a long one for Lacey. She wondered what possible involvement she would have in the Rockwell Kent endeavor, and she was excited because the request indicated career movement—and not just stolid up-the-ladder movement, either, but a skip-step that put her near the center of the action. At parties, Lacey's fearlessness always guided her to the top person in the room, and her cleverness made the top person in the room believe that he had guided himself to her. But the Sotheby's feeler seemed to come from nowhere, maybe even merit. She figured out that Talley had called Cherry, and Cherry had recommended her for something. What, she did not know.

16.

LACEY NOTED THAT days moved faster when nightlife was involved, so she planned to meet up with Angela and Sharon in Chelsea for drinks. Art galleries populated the area, but Lacey didn't normally frequent them. She was East Side, and the art she represented was understood; Chelsea was West Side, and the art it represented was misunderstood. She had been meaning to go but never did, as her travel in Manhattan was vertical, not horizontal.

Lacey's new dress was, as she described it to me, "schoolgirl with possibilities." She knew that the conservative quality of the outfit set her apart from the other females who stuffed themselves into jeans and four-inch heels on Saturday night and then, after two too many drinks, bellowed in the bar with resonant horse laughs. Her rule for weekend dressing was excess during the day and sophistication at night. After pulling tight her wide patent-leather belt and leaning over and shaking her hair into a perfect mess, after hurriedly sticking blue Post-it notes on furniture in her apartment that she meant to get rid of, she taxied sideways across town to catch a few galleries on their last gala Saturday before the onset of summer.

The confidence that she wore so comfortably on her home turf was less present on the new shores of West 25th Street. She had touched down like an immigrant and hadn't even planned a route. For a moment, in the midst of an active street crowd that didn't need her, she experienced a rare feeling: invisibility. She passed active galleries with wide windows and unmarked entrances, with modest signage announcing artists she had never heard of. She stood on the street and looked down at dozens of galleries from which new art was mined and then trucked into Manhattan residences.

By the time she got to the end of the street, after quick ins and outs, shouldering through crowds for partial glimpses of this and that, she had a movie montage in her head of artworks spinning in an aesthetic vertigo. These objects were not old paintings bound in gold frames like their uptown counterparts; these were free-growing sprigs of wild grass, curving around corners and hanging from ceilings. They were lying on floors, making noise, glittering with mirrors and alien parts, stuck in the walls like spears, and looking at you with human eyes. There were good old college tries mixed in with older artists on the edge. There were blatant messages hanging opposite indecipherable jabberwocky. There was kid's stuff, crass stuff, smart stuff, and porn stuff. There were labor-intensive works that sold for two thousand dollars and flimsy slap-ups that cost thirty thousand. And taking it all in were the muscled, the pretty, the pretty strange, and the thoughtful. Lacey felt like a Martian lander, scooping up dirt samples and having no luck analyzing it. As exciting as the carnival was, the art she saw left her unmoved. It was not comparable to the Picassos and others she navigated around every day, but her addiction to energy kept her pushing on, snaking between Tenth and Eleventh Avenues, down to 20th Street and beyond, until the mood gave way to mundane galleries presenting new art made in the old way.

Lacey met Angela and Sharon at Cointreau, where they sat at the hundred-decibel bar for thirty minutes, until they were shown to a table. Of the three of them, Lacey was the easiest to pick up, Sharon was unlikely, and Angela was impossible. This rule also coincided with their physical appeal, with Lacey at the top, though it was Sharon who was often pointing Lacey toward mischief, like a dare, because she knew Lacey was often up to it. Angela saw intrusions suspiciously and couldn't open up to lengthy chats with strangers at the table. But Lacey was also loyal to girls' night out and never flew away before the evening was officially over. If Lacey met a man she enjoyed, it was she who was the sole determiner of the sexual possibilities, and if emotions were invested, they were his and not hers.

The three of them, well dressed but a mismatched trio of varying styles, made outsiders wonder at the nature of their dinner. Three women who couldn't get dates? Impossible. Each was appealing in her own way. Lesbians? Too easy a guess, the fantasy of frat boys, who were not to be found in the pricey restaurant. The way they talked in animation, leaning forward with palms on the table, stifling giggles that led to champagne hiccups, said clearly that they were having a good time, hadn't seen one another in a while, and were quite sufficient on their own.

In the room was a noted television actor, Stirling Quince, who was forming a collection and hosting fund-raisers. He was in rare company: Larry Gagosian, the powerful art dealer with growing influence reaching to Europe and Los Angeles, whose eye for pictures made him competitive with museums of the world; Roy Lichtenstein, the most congenial of the new old masters, anointed at a time when consensus took twenty years rather than months to point its finger at genius; his wife, Dorothy, the most likable of all the artists' spouses. At the actor's side was Blanca, a Czech model whose body seemed to be assembled from schoolboys' dream bits.

Neither Angela, Sharon, nor Lacey knew who anyone was by sight, except the actor. Yes, he was handsome. Yes, he was smart. Such a man, Angela and Sharon agreed, but Lacey balked.

"A man? He wakes up every morning and goes into makeup."

Angela caught the conversational trend: "And holds a pretend gun."

"And shows his bare ass on TV," Sharon added as she slapped the table a bit too hard.

"His girlfriend is supposed to be smart," said Angela.

"Smart?" said Lacey. "She's supposed to be smart? She *poses*."

When the check came, Lacey reached for it. "No!" said Angela.

"I've got it," said Lacey.

This was not a cheap bill. The routine was that it would be split, as none of them could easily afford to treat except at the cheapest of restaurants. The ease and snap with which she picked up the check had a second-nature quality that said Lacey was not extending herself uncomfortably. Both Angela and Sharon thought this was odd.

On the street, Lacey hailed a cab, and they all bowed low as they filed in. "Driver," said Lacey, "follow that street," and her finger pointed uptown.

"Where're we going?" they chirped.

"I'll show you," said Lacey.

The cab wheeled up to 83rd Street and Broadway and, according to Lacey's exact command, hung a left, meandered over a few streets, and stopped at a corner. Lacey rolled down the window and leaned out, and so did the other two as best they could.

"Look up," Lacey told them.

"What are we looking at?" asked Sharon.

"Count three floors up and look at the apartment on the corner, then count five windows in."

They did and saw a nicely framed window in an old building. From what they could see of the apartment, it was empty, freshly painted white inside, and illuminated by a contractor's light standing in the center of the room.

"It's my new apartment," said Lacey. "I move in tomorrow."

"You bought it?" said Angela.

"Yes."

The girls were stunned. As recently as several months ago, they had shared financial recaps, and both Angela and Sharon knew this apartment was out of Lacey's reach.

"Lacey," said Sharon, "how'd you pay for it?"

"Think of it as magic," she said.

Lacey had come into money not by magic, but by prestidigitation. No one had seen her sleights except her and me, and I was bound to silence by complicity. I was guilty, too, but I did not know exactly of what. Lacey and I had collaborated on a feint—I delivered on the requested favor—for which I went mostly unrewarded, but Lacey had seen hundreds of thousands of dollars come her way. It was her will that brought money to her, and it was my lack of will that kept it from me, so I considered her deserving of this newfound rootless cash. But sometimes money falls like light snow on open palms, and sometimes it falls stinging and hard from ominous clouds.

17.

MONDAY MORNING, Lacey climbed the steps of Barton Talley's gallery on East 78th. She rang a buzzer, looked into a videocam, then pushed on the door when she heard a solid click. She entered what was once the foyer of a grand residence, now painted white and accommodating half a dozen paintings of varying size and period and one freestanding Miró sculpture, illuminated only by reflected sunlight as the gallery lights were off.

There was no assistant on duty, and she faced a carpeted staircase, at the top of which sunlight spilled around a curve of banister. Voices, too, tumbled around from somewhere up above. She stood, not knowing what to do. Then two men in narrow suits and cropped hair appeared at the top of the stairs, talking low to each other as they descended the steps. One of them said to Lacey, "He said to come upstairs and walk back to his office." The two men left, and Lacey thought how in the art world even well-dressed, intelligent-looking men could look like misfits.

At the top of the stairs she entered a hall, unsure which way to go. She looked left, toward the street, to a sunny, blindingly white front room, then right, to a hall that extended back to another half-open door, which she guessed was her destination. She walked down the hall, passing a few offices housing an art library, open books on desks, transparencies leaning on light boxes. She got close enough to the end of the hall to see, through a door cracked open not more than a few inches, a sliver of a painting on an easel, an old master type, of a woman singing in a parlor.

"Not there, behind you," Talley said. She turned and saw Talley silhouetted against the window, waving his arm for her to come the other way. "That way, evil and darkness; this way, goodness and light," said Talley, then added, "We're all in here."

"Thank you, Mr. Talley. I'm Lacey Yeager, just in case—"

"Oh, I know," he said. "Thank you for coming. This is Patrice Claire..." Lacey saw the open-collared European whom she had met briefly at Sotheby's a little over three years ago.

"We've met," she said, recalling a memory that had set firm in her by a feeling of premonition.

"Ah, you remembered," said Claire.

"Ah, *you* remembered," said Lacey.

Lacey sat; they all sat. "Have you ever been to Russia?" Talley asked her.

"It's on my to-do list," she said.

"Well, move it up a few notches. Did Cherry explain about the Rockwell Kent situation?"

"Yes, she—"

"So the Russians have these pictures that they really don't care about, but America does care about. Mr. Claire has some pictures that the Russians really do care about, and we don't care about at all."

Patrice Claire picked up the story. "I collected about twenty nineteenth-century Russian landscape painters through the years. All these Russian pictures are painted tight, very photographic, very realistic, the respected standard for the period. Russian artists never got into Impressionism until it was practically over—"

"Neither did the Americans," Talley interjected.

"Yes, neither did the Americans. A hundred years later they turn out to be unimportant, pretty pictures, but they are still amazing. Amazing light, amazing detail."

"Patrice contacted me with the thought of an exchange, a sort of prisoner exchange," Talley explained, "and I contacted Sotheby's for added clout. The art world wants an opening in Russia, and this could be a civil way to begin. We need an assistant for the trip, someone with an American look and nature, preferably from Sotheby's, and Cherry recommended you. Do you think you might have an interest?"

Not wondering, or caring, whether she was picked as a sexual possibility on a lengthy trip for gentlemen, Lacey said yes.

"We would leave in a week for a three-day trip to St. Petersburg. Many of the pictures are at the Hermitage, stowed away. My Russian pictures are being sent there now. Russia's a bit chaotic these days, so it might be easier to make a deal now than in five years."

The conversation loosened; anecdotes were told about travel, foreign ways, differences between Europeans and Americans, and everyone relaxed. Barton Talley fussed with a letter opener, finally laying it precisely square on his desk, leaned back in his chair, and said, "One night in Paris, I was faced with the choice of flying to the South of France to meet Picasso, or staying in Paris and fucking Hedy Lamarr. I chose to fuck Hedy Lamarr.

"That I would call a mistake."

"I'll try not to make the same one," said Lacey.

18.

WITH LACEY ACTING as passport holder and ticket captain, the three of them landed at the St. Petersburg airport, which had a lonely, neglected quality. Weeds grew in the centers of the runways. Broken-down Aeroflot jets seemed to be parked randomly, but upon closer look, Lacey realized they were not broken down at all and there were rattled passengers disembarking from them.

After a sour-faced customs agent rubber-stamped their papers, they checked into the Grand Hotel in St. Petersburg on a rare hot day of the Russian summer. The hotel was built around an indoor courtyard that was now a mecca for the traveling businessman. In 1997, Russia was "between regimes," and a Wild West lawlessness gripped the major cities. Danger marked the streets, and Lacey had been warned that evenings out could be trouble, and that the food in restaurants could not be trusted. It was wisest to eat only at the hotel and walk no farther than around the block. This made her job as tour guide and car arranger easier. Everything was done through the hotel desk.

Before sundown, Lacey took a jet-lagged stroll in the permitted area. Magnificence surrounded her, but the city was tattered at the edges and had a run-down feeling that affected all the stately build-ings, except for the busy churches. The government buildings were shabby and tired; she could imagine the hunched shoulders of weary Kafkaesque protagonists trudging up their unending staircases. Street vendors sold assembly-line paintings only a few blocks away from the Hermitage, which made the junky pictures seem better by its beatific proximity.

Cavernous government offices had been converted to gigantic marts with stalls that offered household cleanser next to plastic baby Jesuses, and the variety of products from stall to stall was so extreme as to be illogical. The streets were alive, though; the warm day brought everyone out as if to stockpile sunlight and warmth for the battering winter. The people seemed to be of two types only, sculpted beauties or squat beer kegs. Lacey's flirtatious imagination made fantasy contact with a few of these Adonises, but she knew that if she was to sleep with anyone on this short trip, it might as well be one of her employers.

The food plan for the day would be the same for every day: breakfast in, lunch in, cocktails in, dinner in. Tomorrow morning they would be given a private tour of the Hermitage, tomorrow afternoon they would meet with the director, and the next day they would fly home. So they would be three musketeers for the next few days, all for one and one for all, relying on, or perhaps stuck with, one another for camaraderie. When Lacey returned to the hotel, she saw Patrice Claire already in the bar, talking to a man in black. He saw her and signaled her over just as the man was leaving.

"Are you passing secrets?" said Lacey.

"Oh no, just making use of my time here for commerce. How about a drink?"

"I'll have a black Russian...oh, wait, you said drink. Scotch." The joke didn't make it through the language barrier, and Patrice ordered the Scotch.

She slid onto a stool. "So, Patrice, what's with the hair?"

He looked at her, puzzled.

She continued, "You know, what's with the oily look?"

"I am European. It's what we do."

"Maybe forty years ago . . . but come on."

"Anything else you find objectionable?"

"Just the gold chain. And the open shirt. Chest hair doesn't have the same effect on American girls. Oh, and I'll pay for your drink. It's the least I could do."

"I should pay. I'm so grateful for the personal instruction."

"Just thoughts."

"If I don't grease my hair, it's like an Afro."

"No way. Euros don't have Afros. Something matte would do it. Same effect, no shine."

"Now should I criticize your hair?"

"You can't. Unfortunately for you, I have perfect hair. I have hair that women sit in beauty parlors for hours to try and achieve. Natural streaks, natural highlights. I think my breasts are slightly low, so I'm vulnerable if you want to get even."

"Do you get a lot of complaints?"

"No," said Lacey, then flatly: "Oh, my God, it was a trick question."

"Tell you what," said Patrice. "After dinner, come to my room. I'll show you something."

Lacey went to change for dinner. Her "luxury" room, one third the size of a room at a Holiday Inn, had electronics from the 1940s and buttons for valet, maid, and room service, all out of commission. A fat hunk of telephone sat by the bedside. Out her window, she could see the Russian Museum, which she found uninviting. Its repeating vertical windows reminded her of a pair of wide, frilly underpants.

She lay down on the bed for just a minute, and the overwhelming weight of jet lag settled on her. Lying there, unable to lift even an arm, she went into a trance of sleep, waking only a few minutes before the eight-thirty dinnertime. She forced her body to sit up, her head still hanging heavy with double gravity. She sleepwalked to the bathroom and dipped her face in cold water. She looked at herself. Passable, she thought. She bent over to let the blood run to her head, rose slowly, and got dressed.

At dinner, Lacey didn't uncap her wit; she thought it would be inappropriate. She was there to listen. She quietly smiled at Patrice, whose hair was now minus the sheen of whatever it was he had been greasing it with. She understood this dinner could be an opportunity to learn something, and her serious question—do museums often swap works of art—was answered quickly by Barton.

"Oh yes," he said. "How do you think the National Gallery got its Raphael? Andrew Mellon swept in and bought a ton of pictures after the revolution because the Reds thought paintings were bourgeois."

Diners in Russia smoked feverishly at the table, and when Barton pulled one out, Lacey inhaled the secondhand smoke and eventually, wanting the nicotine boost, asked for one herself.

After dinner, Lacey, wrongly assuming her rendezvous with Patrice was a secret, excused herself, said good night, and left. At eleven p.m., only a few minutes after dessert and coffee, she rapped on his door, heard shuffles and voices, and the door was opened.

Patrice invited her in—his room was a suite—and she saw the man in black who earlier had spoken with him at the bar. Patrice introduced him, Ivan something. He spoke French with Patrice, English with her, and Russian whenever he felt like it.

"I wanted you to see this," Patrice said, and gestured to the man, who laid an ostrich briefcase on a table. The man turned the case toward them and opened it presentationally. In the case, against black velvet, was amber. Amber rings, amber necklaces, amber jewelry.

The salesman stood with firm confidence, as if he were getting out of the way of a knowledgeable collector and a premier object.

Lacey sat at the table. "May I?" she said.

"Certainly."

She picked up several pieces, rotating them in the light, seeing fissures in the honey-colored transparent stone that pierced the gem like frozen lightning bolts. Occasionally there was an insect trapped in the petrified resin, which brought a vivid picture of the amber's formation, the slow ooze of ninety-million-year-old tree sap flowing over a prehistoric bug.

"Pick something," said Patrice.

Lacey chose a small pendant, with the amber hanging from a filigreed silver claw, laid it across her neck, and smiled. "It's so lovely."

Patrice pointed to two other pieces—Lacey figured they were for other girlfriends—and the man in black scooped them up with, "Excellent choice. Beautiful, so clear."

Lacey held her pendant, warming the amber to her touch as the two men finished their business. She sensed that the amber jewelry was not that expensive, but connoisseurship mattered from piece to piece.

The man in black left, leaving Lacey to wonder what was next.

"Vodka?" said Patrice.

Ah. Vodka was next.

"Sure." Sounds of pouring as Lacey pinched the amber between her fingers and held it to the lamplight.

"Come look out the window."

She went to the window, which was in the bedroom, where the lights were off. Moonlight and city lights gave the room a blue hue, and the fanciful, spiraling towers of cathedrals could be seen poking up over the top of the city's otherwise rigid architecture. Patrice pointed with his finger, circling his arm around her, resting it on her shoulder. He turned half toward her. Sensing permission, he slid his other hand to her breast and caressed it, to the accompanying crinkle of the starch in her blouse.

"I haven't been felt up since high school."

He said nothing but continued his exploration. There was a moment of unbuttoning, and his hand edged toward her skin, which was becoming dewy from internal heat. He stood there like a boy, holding, cupping, grazing her skin with his fingertips. His lips brushed her neck and shoulder, and Lacey's arm dropped. The back of her hand moved toward his pant leg, where she felt what she expected. Minutes passed without advancement, just a steady state of touch.

They stood at the window, in the darkened room, in the same posture, without an instinct to relocate, her hand exploring him, unzipping, reaching in, to which he responded by lifting her skirt and pressing the back of his hand against her. Their heads were both bowed now, their foreheads resting against each other, breathing in what the other breathed out. Lacey lifted her leg against the sill, widening his access to her. He moved her underwear to one side and his fingers slipped in effortlessly, as though they were being drawn up by osmosis. Lacey reached between her legs, lubricating her hand and moving it over to him. They now understood that they were not moving from the window, that this stance was to be the extent of their dalliance. Their breathing intensified; there were adjustments of their bodies, rings clunking on metal, and shoes hitting walls. Lacey's back rested on the windowsill, and one arm stiffened against the opposite side to hold her firm against his hand while her other hand pulled and pushed on him until the end came for both of them.

Lacey got a towel from the bathroom for the gentle mop-up, and then, their legs shaky from their unbalanced stances, they laid themselves on the bed.

"Whoosh," said Lacey.

"You are a very beautiful creature."

"Well, I'm definitely a creature."

There was an unawkward silence.

"Tomorrow," said Lacey.

"Yes, tomorrow. Tomorrow the Hermitage."

"Are you a dealer?"

"No, definitely not. I must move pictures around only to acquire more."

"You have the collector's disease."

"Not a disease. A disease makes you feel bad. I have a mania, an acquisitive gene. Pictures come through me like a moving train through a station. I only need to own them once."

"Like you owned me tonight."

"I don't think of it that way. You, pictures, two different things."

"Momentary objects of desire." Lacey was cornering him, in a friendly way, and she could tell he was rethinking.

"It's true," he continued, "that both you and paintings are layered. You, in the complex onion-peel way, dark secrets and all that. Paintings operate in the same way." He didn't say anything more.

"Uh. Hello? Go on," said Lacey.

"Well, first, ephemera and notations on the back of the canvas. Labels indicate gallery shows, museum shows, footprints in the snow, so to speak. Then pencil scribbles on the stretcher, usually by the artist, usually a title or date. Next the stretcher itself. Pine or something. Wooden triangles in the corners so the picture can be tapped tighter when the canvas becomes loose. Nails in the wood securing the picture to the stretcher. Next, a canvas: linen, muslin, sometimes a panel; then the gesso—a primary coat, always white. A layer of underpaint, usually a pastel color, then, the miracle, where the secrets are: the paint itself, swished around, roughly, gently, layer on layer, thick or thin, not more than a quarter of an inch ever—God can happen in that quarter of an inch—the occasional brush hair left embedded, colors mixed over each other, tones showing through, sometimes the weave of the linen revealing itself. The signature on top of the entire goulash. Then varnish is swabbed over the whole. Finally, the frame, translucent gilt or carved wood. The whole thing is done."

Lacey grasped his forearm and squeezed it, as if to signal that the extremes he went to were all right with her. They lay there for a while, sounds of traffic in a light rain coming from outside.

Lacey got up. "That was a nice shortcut. I don't have to get dressed." She made a move to the door. "Does this mean I have to sleep with Talley, too?"

"They say he's got a girlfriend somewhere. No one knows who."

"Maybe it's a boyfriend."

"You make me laugh, Lacey."

"We'll see," she said.

19.

THE NEXT MORNING, Lacey sat in the courtyard with her breakfast, and when she saw Patrice turning onto the landing from the stairwell, she opened her legs and lifted her skirt slightly, showing him a flash of polka-dot underwear.

At ten a.m., they got in a limo to take them three blocks to the Hermitage. They stopped on a wide street along the Neva where the side entrance was. The museum was closed today, and they were provided a special tour. Tall wooden doors swung open into a small anteroom, where they were given a brief security check, and a guide appeared—a woman with short dark hair and wearing a worn, ill-fitting uniform—to escort them around. Even though the corridor had layers of green paint that reminded Lacey of her high school cafeteria, the oak wainscoting and interior doors had a mellow patina that spoke of history. They were led up a small staircase that opened onto a stairway of renown: wide, hushed, and grand. Then they stepped into the first room of paintings.

The gallery was paneled and dark—translucent shades over the tall windows were raised only a few feet, pinching off the light. The ceilings soared up twenty feet, Lacey estimated, and on the walls were a few Rembrandts, Ruysdaels, and unidentified, musty masters. All the pictures were dingy and brooding, with ornate carved frames that seemed to foam around them.

"This is the beginning of our seventeenth-century collection," said the guide phonetically.

They stood in the center of the room and circled their wagons, each with a back to the other. Lacey wondered why these paintings, made in a century lit only by candlelight and fireplaces, were so dark. How could anyone have seen them? It seemed that Impressionism should have been invented immediately, not only for visibility, but for cheer.

The guard waited patiently, staring toward the daylight with an expression of having been caught in a stagnant pool of unending time. Talley, looking at a nighttime seascape, whispered to Lacey—because whispering was the voice that the hallowed gallery inspired—"You know what I like?" He pointed toward the seascape. "I like it when the moonlight is reflected on the water." He said this as though he didn't want anyone to hear a thought so mundane, as though it were a confession for his priest, who would no doubt impose penance of the harshest kind. Lacey wondered how this connoisseur, this scholar, a man who dealt in Picassos, Braques, and Kandinskys, could care about moonlight on water, a simple effect used by both masters and Sunday painters.

As they moved on through the Hermitage, the ceiling height seemed to grow with every room. Past Jan Steens and even more Rembrandts and through hallways whose second floors, lined with oak paneling holding entrenched libraries, looked down onto galleries below. The tour was punctuated by the appearances of babushkas, stubby little women who served as museum guards and whose word was law. They stood like garden gnomes, wearing head scarves and peasant dresses, and they lurked in the corner of your eye, giving the feeling that if you looked at them, they would vanish into a hidden passage, moving as if on clockwork rollers.

They came into a large hall, tall, wide, and supremely ornate, with glass vitrines extending the length of the room, containing a vast collection of bejeweled clocks and golden boxes, the result of intense craftsmanship applied to useless loot. The quantity of stuff made the most exquisite reliquary seem inadequate when compared with the even more refined one sitting next to it, and after a half hour spent in the room, their response to this treasury had dulled.

They were then led upstairs, to the highest floors, where the oak paneling was replaced by industrial paint and track lighting. However, there was compensation for this depressing change in ambience. The transition from the lower floors was like being taken from the river Styx up to an ascendant sunrise in paradise. Here hung the Matisses and Picassos from the first decade of the twentieth century, paintings so startling, then and now, that they provided a fulcrum on which twentieth-century art was hoisted. To Barton Talley, being in the presence of these pictures—Matisse's colossal painting of elongated figures the color of red clay, dancing against a turquoise blue sky, and Picasso's Cubist women, painted in dark greens and grays—was like being in the presence of the singular gravity around which the modern art world revolves.

Lacey knew she was seeing something she could not quite comprehend. She didn't feel equipped to appreciate these paintings, but she suspected it was a moment that would acquire meaning as her life went on.

She leaned in to Patrice. "How did they get to Russia?"

Talley, looking over to be sure they were the proper distance from the guide, intervened.

"It seems the revolution developed an eye for pictures. Two great rivals, Morozov and Shchukin, were the only two Russians who saw Matisse and Picasso as collectible. They were fantastic competitors, and each made sojourns to Paris to gobble up as much as he could. They double-hung them in grand apartments, until, of course, the Marxists stole—uh, *nationalized* that which the State would never in a million years have collected." Talley looked around warily, as though he might be shackled at any moment.

They toured the rest of the galleries, the endless Kandinskys and Braques, and every picture was enhanced by Talley's sometimes enigmatic expertise ("Poor old Chagall," he said, not adding anything), until they were exhausted by art and longing for food. They went back to the real world, the busy courtyard of the Grand Hotel, where they ordered American sandwiches and rested up for their afternoon meeting.

At three p.m., they met in the lobby and were taken to the director's office in the Hermitage. The director spoke English and welcomed them cordially. "Did you see our few pictures?" he joked. "Come..."

He opened a side door onto a large library. In the room, resting on the waist-high shelf that ran around the bookcases, were eight large Rockwell Kents, the Greenland pictures, inhabited by sled dogs and

The Bay of Naples by Moonlight, Ivan Aivazovsky, circa 1850
47.6 × 75.2 in.

Greenlanders, ice floes and midnight sun. On the opposite railing were a dozen paintings by the Russians Aivazovsky and Makovsky, landscapes, mist-scapes, and village-scapes, some of size, some small and resting on the floor. Not as magnificent, Lacey thought.

"Russia is getting interested in its own," said the director, and with that ensued a negotiation as tough as a missile crisis under Khrushchev. Lacey sat, pretending to make notes in order to justify her presence. Forty-five minutes later all sides were exhausted, and the result was the same as if one of them had said in the first five minutes, "How about twelve Russian pictures for eight Kents?"

They were offered vodka, and they sat around the center table, eventually laughing and toasting. The director looked up at the Kents. "I'm going to miss these pictures."

"Ah, you spent time with them?" said Talley.

"No, this is the first time I've seen them. I didn't know we had them, but they are quite beautiful. Couldn't be hung here, of course. Next to the Rembrandts and Matisses, they would look like . . . what is the word? Slang for shit."

"Uh . . . ," stammered Talley, "turds?"

"Ah, turds. That's the word I'm looking for. Yes, they would look like turds. What about Kent? Wasn't he a . . . what did you call us? Commies? Wasn't he a Commie?"

"Never quite," said Talley. "It's mostly forgotten now. He's too rare to collect; that's been a problem."

"You want to see something? You want to see something wonderful?"

"We would like to see something wonderful," said Patrice.

The director rose, went to his office, and called out, "Sylvie, bring in the gouache we were looking at."

A minute later, a striking brunette entered the room, so beautiful that Lacey's normal confidence was dimmed. She observed the men's response to this sylph, noticing that Patrice was doing the gentlemanly thing and faking oblivion, while Talley stared at her between neck and knees. She brought in a Van Gogh watercolor and set it on the railing.

"Please, take down the Aivazovskys," said the director. "It's for their own good."

The brunette leaned the two paintings on either side of the Van Gogh on the floor, giving the gouache breathing room. The director turned to Talley. "Do you know this picture?"

The subject was a green boat on yellow sand next to a blue sea, eighteen by twenty-four inches, under glass. "Of course I know the painting, but I didn't know there was a gouache. It's wonderfully fresh," said Talley, standing and examining it. Lacey came close. The signature, "Vincent," made her feel the artist was nearby, that his brush had just lifted off the paper.

There was among them—five of them now—a sudden, communal silence. They stood motionless for several seconds, as though the desire to remain still had coincidentally struck each of them at exactly the same time. These were thoughtless seconds. The object was not for sale, not for trade; it had already ascended. It was for them only, to be seen by them only, as though the artist himself had placed it before them, a holy thing. The object seemed, in this brief encounter, sentient. It sat quietly, and everyone was quiet. It spoke in silence, because that was the language of the moment.

"Well," said the director, "thank you, Sylvie." Sylvie picked up the picture and started in motion, a double whammy of beauty. "It's leaving, sadly," said the director. "We've owned it since the war. We got it from the Germans, as spoils, after they looted us and we looted them back, and we kept it all these years. Now we make nice. Give back."

The director poured another round of vodka as Patrice moved the

Aivazovskys off the floor and back to their makeshift easel. Several Russian pictures had been excluded from the trade, the too small and the too inconsequential. Lacey looked, through affected eyes, at one minor Aivazovsky, lit by reddening sunlight, of moonlight on the water. The Aivazovskys were looking more beautiful to her now.

20.

LACEY UNDERSTOOD the ways of men, but she did not know how clever they could be. That night at the hotel, she walked into the bar and saw Talley and Claire sitting at a table with Sylvie. She could not remember any contact or any efforts made in that direction. It all must have taken place after they left the museum, by phone, which was impossible to use, or by messenger, which was even more impossible to imagine, since she was the travel coordinator and had never run across anyone like a messenger. Lacey, in rare confusion, didn't know whether to join the table, but everyone's eyes met at the same time and there was no other alternative for anyone.

"You met earlier at the Hermitage. Sylvie is one of the curators of drawings," Talley said.

Curator of drawings? Lacey thought. Jesus Christ, she can't be thirty.

Sylvie was a five-language European with a soft voice that was raised only to laugh at stories about rich-world: so-and-so's yacht or a Greek's rowdy behavior at a restaurant that ended in broken plates. All this seemed very cosmopolitan to Lacey. She did, however, remain composed. Lacey wondered if Sylvie had been so beautiful from birth that she didn't know her power was unearned. Like the cooing attention lavished on a three-legged dog.

Talley spoke: "Too bad you have to give back the Van Gogh."

"He's not giving it back. He just likes to say he is."

"He can do that?" said Claire.

"In the new Russia, lies and truth are indistinguishable. He may give it back, but it will take years. We gain years of diplomacy with only announcements."

"Will our deal stick?" said Claire.

"Stick?"

"Will our deal *hold*?"

"Oh yes, it's too insignificant. These deals go on all the time. There's no supervision."

Lacey pried into the conversation. "That little Aivazovsky, how much?"

"What do you mean?" said Claire.

"How much is it?"

"It's worth around fifteen thousand."

"I didn't ask how much it's worth. How much is it to buy?"

"You want to buy it?"

"I might."

"It's twelve thousand."

"That's what it's worth," said Lacey.

"I said it's worth fifteen."

"Same difference. Fifteen, twelve. The same."

"I'll sell it for eleven."

"You have nothing in it. You made enough today that your cost is covered. I'll pay you what you have in it. Nothing."

"Maybe you should pay her to take it," Talley added.

"I'll pay six thousand."

Lacey was doing two things at once. She was letting the table know she was funded and letting Patrice know that he owed her. She persisted: "You don't want to take it back. I can put it in my suitcase."

"I would be doing you a favor at ten thousand."

"You would be doing me a favor at six thousand."

"She's eating you alive," said Sylvie, displaying rapport with Lacey and facility with English.

"I've got ten thousand in it."

"You've got nothing in it. It's all profit to you. I'll give you eight thousand."

Talley, amused, spoke: "You are whimpering and wounded, Patrice."

"All right. Eight thousand. But only if I buy the drinks."

Sylvie laughed, Talley laughed, Patrice laughed, Lacey laughed.

Later, in her room, the phone rang. She knew who it was. She did not answer.

21.

SHE HAD WRAPPED the Aivazovsky in a bathroom towel, wedged it safely in her suitcase, and transported the émigré back to the Upper West Side of New York, where she realized, after sending Patrice Claire a check for eight thousand dollars in Paris, that she hated it. It was half as good as an American picture of the same period, and it did not accomplish in her uptown apartment what the Avery had accomplished in her downtown apartment. This was an eight-thousand-dollar souvenir, the price tag on an exotic and egotistical moment far away. However, it was the most expensive thing she owned, so she hung it in a place of honor in her new flat, where absolutely no visitor, art-wise or not, ever noticed or commented on it.

22.

LACEY'S NEW DIGS brought small quakes to her accustomed way of life. Old friends were now subway rides away instead of around the corner, local restaurants had to be scouted, and her route to work was now on a crosstown bus, which meant that on rainy days she had to dodge slush much more frequently than when she was downtown. However, movie theaters abounded, and bars were classier and friendlier to her new, upscale life. On weekends and holidays, she bicycled down the West Side bike path toward Chelsea, sometimes meeting the girls for lunch, dropping into galleries on Saturdays before work, and on Sundays she circled the entire city of Manhattan if the day was lazy enough and warm enough. Nearby, Central Park grew into an oasis of biking, jogging, strolling, street music, tanning, fashion, summer theater, and solitude. For nightlife, though, she eschewed the Upper West Side and would head below 14th Street on weekends for a taste of rambunctiousness.

Barton Talley had given her high marks, and Lacey was more entrenched than ever at Sotheby's, but the summer was under way. The art world was moribund. Promotions and pay increases were unlikely when there was no money coming in. August made Manhattan bake and stink, and her trek to Atlanta for, she assumed, a last look at her grandmother did not relieve the oppression, as Atlanta was under a tidal wave of humidity. There were solemn moments in Granny's bedroom, but in the living room, there were small, quiet talks of inheritance, and Lacey could gather that with priorities going to her mother and aunts, little would come her way. She was thankful for her own sudden wealth.

Labor Day weekend stretched long and slow, and I met her for lunch at Isabella's on Columbus—at an off time, thank God—when we could sit outside and idle away several hours without guilt of table hogging. Lacey's art knowledge had trebled, and she related the entire Russia trip. My face stayed in a frozen grin while she told me of her liaison with Patrice Claire, hiding my real feeling of envy for the lucky Patrice.

"You know what I think now?" said Lacey. "He didn't fuck that Sylvie person. But, oh well, I wasn't up to a second night of high jinks anyway. Plus, I never have sex on the second date."

"Only the first," I said.

"Zackly," said Lacey. "So, Thursday," she continued, then stared at me.

"Thursday. What's Thursday?"

"It's the beginning of the high holy days."

"What are you talking about?" I said.

"The art season! The art season opens Thursday. Why do you think Barneys stays open on Labor Day? To sell clothes for Thursday!"

I laughed. I was removed from the money side of the art world, but I liked that so much excitement was stirring around a subject I had decided to devote my life to.

"There's a show opening at Talley, Giorgio Morandi. Let's go," she said.

"Jeez, Lacey, and then we hop over to Hirschl and Adler for some real kicks? Let's go to Chelsea. There're about a dozen openings that night."

"We'll get Angela and Sharon to come, too."

I said yes, and then I said, "So...how is...you know, the thing?"

"We are fine," she said. "You and I are fine."

23.

I MET LACEY at her apartment. Wet, robed, mouth full of tooth-paste, she pointed me the few steps toward the living room and then flitted into the bathroom. I looked around. I had never been in a young woman's quarters that bore the appearance of success; the ones I'd seen looked assembled from hand-me-downs and junk stores. Bedrooms, if I ever made it that far, usually held a lonely futon. Lacey was no longer dragging furniture from her past life into her new one. Her apartment, now furnished in Craftsman style, with mica lamps and hooked rugs, contradicted its inhabitant, this girl who was barely tame, whose busi-nesslike demeanor was a curtain she closed and opened.

When Lacey reappeared, I changed my opinion. Wearing a dress that uptown looked smart and downtown looked vintage, I realized she was of two worlds, able to exist in either of them without deny-ing her own personality. She had always had flair, even when she had been struggling. She was the type that would be photographed on the street wearing mud boots by *The New York Times* with the implication that, yes, here was commanding style. Yet this was the first time I saw her that she looked like a woman and not a girl.

Lacey had made mint juleps from a *Times* recipe, and we sat by her window at a small round table, sipping them like two grannies. Her window faced south, which meant that the impending sunset ricocheted down the street, turning windows gold and opaque. Lacey always managed to find her light, though I don't think it was conscious: she looked as beautiful as I'd ever seen her. Then we hailed a taxi to the Upper East Side.

People in coats and ties were milling around the Talley gallery, and on the wall were the minimally rendered still lifes by Giorgio Morandi, most of them no bigger than a tea tray. Their thin browns, ashy grays, and muted blues made people speak softly to one another, as if a shouted word might curdle one of the paintings and ruin it. Bottles, carafes, and ceramic whatnots sat in his paintings like small animals huddling for warmth, and yet these shy pictures could easily hang next to a Picasso or Matisse without feeling inferior.

Lacey scanned the party and instantly gave me a look that said, "What are we doing here?" The attendees were on the other side of sixty, and Lacey, observing the clothing of the men, with their gold-button

Still Life with Wine Bottles, Giorgio Morandi, 1957
12 × 16 in.

blazers, plaid pants, and striped shirts topped with starched white collars, said to me, "Are they all admirals?"

Talley came over to us and gave Lacey an extraordinarily warm greeting, hugging her like an old friend. I suppose the adventure they had shared made them comrades. "Isn't Morandi marvelous!" he said. "Every one is the same and every one is different. I opened the season with him because he is uncriticizable! I'd like to hang him in a room with Edward Hopper and see who could outsilence the other. Lacey," he continued, "if you ever get bored at Sotheby's, call me. I could use you in all kinds of ways." Lacey knew there was no double entendre in Barton's invitation, and she felt flattered.

Angela and Sharon rolled in, looking like dressed-up secretaries, which they were, and I could read on their faces the desire to back out the door, hoping no one would notice. But we corralled them, did an obligatory walk around the gallery, and then were standing on the street in perfect September weather, now officially on the town. I realized we were really on the prowl not for art, but for a party. We took a taxi for luxury and charged into the steaming heart of Chelsea, energized and wearing our best outfits. People spilled out into the streets, and the gallery fluorescents did, too, lighting up the sequins on dresses and other glitterati. The plastic wineglasses were appropriate here, where at Talley's they seemed like a lapse in critical thinking.

The gallery names downtown stood out from the stolid uptown houses: Exit Art, 303, Atelier 14, Deitch Projects, Feature, Generous Miracles, Metro Pictures. Some of the names sounded more like bars than galleries, and there was a parallel. Here, the attractive waitresses were the attractive gallery girls, the macho bartenders had become the less-than-macho gallery guys, and the customers' eyes were ever darting around the room, searching for eye contact. The spaces had the buzz of a noisy restaurant, and there were lots of handshakes and kisses for people who only ran into each other at these events. The art on the walls—or on the floor—was duly noted, but if a cynic wanted to make the case that the art was there as an excuse to socialize, he could.

Our group hit about five galleries, in and out, in and out. There were paintings that were intentionally bad, which was an easier goal to reach than those trying to be intentionally good. One gallery had an artificial flower sprouting out of the ceiling; another gallery's interior was coated with dense wax the color of rosé wine, in which the artist had scratched the names of all his rivals; and another gallery had a robotic machine that either saved or destroyed snapshots according to the whim of the viewer. Some of the art made Lacey laugh, some she admired, some made her turn to me and make a vomit sign with finger in mouth.

One artist with the pseudonym (it was natural to assume) of Pilot Mouse had taken over a gallery and installed...another gallery. We viewers went in one at a time, and inside was a simulation of an uptown gallery, complete with gallerygoers—really guerrilla actors—who walked around and looked at the antique store paintings on the wall. It was, I supposed, a comment on gallery going, though I don't know what the comment was. The actors uttered phrases like "The artist is commenting on the calculation inherent in our society" or "The artist is playing with the idea of dichotomies." These phrases were the smarty-pants version of a car dealer's "This little baby only has eight thousand miles on it and gets fifteen miles a gallon." But Pilot Mouse had created something intriguing: I felt a mental disorientation knowing that everything in the room was fake, including the people, especially having just come from a similar real situation uptown; and after I went back into the real world, the feeling lingered uncomfortably. Lacey reported that she had engaged one of the actors in a conversation about a picture, during which neither of them broke character, meaning that she too had become a fake gallerygoer. Afterward, as we walked down the street, Lacey turned to me and said, "How the hell do they sell that?"

The Robert Miller Gallery had one foot in uptown and one foot in downtown, and his image was that of a reputable dealer who had a good eye and knew the market. We wandered in, ambling through a show of Alice Neel paintings, which to me could qualify as either fine art or a student's MFA thesis show. Lacey separated from us and found herself looking through a sandwich of glass that divided the offices from the gallery. She had noticed a small fourteen-inch-square silk screen of flowers.

"Is that...?" she said to one of the employees as he walked into the office, balancing three plastic cups of wine.

"Andy," he said, letting the implied "Warhol" appear in Lacey's head.

She looked at it again, thinking of the few Morandi still lifes she had just seen, thinking it was Morandi deprived of all its energy, squeezed of its juice, that it was as dead as a thing can be, thinking that it was a joyless illustration of one of earth's wondrous things, that it could hang in a dentist's office. After her years of looking at pictures that were working so hard, here was something that exerted no effort at all. And yet, hanging there on the wall, lit, it looked strangely like art.

We finally left Chelsea, our night of art-looking over, but Lacey was about to confront the problem of Andy Warhol.

Andy Warhol died in 1987 and, surprising many historians and connoisseurs, nestled into art history like a burrowing mole. He inched up in stature, casting a shadow over the more accomplished draftsman and less controversial figure Roy Lichtenstein, and could be referred to by

Flowers, Andy Warhol, circa 1965
48 × 48 in.

his first name only, like Jesus or Madonna. As with them, the reference could be either sacred or profane. As Warhol's prices escalated—some said by canny market manipulation from a handful of speculators—there was a strange inversion of typical market reaction. Formerly, when a masterpiece sold for an unimaginable price, as Picasso's *Yo, Picasso* did in 1989 for nearly forty-eight million dollars, it pulled up the prices of equivalent pieces by the same artist. Then, when Van Gogh's *Irises* sold for an equally unimaginable price in the same year, it pulled up the prices of *all* masterpieces. But when Warhol started to achieve news-worthy prices, the value of contemporary art, including art that was yet to be created, was pushed up from behind. Warhol's presence was so vivid, so recent, that he was identified not with the dead, but as the first nugget of gold from Sutter's Mill. The rush was on.

If Andy Warhol had lived to see his conquest of the art world, his response would have probably been a halfhearted "Oh wow." His artistic legacy is rich, but his legacy as a news item is equally rich. He mastered the laconic interview, never seeming to care how he came off and never caring whether he answered the question. He possessed an indifference that said he was not trying to be popular, which had the converse result of making him popular. When asked once what he would do if he was given a million dollars to make a movie, Warhol replied, "Spend fifteen thousand on the movie and keep the rest." This makes sense, when you remember that one of his early films was a seventy-minute continuous shot of his friend Taylor Mead's ass.

If Warhol had stepped into the Cedar Tavern bar, where all the tough-guy Abstract Expressionists hung out, he would have certainly been beaten up for ordering a milk. The shift from muscled, dynamic strokes of an angry brush, intended to reflect inner turmoil, to slack-armed pulls of silk-screened burlap, intended to pose as wallpaper, meant that the slow evolution of art had been upended. Art was no longer tough-guy stuff.

It was easy to give Pop critical status—there were lots of sophisticated things to say about it—but it was tougher to justify the idea that repetitive silk screens were rivals of great masters. If Cubism was speaking from the intellect, and Abstract Expressionism was speaking from the psyche, then Pop was speaking from the unbrain, and just to drive home the point, its leader Warhol closely resembled a zombie.

If you were older and believed in the philosophy of art as rapture, and didn't expect the next great development in art to be a retreat from beauty and an exploitation of ordinariness, then you couldn't endorse Warhol as the next great master. But if you were young, with essentially no stake in art's past, not caring about the difficulty of paint versus the ease of silk screen, you saw the images unencumbered, as bright and funny, but most of all ironic. This new art started with the implied tag "This is ironic, so I'm just kidding," but shortly the tag changed to "This is ironic, and I'm not kidding."

Lacey had been primed in the old art world, so the leap she was about to make took effort, but her heart was leading her head. The flower picture had piqued her interest, and the next day she slipped out of her office, five minutes at a time, to thumb through the library, turning page after page of Warhols, until her desire for the picture had risen to overflowing. She also checked auction prices on Andy Warhol flower paintings. Made in 1964, they were the least expensive of his significant pictures, rounding out at about fifteen thousand dollars for one of the small ones. She came to the conclusion that if Warhol was about deadness, the flower pictures were the deadest of them all. This was, as far as Lacey could remember, the first time she was affected not only by the object itself, but by its theory.

The next Saturday, Lacey went to the Robert Miller Gallery to check in on the picture. It was no longer on the wall, but she didn't let that bother her; pictures were often moved around at galleries. She inquired about it and was taken into an office where the picture had been rehung. A rep came in, a Ms. Adams, who startled Lacey with her youth, and gave her a pitch on the painting. "Comes from a collector who knew Warhol...in excellent condition...signed by Warhol on the back, which is rare...is approved by the Warhol estate." Lacey was instantly relieved that a problem was solved that she didn't know existed. After some haggling, she bought the picture for sixteen thousand dollars.

Robert Miller came in to congratulate her and meet this unknown new collector. "It's a lovely piece," he said.

"Yes," said Lacey, "it reached out and snagged me."

"I like these rich blacks, and how defined the stems are in the background. It's a wonderful example," said Miller, "and it's got great wall power."

"It stopped me from thirty feet away."

"Don't you love the relationship of the colors?" he said.

"Well, yes, but..." She hesitated. "I guess what I really love is..." Miller hung on his toes and looked at her through her long pause. "I love the way the moonlight is reflected on the water."

24.

IN A COUPLE OF MONTHS, Lacey had spent, quite unexpectedly, twenty-four thousand dollars on art. To feel comfortable spending that much in a short time, one must, I assume, have a multiple of that at least ten or twenty times. That is, unless you are far gone. I think Lacey was far gone for several months, perhaps deprived of oxygen from her long Russian flights. She also must have put forty thousand down on her apartment, and she had been generally liberal with cash at restaurants, and tips flowed like Bacchus's wine. No matter what amount she came into, I knew Lacey was not like a lottery winner who would wind up paranoid and broke, muttering, "It's all gone." She saw every action as bearing a response: every penny spent, somehow, would have a return, if not this year, then another; if not in kind, then in another form. But in spite of this practicality, she also—and this is what confuses me—could be rash. She was rash with people, with her body, her remarks. Lacey had an extraordinary sense of position: who was above her, who was below her. However, she considered no one her peer. She was equally reckless with all. So where was I in Lacey's world? I was, officially, a supporter of Lacey, like Angela and Sharon, told I was great, told I was loved. As she would say, "I need you guys so much."

25.

THE WARHOL QUICKLY displaced the Aivazovsky, which was moved to the bathroom. Having an eight-thousand-dollar picture in the bathroom amused her for about a week, then she thought of possible damage that could occur, including being lacquered with hairspray, bubbled by heat from a hair dryer, or sprayed with steam from the shower, and she moved it to the bedroom. For the next month or so, whenever she passed the Warhol, she felt her head crane toward it, as if it were a kid in a cradle that had to be checked in on, not only to see if it was all right, but for the sake of looking at something in which she had so much invested. She did not check in as one would on a stock, to see how the price was doing, but to see how her emotional investment was doing. When visitors came, if they didn't admire the picture—or worse, didn't notice it—she would think them stupid or confused, and they were moved to the bottom of her list of worthwhile people.

In the past few weeks, Lacey had unintentionally balanced her lopsided art world equation: She now knew what it was like to stand on the other side of a transaction. She had experienced the lunacy that can overtake the mind when standing before its inexplicable object of desire, in this case the Warhol, and she had felt the sudden, ego-driven impulses that spark the irrational purchase, in that case the Aivazovsky. She had, in just a few weeks, experienced buyer's remorse, buyer's rejoice, and the extremes of nervousness associated with first dates and executions. She was now able to put herself inside a collector's head, know that she was treating a blessed illness, and determine the appropriate bedside manner.

One night, she lay on her sofa peering over a book at the Warhol, and she retraced her route toward it, which led her to think about Ms. Adams at the Robert Miller Gallery. She liked that Ms. Adams was dealing with customers, unlike her backroom work at Sotheby's, and thought, I could be her.

26.

BECOMING MS. ADAMS began sooner than Lacey was expecting. The 1997 American paintings sales were listless, even though they were given a small boost with the sale of the remains of the property of Andrew Crispo, an ex-dealer whose precise eye for American art was complicated by his proximity to sordid sex scandals—one a brutal torture-murder—and jail time for tax evasion. In the 1980s, he had sold over ninety million dollars in American paintings to Baron Thyssen, and many of them now hang in Thyssen's museum near the Prado in Madrid. Acquitted of the especially seedy sex murder in 1985 that involved leather masks and mouth-balls, he was also a victim, if one could call him that, of tabloid excess when it was reported that sado-masochistic leather masks were found in his gallery, thus indicting him, at least in the newspapers. The press didn't realize that these masks were the work of artist Nancy Grossman—intellectually distant from those found in adult sado-shops—and unwearable. Crispo had vanished from the art world for years, three of which could be accounted for by time spent in the slammer; but this year he poked his head into a Christie's preview, and it was as though the other dealers in the room were pointing at him, shouting, "Unclean!"

But even as slow sales eroded the glamour of older American painting, there was an unexpected upswing in contemporary sales, and Lacey was still a valuable employee who was making connections with collectors and dealers. When Cherry Finch called her into her office in January 1998, Lacey was expecting good news. Tanya Ross watched her go in the office, watched the door being closed, watched and waited, knowing that if the rumor was true, Lacey would be coming out worse off than when she went in. A half hour later, Lacey had been fired, and she explained why to no one.

27.

IT WAS THE coldest day of February when Lacey flew to Atlanta for Kitty Owen's funeral. This conjunction of dire events was not Lacey's world crashing down around her: her grandmother, at ninety-six, was old enough that it felt as though her death had already happened even before it happened, and Lacey's release from Sotheby's was quiet enough and even accompanied by a vague but believable letter of recommendation from Cherry Finch. She told her family in Atlanta that she was moving to a gallery, which was true—that is, if events that have yet to happen but probably will can be counted as true.

Lacey's parents, Hart and Meg, were intelligent and cultured, two qualities that ride along effortlessly in households where the discussion of art is routine, though it's difficult to tell which is the chicken and which is the egg. The memorial was sensible, held in their living room in the early afternoon, with people speaking solemnly about the departed; a delightful letter was read aloud, written seventy-five years earlier from Maxfield Parrish to Kitty, and the Parrish print was featured over the fireplace. The early dark of the afternoon segued into cocktails after the children were trundled off. Hart and Meg had been the ones to attend to Kitty during her waning years, and the estate was passed down to Meg, though there was a will to be discussed, essentially a dispersal of gifts to friends and family.

As Lacey wandered around the house she grew up in, each bit of décor provoked in her waves of either affection or revulsion. The sixties modern stand-alone record player, bought as furniture and now used only for its radio, repulsed her. It had become an antique in her lifetime and had no mystique for her. But she felt an affection for the old records she discovered still stacked inside it, the ones she had played with microscopic precision, laying the needle in the groove like a skilled DJ. She held the jacket of the sound track to *Xanadu* next to her nose and inhaled it as though it were a madeleine, then removed the disk and saw written on the sleeve in her own hand, "Property of Lacey Yeager, age 10." There were antique dishes and silver plate place settings, there were framed paintings that Lacey now knew were worthy only of a junk shop, there were reproductions of famous paintings that showed her parents' good taste. Their furniture was in the style of Danish Modern: pieces that had never been near Denmark, and had been manufactured in the sixties, one decade too late to benefit from a growing craze for authentic fifties furnishings.

Lacey liked her parents, especially her father, but couldn't trace her character to either one of them. Her father's gentleness made her wonder where she got her mean streak. Her mother was practical, but hardly a prototype for her scalpel personality. Lacey was, however, bused as a child to a tough school. She'd often had to defend her modestly better financial status, exemplified by a pretty dress or lunch box depicting the latest TV fad. The usual options for coping were stoicism or aggression, but Lacey chose another: cunning. It had been cultivated from her childhood reading of age-inappropriate literature, encouraged by her mother and book-learned aunts. In children's literature, the clever foxes were often the bad guys, but Lacey never thought so.

Meg took Lacey into a side bedroom. "Lacey, Mom left a little will."

"I don't want anything," said Lacey. "You keep it."

"No, sweetie, it's not money. She wanted you to have the Parrish print. She said you're the one in the family who looks most like her and you should have it."

Lacey sat on a divan with a look of shock on her face, which changed into a suppressed laugh. "Oh, that is so sweet," she said. "I'll keep it forever; I want you to know that." No one at that time knew that her response, which sounded like gratitude, was infused with relief.

Lacey took the print back to her new apartment and shuffled a few things around on the walls until it finally found a home low on the wall, beside her bed. She poured herself a glass of wine, sat in her sole bedroom chair, and stared at the picture, thinking that she had experienced incredibly good luck.

28.

BY THE LATE 1990s, artists' output ranged from the gigantic to the minuscule, from the crafted to the careless, the thoughtful to the thoughtless. Richard Serra made art measured in tonnage, while Tom Friedman carved his self-portrait on an aspirin. Work ranged from macho to fey, regardless of the sexual preference of the artist.

Pilot Mouse edged into the art scene when he spray-painted black bats on walls and doorways around various neighborhoods. He parlayed these art attacks into money by following Jeff Koons's and Damien Hirst's template—and, incidentally, Rubens's and Rembrandt's: he maintained an art factory. The studio, a derelict warehouse teeming with volunteer assistants, produced paintings and sculpture, and in spite of excoriating critical response, the market responded with cash.

His breakthrough had come when collector Hinton Alberg, the American equivalent of the dynamic English collector Charles Saatchi, swept through a modest downtown show and bought every one of Mouse's paintings. The paintings, in retrospect, weren't that good, but when Hinton Alberg bought them out, they suddenly *became* good. The theory of relativity certainly applies to art: just as gravity distorts space, an important collector distorts aesthetics. The difference is that gravity distorts space eternally, and a collector distorts aesthetics for only a few years.

But this purchase was not what made Pilot Mouse a star. It was a

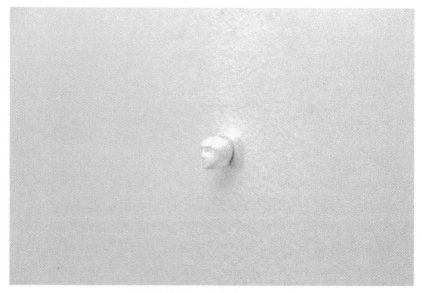

Untitled, Tom Friedman, 1994
.25 × .375 × .375 in.

revelation, made a few weeks later, that guaranteed he would have at least a decade of tenure as an art star. But to explain it, it is necessary to know a little bit about the eccentricities of Hinton Alberg.

Alberg was a collector with a quick purse, which delighted those on the receiving end of things. He donated to the most offbeat art functions, as well as to MoMA, Dia, and the Whitney, and therefore had made himself essential to the goings-on of New York art culture, both newfangled and old established. He had a body shaped like a bowling pin and would sometimes accidentally dress like one, too, wearing a white suit with a wide red belt. His wife, Cornelia, was thin where he was wide, and wide where he was thin, so when they stood side by side, they fit together like Texas and Louisiana. There was always a buzz when he entered a room, a buzz that could be described as negative.

There was a certain unfairness to the bad buzz because Hinton Alberg had at least a sense of humor where his collecting was concerned.

"I went to the Basel art fair last year. Before I left, Cornelia told me to try to slow down. " 'Don't buy everything, honey,' she told me. I told her, 'Darlin', don't you know I'm a *crazy man*?' "

He described his overstuffed warehouse, where he stored his paintings, as either "a junkyard with gems or a gemyard with junk." But he was shy, too, so word of his humor did not leak into the main body of art society; and there was a disdain for his wealth, which was rumored to come from Cornelia's old Detroit money.

Hinton probably had many quirks, but one was highly visible to everyone in the room. He did not drink or abuse himself with anything except food, but he had cultivated or inherited an extraordinarily developed sense of smell, which meant that food was not only devoured but inhaled. Before each meal, he leaned into his plate, sometimes putting a napkin over his head to create an aromatic bell over the food, and took deep, elongated sniffs. From across the room, it looked as though Oliver Hardy had fainted into his food. This exercise was not limited to the entrée, but was employed at appetizer, dessert, and whatever else might appear. It was considered disgusting when a plate of hors d'oeuvres was passed around standees at a cocktail party and Alberg's nose was suspected of grazing the delectables. Once, it is said, he entered a town house off Madison and sniffed the underside of an antique Italian table.

After Alberg bought out the show, Pilot Mouse released the news that when he learned Alberg was coming to the gallery, he came in, took down every painting from the wall, turned them backward on the floor, and daubed the stretcher bars with light touches of truffle oil. He then rehung the pictures. When the story broke, Mouse spoke to *The New York Times* on the phone, saying that he was mocking collectors who bore the smell of money, by making paintings with an odor that was best discerned by a pig.

This comment made Pilot Mouse popular.

29.

BARTON TALLEY HIRED LACEY. She was now the first person a client might see after the receptionist. She was allowed to quote prices, but only after she had judged the client not worthy of Talley. This was a shortcut to success, because what she had learned at Sotheby's was that the Known don't always buy pictures; it was often the Unknown who converted from lookers into unexpected buyers. She had to bone up on a new set of artists, this time ones with famous names: Renoir, Modigliani, Balthus, Klee. The bins, unlike those at Sotheby's, were upstairs, at the end of a suite of offices, and sunlight dribbled in. She had space in one of the many alcoves, even had a private computer. Downstairs was a dimwit receptionist, Donna, who paged her for almost every question that needed answering.

There was less to do here than at Sotheby's. Three or four pictures a month came in or went out. There were shows built from inventory, like "Renoir and His Peers," which needed only one Renoir to ten works by anyone else who had been alive at the same time. "Works on Paper" meant anything that was on paper, regardless of theme or era. Talley also mounted the occasional miniblockbuster, all Giacometti, all de Kooning, some of the pieces borrowed from museums, some from collectors who swore their pieces weren't for sale but who would succumb to an extravagant offer that came after Talley suggested to a client that the owner was reluctant to sell. In fact, Talley did an extensive trade in pictures that weren't for sale, because he understood that anything was actually for sale at some price, and it could be harder to sell something that was for sale than it was to sell something that wasn't for sale. At least in the art business.

Lacey got used to being the front man—attending cocktail receptions, greeting clients—and found she had suitors. Too many repeat visits by a young man asking prices and wanting to be shown other pictures meant that Lacey was the draw, not the art. These were not downtown guys who wanted to fuck her and whom she wanted to fuck back. These were men with jobs who wanted to take her out to dinner and "see if it worked." They wanted to put their best foot forward, which often meant that she couldn't intuit who they would be when the courtesy stopped. The young men downtown were always clearly broke; the men uptown could pay for dinner on credit cards, but maybe they were broke, too.

The downtown men were tolerable because Lacey always viewed them as short term. The uptown men were intolerable because they were presenting themselves as long term. And there was always something fishy about them. She knew what a struggling artist was, she knew what a deejay was. But what was someone in finance? Her worst dates were those on which the other party tried to explain what he did, which was usually prefaced by "This is really boring, but..." and then the explanation would be reeled out in detail. Once, Lacey responded, "You lied when you said it was boring. You should have said it was beyond boring."

There was also a humor gap. Lacey's own wit seemed to blunt itself for lack of response. She thrived on feedback and interplay, but her lines and sparkle seemed to tumble off a cliff before arriving at their destination. The simple problem was that when she was "on," it was a one-man show, and when she was "off," she didn't like herself. But she also knew that her downtown boyfriends were like her downtown furniture: in

117

need of upgrade. So she viewed time spent in the land of the normal as an investigation into the world of marriage-worthy men, even if she was unsure about her own interest in marriage. There must be one solid citizen who also had a spark of life, a sense of humor and adventure.

Lacey was becoming known as an up-and-comer, and her release from Sotheby's was perceived not as a firing, but as conventional art news: who was moving from what gallery to where. People did it all the time. In fact, her position at Talley was seen as a promotion of sorts, and stories about her, stories of audacity, were transmitted along the strands of spider silk that connected the art world.

30.

BARTON STOOD in the middle of his gallery while two art installers stared questioningly at him. He called to Donna, "Please ask Lacey to join me in the main gallery."

Lacey, as if from the ether, said, "I'm standing right behind you."

Barton turned. "Oh," he said. "What do you think? Hang it here?"

"Yes, but it needs to come up a foot."

"You think?"

"Too low," said Lacey.

"Up ten inches," Talley said to the installers. "And Lacey, I donated, unwillingly, to the new Institute of Contemporary Art in Boston. Sunday there's a benefactors' party, but it's, shall we say, 'open' to the Boston Museum board, an entity I'd like to avoid until its current members are dead and replaced with bright, shiny new ones. I think I should have someone there. Can you put in an appearance for me?"

When Talley was unavailable or too tired to show up at the latest cocktail party, he sent Lacey as a rep, because he believed a rep was essential, and a pretty rep had an effect beyond his own venerable powers.

31.

THE DELTA AIRLINES commuter plane to Boston was like having a private jet on call. It left every hour, no reservations necessary, and a ticket could be bought from a machine, so there was very little waiting in line. It returned every night up until eleven p.m., so Lacey could be home in bed by one a.m. She certainly would be given a little grace to arrive late to work the next day, but she preferred to show up on time because otherwise Donna would be in charge and might burn down the place.

She laid out three outfits for the trip: one for the plane ride, one for the evening cocktail party plus boring speech, and one for the next day's trip home. Lacey never chose comfortable clothes for travel, unless it was coincidental, as her instinct was to look at least cute at all times. Naked or well-dressed, was her dictum. And because she was feeling a strong rise in her libido and couldn't foresee a sexual circumstance in Boston that would be appropriate or wise, she reached in a bedroom drawer and selected a vibrator, in this case the one that looked least like a vibrator so she could pass through the X-ray without a glance or wink coming her way. She sometimes used one to promote sleep, although it usually woke her when it finally rolled off the bed and banged on her wooden floor.

Lacey's solo entrance into Boston was less important than Christ's entry into Jerusalem, but not to Lacey. She was a certified representative of a major gallery in Manhattan, and Boston was an outpost of Manhattan that needed to know about her. Lacey had misread Boston as simply a tourist town, but even a short walk from her hotel on this spring day gave her chills of patriotism. She passed the Old North Church and then found herself standing in front of Paul Revere's house. She could feel the immediacy of its revolutionary citizens and the clashes that stirred the community and evolved into legends. Lacey was, in a surprise to herself, moved.

She went back to her hotel for a nap and primp before the evening's cocktail party, but the nap was replaced by a session with a guidebook, in which she read the relevant entries about what she had just seen.

∾

Lacey took a last look at herself: her hair, fuller and longer than usual and still variegated blond even though summer had long since been over; her skin, white against the blue wool of the business suit she had purchased and had fitted just for the trip; and a pair of absurdly high heels on which she was still learning to navigate. Her final swing toward the mirror was one of those moments in a woman's life where she thinks she looks more beautiful than she ever thought she could.

No rain or wind meant that Lacey could walk to the event in Boston's Back Bay without risking a disturbance to her appearance, and it took her only a few yards to find her balance atop her spikes. She stood outside the ICA, a foundation that, if tonight's fund-raiser helped, would be relocated to wider and whiter corridors on Northern Avenue. The current building was too dowdy and cramped to house the needs of contemporary art, which was becoming more hungry for space almost daily. Lacey planned an early arrival so she could familiarize herself not only with the surroundings, but with the guest list. There was a foyer with a table hosted by two young men guarding what Lacey guessed were gift bags to be distributed at evening's end. On each bag was an envelope with a name. There was also a pay phone in the foyer, and Lacey, in a fit of inspiration, went to it, entered in her credit card information, and called Barton Talley.

"It's me."

"Where are you?"

"I'm in the lobby of the ICA."

"Good..."

"And I can see the gift bags for every guest. With names."

"Read them off."

"Mr. and Mrs. Donald Batton."

"Ignore."

"Shelby...something...Fink?"

"Frink. Ignore."

"The Whitzles."

"Oh, my God, run for your life."

"Gates Lloyd."

"Huge collector. Don't ignore."

"Ms. Tricia Dowell."

"Don't mention my name."

"Hinton Alberg."

"Big collector, don't ignore."

The list went on, and Lacey did her best to remember the important ones. As the party expanded to the elite fifty, she introduced herself, was chatty with almost all, and ignored only the most dangerous. Even though she was by far the youngest person in the room, her prettiness was unthreatening because she used it so subtly. She latched on to one group, introducing herself enthusiastically with, "Boston is *beautiful*...I had no idea it was so art-friendly. Hello, I'm..." From this group, she would gather information about another group ("The Frinks are restoring a home on Beacon Hill..."), then walk over to the

Frinks and say brightly, "I heard you're restoring a home on Beacon Hill. That is so exciting!" The Frinks would bestow on her another tidbit, and thus she made it around the room like a square dancer, changing partners when a new bit of information was called out. When asked where Barton Talley was, after she explained her presence, she would say, "He's in Europe."

Droopy canapés were passed around by volunteers, stopping only when a man clinked a glass with a spoon to quiet the room. Everyone halted where they were, and Lacey found herself standing next to a rotund man in brown and his big-haired wife. The man who had clinked the glass spoke with the ease of a natural-born fund-raiser: "Because of you, the ICA is in position to go forward with our grand plans..."

Lacey stood listening, wondering if she was in the best group. She spotted a few married men looking over at her, then noticed the rotund man signaling for canapés. A young woman brought them over, balancing a tray on her open palm, offering a paper napkin with the other. The man bent over the tray, took a whiff in the shape of an S, and then selected one, then two, then three. The tray was offered to Lacey, and she leaned over, took a whiff of similar length, and selected only one. The man looked at her, wondering if he had found a compatriot or a satirist, and Lacey said, "I'm with you."

Cornelia Alberg leaned over to Lacey and said, "You have a friend for life."

After the speech, Hinton and Cornelia Alberg introduced themselves. Lacey was a perfect art crony for them. The Albergs collected contemporary and Lacey sold modern masters, two very different fields, so there was no feeling that Lacey might have ulterior motives; but here was a person, they thought, who should be converted to the new. Yes, they knew of Barton Talley, "marvelous eye, marvelous eye."

"But," said Lacey, "he deals in modern."

Alberg puffed up, and a big grin spread out across his big face. "But we love it all! Lacey Yeager, we love it all!"

Cornelia looked at Lacey and, erroneously, saw herself at a younger age. "We're having a private tour of the Isabella Stewart Gardner tomorrow, why don't you join us?" she said.

While Lacey was hearing Barton Talley's voice in her head saying, *Hinton Alberg, don't ignore,* her own voice was speaking: "I would be thrilled."

She walked out of the event, mingled with a few people who stood outside with drinks, and started her walk home. She was approached by two men—Lacey thought stealthily—who seemed to have been waiting for her. They were not more than thirty, wore suits and thin ties, and one said, "Excuse us, Miss Yeager?"

"Yes."

"You work with Mr. Talley?"

"Yes."

"Sorry to disturb you, but we were told you could deliver this to him."

He pushed a small manila envelope toward her. Lacey thought the men seemed oh-so-American, like handsome heroes in adventure movies.

"Yes, I could."

"It's important, and fragile, if you don't mind."

"I'll take care of it." And the two men left.

That night, after placing the envelope in the safest part of her bag, Lacey bent back her guidebook pages that referenced the Isabella Stewart Gardner Museum. Isabella Stewart Gardner was a grand dame *terrible* of late-nineteenth-century Boston who inherited an inexhaustible fortune and spent as much as she could on art. She built a Venetian fantasy palazzo in demure Boston and, to fill it, began an art sleuthing partnership with the scholar and quasi-dealer Bernard Berenson.

Berenson located and authenticated masterpieces for her that were then spirited out of Europe, sometimes disguised as worthless antique store paintings. This was at a time when "spiriting" was a polite word for "smuggling," but also at a time when nobody cared that much.

The house was three stories high and surrounded a courtyard filled with exotic plantings, Moorish tiles, and ivory carvings. Gardner dedicated it not only to the housing of art, but to concerts, salons, lectures, and company of the bohemian kind, creating a lively and, presumably, stimulating life for herself.

Lacey met the Albergs, now with their son Joshua along—perhaps this was the purpose of the invite?—at the front of the Gardner Museum at ten a.m. Joshua, who was a very young twenty-six, and Lacey, who was an old twenty-eight, recognized each other as compatriots. His parents, longing for a romantic match, failed to recognize their son's guessable homosexuality and Lacey's need for much more varied sexual intercourse before marriage. The parents' illusion of their compatibility was strengthened by the excited squeals of gossip between Lacey and Joshua, which passed for romantic spark.

They were greeted at the door and checked through a metal detector, which Lacey thought was extreme thoroughness given the status of the Albergs.

A guard led them into the dizzying grandeur of the house, which was dark even on sunny days. They were met by a docent who necessarily had to stay with them for the tour, and when the docent asked if there was anything they specifically wanted to see, Alberg replied, "Sargent."

"Sargent?" Lacey said to him. "How do you know about Sargent?"

"I know about Sargent because my father owned one."

"Still have it?" was Lacey's autoresponse.

"That's the dealer in you. Long gone, sorry to say."

At the end of the wide corridor, she saw a painting so familiar that it made her gasp.

"Look at this," said Alberg. "If my knees weren't bad, I would kneel."

In front of them was Sargent's *El Jaleo*. At almost twelve feet long, it had not been imagined by Lacey to be so monumental, and she felt now that as she approached it, the picture would engulf her. A Spanish dancer, her head thrown back, an arm reaching forward with a castanet, her other hand dramatically raising her white dress, steps hard on the floor. Behind, a bank of guitarists strum a flamenco rhythm that is impossible for us not to think we hear, and one hombre is caught in midclap, a clap we finish in our minds. Another is snoring. The scene is lit from below, as though by a fire, throwing up a wild plume of shadow behind the dancer. The frenzy and fever of the dance, the musicians, and the audience are palpable.

In Lacey, the picture aroused her deeper hunger for wild adventure

El Jaleo, John Singer Sargent, 1882
93.375 × 138.5 in.

126

that could not be fulfilled by a trip to Boston in modern times. She longed for wanton evenings spent in a different century, her own head tilted back, flashing a castanet and a slip of leg, and sex with young men no longer among the living. Just then, Joshua leaned in to her and whispered, "That dress is fantastic."

Hinton spoke: "The amazing thing is, Sargent painted this in his Paris studio *from memory.*"

"Mr. Alberg...," said Lacey.

"Mr. Alberg?" replied Mr. Alberg. "Who's that? I'm Hinton."

"How do you know all this?"

"Honey, I told ya, I love it all."

Cornelia jumped in. "He's had more collections than the IRS."

"So why do you buy contemporary?"

"This stuff," he said, waving around the room, "you can buy one, maybe two every other year. Too rare. Contemporary is cheap. I can buy all day. 'Collector' is too kind a word for me. I'm a shopper."

The group marched up the stairs, which were lined with tapestries, odd birdcages, and furniture that, though authentic and valuable, was also grim and sullen. Through the low-slung hallway, they came into a room with soaring ceilings, again lightless except for courtyard windows stingy with the amount of rays they were letting in. They saw Sargent's portrait of Mrs. Gardner, a picture that looked as though the artist wanted to do something wonderful for the enthusiastic patron but couldn't. It suggested there might have been a wee lack of sex appeal about Mrs. Gardner, because if it were there, Sargent could have painted it. Perhaps she commissioned the portrait, longing to look like Sargent's exotic Madame X, but it's clear that she lacked the X factor.

Lacey stepped back from the picture and looked to its left. "Did she collect frames?" she asked.

"No, no," said Alberg. "Sadly, that's where the Degas was. They kept the frame hanging empty as a kind of memorial."

"Stolen?"

"Don't you know about this?" He turned to the guard. "When were the pictures stolen?"

"In 1990, sir."

"How many?"

"Thirteen, sir."

"They never got them back?" said Lacey.

"Never found them," said Cornelia. "They tied up the guards at gunpoint. There're empty frames all around this place. Vermeer, Rembrandt. I always find it sad to come here."

On the way out, they gave Lacey a brochure of the collection, and she put it in her overnight bag, stowed in the coat check.

"Got time for lunch, Lacey?"

"I'm trying to catch the two o'clock."

"Good. The way Hinton eats, there's time," said Cornelia.

"I don't eat that fast," Hinton protested.

"Remember the bag of marshmallows? I turned my back and they were gone."

"That's unfair. I put four of them in my pocket for later."

They stopped in a Boston chain restaurant, high up the chain because it was pretty good. Hinton got the waiter on his toes with, "We gotta catch a plane," then he leaned back in his seat and looked at Lacey. "Tell me," he said, "do you know who Pilot Mouse is?"

"If I didn't, I couldn't be in the art business."

"I've got nine of them I want to sell. Talley could sell them. Do you think he'd be interested?"

"Well, that's not his area, but—"

"That's the point. I don't want them 'on the market.' Quietly, to clients who aren't downtown every day. I want them to go to Mexico, Europe. Those are Talley's clients. I don't want it known I'm selling them."

"I know that Mr. Talley..." said Lacey, making up facts she hoped were true, "...has many clients who buy both modern masters and contemporary. He's perfect for this."

"He can keep it secret?"

"Have you ever heard gossip of any major sales by Talley? They're always discreet. I work there and I don't know anything. I didn't know who you are."

Lacey boarded the plane feeling she had impressed two men. One was Hinton Alberg, who had plucked her like the one bright rose from a monochrome Boston garden; and the other was Barton Talley. Not only had she ignored those to be ignored and attended to those who needed attending, she was returning with a consignment from one of the most freely spending collectors on earth.

32.

LACEY CHECKED IN at the gallery late Monday, stopped by the front desk, and asked Donna if there were any messages.

"Yes, one from the Goodman Gallery and one from Patrice Claire."

"Were the messages for me or Mr. Talley?" she said, hiding her exasperation.

"I'm not sure."

"Did Mr. Claire ask for me?"

"Yes, he did."

"Did he leave a number?"

"He said he's at that hotel...down the street?"

"The Carlyle?"

"Yes."

Impeccable and expensive, the Carlyle Hotel was art central. Its tower stood over Madison Avenue like a beacon. Buyers and dealers came to the Carlyle from around the world, but they were social pikers next to the princes and princesses, presidents, prime ministers, and mysterious international travelers who amassed there, and who thought nothing of paying sixteen dollars for a glass of room service orange juice and who didn't blink when the occasional actor crossed the lobby wearing jeans and a headband. Ursus Books was on the second floor, dealing exclusively in art books and rare editions, and was the place to go to buy the thirty-three-volume *catalogue raisonné* of Pablo Picasso at somewhere around fifty thousand dollars, which all Modernist dealers had to have, whether or not they ever opened it again. Across the street was the Gagosian Gallery, about to expand vertically, horizontally, and internationally. Up Madison was Sant Ambroeus, the flawless Italian restaurant where dealers gathered at feeding time. When Larry Gagosian, the champion art world muscle-flexing aesthete, and Bill Acquavella, the connected and straight-shooting dealer in Impressionists and beyond, were at their separate tables, the place had a nuclear afterglow. The rivalry between the two was friendly, since officially they dealt in different corners of the market, though temperatures could rise to boiling when their merchandise overlapped. Picasso was implied to be Acquavella's, and Cy Twombly was implied to be Gagosian's, but what if some Saudi prince wanted to swap his Picasso for a Twombly? Star wars.

"Is Barton upstairs?" said Lacey to Donna, who sipped coffee with no steam coming from it.

"He left. But he said for you to call him."

Lacey turned toward the stairs. She remembered the first time she'd climbed them, before her Russia trip. Like an echo, one that reverberated with memory rather than sound, she recalled that the two men who handed her the envelope in Boston were the same two men she had passed one year ago when she came to the gallery for the first time. She paused, her eyes downward, letting the memory come back fully. Then she moved up the stairs and into her office.

Lacey called Barton at home, but there was no answer. She left a message, then called the Carlyle and asked for Patrice Claire.

"Oh, Lacey. I'm in town. Let's have a drink. Where are you?"

"Hi," said Lacey.

"Oh yes, hi. The Kents have done well. Let me buy you a drink."

"Not dinner?"

"I thought you hated me or something," he said.

"Hate can be so fleeting."

Patrice hesitated, trying to interpret her. "Well, good. Drinks and dinner. Where are you?"

"I'm at the gallery."

"I'll meet you there and we'll walk to Bemelmans and see where we end up. It's beautiful out."

Lacey consented and hung up the phone. She reached in her travel bag, took out the small envelope, and set it on her desk. She unpacked an outfit from her trip and stepped into it, changing her underwear and bra, too. This was a sudden fix-up that worked. Her hands went to the side of her head, and she raised and lifted her hair, fluffing it outward, making her look like what she was: reckless.

She walked the envelope down to Talley's office and set it on top of his desk. A Matisse hung on one wall, a Balthus drawing in colored pencil of a young girl hung on another. The Matisse was sublime. It was an unreal thing, a windowsill still life with the colors in the wrong places, where flowers were black, and trees were blue, with a pink sky above a floor that was plum purple; and it was, incidentally, a painting at the impossible end of Matisse prices. The picture was being encroached by a harsh streak of sunlight, so Lacey canted the blinds.

The Matisse seemed to respond to the decreasing light by increasing its own wattage. Every object in the room was drained of color, but the Matisse stood firm in the de-escalating illumination, its beauty turning functionality inside out, making itself a more practical and useful presence than anything else in sight.

Lacey retrieved the envelope from Talley's desk, because now she had plans for that desk, and walked back to her own office. She picked up the intercom, almost saying "Dopey," but she caught herself in time. "Donna, you can go home. There's nothing to do here now. I'll lock up."

"Should I set the alarm?"

"No," Lacey said, "I'm still inside. I'll take care of it." Lacey put the small envelope back in her purse.

She watched from the window until she saw Donna leave, then walked to a drawer in Barton's office and pulled it open until she could see bottle tops. She picked out a vodka and made herself a drink, meaning she poured an inch into a glass without a mixer or ice. Then she drank it down.

It was twenty minutes before she looked down and saw Patrice Claire's head at the gallery door. She buzzed him in and met him in the downstairs gallery. Patrice's hair was now straight, combed back over his head, his collar was buttoned higher than his chest hair, and he appeared to have undergone a stylistic transformation.

"Bonsoir, Lacey!"

"Bonsoir, whoever you are."

"You like my new image? I took a look around me and cleaned out the closets."

"How's it working?"

"Fewer European girls, more American girls."

"Good for you."

"I'm joking, Lacey. I've been all over. Europe, Brazil, Mexico. But I still remember Paris."

"It was Saint Petersburg."

"To me it was Paris."

"Patrice, you can also lose the winking."

Patrice peeled off to look at the walls. "Nice Gorky drawing. Hard to find. You still have your Aivazovsky?"

"Neatly in place."

"Barton here?"

"Nobody's here."

"Just the three of us?" asked Patrice.

"Three?"

"You, me, and crazy you," he said.

"You want to see something great?" said Lacey.

"Absolutely." He knew she meant a painting.

"You won't mention it to Barton?"

"I never mention the surreptitiously viewed thing."

She flicked off the downstairs lights, leaving on one ghost light in the back gallery.

Patrice kept his eyes on Lacey as she led him up the stairs. "We sold a Kent in Canada. Sold one in New York. One to a dealer here," he told her. "Our Russian trip was successful."

They turned into the upstairs hallway, toward the office. "You want something to drink?" she asked him as they entered. She set the rheostat to half, spotlighting the Matisse.

Patrice stopped at the doorway. "Oh, that's so nice," he said.

"Vodka? Is it calling you?"

"Yes. Vodka. Thanks."

Lacey poured, got ice from a small refrigerator, handed him his drink, and leaned back on a bookshelf while Patrice stepped around the room, looking at the picture, farther back, closer, farther back. "Nice condition."

It was dark outside now, and Lacey had decided she wanted to have sex under the Matisse or thereabouts. Things slowed a bit as they looked at the Balthus, a sexy image that became officially unsexy when the age of legal consent started to settle in America's mind. They had second drinks, and Lacey sat on the sofa opposite the picture.

"I don't know where to look," said Patrice, who was starting to get the idea. He moved toward her. "You're moving up in the world, Lacey."

Lacey shrugged it off as if it hadn't even been said. He started to speak again, but she put her finger to her lips. "Shh. Lights," she whispered.

"Lacey, let me take you to dinner first..."

She stared at him. He continued, "All right, I'll take you to dinner after."

He walked over and pulled her up from the sofa. His hands ruffled her clothes as he felt all around, finally raising her dress, his palm on the back of her leg. He moved her over to Talley's desk, then pulled down her underwear, and Lacey stepped out of it. He sat her on the desk and slid down the length of her body until he was on his knees, his head pressed against her skirt. Slowly he lifted the cotton fabric until his head was between her legs. With a deep breath, Lacey leaned back, and, stiff on her arms, spread her knees by inches. Patrice's hands were on her thighs, his head now covered by cloth. She raised her eyes and saw the Matisse. She pulled up one leg, hooking the heel of her shoe on the desk, and she stayed in that position until it was all over.

There was a lot of neatening done to Talley's office. Lacey tried to get herself back together, but it had been a long day for her.

"Patrice, let's go to dinner now. I flew in from Boston and I'm dead."

"We'll go to the Carlyle," said Patrice. "Nobody will be there this early."

"Will that make us nobodies?" said Lacey.

The maître d' at the Carlyle went over his reservation sheet for a solid minute before allowing these walk-ins to get a table. He seemed to be on their side, scanning the list as though it were a long equation in which he was trying to find a scientific loophole, even though the place was practically vacant. At last, yes, there was a table. He took them into the blissfully old-fashioned restaurant, with French wallpaper bearing rococo vignettes of women stepping up into carriages, a dining room lit by chandeliers and sconces, and a center flower display that had to cost as much as ten dinners. They were seated at a dream corner table, on a tufted banquette, catty-corner to each other, and the only other people in the restaurant were stragglers just paying their check for afternoon tea.

"Lacey, just so you know, I didn't call you up to have sex with you."

"And if you had?" said Lacey, implying that would not have been a problem.

Patrice angled himself toward her. "Lacey, do you realize you've never said one thing to me that is not banter?"

"I'm doubly shocked," said Lacey.

"Why?"

"Well, one, you're right, and two, that you know the word *banter*."

They ordered food and drinks, and Lacey settled back comfortably.

"There's a Warhol *Marilyn* coming up for auction. They're estimating it at four million," said Patrice.

"Four million," said Lacey, thinking of her own small Warhol; if the *Marilyn* did bring that much, there was a good chance some financial goodwill would spill over onto her flower picture.

"Want to go look at it next week?"

"Where is it? Christie's or Sotheby's?"

"Sotheby's."

"Uhh...maybe. I was in Boston today, at the Isabella Stewart Gardner. Have you ever been?"

"Don't think so. A long time ago, maybe."

"Look at this," she said, reaching in her purse and pulling out the black-and-white brochure from the museum. She put it on the table and flattened it with her palms. "Look at these pictures." She stabbed her finger at each one. "Stolen. Stolen. Stolen..."

"Oh yes, I remember that. A tragedy."

"Rembrandt. Degas. Manet. Vermeer..." Lacey stopped her finger on the Vermeer, and her expression changed to quizzical.

"What?" said Patrice.

"I've seen this somewhere."

"It's a famous painting."

"No, I've seen this, recently, I think. Where did I see it?"

"There was a Vermeer show in New York at the Met. I can't remember when."

"I wasn't in New York before it was stolen."

The rest of the dinner, Lacey would periodically renew her question, as if she were trying to remember a movie title that escaped her, shouting, "Oh, oh!" and hitting her head with her fist. But still, she hadn't found the answer. Patrice observed her like a child interested in an automated toy; he kept wondering what it would do next.

The lights in the restaurant were turned low. A pianist could be heard from the bar playing "The Way You Look Tonight," which worked subconsciously on Patrice. Lacey, now lit by candlelight, her hair relaxed and heading toward unkempt, her concentration diverted, would include him by holding his wrist with one hand and pounding the table with the other when the answer she sought appeared near. In these few seconds, deep inside him, so deep as to be insensible, a passion of viral intensity was slowly infecting him. In spite of their odd beginning, he was deciding not only that Lacey Yeager would make his life wonderful, but that her absence would make it tragic.

Outside, Patrice was shocked to learn it was nine p.m. That meant he and Lacey had spent at least four hours tête-à-tête, talking, eating, flirting, wooing and cooing, and oh yeah, much earlier, fucking. Lacey was exhausted and said good night to him in front of the Carlyle, and a further discussion of another meeting was aborted by the arrival of a cab. Lacey threw her bag in the backseat and said, "Au revoir, baby."

Lacey crossed the park at 79th Street and rested her head against the door of the cab. Her mind relaxed, allowing a sunken memory to bob to the surface. She had seen the Vermeer, or at least a sliver of it, through a crack in the door on her first visit to Barton Talley's gallery, when she was there to be interviewed. She straightened up and the image came into focus, a young girl singing to a gentleman whose back was to the frame, all in Vermeer's unmistakable colors.

She hurried into her apartment, standing vacantly in the center of her living room, wondering what to do. She saw her message light blinking. There were three messages from Talley, saying, "Call me when you get in," "Call me when you get this," and "Where are you? Call me."

She picked up the phone and dialed.

"Oh, Lacey. Gee, darling, where were you? I left word everywhere. I'm getting you a cell phone. Did you get a package? Did someone give you a package?"

"An envelope."

"You got an envelope. Where is it?"

"I have it here."

"Is it thick? Thin?"

"Thin, they said it was fragile."

"Can you bring it over? Can I come get it?"

"You can come get it. I'm dead."

"I'll be there in a few minutes. Where are you again?"

Lacey hung up the phone and went to her purse. She took out the envelope and examined it. It was stiff in the center but otherwise flimsy. She filled her electric kettle with water and turned it on. She took out a white cloth napkin and laid it on the counter. She went and lay on her bed, closing her eyes, not to rest but to blot out the overhead light, her heart beginning to accelerate. The kettle started to spit.

She went to the kitchen, picked up the envelope, and began to steam it open. After a while, there was success, though she left a few faint tears in the flap. She opened the envelope and poured its contents onto the cloth napkin. She saw two pieces of shirt cardboard, cut to about the size of a playing card, taped together and bulging slightly at the center. She went to her bedroom and got a pair of scissors and a roll of tape. She cut one end of the tape and squeezed the cardboard like a change purse. A small, rectangular piece of canvas fell out, ragged at the edges as though snipped by shears, hard and stiff like plastic.

She turned it over and saw brown, old brown paint made rigid by layers of varnish, and she could see its amber tint affecting the color of what was underneath. She put it under the light. She could see words, and she read, written in script, "Rembrandt van Rijn."

Lacey took the piece and sealed it back inside the cardboard package. She went into the bathroom and turned on her hair dryer, aiming it at the flap while she stood and waited, waving the envelope through the blasting air.

Her doorbell rang. She checked the envelope, which looked good, and put it back in her purse. She buzzed in Barton Talley, and his first words were, "I'm glad I remembered where you live. Do you realize you gave me the wrong address? You inverted two digits."

Yes, Lacey thought, while saying, "Oh, sorry, I do that sometimes."

The teakettle gurgled. "You want some tea?" Lacey asked him.

"No thanks, too late for me. Did you have a good trip?"

"Fabulous. I got a consignment from Hinton Alberg."

"Really?"

"Nine Pilot Mouse paintings."

"Well, that will be interesting. Difficult and interesting. How are we supposed to sell those? Anyway, good job. Fill me in."

"Tomorrow, I'm so tired. Here's the envelope…" Lacey started to root around in her purse. "What's in it?" she said, handing it over.

"Come in an hour late tomorrow, Lacey. You've worked hard."

33.

THE NEXT DAY, Lacey banged around the office like a sit-com wife signaling anger. She shut doors with extra force, slammed phones down on their cradles, walked with harder steps on wooden floors. Talley's door was shut, and Lacey was stuck outside like a cat who wanted in. His phone line would be lit for a solid hour, then he would hang up for seconds, and it would light again for another forty minutes. His voice could be heard, but the closed door gave the effect of a voice in the next room of a cheap motel: you could hear someone was talking but couldn't understand one clear word. Once, he got angry and his volume rose.

She heard: "Well, they're idiots! They're not art people. These people are not art people."

Lacey continually checked his door and his phone extension light. Closed and on. She went down the hall to the bins, treading lightly even though the bins were a normal place for her to be. The paintings were arranged on shelves covered in carpet and separated by cardboard flats to keep frames from knocking into each other. Some of the pictures were sheathed in bubble wrap, some were in their own pasteboard containers, and some merely had gaffer's tape stuck on the sides of their frames with the name of the artist written in marking pen. She was familiar with most of the visible stock, but the bins lined both sides of the room and the dark areas toward the back wall remained unexplored.

She wandered down the aisle, her hands touching the frames, left and right, her head doing a tennis match scan of the shelves, pulling the unfamiliar ones out a few inches to check labels. Her head twisted around to the wall phone, and she saw that Talley's light was still burning. She got to the end of the storage and saw in the last, lower bin a picture wrapped in cardboard and sealed tight with wide, clear tape. Under the tape was written a number, 53876, which she committed to memory. She estimated its dimensions by spreading her hand and counting spans. She had long ago measured this distance for quick calculation of a painting's size.

She then went back into the hall, which was lined floor to ceiling with art reference books. A never-used section on museum collections had migrated to the bottom row—because nothing in them was ever for sale—and there she found a Gardner catalog published before the theft, in 1974. She didn't want to be caught holding the book in case Talley suddenly emerged, so she quickly turned back to her office, impressed at her own detective work as she edged out of sight. All this sneaking around was making her agitated, even though every one of her actions could be considered ordinary office maneuvering.

She opened the book and went to Vermeer. There it was, *The Concert*, one of the world's masterpieces reproduced in muddy, out-of-register ink. Its size was printed as "0.725 x 0.647." What the fuck does that mean? she thought. She figured it was metric, but there wasn't as yet an omnipresent Internet to confirm it. She called the Carlyle and asked for Patrice, but he wasn't in. Before she hung up, the hotel operator came back on the line and asked, "Would you like to leave a message?" The Carlyle was one of the few remaining hotels where unanswered room calls didn't default to voice mail.

"Yes," replied Lacey, "ask him how many centimeters are in an inch."

"Please hold," said the operator, whose accent placed her in the heart of Queens. Thirty seconds later, she came back on the line and said, "It's two point five."

Lacey computed that *The Concert* was twenty-eight inches by twenty-five inches, and she added three inches all around to allow for the frame and another inch for packaging. Yes, the package was the same size as the wrapped, stolen Vermeer. She was convinced that this was the missing painting.

A moment later, Lacey heard Talley's door open. She quickly put the book on the floor under her desk. "Lacey, are you here?" he called.

"Yes," she shouted. "Let's meet."

Talley was flush and distracted. "So what about Hinton Alberg?" he said.

"I called him this morning," Lacey told him. "He's sending us transparencies. Nine early paintings by Pilot Mouse."

"Early? The guy's thirty."

"Yes, but it seems that in the contemporary world, early can be four years ago."

"What's the deal?"

"He paid a hundred eighty thousand for them, and he wants to double it."

"Can we?"

"Well, if they were on the New York market, we could, but he doesn't want them on the New York market because he doesn't want it known he's selling."

"Well, we'll do our best."

"Who's your collector in Mexico? Flores? He bought a Hirst, didn't he? It was in the *Art Newspaper*," she said.

"Flores buys Légers and Braques."

"He also buys Hirst."

"Who's Hirst?"

"He's my dry cleaner."

"Are you joking?"

"Yes, Mr. Talley. You've got to get out more."

"I'll call him. Tell me about Pilot Mouse."

"I don't know much about him. He was with a small gallery, Alberg bought all the paintings, then Pilot Mouse jumped."

"Jumped?"

"Jumped to another gallery with a higher profile. Then he started doing conceptual pieces, and raids."

"What are raids?"

"Like happenings. He fills the gallery with nudes, nudes standing around, lots of things banging and sound effects, clatter. He calls them raids, as in raiding the conventional art establishment."

"Sounds unsalable."

"I agree. That's the part I don't get."

"What's he look like?"

"Never seen him."

"What do I tell Flores?"

"You just say Pilot Mouse and he's either heard of him or he hasn't, I guess."

Talley was not used to talking about living artists. "The deader the better," he would say. The antics of the long dead, like Duchamp sending a signed urinal to an art show or Salvador Dalí giving an interview with a lamb chop on his head, had transformed in time from pranks to lore, while the actions of Pilot Mouse just sounded juvenile or, at best, lacking in originality. But Talley was not stupid. He knew that "derivative" was an epithet used erratically and that generations of collectors grew up believing that the art of their time, however derivative, was wholly new. He understood that markets could be blinkered, with activity hotly occurring and nobody ever hearing about it. So while Pilot Mouse's status as an artist of importance was doubtful, his status as a name that could be sold, at least for a while, was probably assured.

I met Lacey for lunch, and she alternated between fretful and enthused. She described the trip to Boston and the consignment from Alberg. When she told me about the office tryst with Patrice Claire, again I felt an involuntary electrical jerk pulse through me, which I interpreted to mean not that I had a crush on Lacey, but that I wished she had commandeered me instead. When she elaborated on the intrigue, she never once asked me what she should do. I only listened. Once she said, "Am I in trouble?" but she answered her own question by placing herself at such a distance from the initial crime that she tried and exonerated herself in a matter of seconds. Whether Talley was complicit or innocent was open to her. He could be working to get the pictures back, but if the Vermeer was indeed in his gallery, didn't that make him a criminal? And if Talley went to jail, would that hurt her career or help it?

Finally, Lacey said to me, "How are you doing?"

"I'm still writing, got a piece in *ARTnews*, doing an essay for a photography catalog. I keep trying to start a novel."

"About?"

"About my growing up."

"Daniel, jeez, get a subject."

"Well, I'm rethinking."

"Girlfriends?"

"They come, they go. Nothing sticks."

"You know what you are, Daniel? You're too kind. Girls like trouble until they're thirty-five."

"I thought I was an intellectual nerd."

"Wow, if you were an intellectual nerd who made trouble, you would be *potent*."

Lacey paid the bill, and we walked out of 3 Guys onto Madison Avenue, and in the air were the first real hints of summer.

34.

"IT DOESN'T MAKE SENSE to me, Mr. Talley."

"What is that, Lacey?"

"Why you didn't go to Boston."

"I told you—"

"I know what you told me, that you didn't want to see people from the Boston Museum. But that's never stopped you. You're not shy. And the room was filled with collectors. That's like Ho-Ho's to a fat man."

"I'm breaking you in, Lacey."

"Baloney. Is it that you didn't want to carry back what was in that envelope?"

Talley looked up at her. "What was in the envelope?"

"I don't know."

"Lacey, you carried something back. I didn't even know what it was. You have to stay out of this."

"But I'm in it. Your fault."

"Aren't you afraid of being fired?"

"But you can't fire me now, can you? Can you put me loose on the streets?"

Not sure what she meant, Talley squinted fiercely and leaned back, and although he was taking himself farther away from her, his total area seemed to expand. "Oh, I could, Lacey. But truthfully, I wouldn't.

Go back to work. Zone out. Stare at the Matisse for a few minutes. Use it like Zen."

Lacey crossed her arms and looked up at the Matisse. "Wrong time of day," she said.

Busying himself at his desk, he said, "Well, take a last look because it's leaving. Sold it this morning."

"Oh, who bought it?" said Lacey.

"A European," said Talley.

"That's specific," said Lacey.

"A Western European," said Talley.

35.

LACEY WAS SURE she was going to open the wrapped picture, but she would let several weeks elapse without drama to make Talley believe that the matter was a blip, now forgotten. Auction season was settling upon Manhattan, so there was much to be distracted by. Patrice Claire invited her to the previews, and Lacey decided she couldn't avoid Sotheby's forever, so she made the trip on her lunch break, understanding that it would be Sotheby's lunch break, too, and perhaps she would not run into those she would rather avoid. As she stepped out onto the tenth floor, she saw a newly promoted Tanya Ross leading clients around the room. Lacey was not and never had been unnerved by her—she only resented her for being competent, nice, pretty, and prim. When Patrice, reacting to her "Ugh," asked her why she didn't like Tanya, Lacey said, "Because I'm a petty person."

They turned the corner into the main gallery and saw, in the premier spot where a 1909 Picasso had hung last week before selling for eleven million dollars, the Warhol *Orange Marilyn*, a silk screen done in 1964. While the Cubist Picasso had gravitas, the *Orange Marilyn* had exuberance: it was as though a fruit-hatted Carmen Miranda had just shown up at a funeral.

However opposite these pictures were, they both worked as historical objects, and they worked as objects of beauty. While the Picasso was deep and serious, the Warhol was radiant and buoyant. The Picasso

Woman with Pears, Pablo Picasso, 1909
36.25 × 28.875 in.

added up to the sum of its parts: artistic genius combined with powerful thought combined with prodigious skill combined with the guided
hand equals masterpiece. The Warhol was more than the sum of its
parts: silk screen, photo image of popular actress, repetitive imagery,
the unguided hand, equals... masterpiece.

"How," said Lacey, "can an artist have no effect on you for years and
then one day it has an effect on you?"

"What are you talking about?"

"Warhol. I'm a proud owner, you know. A small flower picture, but
still..."

"Darling, I call that the perverse effect. Those things that you hate
for so long are insidiously working on you, until one day you can't resist

Marilyn, Andy Warhol, circa 1964
40 × 40 in.

them anymore. They turn into favorites. It just takes a while to sort out the complications in them. Those artworks that come all ready to love empty out pretty quickly. It's why outsiders hate the art we love; they haven't spent time with it. You and I see things again and again whether we want to or not. We see them in galleries, we see them in homes, we see them in the art magazines, they come up at auction. Outsiders see it once, or hear about it after it's been reduced to an insult: 'It's a bunch of squiggles that my kid could do.' I would like to see a kid who could paint a Jackson Pollock. In a half second, any pro could tell the difference. People want to think Pollock's not struggling, that he's kidding. He's not kidding. You want to know how I think art should be taught to children? Take them to a museum and say, 'This is art, and you can't do it.'"

"And I thought you were just in the service industry."

"That's my night job," said Patrice.

They stopped at Sant Ambroeus for a panini at the bar. Patrice set up a dinner with her the next night at the Carlyle. "I'm leaving in four days, Lacey."

"Oh," she said with an edge of disappointment. "When are you back?"

"It depends on how the auction tomorrow night goes."

They ate their sandwiches, and Lacey left for the gallery. Patrice stayed seated and watched Lacey through the glass window as she spoke with a young man on the street whom she seemed to know. Lacey was so vital with him, so animated, that Patrice wondered if she was as vital and animated with him. This moment, innocuous as it was, functioned as an ax blow to a tree: it didn't knock him over, but it left him less steady. Then he was invited to join a Minnesota collector and Larry Gagosian at their table, where they would engage in a conversation about art so lustful that an eavesdropper would assume they were three randy guys discussing babes.

At the gallery, Lacey stopped by the front desk for messages. Donna, who had unveiled a new, unbecoming hairdo, handed her a few, and Lacey read them as she climbed the stairs. One was from Hinton Alberg, inviting her to join them for cocktails after the auction on Thursday. And one was from her old boyfriend Jonah Marsh, asking her to call back. Lacey hadn't thought of Jonah Marsh for three years, and she guessed he had heard she was with Talley now, and would he look at my paintings? Lacey threw the message in her lowest drawer.

Talley summoned her into his office. "Eduardo Flores is going to be in Los Angeles next weekend, so I'm flying out with a shitload of transparencies," he told her. "You'll have to hold down the fort. The town will empty out after the auctions, so I think you'll be fine. Just remember, 'First, do no harm.'"

"And if I sell anything, do I get a commission?"

"You won't sell anything."

"I'll settle for five thousand on every million dollars I sell."

"Oh hell, all right."

36.

LACEY ARRIVED AT the Carlyle for her dinner with Patrice. Her salary at Talley's had given her not only a living wage, but enough spare money, if there is such a thing, to keep her well clothed without having to dip into her reserves. She looked elegant enough that she could move across the lobby without a disapproving head turn, and in fact she got a few approving, inviting, head turns. Elegance in the Carlyle lobby was common, but *youthful* elegance was not.

She went to the desk and asked for Patrice Claire. The clerk rang the room—after getting her full name—then pointed to the elevator. The operator pulled aside a brass folding gate and cranked an iron lever around to 21. His head tilted back and he looked just above her eye line during the ascent. The elevator landed, and the operator did a precision adjustment to ensure there was no fault line between the cage and the hallway floor. "To the right," he said.

Patrice opened the door, and over his shoulder, the first object Lacey saw was a small Picasso drawing: a nude reclining against nothing, all line and space, set in a dusky gold frame. He gave her a European kiss on each cheek and brought her into the small corner apartment; a hotel room that he owned. A large window looked over the rooftops to Central Park as the lights of the city beyond it were starting to twinkle on.

Lacey looked out over the city, south to the Plaza Hotel and north to Harlem, and said, "This will be a nice place to watch the apocalypse."

She turned and looked at him up and down as he waited for her full attention. Patrice did look attractive. He had completed his transformation from the oily Euro she had met at Sotheby's almost four years ago into an Armani guy with regular hair that no longer made her queasy to touch.

"I thought we'd eat in the room. The food is from the restaurant, and with the view—"

"Let's go get a drink in the bar first," Lacey said.

"But we can have one here."

"Yes, but then no one will see how great we look."

They walked around the block first, each proud to be on the other's arm. The sun was just dropping, and the bedecked, bejeweled mannequins in the store windows were like saluting soldiers as they strolled in their enchanted state of opulent seduction. They walked a few blocks and asked for an outside table at La Goulue. They explained they were just going to have drinks, and even though prime dinner hour was approaching when the outdoor tables were prized, the restaurant could hardly refuse such a civility.

Like their drinks, their date was perfectly blended. Patrice, desirous of Lacey, was the subtle engine driving them back to the Carlyle, and Lacey's nonchalant "let's wait and see" demeanor kept the ending unknown to both of them. This was Patrice's chance to legitimize their previous dalliances with a full courtship press.

Now, feeling the kind of euphoria that can overtake you at this time of day, at this temperature, at this level of breeze, after one drink, when the person beside you is making you alert and keen and the idea of being with anyone else is not imaginable, Lacey and Patrice went back to the Carlyle. Patrice knew that tonight would be their first opportunity, if her signals were interpreted correctly, for real sex, real lying-down sex, not standing-up sex or sitting-on-a-desk sex.

They ordered room service, sat at their own corner table with views across and up Manhattan, and sipped a bottle of wine until there was nothing left to do but kiss, and kiss again, for anyone with a pair of binoculars to see. Lacey led him into the bedroom, where the hotel sheets were fresh and rich, where the lighting had been preset, and where, placed opposite the bed, illuminated by two candles that threw their light upward, was the Matisse that had overseen their last coupling in Talley's office. Patrice had bought the moment, and it had cost him six million dollars.

"So it was you," Lacey whispered.

"With what it had seen, I couldn't let it get away." Then they made love.

Afterward, Lacey put on a robe that swathed her like meringue, and Patrice ordered dessert, which was wheeled into the living room while Lacey waited hidden in the bedroom. When the door shut, Lacey emerged and they sat again by the window.

"And now...," said Patrice as he picked up the phone. "Auction results."

"Oh, yay," said Lacey.

Patrice dialed someone. "How'd the auction do?... You're kidding... Oh, really?" He covered the phone and mouthed to Lacey, "The Warhol *Marilyn* brought seventeen million dollars."

Patrice continued on, asking other prices, but Lacey was stunned. She knew not only that the price was phenomenal, news-making, but that there would be a sympathetic rise in all of Warhol's works and that her small flower painting had at least doubled in value while she had been in the bedroom with Patrice.

Patrice hung up the phone. "So," he said, "there's been a revolution." Lacey looked at him.

"Warhol has brought more money than an equal Picasso. The baby boomers are starting to buy their own." What Patrice was saying was true. The vague rumors of strength in the contemporary market had been made manifest, and contemporary art, over the next ten years, was about to inflate like the *Hindenburg*.

Lacey spent the night and left early to change clothes at her apartment. She said good-bye to Patrice with a kiss. He was flying out before lunch for Paris and had already made arrangements for flowers to be delivered to her at Talley's, with a note that read, "I am missing you right now." When Lacey got to her apartment, she paused in front of the Warhol. The feeling that swept over her was a bit like that of a gambler who gets lucky the first time out and leaves the table thinking, This is easy.

At work, Lacey bounced up the stairs and stiff-armed one hand on Talley's doorway. His eyes rose, and as she fluffed her hair with the other she said to him, "You owe me a commission on the Matisse." Then she turned and strolled down the hall, dragging her jacket by one finger before letting it fall to the floor as she turned the corner into her office.

37.

TALLEY PACKED A BAG and flew to Los Angeles, and Lacey went to the shipping room to get an X-Acto knife. She was going to perform surgery on the unknown carton in the bins, just as she had done on the envelope from Boston. The cardboard of the box had already been reused several times, so it wasn't likely that her tinkering would show. Donna never left her post downstairs, and Lacey was her overlord anyway, so she proceeded fearlessly, if secretly.

She turned the box upside down and sliced through the tape, then opened a flap that she bent back, revealing the framed painting inside. She pulled it a few inches from its sleeve, and even though it was now upside down, she could make out the distinct shapes of the now very familiar picture. She pulled it halfway out and bent her body sideways to make the view as upright as possible, and yes, there it was, *The Concert* by Johannes Vermeer. She slid the picture back in its case, retaped the bottom, turned the whole thing right side up, and seated it exactly where it had been. The whole enterprise had taken only a minute.

She walked back to her office and sat at her desk. She did not believe that Barton Talley had stolen a dozen pictures and tied up four night guards at gunpoint. She did believe, however, that Talley was involved in negotiations to get the pictures returned, but whether he was Jesse James or Marshal Dillon she did not know. What she did know was that she did not want to be a detective anymore. Her pulse was not handling it well, and she now, whatever the caper was, had her fingerprints all over it, literally.

Lacey went to the restaurant Sofia and sat upstairs, where she was nominally outdoors, and ordered a truffle-oil pizza. She never looked up while her mind rotated the facts, trying to see them from all sides, trying to piece them together into theory. All she could think was that she was flunking an IQ test.

38.

THE NEXT DAY was Sunday, and Lacey half-walked and half-rode her new bicycle over to the West Side bike path. The path, which ran from the George Washington Bridge all the way to Battery Park, was the great hope for bikers who were tired of dodging car doors that opened incautiously into the street. Even so, she noticed the occasional memorial to riders who were killed in action, a bicycle frame that had been painted ghostly white, including the tires, and bearing flowers that were usually desiccated and drooping. She also noticed that if she didn't wear a helmet and let her hair fly, male riders would tag alongside her for a hundred yards, as though it were all coincidence, hoping for an exchange of glances that Lacey never offered.

The bike path was her sacred time of contemplation, today especially, as she tried to sort out whether she would go to jail for a hundred years or be a heroine who selflessly and cleverly returned a Vermeer to the nation. If she returned a Vermeer to the United States of America, it would be very good for her career. If she was implicated in grand theft, even though she would undoubtedly be cleared, it might be bad for her career. But while Lacey biked farther along, she began to imagine what she would wear on the witness stand, her handkerchief in hand to catch a sudden flood of tears, and the dinner parties she would be invited to. She pictured all the ears listening attentively as she told her story, and decided that either outcome would be okay.

She pulled off the route at 22nd Street, locked her bike to a tree, and strolled through gallery-rich Chelsea, looking in windows, seeing names that instilled in her a spore of initiative: Andrea Rosen, Mary Boone, Angela Westwater, all women who had opened their own galleries and succeeded. She then went to the Empire Diner—the busy café that served irresistible grits at any time of day and had a dozen unattainable tables on the sidewalk—sat at a back table, and ordered lunch. She took out a piece of stationery and carefully penned this letter:

To Whom It May Concern:
On May 10, 1998, I was sent to Boston by Barton Talley to attend a party celebrating funds raised by the ICA. On the way out, I was approached by two men who asked my name and confirmed that I worked for Mr. Talley...

Lacey went on to describe the entire misadventure, including her steaming open of the envelope, the discovery of the Vermeer, and her intent to confront Barton Talley. She expressed concern that if she exposed the presence of the picture without consulting him, she might ruin some plans to get the other pictures back, and that this letter was a dated testimony to her righteous intent in case there were developments before she could ascertain what to do by interrogating Talley. She then sealed the letter in an envelope and addressed it to herself. The idea was that if there was ever a trial, she would produce the unopened letter, with the postmark verifying when it was sent, to be opened in front of a judge, who would immediately send her home. She finished her meal, went outside, and dropped it in a mailbox. When she heard the letter hit the bottom, she realized its futility. Any crook could write himself a letter of righteous intent after a crime, but it wouldn't make him innocent.

39.

BARTON TALLEY'S SHOES were impeccable. He traveled with them in a separate suitcase, each shoe in its own velour slipcover and polished to a hard enamel shine. The Beverly Hills Hotel had expertise in the old world craft of shoe pampering, but Talley's care and maintenance was so self-contained and ritualized that he rarely used their service. Also, the hotel had recently changed hands and it was unknown if the degree of seemingly telepathic attention would remain constant, slide, or rise.

If cities could be given an EKG, New York's readout would be Andean and Los Angeles's would be a sandy beach. Talley already felt himself rocking to the slower rhythm. He dined Saturday night at the Ivy, a restaurant that years ago had ushered in the era of Cajun spices and had been in business so long that it had seen its initial clientele of young celebrities grow old, die, and be replaced by new ones. He ate with Stephen Bravo, a dealer with galleries on both coasts who had clout almost as thundering as Gagosian's. Talley showed him the Pilot Mouse transparencies, and Bravo bought four paintings essentially sight unseen. He wondered how Bravo could even see them as he held the five-by-six-inch transparencies up to the dim lamplight of the Ivy. But Talley understood. Contemporary paintings usually posed no condition problems or questions of authorship, they were valuable only by fiat, and there was rarely anything to research. Back at the hotel, he woke Lacey with a phone call to let her know of the sale and, unprompted, gave her her first small taste of profit participation.

His lunch the next day was taken alone at the Polo Lounge, the tourist-destination restaurant at the hotel. Agents and movie stars still patronized the place because its tables recalled Hollywood's most glamorous era. Out-of-towners who dared approach a celebrity table were nearly tackled by waiters or intercepted with a harsh arm signal of "foul" by the attentive maître d'. Talley ate a deceptive salad that had enough goodies in it to raise the calorie count to over a thousand and waved good-bye across the room to Bravo, who was off to catch a plane to somewhere kept secret from other art dealers.

There is art in Los Angeles that rivals New York's, but to see all of it you would need General Eisenhower to plan the attack. The Los Angeles County Museum of Art is miles from the Getty, which is miles from the Hammer, which is miles from the Norton Simon, which is miles from the Museum of Contemporary Art, and if the dots were connected on a map, you would see a giant circle running around the periphery of Los Angeles with no convenient route connecting them. The viewer of this map would realize that the best way of commuting among these five significant art museums would be by Swiss gondola or light aircraft.

But Talley was not there for the art museums. His main concern was dinner that night with Eduardo Flores. Flores was capable of expenditures the size of movie budgets, and to prove it he had just finished remodeling a house in Los Angeles that was the architectural perfection of 1961, before anyone thought of 1961 as a year of exceptional style. This was sixties modern, distinct from the kitsch California architecture of the same period marked by electrons swishing around nuclei on top of bowling alleys. But there was a high style floating around then, though no one knew it yet. It was the furniture of Knoll, Nakashima, and the Eameses. Flores's house had been redone to satiny perfection, and the effect was spectacular. When you entered the house for the first time, it felt as though you had just stepped into the pages of a *Life* magazine layout of the modern home.

The house was walking distance from the Beverly Hills Hotel, but Talley wasn't about to risk it. Even a taxi or limo drive threatened to burr his shoeshine, and a walk would have to be done so carefully that he might look silly. So when he ran into Gayle Smiley, who was the highest-ranking representative of the Stephen Bravo gallery and who was also attending the dinner, he angled for a ride, as a front seat was safer for shoes than the backseat. But Stephen Bravo was Eduardo's number one dealer, and Gayle protected the franchise like a mother bear would a cub, claws and all. She did not want to arrive with Talley next to her, especially since she was morbidly unhappy that he had been invited in the first place. Gayle mumbled, stumbled, took a phone call, and withdrew.

In the end, Talley settled for a taxi. Though he was expecting to be berated by the driver for such a short hop, the turban-wearing cabbie said a cheerful good night and gave him his card in case he needed a ride back.

The houses in Beverly Hills were either low-slung or high-slung, and Flores's was as low as a sixties modern would allow. Yet the house had a view not only of its own sculpture garden, but of the city of Los Angeles. This mysterious effect belonged to many houses in Beverly Hills that appeared to be in the flatlands but were actually on an imperceptible uphill slope that positioned the house for a view to the sea. These views that skimmed just over the top of the city gave sunsets an extra redness and positively affirmed that Los Angeles could be beautiful.

Talley stood in the entry of the house, which he had been in before, and realized something was up. The art on the walls—formerly the modern masters that Talley sold—was now shifting toward contemporary, and because of it the house had been infused with energy. A

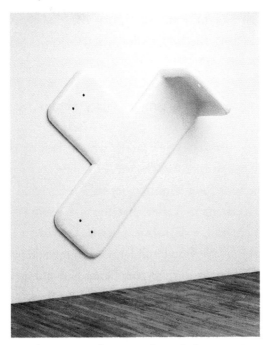

Three Parts of an X, Robert Gober, 1985
81 × 81.5 × 25 in.

Robert Gober sculpture, an interpretation of a porcelain sink that had been unfolded like a Chinese take-out box, hung on the wall in the dining room, and a Damien Hirst mirrored pharmaceutical shelf the size of a plate-glass window hung over the fireplace. The livelier environment felt good even to Talley. He was grateful to Lacey for delivering unto him some contemporary art that made him feel much more up-to-date. His normal world of modern masters made him feel snug and comfortable, but these new objects, hanging with such bewildering cheer, made him feel as if he'd already had one drink. One drink was not enough for any of this group, though, and they gathered in the living room, where the hard stuff was being served.

The host had not made his entrance yet, but Gayle Smiley had, and she made it clear that it was she who had sold most of these

163

contemporary works to Eduardo. "Isn't the Gober fabulous?" She was already pumping the bellows for the art she was promoting. The party was livening with the arrivals of actor Stirling Quince and his enduring girlfriend, Blanca. Stirling had been a solid TV star for five years, and despite escalating annual salary bumps, he was still only *wealthy.*

Talley looked over at Gayle's purse, which she had put on a small divan. Sticking out from it was the very envelope containing the transparencies of the four Pilot Mouse paintings he had sold Bravo the day before. It was apparent to Talley that she was going to offer them to Flores. This made Talley slightly sick, as he knew he had the remaining transparencies at his hotel and hadn't brought them because, one, it was tacky, and two, he didn't know Flores had shifted gears. He also knew he had an advantage because he could beat Bravo's price, since he knew what he had paid for them. It wasn't that Talley wanted to make fifty thousand dollars; he simply wanted to sell Flores a contemporary painting right under Smiley's nose.

"Oh my," said Talley. "I left my inhaler back at the hotel."

Talley didn't really know much about inhalers, but he knew it sounded much better than saying "transparencies." He walked out the door, and because the hotel was downhill from the house, he made it in less than five minutes. This run was done with a strangely high-stepping gait, as each shoe had to come down squarely on its sole. At the hotel, he put the transparencies in his coat pocket and gave Lacey a quick call, waking her up for the second time in two days. "Give me the run-down on Robert Gober," he said to her.

"Sculptor, expensive, conceptual, very respected," she said. "Mention sinks, drains, and 'the playpen.'"

"Thanks, Lacey," he said.

When he walked back in, the party had grown to a total of ten, minus the host, who still had not appeared. One of the new additions was a stray young man whose name sounded like Fortunato, but Talley couldn't be certain and he was afraid to call him by name until it was verified. What worse blunder was there than calling someone Fortunato if that was not his name? The young man wore tight leather pants and a tight black T-shirt and would occasionally sally down the hallway, indicating he was a houseguest or perhaps more.

After one of these hallway dashes, Fortunato—yes, the name had been confirmed—appeared with Eduardo Flores on one arm. It was hard to tell whether he was escorting him in affectionately or propping him up, as Eduardo looked glassy-eyed.

Gayle, with rabbit quickness, bounded across the room to greet him. "Eduardo! The new Warhol looks incredible there. You were right!"

Eduardo said little as he was taken around the room and introduced to guests. Possibly he was uncomfortable with English, possibly he was just uncomfortable. But his discomfort was certainly social and not pharmaceutical, as he had the happy grin of a patient on morphine.

Talley looked into Eduardo's face and knew that neither he nor Gayle was likely to get his attention to look at transparencies. He would call Eduardo's curator tomorrow and make the pitch. The curator in Eduardo's case was a smart coordinator only, as Eduardo made all the final decisions with an uncharacteristically sober acuity. The group was then led around for a tour of the house, which was a showcase and had been meticulously detailed. Even the light switches were period and flawlessly installed; it was as though a heavenly contractor had floated in, waved a wand, and perfected every corner. In the bedroom, a surprising and satisfying art reference library was arranged alphabetically in a splendid Nakashima bookcase. Nakashima, who elevated the craft of driftwood furniture from beachside tourist shops to high art, was now being rediscovered after a lengthy fallow period, with Flores leading the way. Over the bed hung a Wilfredo Lam, the Cuban painter who was a Picasso acolyte but distinguished himself with a unique, surreal-istic diversion from Cubism.

"Cubanism," joked Flores, indicating he was not as potted as he looked.

"Where the hell do you find one of those?" said Stirling, asking the question aloud that was on Talley's mind.

"Where'd we get that?" said Eduardo, looking around.

The other question that was on Talley's mind was one that only Stirling could answer: "What can it be like to sleep with Blanca?" Talley stood behind her and stared at her bare neck when he was supposed to be looking at the Lam.

The narrow hallway forced them to line up, Gayle shoulder to shoul-der with Eduardo, squeezing Talley to the rear, making him leave the

Initiation, Wilfredo Lam, 1950
72.8 × 66.9 in.

room last. But he could still hear her remark to Eduardo: "You know what would look good in the guest bedroom? Pilot Mouse! I have some transparencies I was going to show to Dean Valentine, but I'll show them to you first." This remark was intended to get Flores's blood flowing, as Dean Valentine made every other contemporary collector a pretender. Hinton Alberg's collection of seven hundred paintings seemed paltry compared with Valentine's twelve hundred. His sweet-science combination of a keen eye for new work and a vacuum cleaner mentality meant he got everywhere first. He once sneaked into a Manhattan art fair a day before it opened by disguising himself as a janitor in order to get first crack at the best in the show. But Talley thought Gayle had misjudged her man. Flores never thought of himself as a competitor; he just liked art.

Dinner was called. The service was stealthy and invisible; new plates were slipped in like playing cards. The conversation was exclusively about art, not so much art as spiritual metaphor, but art as advanced thing, with beauty being an asset like the sleek lines of a Buick: a really nice thing to have, but it still had to get you there. Gayle Smiley perked up at every mention of artists she represented and fell into irritated silence when any other artist was mentioned, including Goya. Talley scored points by mentioning Gober's playpen, but he still didn't understand what it was.

Gayle was more like a great basketball player than an art dealer: she unfailingly covered her man, making it impossible for Talley to throw him a pass. However, Talley knew that there would be a moment after dinner when Gayle would have to go vomit, leaving her man wide open. When she left, precisely after dessert, Talley took Flores aside and said, "I like the new direction. I left a transparency of a Pilot Mouse picture next to your bed. There could be some fakes out there, so be careful. This one is genuine. I'm assuming the Lam's not for sale, but if it ever is…"

Dinner wrapped up with everyone in a stupor, and Talley made his way to the hotel on foot, whistling drunkenly in the balmy night, one hand in his pocket, the other dangling his coat over his back with one finger like Sinatra. Back in his room, the phone rang.

"Hey, you in?"

"Yes, darlin', come on up."

A few moments later, Cherry Finch was at his door, and soon they were tugging at each other's clothes. These rendezvous remained undisclosed even to their closest friends, and their total discretion meant that they could go on forever.

40.

PATRICE CLAIRE was in Paris alone, and he didn't know why. Every bistro lunch, every café dinner, every evening engagement, would have been better with Lacey present. He wanted his social group to meet her, to like her, to see her as he did, as an extra measure of sunlight in the room. He knew she would stand up to his friends' rigid appraisals, because Lacey never tried to impress with manners; she impressed with wit and daring. He could imagine his stuffiest Parisian cohort tilting back on his heels, trying to get a wider look at her. Patrice wanted Lacey's take on everything in his world: what was the best food, which were his best clothes, what was his best quality.

It was eight a.m. in Los Angeles, eleven a.m. in New York, and five p.m. in Paris. Barton Talley was boarding a plane at LAX, and Patrice was calling Lacey at the gallery, his first communication with her since the rapturous Carlyle night. Donna put him through upstairs, announcing who it was. Lacey bowed her finger on the extension button.

"What are you doing?" he asked.

"Thinking about your dick," she said. Somehow, this was a more welcome response than if she had said, "How do I love thee? Let me count the ways." They talked for one hour, ending with phone sex that was as frustrating as it was fulfilling. Lacey's palm gripped the front of her chair as she rubbed against her wrist, her other elbow on the desk with the phone held under her hair. Afterward, she walked down the gallery stairs with a just-fucked look so evident that it made Donna wonder if a deliveryman had slipped by her.

Patrice had promised to be back in New York in two weeks, but Lacey knew he would be there by Thursday, so she kept her evenings open.

Talley stopped by the gallery after his plane landed. He looked exhausted, so she postponed until tomorrow the grilling she was about to give him. If he was going to be dragged off to jail, she thought he should be freshly shaven.

41.

I SHOWED UP at Lacey's that night at eight p.m. She was making pasta for Angela, Sharon, and me, the recipe for which she had gleaned from *The New York Times Magazine*, and tossing together a clarifying drink called an Aviation, which has to be made in a batch because after the first one you're too drunk to make any more.

When the drinks had taken effect, I was treated like the gay friend, privy to all gossip, allowed to hear the girls' most detailed sexual experiences. I even found myself retorting with catty comments that I imagined a stereotypical gay invitee might interject amid the squeals and coughing fits generated by spit takes. Lacey detailed the earlier phone encounter with Patrice and then would repeat it this way: she would say, "It was an ordinary, boring day, except for the..." then she would mouth the words *phone sex*. "Yes," she would go on, "except for the [mouthed] *phone sex*, it was a very ordinary day." Once, the phone rang during dinner. Lacey looked over at us and said, "That must be my *phone sex*." This sent us into fits whenever we could work "phone sex" into the conversation, and things got sillier and sillier as all of us contributed, intoning the unimportant words at full volume and finishing the sentence by mouthing the last two words only: "Now where did I put that *phone sex*?" We were aching so much that we imposed a moratorium on saying "phone sex," which, like an Arab/Israeli cease-fire, took longer to take effect than it should have.

During an interlude of sobriety, figurative only, we each filled in the others on our lives. Angela, the most practical of us, was likely to be married within the year and living in Seattle. Sharon had fallen in love with a downtown theater actor and was focusing on theater fundraising so her boyfriend would have a place to act. And I had broken through at *ARTnews* magazine with an article on Jeff Koons's relation to Pop Art, where I made the case that Pop had become a genre unto itself, like landscape and still life, and was therefore no longer ironic by definition. I didn't get to explain the premise of my piece to the women, because my floor time had been cut short by a contest to see who could say the word *dirigible* without laughing.

Angela and Sharon shuffled out when the evening had deflated like a whoopee cushion after the joke's over, and I lingered because Lacey indicated for me to linger. She wanted to get my take on the Vermeer situation, and I sat rapt as she unfolded the story. She really didn't need me to hear it, because she never asked me what to do, and I had no clue what to tell her. I did think that it was symptomatic that her life fell naturally into states of intrigue, while I was always moving in a world where nothing changed.

Lacey finally arrived at the conclusion that the only questionable evidence was the Vermeer in the bins and that everything else could be explained as being on the right side of the law. This frustrated her. She wanted to go into work tomorrow steaming, but she couldn't quite. She finally found an angle that could work her up into a frenzy.

Tuesday morning she left a note on Barton Talley's desk: "I need to talk to you." Each word was underlined for emphasis. An hour later, Barton appeared at her office door with nonchalance, not picking up on the underlining.

Lacey looked up. "Oh," she said, "I need to see you."

"That's what the note said," Talley responded.

"In your office," she commanded.

Lacey was trying to funnel her energy into one pure welder's arc of white heat that would sear Talley's forehead, but she kept feeling herself slipping back into unwelcome calm.

"Sit down," Talley invited her.

Lacey, thinking she was being stern, said, "I'd rather stand," then she sat down.

"Look," she said, "why didn't you go to Boston?"

"When?"

"When you sent me."

"Lacey, do you realize you work for me, not the other way around?"

"You used me."

"You work for me. I'm supposed to use you."

"You used me in an off-contract way."

"We don't have a contract." Talley's responses were all said with a half-smile that indicated to Lacey he considered this repartee and not grounds for dismissal. So she went on.

"Why didn't you go to Boston?"

"I told you, I was trying to avoid a certain group of trustees."

"Okay, so that's bullshit. Next."

"Uh, you go next."

"As long as I've known you, you have never been shy, perturbed, or cowed. An art dealer doesn't live on tact. You sent me because of the two men. You wanted me to carry something back that you didn't want to be caught carrying back."

Talley got up, walked to the office door. "I didn't know what it would be," he said, and then he closed the door. "Do you know what it was, Lacey?"

"They showed it to me before they sealed it," she said.

Talley paused and thought over this statement, assigning numeric value to its possible truth. The number came up low.

"No, they didn't," he said.

"I steamed it open," said Lacey.

"Do you know what it is?"

"I think I do."

"It was like sending back a finger of a kidnap victim. Grotesque. I didn't expect it."

"And the two men?"

"FBI."

"Oh, good."

"Why 'Oh, good'?"

"Because if they were the crooks, you'd probably ask me to sleep with one of them. Wouldn't you."

There was a second of silence, then they both broke into laughter.

"Wouldn't you, you fucker!" said Lacey, simultaneously screaming and muffling her own voice.

"Only off-contract," Talley said.

Then Lacey got serious. "Don't mistake this smile for 'problem solved.' I don't want to be the dupe who gets ten to twenty."

"We wanted evidence that they had the pictures. The FBI guys acted as go-betweens to the thieves. I was expecting a photograph of the painting next to today's paper, something like that. But these jerks are not us. They don't handle with care. I didn't know they were going to deliver that night. I got a call and told them to give it to you. I didn't realize you were Nancy Drew."

"And why you?"

"It started years ago when I was in Boston. I was the expert; I had written essays on the Vermeer. The FBI came to me to authenticate if the situation ever came up in New York. The thieves tried contacting the FBI years ago, but the agent couldn't confirm that the picture they let him glimpse was the real thing, and the deal fizzled."

"So none of the pictures have been returned," Lacey said, which was her own test of authenticity.

"No. These pictures probably won't be returned until the next generation. Deathbed confession sort of thing."

Lacey had heard nothing but plausibility, yet everything Talley was saying was rendered implausible by the corpus delicti in the bins, and she didn't know how to handle it. But directness had worked so far, so she decided to produce the body. She stood up.

"Sit, just sit," she said to Talley, and she left the office. She went back to the bins, looked at the slot where the Vermeer still dumbly sat. She pulled it out and grabbed a box cutter on the way back to the office.

When she walked into the office with the package, Talley said, "Oh."

She carefully sliced open the tape and took out the painting while he sat. She rested it on Talley's office easel and stood back, crossing her arms.

"And?" said Talley.

"And you're under arrest if you don't explain."

"You're one to be talking about arrest, Lacey."

"What do you mean?"

"I've had a few conversations with Cherry Finch."

Lacey stopped still. She turned her attention back to the Vermeer. "What about this?"

Talley put the intercom on speaker and rang Donna. He indicated to Lacey to show him the edge of the cardboard box. "Donna, what's inventory item 53876?"

"Oh...okay...," said Donna, rattling around on a keyboard. "That's the...let's see...that's the Johannes Vermeer," she said, pronouncing the J in Johannes.

"Okay, thank you," said Talley. "Now, Lacey Drew, if Donna, who is my Connecticut client's quidnunc daughter—"

"What?" said Donna, who was still on the phone.

"Oh, sorry, Donna. I meant to hang up." Talley pressed the intercom button. "If Donna knows we've got a Vermeer in here, do you think we have a serious problem?"

Lacey put her index finger to her chin and shifted her hips, posing herself like a Kewpie doll.

"Turn the Vermeer around," said Talley.

Lacey did, resting it backward on the easel. "Read the label."

"Johannes Vermeer, blah blah, Metropolitan Museum of Art."

"What does that tell you?" said Talley.

"What's it supposed to tell me? It sounds like it's getting worse for you."

"Wrong museum," said Talley. "The stolen Vermeer's from the Gardner. The label says the Met. This is a nineteenth-century copy. Vermeer didn't bring much money until then; that's when the fakers got busy. Very precise, meant to fool. The size is correct to the centimeter. Bernard Berenson vetoed this one and found the real one for Mrs. Gardner. He was a dog, but he had a good eye. In the twenties this picture got donated as a study picture to the Met. There was a moment where we thought the bad guys were going to produce the real one as evidence, keeping the rest hostage while we examined it. We intended to swap the real picture out of its frame and stick in this pretender. The Met agreed that this was a lamb that could be sacrificed."

Lacey was deflated. "Rats. I wanted there to be a crime," she said. "It would have been so much more fun."

42.

PATRICE CLAIRE sat at his favorite restaurant in Paris, Le Petit Zinc, surrounded by cheerful friends who were toasting his fortieth birthday on a beautiful and still summer night when the sun wouldn't set until ten p.m., and all he could think was, What am I doing here? He had made several trips to New York during the summer to see Lacey, and each seemed to enforce his suspicion that she was in love with him. While his friends laughed and chatted, he left a phone message for Lacey: "Lacey, dinner Thursday?" He would fly to New York for no reason at all except to see her, unable to wait the two weeks to return to Manhattan that was his usual cycle. He had noted that phone sex with Lacey was better than real sex with his standby Parisian girlfriend, who once had intrigued him—but now looking at her was like looking at cardboard. Later that evening, when he told his standby that he was breaking it off, she responded with a "puh" so indifferent that he thought she had misheard him.

Patrice left Lacey a message with Donna, and wondered whether to go ahead and book the flight and just chance it. When he finally got a message back ("Come on over, sailor boy, I'll let you swab my decks"), he booked a Thursday Concorde, not because he didn't want to risk being late for dinner, but because he was so eager to get there that he wanted to arrive before he took off, which only the Concorde could accomplish.

As Patrice waited in the Concorde lounge, he noticed a change in the usual demographics. The Americans, English, and French were being displaced by Russians, Asians, and Arabs, who not only could afford to bring their entire families on the plane even though there was no discounted child's fare, but would also buy blocks of seats so no one could sit next to them.

A new level of wealth was emerging from the former Communists and the capitalist Chinese. Businesses lacking glamour, like mining and pipelines, bestowed riches on Russian entrepreneurs who had stunningly outmaneuvered organized crime and political kingpins. What one thousand dollars was to a millionaire, a million dollars was to the new billionaires. And what they spent on art was irrelevant to them and their lifestyles. Art was about to acquire the aura of an internationally recognizable asset, a unique and emotional emblem of the good life. While Patrice Claire was only a normal millionaire, incapable of the extended reach of the new global money, he had the advantage of expertise and intuition in a delicate business.

Even though the Concorde was sleek and magnificent, looking like a perfect robot bird, it was still a crate. It rattled like a jalopy as it hypersped down the runway, it jerked and clanked as it climbed, and it gave the illusion of stalling as engines were suddenly cut back because of noise regulations. And once aloft, it sailed dully like any other aircraft. The seats were cramped, and if someone took the seat beside you, it was easy to feel that your costly flight had been downgraded to a Bombay train.

When Patrice landed at JFK, he felt as though he had been inside a dart that was launched into the Paris sky and stuck into a passenger gate in New York. He called Lacey from the taxi, but six p.m. was a bad time to reach anyone, and he got message machines all around. He made reservations at Le Bernardin, which was intended to send a message to Lacey, and to himself, that this was a special night and she was worth every extravagance. It was seven p.m. by the time he arrived at the Carlyle, having already left another message for Lacey at her apartment. In case they don't connect, he said, meet him at nine p.m. at the restaurant. His actions, his mood, his methodology, indicated the presence of an unrealized kernel of hope in his soul: this night they would walk into the restaurant as two people on a deliciously serious date and emerge as two people in love.

The Carlyle was still old-fashioned, and phone messages were delivered on handwritten notes that were slid under the doorway by an unseen hand. After his shower, and after dressing in a looser-cut suit than his pre-Lacey, tight-waisted Parisian standby, Patrice noticed a small, folded message poking an edge out from under the doorsill. He opened it and read, "So sorry, something came up and I couldn't reach you. I'll call you later. Old friend in town and can't change." Patrice cursed the shower and sat on the bed, the message dangling from his fingers like a notification of death, and he wondered what had just happened.

What had just happened was this: Earlier, I had called Lacey at work and said, "There's an opening tonight at a small gallery in Chelsea. A not very interesting young artist, but Pilot Mouse is supposed to be there. They're friends or something. Want to go?"

"What time?" she said. "I've got a dinner tonight."

"The opening's six to eight. Party afterwards," I said.

"Where do I meet you?" she said.

"The bar at Bottino."

Lacey had picked up Patrice's message but hadn't responded, assuming she would meet him at Le Bernardin. But now there was a stronger pull elsewhere. She left a message for Patrice, not ringing his room, as she dashed out the door.

Lacey came into the bar wearing her usual too-small sweater and a cloche straw hat with a summer umbrella hung over her arm. When she came into the room, there was an adjustment in the hierarchy of women. The most beautiful remained undisturbed in their fixed positions, but Lacey shot to the top of every other list: cutest, sexiest, most fun. We had a drink, and a few other people joined in. Everyone was talking about Pilot Mouse and was he really going to be there. Yes, for sure, they said. He's supporting his friend's show. You know he's not reclusive, he's just wanted everywhere, so when he doesn't show up he's missed and mythologized. He's handsome, oh yes, he's handsome and mysterious. Doesn't speak much. Very serious. Gay? Maybe, someone said. I heard not, said another knowingly.

We all marched around the corner and entered an industrial building with a clanking elevator operated by a guy playing a radio. A dozen people crowded into the cab as it jolted and lurched to the seventh floor. The gab was already under way when the door screeched open and we spilled out into the hallway. We filled it like gas expanding and trooped our way around several bends, following hand-drawn signs bearing colored arrows. Finally, the gallery was in sight, indentified by a clutch of young people standing in the hall with plastic conical cups of white wine, a few of them smoking.

We entered the gallery, an unexpectedly large space for such a small door, where perhaps a hundred invitees, friends of invitees, and miscellaneous interlopers gradually raised the volume to crushing intensity. Lacey and I pulled away from our default group, heading toward the table of wine, which was pour-your-own. The art on the walls was the kind that resists normal interpretation: paper, sometimes cardboard, thumbtacked to the wall with collaged images taped or glued to its surface, and nearby, a plinth displaying a spool of thread, or a safety pin, or something else ordinary under a Plexi box. Lacey and I looked at one of these mysteries and then looked at each other, but I couldn't knock it because who knows? A lot of strange art had achieved classic status over the last twenty years, making criticism of the next new thing dangerous. Lacey, however, shrugged, leaned in to my ear, and whispered, "Spare me."

Even though there was no music, the gallery pulsed to a beat. Thursday is the standard night for openings in Chelsea, and when galleries' biorhythms aligned so that a dozen or more openings fell on the same night, there was blastoff. This was prom night for the smart set, a night to be smug, cool, to dress up or dress down, and to bring into focus everything one loves about oneself and make it tangible. It was possible for young men to set their sights on a particular woman and "coincidentally" run into her at three different galleries until there was enough in common to start a conversation, or rue for days one's failure to say hello to the object of desire and then run an ad in the *Village Voice*'s "Missed Connections" column.

Art was being flown in from Europe or carted up from downtown basement studios. It was being made by men, women, minorities, and majorities, all with equal access. Whether it was any good or not, the sheer amount of it—to the dismay of cranky critics—was redefining what art could be. Since the 1970s, art schools had shied away from teaching skills and concentrated on teaching thought. Yet this was the first time in conventional art history where no single movement dominated, no manifesto declared its superiority, and diversity bounced around like spilled marbles on concrete.

If the history of humor could be charted, visual art of this period might be seen as its next frontier. Stand-ups were still doing stand-up, but Jeff Koons made a forty-foot-high sculpture of a puppy built out of twenty-five tons of flowers and soil in pots, and Maurizio Cattelan made a life-size sculpture of the pope flattened by a meteor that had just fallen through a skylight. This piece was made only a year before he convinced his gallery director to walk around for a month dressed as a bright pink penis.

We were about to leave when there was a stir by the entrance. A small coterie of people moved toward another group standing mid-gallery, and there was a moment where I thought they were like two

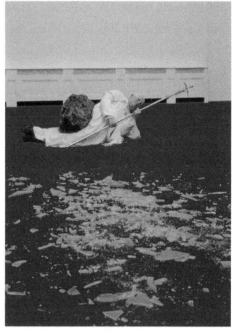

La Nona Ora, Maurizio Cattelan, 1999
Lifesize.

galaxies about to pass through each other. But there was a halt, and the
two groups became one. The galaxy metaphor is apt, as this comming-
ling produced two centers. One was a young man we had identified as
the artist whose work was on the walls, but the second man seemed to
have all the gravity. Lacey looked over, and her first identification in the
lineup was a woman: "Oh shit, Tanya Ross." But her second identification was friendlier. "Oh," she said, "Jonah Marsh." She had not seen
him in three years, and Jonah had grown from boy to man. His black
hair looked uncombed, but the truth was probably a meticulous opposite. Lacey led the way toward the group, and Tanya Ross turned first.

"Hi, Lacey," she said stiffly.

Lacey introduced me, and fixated as I was on Tanya's screen-test
beauty, she seemed not to notice me. Tanya reluctantly introduced

Lacey and me to a few more people by their first name only, then she turned to Jonah Marsh and said, "And this is Pilot Mouse."

Lacey cocked her head and uttered a long, slow, "Hey..." It was the first time I had seen her unsettled. Then she recovered, saying, "I owe you a phone call; I've been out of the country." It was as though she had backed into someone at a high-rise and accidentally bumped him out the window but hoped no one had noticed. Unwanted by Tanya, Lacey shouldered her way into the troupe like a boxer muscling her opponent back against the ropes. Lacey's uptown moves, high-style reserve with a playful edge, had been perfected, but she hadn't used her downtown moves—fearless sexuality with a flapping fringe of pluck and wit—in a long time. There was an instant breeze from her, and she was the new alternate center of this group of stars. When she spoke to the young artist whose show it was and whom she had just displaced, she didn't betray herself by flattering him but instead asked vibrant questions about his intent. And after his unparsable response, including a passage where he said he was "blurring the boundaries between a thing and thought," she said, "Thank you, I get lost sometimes," while laying two fingers on his folded arm.

We walked around Chelsea for a while. I was trying to make headway with Tanya Ross, who was clearly friends with Jonah Marsh, and Lacey, not knowing to what degree Tanya was a friend, was staying in Jonah's sight, crossing his field of vision whenever Tanya got his attention. Then there was a discussion of food and drinks. Lacey declined, peculiarly, saying, "No, I'm meeting a friend." The group mentioned Cia, a sushi bar around the corner. "Oh, jeez," said Lacey, lying, "that's where I'm meeting him."

I was relieved that the evening wasn't over, because I wasn't ready to give up on Tanya Ross. It was obvious to me that Tanya was not Pilot Mouse's date, because she had clearly warmed to me and she didn't seem duplicitous, unlike Lacey. She asked what I did, and when I told her I was a freelance art writer, there was no ho-hum blankness that overcame her. Instead she responded with, "Oh, how interesting!" No one had ever said that to me since birth. She even had the courtesy not to ask if I was published, so I volunteered that I wrote regularly for *ARTnews*, and for gallery catalogs. And when I told her I wrote an essay about the rare bird Arthur Dove for the Whitney show, her face brightened and she said, "I read that. I think."

At the restaurant, there was a seating war that appeared casual but if diagrammed would have looked like an Andy Warhol dance-step painting. With me across from Tanya, Lacey positioned herself so that every time Jonah looked at her, he was forcibly looking away from Tanya. With the seating chart done, Lacey excused herself from the table and walked toward the phone with a small swing of her hips.

⌀⎯

Patrice Claire sat in his Carlyle paradise, which had so quickly turned itself into hell. There was nothing with which to uplift himself; the repair was out of his control and completely in Lacey's. He had canceled Le Bernardin, but this was not an act of power, it was one of grief. Lacey had said she would call. Did she mean tonight? He had ordered room service to keep him close to the phone. When it rang, he felt a surge of hope that he resented in himself. It was Lacey.

"I'm *so* sorry. I wasn't sure if you meant tonight. We never set a time... I'm downtown at Cia. I ran into an old friend. He's great. Come down. I need to see you."

"I'll find it," said Patrice.

Patrice was used to the steadfast responses of paintings, not the unpredictable responses of people. A discussion of a picture was a conversation of ultimate complexity and intrigue, irresolvable and ongoing. A conversation with Lacey was the same, except the picture did not strike out at him. He fantasized that he and Lacey would have a lifelong conversation—also irresolvable and ongoing—because their common subject would be a route to each other. He was stable and sane, an avid art enthusiast with the same mutant gene as the stamp collector, the coin collector, or the model train freak—except that there were glorious buildings erected solely to house and protect his objects of interest, objects that commanded the attention of scholars, historians, and news bureaus, giving undeniable proof that they were worthy of devotion. But because the objects of his adoration were inert, he was unaccustomed to mood swings. Especially volcanic ones that took place over a few seconds. He was angry that Lacey had canceled, unhappy that he would be seeing her in a group, disturbed that her old friend was male—yet he was eager to see her.

Instead of the serenity and anticipation with which he would have arrived at Le Bernardin, he arrived at Cia with anxiety and vulnerability. He was too old for this place. It was a different crowd, with different slang and different references, a crowd ignorant of the nomenclature of the uptown art world. He did, however, understand sushi.

He passed through the bar, and thankfully, it was an art bar and not a sports bar, so he wasn't the shortest male in the gauntlet. He looked around the darkened restaurant when he heard Lacey shouting from the murk, "Patrice!"

From my seat, I watched as Lacey ran up to Patrice, delivering an affectionate hug that seemed to me exaggerated. She took him to the group and introduced everyone, at least everyone she knew, and except for me and Tanya, whom he knew, there were lackluster hellos.

Lacey squeezed back into her slot across from Pilot Mouse, with Patrice having to turn sideways to sit down. She seemed genuinely in love with Patrice, and genuinely trying to rekindle Jonah's fleeting interest of three years ago. Looking back, I think that both behaviors were valid. To her this was natural, to Patrice it was unsettling, to me it was bewildering, and to Tanya Ross, who had matured normally, it was creepy. Tanya occasionally looked at me with an expressionless stare that I knew signified disgust. Although it seemed that Jonah Marsh was with Tanya tonight, I did notice his eyes glancing over to Lacey with metronomic regularity.

As I reached over to refill her sake glass, Tanya looked at me oddly and said, "Have we met?"

"I would have remembered," I flirted.

"You look familiar," she insisted, and she sat in silence for a minute, trying to work it out.

The party broke up, and Lacey hugged Pilot Mouse good-bye, her actions maintaining that they were just old friends, while Patrice stood by, correctly assuming that Pilot had already fucked her, or was about to again, which made him queasy. They took a taxi to her apartment, and Patrice came up for a few minutes, but this was not the end that he wanted for the night. So he made, enthusiastically, a date for the next night, but he knew Le Bernardin would be impossible on a Friday and he would be settling for a restaurant less major, less symbolic.

He had been knocked backward, but a previously untouched part of his heart kept driving him forward, fueled by fresh emotions emerging from the wound, unknown and uncontrollable. Lacey gave him a ravishing kiss good night, then he walked east to Central Park, where he flagged down a cab. On the way back to the Carlyle, his mental reenactment of their last kiss told him, yes, she loves me, and he once again saw Lacey as an illuminating white light, forgetting that white is composed of disparate streaks of color, each as powerful as the whole.

When Patrice called that afternoon, telling her the restaurant was Nello on Madison, walking distance from the Carlyle, Lacey said, "Can I shower at your apartment? I brought a change." The idea of Lacey showering and changing at his apartment made his heart leap. This was a special gesture of ease, of closeness. Where he had been thrown down last night, he was now proportionately uplifted. This evening was suddenly more than a date; the details bore the assumption of attachment.

Patrice opened the door after Lacey's light rap. "Hello, lover," she said, hitting at least three separate musical notes. Patrice, with comic timing, turned to look behind him. She kissed him hello, strutted into the apartment, and threw herself down on the sofa with a sigh of homecoming. The red lights from last night were turning to green. The bag on her arm slid off onto the carpet beside her. She pulled her knees up, draping her skirt between them as her fingers combed through her hair, spreading it out on the pillow like a peacock's tail. Patrice sat and enjoyed the show.

"Can you see my place from here?" said Lacey.

"I don't know," said Patrice, "I haven't tried."

"Liar."

"I'm an adult."

"I can see the Carlyle from the park, but I couldn't tell which apartment was yours," said Lacey.

"Twenty-first floor. Can't count to twenty-one?"

"I can't see the street level, smart guy. There's no place to start counting."

Patrice looked at Lacey and wanted her right then, but he knew that immediate sofa sex would be an intense but short engagement, and he preferred the promise of a long entwinement between the perfumed sheets of the Carlyle's king-size bed.

After a shared glass of wine taken from Patrice's personally stocked minifridge, Lacey took over the bathroom while he sat in the living room and listened to the sounds coming from behind the door. When he first heard the hard rain of the shower, the image of her naked, with her hands slipping over herself, rose and stayed in his mind. He visualized every move she might make with a washcloth, until finally he pictured her standing motionless under the rich flow of water, taking in the enveloping steam that cumulated around her like summer clouds.

The jet-engine volume of the hair dryer went on for about ten minutes, then it stopped, and there was another ten minutes of intermittent jangling. He saw a quick flash of her, nude, as she dashed across the hallway to the bedroom, where she had hung up her change of clothes. A few minutes later, she came out dressed, still pulling her hair with a brush. "When are we supposed to be there?"

"We are supposed to be there when we get there," he said.

"Yes," she said, "but for normal people what time are we supposed to be there?"

"Eight o'clock." Patrice liked what he saw in this snapshot. She looked sophisticated and confident. He liked that she still had a sense of the normal, and she was treating him as if they were living together. When she finally presented herself, she was wearing the amber necklace he had given her in St. Petersburg.

She leaned against the wall and snaked the amber around her finger. "Remember this? You gave it to me on the night we *got hot.*"

Madison Avenue was just beginning to flicker on. They walked down the street, sometimes arm in arm, sometimes with Lacey breaking away to physically exaggerate a point, walking backward, then slue-footing around to take his hand or slip her arm through the crook of his elbow. Her strut appropriately modified, her girlishness tempered and grown up for the richest shopping promenade in Manhattan, Lacey had artfully tailored her downtown vibrancy to an acceptable uptown chic.

Nello was filling up quickly, but Patrice had clout. After being greeted with a genuine smile and handshake from the maître d', they were taken to a small, intimate table that was prime Nello real estate. They had a broad view of the restaurant and its select clientele, who were not the same habitués from even a few blocks down the street.

Lacey scanned the room, able to take in all the faces because of a narrow strip of mirror that ran around the entire diameter of the restaurant.

"No art dealers," she said. "What are you going to do?"

"Art dealers don't have dinners. They have lunches."

"Let's have a prosecco." Lacey laid her calf over Patrice's ankle.

A couple next to them was speaking French. Patrice turned and said in stern French, "You should mind your own business."

"What was that about?" asked Lacey.

"It was about rude snobs who think that nobody in America can understand it when they are insulted."

"You don't look French anymore, Patrice."

"Because of you."

"No more skinny pin-striped suits with pinched waists in your Paris closet?"

"No more cuff links, either."

"And Patrice, no more tanning."

"I shouldn't tan?"

"No," said Lacey, "no more tanning no matter how you're getting it." Then there was a pause while they waited for a new subject to appear.

"What's on your walls?" Lacey asked him.

"Of my apartment? I will give you the virtual tour. Close your eyes."

"I *will* give you the virtual tour, not *wheel* give you the tour. *Will...ill...* not *wheel.*"

"I *will* give you the tour...," Patrice struggled to say. "Now close your eyes."

"I *wheel* after the prosecco arrives."

She stared at him, unwavering, until the waiter placed the fizzy glass in front of her. Then she shut her eyes. "First," she said, "what's out the window?"

"The Seine," said Patrice.

"Okay, I'm situated," said Lacey.

"On the first wall you see a Miró *Constellation* gouache. You know what that is?"

"Expensive."

"To the right is a matched pair. A Cubist Braque and a Cubist Picasso. To tell which is which is a game only fools play. Over the sofa—and yes, it matches the fabric—is a Cortès."

"Okay, I'm stumped. Who is Cortès?"

"Cortès is a terrible French street scene painter."

"How can you hang it next to the Picasso?"

"It's the best picture Cortès ever painted." At Lacey's look, he continued, "Look, if you want to be strict, there are only six twentieth-century artists: Picasso, Matisse, Giacometti, Pollock, de Kooning, and Warhol. But I don't want to be strict, which is my downfall. I like sentimental Pre-Raphaelites and dumb Bouguereaus, insipid Aivazovskys, and dogs playing poker. As long as they're good, relatively good, I just can't help myself."

"Everyone you collect is dead."

"They're much easier to negotiate with."

"Wouldn't you rather talk art with an artist than a dealer?"

"Oh please, no! Have you ever heard an artist talk about their art? It's Chinese! What they describe in their work is absolutely *not there*. And it's guaranteed that what you think is their worst picture, they think is their best picture."

Patrice was the funniest unfunny person Lacey had ever met. She liked him, yes, and when they got back to his apartment, she told him so without ever saying it. She treated him as though he were the first and last object of her passion, and their ardor was pitched precisely between lust and romance. Eventually, when it was all over, sitting pegged on him with her knees brought up by his waist, their fingers interlaced palm to palm and her hair falling forward over her face, she looked at him with an expression of immutable love.

43.

THE NEXT DAY she went to work, dug out a phone number from the back of her drawer, and booked lunch with Jonah Marsh. The gallery was closing early for summer hours, and Barton Talley had already gone off to the Hamptons. She was to rendezvous with Patrice later, so she went home, wrenched her bicycle from its vertical slot in her closet, and rode down the West Side bicycle path to Chelsea. It was now the glory days of biking, which began in May and sometimes ended not until late October. She could go in shorts and halter tops and let her hair fly free, and she imagined every metallic rattle behind her was an accident caused by the male bikers who swiveled their heads to get a look at her going away.

She got off the path at 26th Street and slowed to a walk as she gazed into the buildings that had stacks of gallery names listed outside. Here was the kind of activity that separated contemporary art from the sticky pace of the modern masters. She was never going to sleep with Chagall, but she had already slept with Pilot Mouse. There were no exciting studio visits to see Mondrian's strict output, but south of 26th Street there were iron staircases that led to grungy spaces still fresh with the smell of paint, or fiberglass, or horse manure, or *whatever*, and occupied by struggling artists who were morosely fucking each other. Lacey could imagine her name headlining a storefront, Yeager Gallery, or perhaps Parrish Gallery, a pseudonym in honor of her first introduction to art. Parrish had a nice sound to it, she thought.

She met Jonah Marsh—Pilot Mouse—at the Empire Diner, and they sat inside rather than join the cattle line for outside. Jonah introduced Carey, his buddy, his buddy with paint splattered on his jeans, and Lacey thought these two cute guys must have their own kind of waiting list.

"I'd heard you worked at Talley. So I called to catch up."

"Well, I caught up last night. Pilot Mouse. Where did you come up with that name?"

"The night we did X. And thus I am born."

Lacey laughed. "Oh, my God. And Carey, where did you get your weird name?"

Carey laughed, catching the joke, and said, "When I took aspirin."

Jonah Marsh had really called Lacey because he was not finished. Their dissolution had been so abrupt, he felt as though he had been left teetering on a precipice and not quite fallen, his arms still circling for balance. I don't think Jonah was in love with Lacey anymore, but he still wanted to sleep with her; he felt she owed him that. Jonah had interpreted their drug-driven intimacy as genuine, and the enhanced sex that accompanied it stayed in his memory as something that was unique to them, and he believed, correctly, that Lacey wouldn't mind the occasional experiment.

It was to Lacey's advantage to keep Jonah interested. It was to her advantage to keep the newly discovered Carey interested—maybe he was a sellable artist. It was to her advantage to keep everyone interested.

44.

THROUGHOUT THE SUMMER, Lacey continued with Patrice Claire. There were parties and introductions, there was a trip to Paris to see his apartment and be shown off to friends. When the dinners were in English, Lacey charmed; when conversations would drift into French, she sat and waited, a pretty young thing. Her high school French was no help when the speakers sped through words and sentences, leaving nothing for her ear to latch on to.

Patrice's travel kept the relationship from becoming routine, but it also kept him from advancing it. They were still in the romantic phase, extended because of their discontinuous time together, which meant that every two weeks there was an exciting renewal. Lacey's indiscriminate joie de vivre, her openness to adventure, never let Patrice feel he was on solid ground. Though he had tacit commitment, he waited for actual commitment. He also believed their relationship deserved a phone call a day, but sometimes she would not return a Wednesday call until Saturday. Once, he decided to punish her by not calling or returning her calls for four days. It was torture for Patrice. He felt cruel, and his imagination pictured Lacey worrying about him. But this behavior would have been better left to expert manipulators. When he finally called, ninety-six hours after they last spoke, which Patrice had timed exactly, he was twittering with nervous energy. She answered her cell phone with party noise in the background.

"Hey," she said, "I'm at a party downtown. All art people. Are you coming in?"

Absent from Lacey's conversation was the simple inquiry that Patrice had expected and had suffered to obtain, which was, "Where have you been? I missed you so much." She was certainly not in mourning; it seemed she had barely noticed he was missing. Patrice's plan had been a trick on himself, one that left him hurting and alone in the City of Light.

The next day, Lacey called Patrice in Paris as though nothing had happened—because to Lacey, nothing had happened—saying, Come in, we'll go to Shakespeare in the Park. Patrice humbly packed his bags, unable to resist the command. But he didn't take the Concorde, as a personal sign of civil disobedience.

Lacey's display of excitement at seeing him compensated for all her misdemeanors of the past month, and she gave her all in bed that night, which brought him back to the mountaintop. While making love to her, he was also watching her. Yes, this was real passion, centered on him, focused and indivisible. He felt he was taking her to a place no man had taken her, that she had given herself over to him entirely. But afterward, when she rested beside him and he watched her sink into her own thoughts, he could feel the communion slip away, and he knew that she was not his.

Patrice was still unable to give up his fantasy of perfect love and a changed life, even with the surprise blows of reality that Lacey delivered. He could distort her shortcomings and make them his own: it was he, he thought, who was not vital enough to make her fully his.

His week with her extended over Labor Day, and they went to Larry Gagosian's house in the Hamptons for an all-day party. Barton Talley was not invited, being a rival dealer, but Hinton Alberg was there and he greeted Lacey warmly. The ovoid Hinton didn't register a blip on Patrice's jealousy sonar, and he felt almost fine the whole day. As they drove back late in the evening by limousine, Lacey fell asleep against his shoulder. He felt that if he moved, she might be displeased with him, so he stayed stiffly in place the entire two hours.

45.

TOWARD THE NEW MILLENNIUM, Lacey began to throw accurate strikes for the Talley gallery. At the end of 1998, she sold a small Léger for over a million dollars (to a French couple Patrice Claire had directed her way), and early in 1999, she negotiated a sale of little-known Warhol black-and-white photographs to Elton John, whose Atlanta-based collection of photography had grown into a treasury. Large numbers were beginning to be easier to say. She had had an initial reticence about saying "one point two" instead of "one million two hundred thousand." It seemed as though "one point two" should be said by people partying on a yacht, not a twenty-nine-year-old woman who still felt like a downtown girl. It remained hard for her to say "three" when there could be a confusion as to whether she meant three million or three hundred thousand. When Talley said "three," the client always understood its meaning.

As comfortable as Lacey was becoming with prices that would have stuck in her throat a year earlier, she was working on salary rather than commission, except for the occasional generous gratuity from Talley, meaning that she was not participating in the newly inflated profits the art market was starting to generate. She continued to imagine a gallery with her name out front. She could likely afford a new gallery that showed younger artists, while she couldn't fund even the frames required to show modern masters, despite her windfall from a few years ago.

To further enhance the viability of downtown galleries, a new category of art was being created. Already in place were "old masters," "Postimpressionists," "postwar," and "contemporary." When collectors said, "We collect contemporary," their scope and interest—and their prestige—could be fairly understood. But when the rubric of "young artists" surfaced, a whole new class of collectors had a label. Saying, "We collect young artists," had extraordinary cachet. It meant that they were in the forefront, ferreting out genius, risking money and reputation.

It was impossible to know if this new art was good, because, mostly, good art had been defined by its endurance over time. But even though this new art had not yet faced that jury, collectively it had a significant effect: it made art of Talley's generation seem old and stodgy. It was similar to what happened to crooners when Elvis came along: they were instantly musty. A living room full of Picassos identified the collectors as a certain kind of old money. But a roomful of unprecedented objects, historically rootless, was lively and game, and the collectors who amassed them were big-game hunters.

The nature of collecting changed, too. Formerly, dealers tried to win the respect of their collectors. Now collectors were trying to win the respect of their dealers. A new social constellation had been created linking New York to London, San Francisco, Chicago, and Los Angeles. Collector stars were once again being created on rumors of buying binges and hearsay about private galleries being planned to house their vast acquisitions.

An art renaissance was under way. Unlike the Italian Renaissance, fueled by science and art nibbling away at a strict anti-intellectual environment, the new renaissance was fueled by an abundance of affordable art that was, in most cases, made by sincere and talented artists flocking to New York, its cultural center. Cortés and Sir Francis Drake were on the prowl, not for land, but for competent artists with an idea.

In 1999, the full potency of young artists was not yet known. Lacey's embryonic notion of starting a gallery had begun before objects that were barely two years old would achieve million-dollar prices.

46.

WHEN AUGUST FALLS on Manhattan, the galleries go quiet, with some of them shuttering until the season opens again in September. Lacey became the gallery sitter while Barton took his Hamptons vacation. By the time the workday ended, she still had hours of sunlight left to Rollerblade around Central Park. Lacey liked the summer heat and the stripping away of sullen winter clothing to near nudity or athletic wear that emphasized the bas-relief of her anatomical landscape. The sky was still dusky when she set out for open ground, the bars and restaurants of young Manhattan.

Patrice Claire still courted Lacey, and Lacey courted him back. But while he was forthright, she was tricky and unreliable. As much as Patrice's every thought was about Lacey, whenever he was wheels up at JFK and heading for Paris, there was an accompanying release of tension, as he no longer felt the need to be constantly interesting or to artificially represent himself to her and her friends as a ceaselessly dynamic person. He made many transatlantic flights that summer, because he knew not to stay too long in New York, not to crowd Lacey with his presence, and not to appear that he was exclusively hers. However, Lacey already knew he was exclusively hers, if she wanted him. As long as Patrice didn't embarrass himself by proclaiming undying love, she was fine remaining involved but uncommitted.

One August night, Patrice landed in New York against a burnt orange sunset and headed for a spontaneously arranged dinner with Cornelia and Hinton Alberg. Unable to call her from Paris without it being a three a.m. wake-up, he phoned Lacey upon hitting the tarmac, and she answered.

"Lacey, tell me you're okay for dinner. Meeting Hinton and Cornelia at Boulud."

"Rats, give a girl a little warning. I've got to be downtown, I don't know how long. Can I come if I can get out of this?"

"Of course. Just come if you can, love to see you."

"Don't wait for me, just start," she said.

Patrice was so polite. "Just come if you can" was not what he meant. He meant "Come. Do it. Show up." But "Just come if you can" made him feel less desperate, more confident. And now he was left with a lacerating curiosity about what she was doing instead of being with him.

Boulud, adjacent to the Carlyle, was the restaurant where upscale dealers took their clients, often to celebrate a sale or to position themselves as matchmaker between an important collector and a museum director. The collectors liked to meet museum people because one approving word from them about a single painting in a hallway could, by liberal extrapolation, validate an entire collection. Directors liked to meet collectors because maybe they would soon be dead and their collection would come to their museum.

But Patrice's dinner with the Albergs was not about business. Hinton could, and would, talk art with anyone, anywhere, and at any time. Patrice and the Albergs liked each other, and Cornelia enjoyed listening to his dating woes and giving him advice and counsel. So when Patrice phoned her to say that Lacey might be joining them and would it be all right, she regarded the request not only as a politeness, but as information about Patrice's heart.

"Lacey Yeager, oh yes, we like her," said Cornelia into her cell phone moments before walking into Boulud.

She and Hinton were seated at a corner table while Patrice's taxi jangled down Park Avenue, heading for 76th Street. There was a moment of repose as they waited. Hinton fit beautifully into the restaurant and its clientele; it was as though he were sitting on an easy chair at home. And Cornelia's frankness made her welcome in an art world so filled with reserve. In came Acquavella with his wife and grown children, clearly not here on business, and Hinton wondered about the practicality of hosting one's family at a restaurant that *Zagat's* rated as $$$$.

Patrice arrived and took the seat with the best view of the entrance.

"Patrice, you look well. Doesn't he look well, honey?"

"Darlin', don't you know I can't look people in the eye?" said Hinton. "That's why I have pictures. I can look over people's shoulders and land on something so forthcoming."

"But Hinton, there's nothing on the walls here, you might as well look at me," said Patrice, coaxing a laugh from him. "Lacey's going to try and come," he continued, "she's got work downtown."

"When did this start?" said Cornelia.

Patrice smiled at her. "Start? I'm not sure it has. She said to go ahead without her."

Patrice always laughed with the Albergs. Cornelia's curiosity about the forceful personalities that populated their collectors' world and Hinton's lack of interest in anything that moved except by art courier made them lively, made them yin and yang, and Patrice could bounce along over the entire spectrum of conversation. But tonight, as their chatter crisscrossed the table, Cornelia noticed something in Patrice: his eyes shifting from the table to the restaurant entrance. Sometimes a glimmer would come to his face as he spotted the tip of a skirt or a sweater-covered arm that edged inside the front door, and occasionally the anticipatory brightening of his face would turn Cornelia toward the door, too, to see nothing, a mistake, not Lacey.

During the dinner, Acquavella dropped by and jousted with Hinton.

"When are you going to get rid of that stuff and get some real paintings?"

"Well, when are you going to offer me something great?"

"Oh, I've just got Van Goghs and Monets, nothing any good."

"I'll come by tomorrow, Bill."

"Okay, I'll dig something out for you; get you into some quality merchandise. All right, see you later, buddy."

Cornelia was amused by Bill, but she again noted Patrice's distraction from the table and attention to the door. They covered no topic that wasn't attended by this little punctuation. By dessert, Lacey had not shown up, and one last time Patrice gave a now mournful head twist toward the entrance. Cornelia looked at him, squinted her eyes with displeasure, and said, "Women can be so stupid."

PART

III

47.

LACEY, NOW AN UPTOWN WOMAN, felt an increasing tug toward Chelsea. She was like a cat sensing the first vibrations of the oncoming earthquake that was about to rumble through the art market. There were plenty of small signs to be successfully interpreted. Years earlier, SoHo, the former New York gallery center, had proven too successful. Rising rents killed all but the strongest galleries. So the smaller galleries moved leftward to Chelsea, stranding and branding the ones that remained in SoHo as unhip. New galleries sprouted in Chelsea overnight, lacking only fungi domes.

Lacey was aware of an unwieldy rhetorical shift that took place between the Upper East Side and the lower West Side. Art on the Upper East Side was referred to as beautiful, exceptional, serene, exquisite, and *important*. Art below 26th Street was described in the "language of relational aesthetics" or something like that, an argot with a semantic shelf life of about six months. Now artworks "related to spatial, representational, and material functions in contexts defined by movement and transition." An artist who painted a face was now "playing with the idea of a portraiture," or "exploring push-pull aesthetics," or toying with contradictions like "menacing–slash–playful," but he or she was never, ever, simply painting a face.

Patrice Claire, who had chased Lacey into the twenty-first century like a horse chasing a train, and who had allowed humiliations to collect unacknowledged in his psyche, was invited to dinner with Lacey's good friend, me, at Jack's Luxury Oyster Bar. "Oh, you must spend time with Daniel," I could hear her saying, "we're so close."

Jack's Luxury Oyster Bar was a vertical restaurant squeezed between town houses. Quaint and charming, it had silver salt and pepper chicks on the tables and tiny dining rooms trimmed in mother's lace curtains and red-and-white-checkered wallpaper. The rooms were connected by narrow stairs that necessitated an excellent grip on the handrail to avoid a deadly, headlong tumble after a round of cocktails. All this atmosphere was reflected in the bill, which soared into triple digits even for single diners. So when Patrice showed up for dinner with Lacey, it would have been romantic, had it not been for me.

I could see his taxi pull up, and Patrice emerged looking windblown, even though there was no wind. Dressed in a dark suit with a white shirt and no tie, he could have been a fashion model who had been directed to get out of the car as though he were carefree, wealthy, and masculine. My theory of his insecurity about me vanished, replaced by my own insecurity about looks, accomplishment, and money, everything that Patrice effortlessly possessed.

But Patrice was generous toward me, asking questions about my writing, about the art world and the way I saw it. I think he liked that I was not cynical about it, this insular collective that is so vulnerable to barbs from the outside ("Three million dollars for *that*?"), a world that can shield itself from criticism by the implication that its detractors are rubes. So Patrice and I hit it off, and Lacey was in top form, funny and caustic. And naughty:

"Oh, Patrice," she said midconversation, "you like Balthus because you like underpants."

Patrice included me in his response: "Could anyone but Lacey make the word *underpants* sound like a nasty verb?"

"Well, you are a horn dog," said Lacey.

Patrice smiled while he tried to parse "horn dog," concluding it was both funny and accurate, and looked over at me. "What am I going to do with this creature?"

I don't know if the next question Patrice asked me came because he was now satisfied that I was not a threat, hence a few personal questions were okay, or if he was still trying to figure out my status with Lacey:

"Do you have a girlfriend, Daniel?"

"I am currently between girlfriends," I said.

"You wish," said Lacey.

Then I stupidly told them my dating stories, which I realized were all nonstories when I saw their eyes glaze over and stare into their drinks.

"There must be hundreds of women in the art world," said Patrice.

"Yes," I said. "They like artists, not so much art writers. We seem to be on the fringe. Plus, I'm benign. Benign is not a trait women go for."

"But Daniel," said Lacey, "you are in the most desirable category of all for women of our age, the employed, handsome dork."

We all laughed, and I secretly thought, Could I have finally entered into a desirable category?

Precisely after the appetizers, when the last dish was cleared, as though she were waiting for elbow room, Lacey said, "I took a lease on a space in Chelsea."

"A gallery?" I said.

"Yeager Arts," she said. "I've got connections uptown and down-town."

Patrice said, "You're tired of working for the man."

Lacey shriveled. "Oh, Patrice, we don't say 'the man.'"

He looked over at me to check; I agreed with a sympathetic nod.

"Where?" he asked.

"It's at 525 West Twenty-fifth Street. Fifth floor. There are lots of small galleries moving in. I grabbed a space."

"Commercial or conceptual?" I said.

This seemed to stump her. The Chelsea galleries were carefully and willfully defining themselves, breaking away from the more established galleries by presenting art that was "difficult," backing it up with the academic grad school rhetoric. This was art that maintained the irony that began in the sixties, and irony provided an escape valve in case the visuals became too pretty. It was as if a pitcher had decided it was gauche to throw fastballs but still threw fastballs in a mockery of throwing fastballs. These were the conceptual galleries, which garnered respect by defiance and distance, which went *young*, which made you feel that they possessed the cabalistic code that unlocked the inner secrets of art.

I had more trouble explaining commercial galleries because the word implies saccharine merchandise headed for the space above the living room sofa. But Cy Twombly, Richard Serra, Agnes Martin, and Robert Ryman are not saccharine, they are simply *known*. Commercial galleries dealt in artists, famous or not, whose work was in the tradition of something before it and therefore was, in some way, understood.

Lacey got it, Patrice got it, but neither cared. Lacey was opening a gallery, and she needed to find artists, conceptual or commercial, and she was excited.

"Why not both?" she said in answer to my question. "It should be ready in nine months."

"How come so long?" I said.

"Because you're painting it and I know you're slow," said Lacey.

We laughed. But Patrice was drifting out of the conversation. With Lacey's adventure would come new men, and he knew she was careless.

He took Lacey to her home that night and slept with her. Afterward, still between sheets, with a drink beside him, he said to a distracted Lacey, "Do you need money for your gallery? I'll be happy to help out."

"What would I be if I didn't do it myself?" she said. "Besides, I have money."

As noble as Lacey's self-sufficiency was to Patrice, he knew that her refusal kept him out, kept her free of him.

There was a long silence, which, if made audible, would have sounded with the jangle and clatter of Patrice's racing mind and the singular drone of Lacey's will. Finally, hoping for a reprieve from her increasing remoteness, Patrice said to her, probing for conversation, "What are you thinking?"

She lowered her voice to a comic gravel to cut the harshness of her response. "You don't want to know," she said. Patrice suddenly felt very tired.

48.

IN THE SPRING of 2001, Lacey took her beloved Warhol *Flowers* and auctioned it at Christie's—she was too uneasy to deal with Sotheby's. When she heard talk on the street—the art street—that a small *Flowers* could bring as much as eighty thousand dollars, a profit to her of perhaps sixty-four thousand, practicality prevailed. Whatever heartache she felt at selling the painting was soothed by the stunning check she received after it brought a warming one hundred and twenty-nine thousand dollars. Warhol was on the move, and so was she. This would cushion her against the hard landings that can occur when one is in business for oneself. Pilot Mouse had promised her two paintings, not to be sold until her gallery opened; and his friend Carey proved to be an interesting painter, and it was decided that he would be her first show. She liked his work because it was essentially inexplicable, and she knew it would keep her gallery from seeming too easy. She was also a regular at the studio of a beautiful African-American girl just out of art school, Latonya Walsh, whose racy and racial images would be her second show. She knew both these attractive artists would show well at their opening night party, both on the wall and as physical specimens.

She stayed at Barton Talley's through the summer running the gallery, and Barton was happy to have her, as it allowed him to have his Hamptons weekends and summer jaunts to Europe. He had no rivalry with her; he was experienced enough to know that gallerists come and go, and he saw her departure not as creating competition, but as developing connections.

Yeager Arts was scheduled to open after Labor Day, when the streets of Chelsea would be teeming, when the festivities would bloom with art openings that included handsome servers bearing plastic flutes of champagne and patrons backing clumsily into paintings as their chat circles grew wider and wider. The hoopla was a month long, because galleries rolled out their events so they didn't all occur on the same night. When Lacey's opening was postponed several weeks for several reasons, she knew there would still be enough excitement to spare for her virgin upstairs space.

49.

ONE MORNING she woke to a late summer day so glorious, she was compelled to take an early bike ride down to Chelsea to sit in the middle of her still-unhung gallery and contemplate the potential of its blank walls. There was one week left before she was to open.

Outside, it was cloudless and already warming at nine a.m. The silken air slipstreamed around her even though she was trying to be as unaerodynamic as possible. She sat erect, steering the bike with one hand while her other arm swung free. Though now, at thirty-one years of age, she was more respectful of helmets and sunscreen, today she was unhampered by safety apparatus, letting the wind blow through her hair as she turned her face toward the morning sun. This was a free day; Barton Talley was in, and she was attending to the impractical side of her business, allowing creative daydreams to overrule the duty call of daily business.

The sounds of New York were lighter today; fewer cars along the highway made the journey more pleasant, and the whir of Rollerbladers reminded her of the ball-bearing rumble of her childhood skates on a sidewalk. There was a siren in the distance, which she barely noticed. Colors were stark and crisp: there was the blue of the sky against the green of the grass, and Lacey's sun-yellow shirt against the pure white of her shorts. And of course there was the occasional butthead who streaked by everyone with near-miss intentions. She thought she might tour the entire perimeter of Manhattan, after a religious stop at her new gallery. Another siren.

She neared 54th Street, where the bike path emerged from under the highway trestle and the buildings retreated, giving the feeling that Manhattan was doing its best to have a prairie. She imagined her gallery and its accidental golden rectangle interior that would make hanging pictures a joy; and she visualized its cozy back room that would make any artwork hanging in it seem more special, shown to the important clientele only. A fire truck blared down the highway, annoying her. These sirens are ruining my day, she thought. When another and then another siren blared by, she understood: Oh, something's happening.

She looked ahead—the sirens seemed to be headed south—but she saw nothing. A police action, she suspected. She continued down the path and sensed a disturbance in the mien of people who populated the next few hundred yards of path. Some were stalled, talking in groups, while some continued on as usual. She saw a car ahead, barely parked off the path, and a man sitting motionless inside with his foot holding the door wide open. As she neared, she could hear that he had the radio on. A few people were listening around the speaker in the car door. She slowed to a stop, putting her foot on the ground, leaning the bike against her thigh.

"What's going on?" she said.

A Hispanic man turned his head toward her. "They think a plane flew into the World Trade Center."

She looked downtown but could see only one of the giant buildings, as they lined up almost perfectly. There was a stream of black smoke starting to billow from a window-size puncture. She imagined that a stray Piper Cub, guided by a Sunday pilot, had misjudged a banking turn over the Hudson and couldn't pull out in time. She ventured farther downtown, and still nothing changed much. People kept biking, jogging, walking. She stopped again when she saw a small group of people who seemed to be aware of the news, and again she said, "What's going on?"

"They think a plane crashed into the tower."

"A Cessna or something?"

"A jet," someone said.

She believed this report would be corrected, thinking the small plane scenario more logical, and she biked another mile down. Within minutes, she could see flames spewing from a high floor of the building like spitfire, and she paused, thinking how two-dimensional, how flat, it looked. She had to remind herself that as surreal an image as it was, it was also real. Horror was going on inside, and her distance from the site meant that the screams inside were falling silent before they reached her ears.

Decency told her she should not press forward, but her awareness that this moment was unique and probably historical drove her farther downtown. But the previously sparse crowds had turned thick. People were now moving en masse uptown along the bike path, talking unperturbedly, a migration of people away from the towers. Lacey could no longer cycle forward. She turned around, pedaled uptown, veered off onto 83rd Street, carried her bike upstairs, turned on the TV, and stared.

She looked at the towers, believing the camera angle was from her bike path point of view, seeing only one. Unaware that the north tower had fallen, she went to the kitchen for a bottle of water, returning in time to see a replay of the second tower imploding into rubble. She figured out that both towers had fallen, one while her back was turned to the south, cycling home, and one while she stood at her refrigerator. She looked out her window. She could see a slow movement of people heading north, walking safely down the center of West End Avenue, as all car traffic had stopped. The silence brought on by terror struck

Lacey as perversely serene, and it took her a while to notice that all air traffic had stopped, too, reducing Manhattan's constant din to what it must have been like one hundred years earlier.

She went alone to Isabella's for lunch and found it a busy restaurant, with patrons talking, laughing, ordering with puzzled looks while pointing at the menu. It wasn't that life was going on as usual, it was that what had happened was not yet fully known. Over the next twenty-four hours, there would be a dampening in people's gestures, activity, and volume.

Lacey stopped at a market, wondering if there would be a run on food; but there wasn't. She bought enough for a few days and returned home. She sank into her sofa, transfixed by the television, her cell phone and landline jammed by traffic. She didn't move until night came, eventually sitting in darkness, having forgotten to turn on even a lamp. The room was illuminated only by the blue glow of the TV news, while banners of text streamed under the newscasters, amid reports of a Pentagon attack, a delinquent president, a crash in the Pennsylvania woods. The nation grew still, an anesthetized giant waiting to figure out what was happening to it. That night in bed, she revisited the searing image of the tower shooting flames. It reminded her of something—which seemed impossible to her—but she didn't know what.

She woke in the early morning and checked her phones: still dead. The TV was alive, however. She sat again watching while news tumbled over itself, and again she sat until ten p.m., never turning on a light in her apartment, because the TV was all she wanted and all that she needed. She assumed her parents were concerned for her, but there was no way to communicate, so she could only wait. She worried for her downtown friends, but the area was closed tight. The bridges and tunnels remained closed, stranding people where they were at the moment of penetration. She sat and watched.

Wednesday came and went. Thursday morning the phones were still dead. Her cell phone had bars, but service was jammed. She walked outside a bit and wondered if New York had been this silent, ever. Even twenty minutes away from the television created an unease that something worse had happened, which required her to focus harder on the news and its flowing ticker tape of rumors and facts in order to catch up. For another day, she remained motionless in front of the TV, hours passing, night creeping over the city.

It was around nine p.m. when the door buzzer rang. She rose, her legs stiff from the last three days of cave dwelling, and spoke into her intercom.

"Hello?"

"It's Carey. You okay?"

She buzzed him in; he climbed the stairs.

"I thought I'd check in. Nobody can reach anybody," he said when she opened the door.

"How'd you get here?"

"I walked," said Carey.

"Sixty blocks?"

"Yeah." His head gestured toward the TV. "Anything?" he asked.

"All the same," she said.

They were now in the dark, all connections to the outside frozen, all considerations for the outside in suspension. Whatever was about to happen was excusable, was necessary to confirm humanity. As carnal as their night was about to be, they would be visited by a simulacrum of emotion that loomed briefly and moved on. They would be reminded of love without feeling love, reminded of deep human contact without having it.

It was now Friday morning after the awful Tuesday. Carey and Lacey watched the morning news, then walked funereally to Riverside Park, where they stood and looked where the towers once were. It was shocking that there was no trace of them, no afterimage left in the sky, no outline traced around their perimeter.

Lacey said, "I know what I was reminded of yesterday."

"When?" said Carey.

"When I first saw the tower burning. The Ruscha."

"What Ruscha?"

"Los Angeles County Museum on Fire."

When Carey left, they agreed to postpone his opening until a more practical date. This was the first time Lacey thought of her business, a demonstration of the numbing power of shock. Their sexual encounter was never mentioned again.

There was still an art world, but there was no art market. Stocks tumbled; who but the crazy would buy pictures when it was unknown if anything would have value, when our main preoccupation was anticipation of further terror? Lacey mourned for her gallery and her dream of self-governorship, but she knew that rage was useless, that this was an act of God, or godlessness, and that she could do nothing until the world righted itself.

Her gallery finally opened in December, a slow time in the art world, when buyers were about to disappear for the holidays and not straggle back until the second week in January. She sold two paintings by Carey Harden, but they were to his relatives at deep discounts, and the opening party was a fizzle. Patrice Claire was in Paris; he was weaning himself away from her, so he and his dazzling friends never came. She waited for the gallery to fill up, to resemble a crowded first night, but it never did. She felt like another hopeful tucked into the warrens of the building, running a gallery that needed a flashlight and compass to be found, and the long, empty days meant that business, real and imagined, was conducted mostly on the phone.

When Christmas came, she went home to her parents in Atlanta and pretended that everything was fine. But now, away from New York, the idea of selling art after the apocalypse seemed frivolous.

50.

ART MAGAZINES SURVIVED—I guess subscription canceling is the last thing to think about after a disaster. My income stayed at parity, and my savings stayed intact, topped off occasionally by my intuitive parents, who had miraculously timed the sale of a dozen prime acres near Stockbridge. New York still moved, mostly on inertia, like a car coasting downhill after it had run out of gas. It turned out there was nothing to do but go on as usual, with a revival of old-fashioned love-it-or-leave-it patriotism coating everything, and the public eventually caught on that the nascent TV phrase *breaking news* could mean a traffic tie-up in Queens.

I made a lunch date with Tanya Ross. I was attracted to her, and we both spoke art, which meant the conversation never ran dry: we could talk about artists, shows, openings, museums, prices, collectors, Europe, the Prado, uptown, downtown, gossip, theory, Bilbao, the Guggenheim, little-known works at the Met, the Frick, Isabella Stuart Gardner, Chuck Close, Florine Stettheimer, and sales. I met her at the restaurant at Barneys on Madison, and she insisted that we split the check. I tried, but she insisted. I couldn't interpret if this was a good or a bad sign. Splitting the check indicates it's not a date but also shows respect for the other person, especially since she suggested the restaurant. There was nothing datelike about our lunch, but once, she touched my hand as she made a point, and at the end of it, she invited me to a lecture sponsored by Sotheby's. I couldn't tell if the invite was social or professional.

"Oh, John Richardson's talking about his new book on Friday. Would you like to come?"

"John Richardson?" I said. "My superhero, my god, and if it were possible, my Halloween costume."

Tanya laughed and looked into my eyes, pleased.

"I'd love to come," I said. "What's the book? A new one?"

"*Sacred Monsters, Sacred Munsters*, something," she said. "It's at five and there are drinks afterwards."

"Drinks afterwards" made me think that Tanya was putting her toe in the water with me, and it turned out she was. She was Lacey's opposite. She didn't leap in ablaze. She was a tortoise to Lacey's hare, perhaps not as effective, but her goals were less grand than Lacey's, and a modest presence can eventually catch the eye in a powerful way.

The lecture took place at Boulud, which Sotheby's had bought out at tea time for the event. I felt this was the way the art world was supposed to be: sophisticated, dressed, with a British accent and raconteur's tongue. Richardson, a real scholar with a bright pen, was a renowned biographer of Picasso; he had already completed two massive volumes of a projected four. He had escaped from the astringent clutches of Savile Row and didn't wear the English gentleman's uniform of a blue-and-white-striped dress shirt with a white collar, pinched gray suit, and pink tie. Instead, he looked sharp but frazzled: in other words, like an author. He enjoyed humor, especially wicked humor, and at age seventy-seven, he seemed keener and more magnetic than any person in the room. His talk, a form of worldly gossip about the fabulously interesting, was too brief, and I wanted more: I didn't know that the Art Deco designer Jean-Michel Frank was a close relation of Anne Frank, the doomed child from Amsterdam.

Afterward, pools of admirers collected in the dining room. I bought his book—it was actually titled *Sacred Monsters, Sacred Masters*—and he signed it. I of course tried to impress him by quoting back his own lines to him, but what I really wanted was for him to simply tell me his writing secret. Unfortunately, I already knew it: brilliance. Perhaps I should work on that. Then Tanya brought Richardson a six p.m. Scotch, and we all were thrilled by his further stories of the naughty elite.

I walked Tanya down Madison, asked her if she wanted to sit for a while. Yes. We stopped at Le Charlot, an authentic French bistro that made me feel authentically inferior. The waiters sped by us, curiously, since the place was nearly empty. The drinks made us loose, and we got only one-third the way through our art world, and world, topics before it was time to leave. She grabbed a cab, and I took the subway home. I thought about her a lot. There was talk of war, it was cold, but our afternoon spent in peace comforted me, and I think it comforted Tanya, too.

51.

IN FEBRUARY 2002, Chelsea was about to be hit with five hundred tons of steel. The Gagosian Gallery was opening a space on 24th Street, which, considering the timing, seemed like a misstep, inspiring glee in Larry's detractors. And he was bringing in the colossal work of Richard Serra, whose favorite medium was difficulty. Fifteen-foot-high walls of rusted Corten steel had to be moved into an old paint factory, and the old paint factory had to look like a slick gallery in a matter of months. The opening was delayed because the cranes that were necessary to move the leviathan works were all occupied at Ground Zero and couldn't be diverted for something as frivolous as an art show. But eventually, the massive leaves of corroded steel were balanced in the Gagosian Gallery like sheets of paper standing on end, and walking among them produced in the viewer equal measures of awe and nervousness.

Lacey timed her second opening to coincide with Serra's. She installed Latonya Walsh's jumpy, jazzy works, and when a thousand art lovers showed up for Serra's opening, giving Chelsea an unexpected kick start, her place hummed along with the spillover. Pictures sold, and sold to collectors, not friends. The idea of a war in Afghanistan and luxury art purchases running along the sidewalk hand in hand struck everyone as mysterious. The war was away, far over there. Here, we were being encouraged to act normally and to understand that this conflict would affect us not at all, a fly to be brushed away. An unprecedented

Betwixt the Torus and the Sphere, Richard Serra, 2001
142 × 450 × 319 in.

and feverish upswing in the art market was about to occur, one that reached beyond the insiders and the knowledgeable, which would draw the attention of stock investors and financial operators, making them turn their heads toward Chelsea.

This was the opening night Lacey had imagined, not the setback of several months earlier, where Carey Harden's work languished. Lacey put herself forth with charm and confidence, and she pushed the equally compelling Latonya Walsh forward as an intellectual, which she was, steering her into collectors' memories as well as their sight lines.

Patrice Claire was there for this one but guarded by a few friends, and Carey Harden was there, too. I was sorry their secret was invisible to Patrice, because at least this would have been a fact he could have digested, acted on, and used as an escape from whatever airy tethers kept him hopeful. In fact, it disturbed me that their one-nighter was so acutely unnoticeable; what did it mean for my larger world? Was every transgression capable of being so well hid? It suggested that one could connect the dots between any two people in any room and perhaps stumble onto an unknown relationship.

Patrice left, suggesting Lacey join him for a drink later. But she never called, and he didn't expect her to. After that night, he never saw her again.

52.

DURING THE NEXT FOUR YEARS, auction catalogs would swell with glamour. A reader could now see his face reflected in their glossy pages. Color foldouts heralded important paintings or tried to make unimportant paintings seem grander than they actually were. All artists, whether they deserved it or not, were, in bold letters on the page, referred to by their last names only. This made sense if the last name was Cézanne, but when contemporary catalogs announced "Jones," the effect was silly. Somewhere, in the dark heart of the houses, it was decided that the catalogs should not just *present*, but should *promote*. A catalog could no longer be flipped through; it should demand time to spread out and absorb these sexy centerfolds. The catalog entries now had lengthy analytical essays and illuminating reproductions of other pictures, whether they related or not: a minimalist Agnes Martin might be accompanied by an illustration of the *Mona Lisa*, whose best connection to the picture in question might come under a TV game show category, "things that are rectangular." The catalogs' weight increased, and weary postmen in expensive zip codes must have hated it when auction season came around.

These catalogs became like a semiannual stock report. Collectors scoured the estimates, then assessed the sales figures and reinsured their pictures, feeling proud that they had gotten in early. Insurance required appraisals, and Sotheby's and Christie's could provide them, thus gaining entrance to hitherto closed collections and coincidentally finding out where all the loot was. They started to make bold guarantees for paintings, bold enough to pry them off even the most sincere collector's walls. It was unclear why all this market heft was occurring, but money was flowing in from Europe, Asia, the Middle East, and Russia. There was, clearly, a surfeit of cash. New billionaires were being created from apparently nothing. They just suddenly *were*. Ten million spent here and there, even foolishly, didn't matter.

Because established artists were achieving out-of-reach prices, collectors turned to contemporary, and New York responded. Uptown galleries, unable to find goods at profitable prices, watched as Chelsea exploded. One could imagine the classy East Side dealers racing downtown, shedding their ties and tossing their papers of provenance into the wind, trying not only to cash in on art whose only cost was materials, but also to stay relevant.

Lacey's business soared. Over the past year, her gallery, quite accidentally, had become known for female artists. Besides Latonya Walsh, she had taken on Amy Arras, who produced exquisitely detailed drawings in colored pencil of warring soldiers that were remarkable both technically and conceptually.

One Saturday, two major collectors, Ben and Belinda Boggs, wandered in and bought two pieces by Pansy Berks, who made small, glowing portraits of her drugged-out friends. They invited Lacey to attend a celebratory dinner that night, and she was not only thrilled, but obligated to attend. She taxied over to Pastis, the new in-spot.

Belinda's hair was golden and high, sweeping back over her forehead and held in place with lacquer and enamel red headband. The look was of a wave about to crash backward over her head. Ben had a fence of white porcelain for teeth, and his hair was styled just like Belinda's. Their hair color matched almost exactly, which raised questions of duplicate bottle use. His skin was mottled red, sanded to a shine by one too many chemical peels.

Lacey started to take a drink of water, but Belinda held up an open palm, indicating "halt." She signaled the waiter, who brought over an open bottle of champagne and poured three glasses. Belinda passed Lacey a flute, toasted to her and then to her nodding husband, and said, "Congratulations, Lacey. You sold us our one thousandth painting."

They drank to it, and Lacey said, "Well, I wish I had met you earlier. I would have preferred to sell you your first two hundred." Though Ben and Belinda couldn't make jokes, they were able to sense them in the same way a blind man sensed the curb after thwacking it with his cane—they couldn't see it, but they knew it was there—so they laughed exactly on cue.

"We like Pansy Berks's work because we can figure it out," said Belinda. "That's what makes a work appealing; I like figuring them out. Berks paints her friends when they're high, but with colors that are unreal, too bright for the room, so she's saying that she's too bright for this room. And that she should change her friends. Right?"

"Wow," said Lacey, "right." She cringed inside.

"We bought a painting from Yasper," said Belinda, "and Yasper said there was no way we could figure this one out."

Ben jumped in. "We had always figured out Yasper's pictures before, but this one he said we never would. It's one of his paradox paintings."

Lacey figured out, in time, that they were talking about Jasper, Jasper Johns. "Did you figure it out?"

"No! That's what's so amazing. He said we couldn't figure it out and then we couldn't," said Belinda.

"I thought it was a hat; I was convinced it was a hat. But he said no," said Ben.

"It's not a hat," Belinda said.

"It's not a chicken, either," accused Ben.

Felt Suit, Joseph Beuys, 1970
66.9 × 23.6 in.

"I said it was a chicken and Yasper said it wasn't," said Belinda.

"Do you know Joseph Beuys?" Ben said. "We bought one of his felt suits."

Lacey knew. Her days at Talley's always paid off somehow. Beuys made the suits in an edition of one hundred in 1970. They were meant to hang on a wall on a coat hanger, with the pant legs hanging long, almost as though inhabited by an invisible person.

"I love this story," said Belinda.

"We were having a sit-down dinner at our opening of the collection at our gallery," said Ben. "When was this, honey?"

"In the early nineties," she said. "That's when we opened our gallery." The Boggses had a private gallery on their property in Connecticut.

"Big, gala opening," said Belinda.

"I'm in a tuxedo, and let's just say a tuxedo, white frosted cake, and a clumsy waiter don't go well together."

"Oh God, this is so hilarious," said Belinda, who did her hand thing to Ben, stopping him. "So what does he do? He takes the suit off the wall, goes into the men's room, and changes into it. He comes out in the felt suit and there's applause!"

"Most of the people there weren't art people, mostly financial, so I was lucky. The story's a legend now, though."

Lacey laughed, but she knew that Beuys was an emotional artist and that the felt suit was a serious work, probably stemming from his post-war days in Germany, days of guilt and regret.

"The suit got wrinkled, so we bought another one. But it was worth it," said Ben.

"We donated the wrinkled one to a museum in Tulsa. They were happy to get it, after we explained what it was," said Belinda. "We didn't tell them Ben had worn it. We had it steamed."

Midway through dinner, Lacey could see that Ben was drunk. His head would swivel and fall toward Belinda while she ran on, and Lacey could see him try to focus. Lacey worried that someone might think that these were her parents. She excused herself to the restroom, then met them on the sidewalk. When Ben asked if she wanted a lift home in their chauffeured car, she declined, worried that his drunkenness might somehow infect the driver.

53.

WITH THE NATION AT WAR, I went to an art fair. Financed by *ARTnews*, for whom I was writing an article, I landed in Miami for the big mutha expo of galleries from all over the world, or at least countries that participated in the art market. Lacey, as a new gallery, was offered a small auxiliary space, and she took it.

This visit was perfect for me in at least two ways. One, I got to go where the latest and greatest were gathered, sparing myself thousands of miles of travel that neither I nor the magazine could have afforded. Two, Tanya Ross and I were now going out on a date most weeks, and I was glad to have something self-important to say to her: "I'm flying to Miami for the fair." This credited me, in my view, with special involvement and stature: I was the one *ARTnews* was sending. I would, by the way, have asked her out every night of the week, but I could tell she was slower-paced than I, and with each date she leaned my way a slight degree more. And she always seemed happy to see me.

I stayed at a fabulously shabby Art Deco hotel that was walking distance from the humongous convention center, with its seventeen entrances, vast plains of space to fill, and the worst Miami-ugly facade of bleached white stucco. Inside, though, the expo teemed with galleries, some of them so upscale that their booths were covered in brown velvet and had paneled ceilings, and some so slapdash that they could have been selling tattoos and moonshine. There were Picassos near the front of the expo, and as you moved toward the rear, name values diminished to pinpoints. I've heard of museums so large that they're easy to get lost in, but I never did. However, I did get lost in this labyrinth, and I was so befuddled for a few anxious minutes that if I had been five instead of thirty-two, I would have cried.

Lacey had taken a small space at a satellite fair, which by virtue of being labeled a satellite gave the art that was shown there extra cachet. But it put her far from the action. Spots inside the main fair had to be earned.

I walked and took notes, which gave me away as a journalist and not a buyer, but I was still welcomed as I scratched on a notepad while staring at whatever, and I would exchange smiles with the assistant or owner when I left. A few smiles were returned warmly, or perhaps provocatively, but I'm not a pickup artist. Like Tanya Ross, I prefer to talk for months.

The art fair was designed to appeal to almost any type of collector, and there were throngs of people to maneuver through. There was no way to go from start to finish without doubling back, which created an ongoing loop of déjà vu, and I was surprised to see a painting for the second time yet have no recollection of the other pictures around it. It became impossible to evaluate the artworks but easy to enjoy them; they were like a steady parade of beauty queen contestants where you find yourself saying after the fiftieth lovely one, "Next."

Around two p.m., I felt a quiver in my legs and realized I was fatigued and famished. I went to the center of the arena, where wrapped sandwiches were served after a twenty-minute wait in line. Coffee, illogically, was at another line, infuriating me. There was impractical seating, a dozen ottomans strewn around the sandwich bar. I found a tiny corner on one and perched on it, the sandwich balanced on my knee and the coffee set on the floor. As dense as this place was with art world heavyweights, lightweights, and underweights, I realized just how few people I actually knew. Artists weren't likely to show up here, and Lacey was in the hinterlands.

My cell phone rang. The caller ID said Alisa Lightborn, my editor at *ARTnews*. She was pretty, too, and pretty married.

"Where are you?" she said.

"I feel like I'm in Calcutta."

"Me too!" she said.

"I'm at the sandwich bar."

"Oh, jeez…" The woman in front of me turned around. It was Alisa. We laughed and both closed our phones.

"Are you coming tonight?"

"Coming to what?" I said.

"Ah, I was right: you didn't get it. *ARTnews* is hosting a dinner at Joe's Stone Crab, at least a dozen people. We have the glitterati, you could be the literati. And you could take notes."

"Would that be okay with them?"

"When a magazine hosts a dinner, everyone knows it's on the record."

I wasn't so sure they did, but I was chuffed to have a dinner invite at one of the most desirable restaurants in Miami.

I trudged through the rest of the fair and its satellites, and even revisited standout displays. These second visits were valuable; what had charmed me on first glance often bored me on the second. I said hello to Lacey, whose booth was a standout because of both the art and her dress. But I didn't tell her about the *ARTnews* dinner because I figured she'd invite herself, and I didn't want her there. I knew that she could turn an evening upside down and somehow make it about her. Still, when I left her booth, she said, "Have fun at that dinner tonight."

I was glad I had brought a suit and tie. I clean up well. Joe's was an easy taxi ride from my Deco splendor, but I walked in the warming night, glad to be out of New York during a particularly blustery

December. I neared the restaurant, which was as much high-end tourist spot as it was a chow-down family restaurant. Crowds waited in an expansive lobby for a table, and although Joe's ostensibly didn't take reservations, the maître d' dealt with people like a shrink, eagle-eyeing the famous and connected and treating the RV-touring family with equal respect and facility.

I asked for the *ARTnews* table and was guided through a vast dining room where robust waiters with pins on their lapels indicating twenty, thirty, or forty years of service cheerfully entertained while taking and delivering orders. This was not an art world restaurant, even during the busy Miami Basel week. There were families, and there were businessmen sporting lobster bibs. There wasn't a solo diner to be seen; the place was too much fun for that. I was taken to a private dining room with paneled walls and a wagon wheel chandelier looming over an empty table for fifteen. I guessed I was the odd man. The din from the main dining area reverberated in this small room, so things still felt active.

Alisa was there—it was her job to be there first—and there was a well-dressed Englishman already holding champagne. I debated abstaining since I was, in fact, working, but as I might be a poor reporter if I didn't blend in, I took a glass. The Englishman was Kip Stringer, who was in the vanguard of the coming vogue: curator as artist. It was he, he decided, who determined that he could use artists' works to make *his* point, not theirs. He took the artists' right to be obscure and turned it into a curator's right. This resulted in a show in Milan where artists were forced together as though in a hadron collider. Pollock and Monet were hung in the same room under the premise that the heading "Material/Memory" or "Object/Distance/Fragility" clarified everything.

I joined Kip and Alisa just in time to hear him bemoaning the fair, saying that the auxiliary shows that sprang up to capitalize on the influx of art enthusiasts into Miami were much better than the shows in the main room, but he did like that Pace Gallery had hung an Agnes Martin opposite a Robert Ryman so that they were "in dialogue" with each other. "In dialogue" was a new phrase that art writers could no longer live without. It meant that hanging two works next to or opposite each other produced a third thing, a dialogue, and that we were now all the better for it. I suppose the old phrase would have been "an art show," but now we were listening. It also hilariously implied that when the room was empty of viewers, the two works were still chatting. I was tolerant when he said "in dialogue" because I can get it, but when he said "line-space matrix," I wanted to puke.

The air was cleansed when Hinton and Cornelia Alberg entered, Hinton emitting a big laugh for no reason except to greet everyone. Next came another idol of mine, Peter Schjeldahl, the great art critic for *The New Yorker*, and his wife, Brooke, who gave off such a vibe of fun that I knew it was she I would try to sit next to.

A quorum was struck when the Mexican collector Eduardo Flores and a young man entered, along with Gayle Smiley, his default dealer, who stuck to Eduardo like a barnacle, lest he be spirited away by the ghost of Larry Gagosian. The Nathansons, Saul and Estelle, were next, and I started to wonder how *ARTnews* could draw such a diverse crowd. When the actor Stirling Quince and Blanca entered, I thought maybe they were the main attraction, but it didn't seem likely. But soon, a woman ninety-one years of age but a dyslexic nineteen years of age in her soul, entered the room, and everything made sense. It was Dorothea Tanning, a painter whose career had slid into being when this Illinois born woman found herself in Paris married to Max Ernst and aligned with a slew of Surrealists and other "ists," including, in her words, "Yves Tanguy, Marcel Duchamp, Joan Miró, René Magritte, Salvador Dali, Pablo Picasso, Max Ernst, and Max Ernst." After a decade of accomplishment in Surrealist painting, she climbed aboard *The New Yorker* magazine and became a poetry contributor, active into

Eine Kleine Nachtmusik, Dorothea Tanning, 1943
16 × 24 in.

her eighties. An upcoming retrospective at the Metropolitan made her not only hot stuff, but enduring stuff, and her painting, *A Little Night Music,* executed in 1943, made her unassailable, and *ARTnews* had the story. She charmed us with her greeting: "I apologize for being alive."

I wondered how Lacey could have managed to miss a dinner attended by so many of her acquaintances, which in turn made me wonder if perhaps this dinner had missed her.

I knew I was at the position on the totem pole that got chipped by the lawn mower, so I stayed away from Ms. Tanning except to say I admired her work, which I do. With her at one end of the long table, I planted myself at the other, more gossipy end. I was delighted because all I could have done with Ms. Tanning was compliment her, but here in the panhandle I could hope for some loose lips. The conversation started when thespian Stirling Quince stopped everyone with, "How about this war?" referring to the born-again Iraq war, but before we could even nod sadly, he added, "Nobody's makin' any movies!" After the silence and a poor attempt at commiseration, talk of the art fair nicely combusted.

"What do you think of the fair, Mr. Nathanson?" I asked. I remembered him from Lacey's Milton Avery story years earlier.

"Well, things are different. What happened to paintings? Nobody's painting. We found a little Nadelman drawing, but they wanted too much. We went back a few hours later and someone had bought it."

Hinton Alberg broke in. "You gotta snatch! These things aren't lasting. You pause, you missed it."

"Did you see the Gober?" asked Eduardo Flores.

"Too much," said Hinton. "Too much. A million two or something. Even so, I went back. It was sold."

"I bought it," said Eduardo. Fortunato, his young friend, sat prettily next to him.

When he said, "I bought it," Gayle Smiley went white. When, she must have thought, did he leave my sight?

Schjeldahl was uninterested in money talk, so he sat mute. But his wife, Brooke, was forthright and funny, which made Brooke and Cornelia instant friends.

"What was the Gober like?" Brooke asked.

"It's a kitchen sink," said Hinton.

"A what?" said Saul Nathanson.

"It's like a kitchen sink that hangs on a wall, but with an elongated back," Flores told him. "Plaster and wood; it's an amazing piece."

Kip Stringer couldn't resist: "The sink is evocative of cleaning, but the fact it is on a wall, without plumbing, not functioning, creates cognitive dissonance. It embars the viewer from the action it implies."

Schjeldahl, whose art criticism goes down like good wine, said, "Huh?"

"Sort of like a locked door," said Saul. Saul Nathanson did not mock art, so his response was probing rather than cynical.

"Well," said Kip, "Gober actually did install a locked door in the wall of a gallery."

"I would only pay a million for that," said Brooke.

"Not if I'm there first!" said Hinton.

Kip tried to laugh but couldn't.

"No kidding. Hinton would buy paint in a bucket," said Cornelia.

"Is he a bad boy?" said Brooke.

"You would think each gallery had a pole dancer," Cornelia said with a grin, "but honestly, art has enriched us. With things, with thought, with conversation, with people. Don't you think so, Hinton?"

"Art has de-riched me, honey. You know what I thought when we bought the house in Montauk? Walls! More walls! You know what I think when I buy a car? No walls. No goddamn walls."

Nathanson jumped in. "I find it strange that when we have people over for dinner, no one, not one, mentions or ever looks at the paintings. We have all these beautiful works, and it's as though they don't exist. And if we give them a tour, I can feel their struggle to enjoy it, but really they don't care."

"They will notice my sink on the wall," said Flores, now on his third vodka.

"And if they don't, they're not invited back," toadied Gayle.

"I find the fair very hard to navigate," said Saul. "As I wander around, I don't know what anyone *is*."

"There is tremendous diversity," said Kip.

"Look," said Hinton, "up to the seventies, art proceeded in movements. Cubism, Surrealism, Abstract Expressionism, Pop, Minimalism, so everyone, including me, was on the lookout for the next movement. But instead, art in the eighties was at an evolutionary moment where it split into chimps, birds, fish, plants, and cephalopods all at once. Saul, artists can make a living now as a *bad painter*. I'm not kidding. You ask them what they make and they'll say 'bad art.' And they can put the implied quotes around it, too, with just their voice. And you know what? It's bad, but not that bad."

"Do you have any?" said Brooke.

"We've got a roomful of it," said Cornelia.

Hinton went on, "We sure do, and sometimes the bad stuff can make the so-called good stuff seem boring and stiff."

Kip Stringer didn't go for this kind of plain speaking. "The artist has fractured the iconicity," he said.

"Exaaacctlly...," said Brooke, looking over at me with her mouth agape.

"There are a hundred categories," said Hinton, now getting revved up. "There's 'pale art,' faint things with not much going on in them. There's 'high-craft OCD,' you know, those guys who take a thousand pinheads and paint a picture of their grandmother on every one. There's 'low-craft ironic,' a fancy name for wink-wink nudge-nudge."

I dared to speak. "What about 'animated interiors'?"

"Good one," said Hinton. "Apocalyptic scenes of stuff flying around a room. And don't forget 'angry pussy'!"

"Hinton!" said Cornelia.

"Oh, do go on," said Brooke.

"Oh, you know. Stuff made with menstrual blood."

"I'm *so glad* I asked," said Brooke.

"How can we forget 'junk on the floor'? You walk into a gallery and there's stuff strewn everywhere. I've got three of those. Wanna buy one, Eduardo?"

"So if you think it's silly, why do you stay involved?" I asked, reporter style.

"I don't see it as silly. But outsiders do. What was that guy today, honey? Oh yeah, there's an artist who's documenting his own peeing. Photos, videos, he's...

"The artist is making us question the act of urination," said Kip.

"Right. Now, that line should never be quoted or they're going to use it against us at our *trials*."

"How would you defend yourself?" I asked.

"Well, let's see... Hey, what was that piece that won the Turner Prize last year?"

"The Lights Going On and Off," said Kip.

"Right. So the Tate buys it for twenty thousand pounds, and it's an empty room, with a lightbulb going on and off. This hit the news so fast... two-inch headlines. They tried to make the art world look stupid. But, you know, I saw the thing and liked it. So at my trial I'd start to say, 'Twenty thousand pounds really isn't that much,' but I'd stop myself because I wouldn't want to be executed right off.

"But then I'd face the jury: 'Let's say you're going to buy a puppy. You're going to buy a yellow Lab. A cuddly yellow Lab. So you read that you should go to a breeder, because you don't want to get one that's going to go sick on you. Now you get to the breeder and you find out there's English Labs and American Labs. American Labs are good for hunting because they're kind of lithe. But you don't want to hunt him, so you go for an English Lab, more stocky. Then you're told that the real prize of the Labrador breed is one with a big head. So you wait and wait, and finally you get one with a big head. Now you take it home and proudly show your big-headed puppy to a friend. You're thinking, I've got this great show dog, an English Lab with a big head, and your friend is thinking, What an ugly puppy."

By now the other end of the table was tuned in, Tanning enjoying Hinton. He turned to her and said, "Excuse me, Miss Tanning, I'm orating."

"Please, go on." She smiled.

Hinton smiled back. "I would rather hear what you have to say."

Tanning paused thoughtfully. "I believe the last twenty years has been the most desperate search for artistic identity in the history of the arts. Don't you think so, Peter?"

Schjeldahl, now that the conversation had turned to art and not money, finally spoke: "All the cocksure movements of the last century have collapsed into a bewildering, trackless here and now."

The table went silent, then the chatter resumed at the same tempo as after a distant gunshot.

When we left the restaurant, I saw Lacey canoodling at a corner table with a known Russian collector, also known as a playboy, also known as very rich. Now I knew why she'd missed this dinner. Cornelia saw it, too, and she did not like it.

54.

BY THE END OF 2003, Lacey had solidified her business. She had
several employees and was making a profit. I dropped by the gallery,
meeting her for lunch; she was on the phone, and I could hear her voice
from the back office as she closed a deal:

"You know it's a good picture... Still, you know it's a good picture.
And your Basquiat, how much did you overpay for that at the time?
And now it's worth whatever... Okay, sorry, millions... Look, you
know you love this piece. You should buy it because you need it... No,
you're right, nobody needs art. Nobody except for you. You need it.
You know I'm right... Okay, then, I'll take it off hold... No, I'm going
to take it off hold. I'm taking it off hold in thirty seconds."

Then I heard her laughing. "I'm telling you, off hold in twenty-four
seconds."

She laughed some more, and I could intuit that the person she was
speaking to was laughing, too.

"I've got another buyer on my speed dialer. Twenty seconds..." Then
she said, "Smart move. I'll have it delivered. When's a good time?"

I took her to lunch, which began with her saying, "I'm dating a
vibrator. I think I love it... him... whatever." I laughed. "And it never
cheats on me."

"Have you been cheated on, Lacey?"

"Never. I always strike first."

"Where's Patrice these days?"

"Nowhere. He was a bit too interested, wouldn't you say?"

"I don't know him that well."

"Plus, I'm thirty-three, he's forty-five. And when I'm thirty-three, he'll be fifty-five, and when I'm thirty-three, he'll be sixty-three."

I laughed. "You don't plan on aging?"

"Why would I?"

We both had news, and we both waited until the entrées to report it.

"I'm moving into a new space," said Lacey. "Around the corner, window to the street, a real gallery. Like Andrea Rosen and Matthew Marks...well, not that big, but it'll have clout. Daniel," she said, "it's ten thousand a month. I'm going from seven hundred to ten thousand a month."

"Jeez."

"But I've been making ten thousand a month, or I'm starting to. I figure the added square footage will pay for itself and attract more artists. I'm doing resale, like at Talley's. Nobody down here is doing secondary market stuff, nobody. It's like they never think about it."

Secondary market is what all the uptown galleries are, what Sotheby's and Christie's do—they resell previously owned works. Lacey was right: the contemporary market had little outlet for private sales of this nature.

"I do it in the back room, on the phone."

"Do people want to buy such a recent picture? Don't they wonder why it's being sold?"

"I say divorce, distress, and people love it. Somehow it makes the piece more desirable. And these pictures are going nowhere but up, so no one's afraid."

"But ten thousand a month."

"Plus I have to remodel. With a fancy architect. Look, the only money

I need is lunch money. I put everything back in. So I'm not strapped. Clothes cost, though. They're like a car for a Realtor. They've got to be all class. Lots of evenings out. And you, what's new with you?"

"Are you sitting down?"

"I could sit on the floor, I guess."

"Remember Tanya Ross?"

"Lovely girl, nice person," she said with a tinge of color.

"I'm dating her. Exclusively."

"What happened to what's-her-name?"

"Lacey, that was so long ago."

"But what happened?"

"No fireworks."

"And there are fireworks with Tanya Ross?"

"Well, she's not a fireworks person; she's a different kind of person."

"So, no fireworks."

"I'm not looking for fireworks with her. I'm enchanted, maybe in love, with the idea that she's someone who would always do the right thing. It's taken a while to get through to her, but I think she's bending."

"Over?"

"Lacey."

"Have you kissed her?"

"Lacey."

"Sorry. She probably wants to punch me. Tell her she can, and invite her down to the gallery. After the new one's open. I can make peace; I have that in me."

55.

I CONTINUED TO SEE Tanya that winter, twice a week, then three times a week, ending with an all-out-effort dinner at Del Posto, paid for by one paycheck for five reviews from *ARTnews*. She dressed up for it and so did I, and she looked so beautiful that I thought I didn't belong with her. But my best behavior makes me look better: I stand up straighter, and I'm more polished, the way I've seen other men be.

She had one glass of wine to my three, but mine were spread out over two and a half hours, so I was never tipsy, just loosened, and she was constant and forthcoming by choice, not alcohol. This night, so memorable, seemed like the last step before unspoken commitment. And when I kissed her good night, it seemed as though little animated larks circled around our heads. She reminded me of a song... what was it? And when she said, smiling broadly, "I think I love you," she put her hand over her face and smiled into it. I felt as though I were Fred Astaire, my top hat and tails magically appearing, and I sang to her, making up the lyrics, which made her laugh on the dark stoop. Then we paused and looked at each other. She said, "Come up."

So I was surprised, three days later, when I called her to confirm a dinner date and she said, "I could see you for lunch."

I can't think of anything that unnerved me so quickly. My response was so shaky, it meant I had been walking on air, not solid ground. I assured myself that nothing, nothing could have happened between our flawless night spent together and this phone call. But Tanya, I knew, does not mislead. So the bliss of the good-night kiss and the frost of our latest exchange were both true. This state of unease could properly be called "disease," because I felt sick. But at least disease has the courtesy to develop over time; this infection was abrupt and arrived all at once. By the time the receiver was replaced on the hook, I was fully in it. I had an elevator-drop loss of appetite and found it difficult to stand: my legs were shivering like a tuning fork. Had she met someone? Impossible.

The two events I am about to describe did not happen simultaneously, but I will present them as though they did, because they are so intertwined by cause and effect that they may as well be connected in time.

I met Tanya for lunch, not at one of our romanticized regular spots, but at the place of one of our first, pre-romantic, all-business lunches. Tanya picked it. On 68th Street, a short distance from Madison Avenue, the restaurant was detached from our previous dating life and empty enough that we could have a conversation without being overheard. I arrived first, my timing sped up by anxiety, and when she arrived, each of her steps toward me was freeze-framed in my mind while I analyzed each inflection of her body language. I perceived nothing, except that she was withholding what I was searching for, intimacy, and that for several minutes there was a faking of normalcy.

"How's work?" I said.

"Oh, that," she said. "Just going on. We have a beautiful early Picasso coming up; lots of talk about that."

"Which one?"

"*Garçon à la Pipe.*"

"Wow, important picture."

"It's going to bring a lot."

Then the conversation withered like a dehydrating prune on the science channel. I requested menus, not wanting to start anything with this sudden stranger until we got our first course.

While Tanya and I diverted into art small talk, two men walked up the seven flights of metal stairs of 525 West 25th Street and spent minutes turning a guide map this way and that before they found Lacey's gallery. The Chelsea galleries always look closed and unwelcoming, and they swung her door open a few inches to make sure the lights were on and the place was operating. They went into the gallery and stood at its center, and Lacey, having heard the shuffle of feet and low voices, appeared from the office doorway. These men were familiar. It wasn't so much their faces that jarred her memory as their clothes—plain suits, dark fabric, beige trench coats that were too thin for the cold outside—and the short army hair.

These were the two men she had seen at Talley's on her first day in the gallery. They were also the men who had approached her in Boston, covertly handed her an envelope, then faded back into the alleyways.

"Miss Yeager?"

"I probably am," she said.

"We're with the FBI."

"Show me your stinkin' badges. Or don't you need them?"

The two men looked at each other, confused. "I'm kidding," she said.

They tried to smile. "Could we talk with you?"

"Sure," she said, and they entered her office, knocking about like Rosencrantz and Guildenstern.

The salads arrived, and I finally began to speak with Tanya. I had no appetite. I suppose I ordered food so I would have a plate to look down into, some reason to look away from her if the conversation turned uncomfortable, which it already had.

"Something's up," I said.

"Yes." She nodded.

"I'm so curious. And a bit worried."

"Do you remember the first night we met?"

"At the opening."

"Yes, and do you remember I said you looked familiar?"

"Yes."

"Well," she said, "I remembered where I saw you. On the video. Do you know we tape all our auctions?"

Lacey did not sit behind her desk; she sat in a chair across from the two men and deliberately crossed her legs in front of them.

"I'm Agent Parks and this is Agent Crane."

"Yes, with the Isabella Stuart Gardner case."

"Well, that case is dead, at least for now. We investigate art issues, and with nothing happening on that front, we had time to take a look at some other unclear activities."

Agent Crane then spoke. His eyes kept shifting involuntarily to her crossed legs. "The statute of limitations on fraud is six years, so we asked around the auction houses about questionable events at the furthest end of that time frame and came up with a bothersome issue."

Tanya was a bit nervous. "You know Lacey, right?"

"A long time."

"Is she trouble?" asked Tanya.

"I think some people would call her trouble."

"We tape all our auctions, mostly so the auctioneer can check his performance, but also to confirm bids, just for records. About six years ago, there was an American sale. Lacey is standing by a phone desk, holding a folder with some papers, near the auctioneer. Her arms are crossed around it. There are a few people bidding on a Parrish."

"And one of them is me," I said.

"Yes, one of them is you. That's unlikely, isn't it? That you would be bidding on a six-hundred-thousand-dollar Parrish?"

I looked at her, unable to answer. I felt a surge of adrenaline's opposite.

"Anyway, it comes down to you and one other phone bidder. And just before the six-hundred-thousand-dollar bid, the last bid, Lacey unfolds her arms and leans forward. And when she unfolds her arms and leans forward, you stop bidding."

Agent Parks rose and walked over to a window. "So we recently reviewed this tape…a tape that was the reason you were dismissed from Sotheby's, isn't it?"

"Unfairly dismissed," said Lacey. "They never accused me of anything. I could have made a fuss, but I had a place to go. We all parted friends."

"Don't you find it odd that exactly when you leaned forward, a bidder, who you evidently know, stopped bidding?"

"No. People stop bidding."

"We think it's pretty clear that this was a signal of some kind."

"Well, you can amuse yourselves with that thought," she said.

"Why would you want someone to stop bidding?" they asked her.

My heart was racing as Tanya paused. "We checked out the Parrish sale," she said. "The painting was represented by a lawyer, so we really don't know who sold it. But I can't figure why you were bidding. Something's wrong. Can you explain it?"

"I was asked to bid for a friend. I didn't really know it was wrong."

"Have you ever owned a painting by Parrish Maxfield?" said Agent Crane.

"You mean Maxfield Parrish," said Lacey.

"Oh yes, Maxfield Parrish."

"I own a print. I inherited it from my grandmother and I still have it. It's on my wall in my apartment if you want to see it."

"I might like to see it," replied Parks. "You can give me your contact information."

"We looked at the tape recently," Tanya said. "It's a definite move. It's clear. And it's clear you're cooperating. It's clear, Daniel. It's clear." Then she looked down at her plate before I could. Her eyes moistened, and she stayed bowed.

"I checked your paddle number: 286 was registered to Neal Walker. How did you get a paddle?"

"The paddle was arranged."

"I know how rigorous we are. Arranged how?"

"Tanya, I thought it wasn't much. Afterwards, I found out it was worse than I thought."

"Tell me."

I told her what I knew: "I was told to stop bidding when Lacey leaned forward."

This information made her face go slack. She got up and left the restaurant, but unfortunately she wasn't angry. She was finished with me.

56.

AGENT PARKS came to Lacey's apartment around seven p.m., in the middle of New York's deep winter darkness. He came alone, without Crane, which was fine with Lacey because she knew this was both an investigation and a date. She guessed he was an all-American boy with a dirty side, and she guessed that an affair with him would put a legal end to this annoying stumble. Someone investigating her seduced her? It certainly could be implied that the seducer would have a conflict of interest, though of course it would be Lacey who would be in charge of the seducing. All this did cross her mind, in fact, but here is the fine point on Lacey's sexual conduct: She never did it for gain, only for excitement. The *promise* of sex was what she did for gain.

She took Agent Parks into the bedroom to show him the Parrish print. She told him the story of its acquisition.

"How long has it been in the family?" he asked.

"Eighty, eighty-five years."

He looked at it; she could tell he did not know how to look at a print. He might be on the art squad, but he was not an art person. He left the bedroom after glancing around, and Lacey followed him into the living room.

"Sit?" he said.

"Sure."

"So what do you think of all this leaning forward stuff, Miss Yeager?"

"If you call me by my first name, I'll call you by your first name."

"Bob."

"Lacey." Then she said, "Take a look at that tape. I'll bet at the same moment there are people coughing, scratching their ears, tapping their chests."

"Who's the guy? Bidder 286. Neal Walker."

"I'm supposed to know bidders; it was my job. But I don't know Neal Walker. Would you like a cocktail?"

57.

I WILL TAKE YOU back six years:

"When I lean forward, you stop bidding."

That's what Lacey told me to do. It seemed like a crime in the negative. It seemed untraceable, not provable. We sat in a restaurant, drinking Kirs, and she was all but hanging out of her dress, which reminded me of when I slept with her. But that was so long ago, and even though I was unattached at the moment, I still maintained to myself that she was an object of human, not sexual, interest.

"I will be giving out the paddles; you come up to me, tell me your name: Neal Walker. I'll check the list and give you one. You might not even have to bid at all; there could easily be other bidders. As soon as the action starts, I'll move to the podiums in front to be a spotter. When I'm standing, you bid. When I lean forward, you stop."

"What if I get stuck with the picture?"

"You won't."

This seemed to me like an art world game, a mystery of sorts, and Lacey was convincing and fun. So I went to the auction and Lacey gave me a paddle. I sat through the auction for about forty-five minutes. Finally, the Parrish came up. And when Lacey leaned forward, I stopped bidding. She had never once looked at me.

After the sale, there was a phone message waiting: "Call me." I did. "Come over," she said. She was jubilant. "Let's take X."

"Not for me, Lacey."

"Come over anyway, we'll celebrate."

"Celebrate what?"

I walked up the steps of her 12th Street apartment. "It's open," she shouted when I knocked. I came in and she locked the door behind me. She handed me a check for one thousand dollars.

"What's this for?" I said.

"For helping," she said.

"Did I break the law?"

"No, darlin', you helped an old friend. There's no law against that." I kept the check because I needed it.

Then she opened her fist and revealed two small pills with pentagrams etched in them. "This could be so much fun," she said.

"Lacey, I'm spooked by drugs. You take it. I'll watch the floor show."

I didn't know much about the effects of the drug, its duration, its downside. But Lacey made me promise not to leave without her okay. She opened a bottle of wine, but she took none. She poured me a glass of red, then picked up the tiny pill between her fingers, clinked my glass with it, and swallowed it down. She pulled the sheers closed, darkening the room by half, and threw a towel over the lamp, darkening the room further. Then the winter sun dropped so fast that the room went blue.

Lacey walked the two steps to the kitchen. "Do you want a sandwich?"

"Yes," I said, and she quickly prepared a deli-worthy pile of ingredients, including tomato and mozzarella, that looked as good as a food section photograph. While she worked, I asked, "So what happened today?"

She turned to me, exaggerated a shrug, and spoke in the voice of Minnie Mouse: "I dunno, Mickey." As she put the last slice of brown bread on the stack, she paused and said, "Oh," her movements slowing down perceptibly. She took a breath and walked the plate over to me, handing it off. Standing in place, she closed her eyes, raising her right arm and moving it through the air as though she were hearing and conducting a Satie étude.

Then she walked over to her bed and lay down, staring out through the sheers of the window, not saying a word. Sometimes she would sigh deeply, shift, or feel her face. I sat in her only upholstered chair and watched as she drifted through an internal space. I thought of the Warhol movie *Sleep*, in which he filmed someone sleeping for eight hours. I saw it as a gung ho college student and remembered how the slightest movement of the sleeping man had the same impact as a plot twist in *The Maltese Falcon*. When Lacey moved, I was fascinated.

The drug began to affect me, too. It was as though it seeped through Lacey's skin and emanated into the local ether. I, too, was happy not to move, and eventually I realized that an hour had passed since Lacey had lain down.

She began to make an occasional noise, like someone reacting to a dream. I could tell she was watching an internal drama, sometimes speaking to the characters, saying, "no," or, "I didn't." Her eyes opened and she looked at the ceiling, blinked once or twice, and then closed them again. She was seeing something or reliving something. Then she turned her head and looked at me.

"You are such a good friend," she said.

"You are, too," I said. Though I know now that the statement was incorrect, at the moment it seemed like an eternal truth.

"Come over..." And she made room on the bed for me. The invitation was delivered with a love that was neither romantic nor sisterly, but some other kind of love discovered in the moment, one of the least complicated invocations of caring I had ever witnessed. I walked to the bed and lay down next to her. She snuggled into me, holding my arm the way a child holds a teddy, burying her face between my shoulder and the bed.

"My grandmother will die soon. She will die."

I said nothing. It seemed to me that she was speaking to herself.

"So beautiful. When she was eighteen, he made paintings of her. He painted her like she was; I'm sure of it. I think I look like her."

She turned on her side again, toward me, and put her hand on my stomach. She began to rub me, lifting my shirt, touching my flesh. She would lower her hand across my jeans, gliding around, moving back up to my stomach. Each visit to my penis got a little longer, but it was absentminded motion, and my dick got absentmindedly hard. She treated it like a curiosity that was third or fourth on her to-do list. I was glad when she just as casually stopped, which meant I had no decisions to make. Then she turned toward the window, and for the next thirty minutes she either slept or dreamed.

It had been two hours since she'd ingested the drug, and she was beginning to stir. She sat partially up, opening her eyes and looking around, as if trying to determine where she was. She looked at me, hugged my arm again, said, "I'm sorry you didn't take any." She got up and found her legs, stretching long, the high starting to recede and the drug's amphetamine base starting to take over. She opened the refrigerator, poured from a pitcher of ice water, and drank it down, pausing between gulps as if it were a hard Scotch.

She sliced some fruit onto a plate. We sat at the small kitchen table. "Daniel, I have money now."

I thought she would stop talking if I seemed too interested, so I tempered everything I said. "Because of today?"

"Yes. Today."

"Oh," I said.

"I can't see the wrong in it."

"In what?"

"The Parrish print. A couple of years ago I visited my grandmother, who was very sick. Remember? I told you."

"Yes."

"I've worked at Sotheby's for years; I've seen a million pictures. I'm used to looking at things close, trying not to be tricked. I went into my grandmother's room, we spoke a bit, and I took the Parrish print over for her to look at. It was a sunny day. If not, I might have missed the whole thing. I took the print back to put it on the wall. I used my coat to clean dust from the glass. But something wasn't right with the print."

"How?"

"The surface was odd. There were textural changes. The surface of a Parrish print would be uniform, except for the blacks. The prints were extremely well done, very easy to distinguish copies from the real thing, because their surface is so remarkable. I went into an empty bedroom and closed the door. The frame hadn't been touched in decades. There were rusted metal points holding in the glass, pressing against a wooden back. I got a nail file and moved them aside. I turned the frame upside down on the bed, and the picture and glass fell out. I took away the wooden back and saw another panel, with an old sticker on the back, 'Maxfield Parrish Studio.' I picked it up, expecting the print to be underneath. It wasn't. I turned over the board, and there was the image. Maybe they glued the print to the studio board. I looked; I looked closely. I looked at the edges. There was no paper trim. No, they hadn't. I looked at the surface. This was not a print. It was a painting. Parrish had given my grandmother the painting of herself. She had assumed it was a print."

"How could she not know it was a painting?"

"Parrish used his own framer. And his prints were often framed close in like paintings. He must have given it to her framed, and she assumed it was a print. She had said he gave it to her in his studio and there was a stack of prints nearby. We've always assumed it was a print because that's what she told us."

"What did you do?"

"I reassembled it and put it back on the wall. And I didn't tell my grandmother or my mother."

"And today?"

"I thought about the painting, how valuable it was. Circumstances got worse for me. I could not fail. I could not be driven out of New York by a simple lack of money. And my taste was improving. I needed better things.

"I went to New Hampshire where Parrish lived and found a dealer. I told him the print I wanted, and a few months later, he found one and I bought it. It was the print of the painting. I paid two hundred fifty dollars for it. The image had advertising around it, for Fisk Tires, but otherwise the image was the same size as the painting. I trimmed away the margins that included the advertising. I went to a framer and had them glue the print to an antique artist's board. My next trip to Atlanta, I took out the painting and replaced it with the print. It was an incredible match. The Parrish print surfaces are remarkable, exactly like his paintings. I wrapped it in a towel and put it in my suitcase.

"I put it at auction through a lawyer."

"And me?"

"I knew there was a bidder hot for the piece. He was going to leave a maximum bid, but I didn't know what that bid would be until just before the sale. I wasn't going to let him get it for four hundred thousand if I knew he would go to six hundred. Just before the sale, I made sure I glimpsed the auctioneer's cheat sheet, and beside the lot number for the Parrish was written, 600k. So I had you stop bidding at five eighty. There was no bidder on the phone; it was a Sotheby's rep, bidding for the absent client."

I was a beginning art writer, just starting to make my way in New York, and now I was a participant in a newsworthy fraud.

"You will never tell."

"No," I said, "I will never tell."

58.

IF YOU EVER get lost heading for Chelsea, use your X-ray vision to find a truck bearing hundreds of gallons of white paint; it will lead you to where you want to go. White became the default color for modern gallery walls as early as the 1920s, when Bauhaus rigor dictated it. White feigned neutrality, but it was loaded with meaning. It was the severe reaction to Victorian darkness, to the painted walls of Art Nouveau and the elegant wood panels of Art Deco. A painting looked good against it: there was only it to look at.

Even older pictures took on an air of modernity when surrounded with white paint. Chelsea was awash in it, and so were collectors' homes and museums. The only things that didn't look good against it were people. Light was coming from everywhere, windows, ceilings, and walls, illuminating every makeup smear, skin flaw, and case of thinning hair, no matter what efforts were made to disguise them. Collectors' homes, now high-ceilinged, spare, rugless, and chromed, became echo chambers.

The theoretically ideal space for showing pictures was deemed a windowless white cube, an idea that was cumulative rather than birthed, and a gallery called White Cube opened in London in 1993, further solidifying the concept. Frames were dispensed with, as much for reasons of economy as taste.

Lacey's new gallery, drenched in white though not quite a cube, was located on the north side of 22nd Street, between the ultracool 303 Gallery and the architecturally oriented Max Protetch Gallery. Her gallery was flooded with sunlight, and only the gray concrete floors diluted the glare. When Lacey wore yellow, which meant that she was blond from head to toe, she stood out against the bleached walls like the Sun King.

But during the few months it took to relocate, there was a slow desertion of Lacey's friends and acquaintances. Hinton Alberg never visited the gallery because of Cornelia's disapproval of the way Lacey had treated Patrice Claire, whose life went on fine without her, though he still felt shivers at the mention of her name. Pilot Mouse had been collected by celebrities and major dealers and didn't need Chelsea or Lacey. He had delivered on his promise to get her two paintings to sell, but his new girlfriend made sure he stayed away from her. Carey Harden was never given another show and resented her for it, and he spread around the art world a weak, self-serving ill-will toward Lacey and her gallery. Sharon, her formerly impetuous cohort, had gotten married and settled into life with her new baby, and Angela had moved out of state to work as a writer's assistant.

After my breakdown with Tanya Ross, I, too, bore a grudge against Lacey, and it kept me at an angry distance from her. I hoped that Tanya might view my rejection of Lacey, if she ever heard about it, as remorse, and the memory of our romance might settle on top of and obliterate the stink of the nasty event at Sotheby's that had taken place now seven years ago. But I also knew she would always think of me as a crook, something that was beyond her nature to forget.

I had tried to repair my relationship with her, but my calls were not returned, and intermediaries I enlisted did not succeed in even framing a tea time with her. Eventually, I heard she was taking dates with a financier, which made me ill. I wanted to write her a letter explaining that a financier was more likely to engage in misadventure than an art writer, but wisely, I didn't. I could not imagine that Tanya was any less sad than I was; we had both said I love you—something neither of us would have said frivolously. We had moved easily as a couple through the art world waters. I found her attractive; I felt she reflected my own good taste in a mate. But I knew now that I would never reflect her own good taste in a mate, even though the case against Lacey and me was never pursued. I was now cast down with the sleazeball hustlers who inhabit the back alleys of the art world, whom the legitimate folk can smell coming.

I had heard that Agent Parks was a gallery visitor who was allowed inside Lacey's inner sanctum office at odd hours. And it could only be ironic that I had turned down requests to review Lacey's shows in *ART-news* because of my "integrity."

The missing people in her life, however, were replaced by an influx of new collectors and personalities, raging, competing, socializing. There were dinners and openings, invitations to fund-raisers, and a fluctuating, dynamic mix of people that transformed her impetuous youthful charm into professional adult ease. Lacey poured her profits back into the business, taking out full-page ads in art magazines, funding promotions, delivering guarantees to her hot artists, and financing better-than-average catalogs for her shows. She was living well, if only breaking even, and her gallery, it appeared, was prospering.

59.

IT IS EASY to think that the hot young art stars who were dwarfing prices for old masters at auction were newborn arrivals reaping the rewards of fashion. But most of the celebrated artists only looked like new arrivals. Koons, Hirst, and Gober had all been working since the eighties. Basquiat was achieving sensational prices but at least had the courtesy to be dead. Warhol led the pack, though it was unlikely he would ever have been in a footrace.

Arab money. Asian money. Russian money. The auction houses were seeing most of it, but there was a nice trickle-down from Wall Street collectors, who heard about their clients' investments in art and decided to get in on the action by frequenting Chelsea. Artists flooded Manhattan, then all the boroughs of New York City, and it became inexplicable why one artist would be swept up by a dealer while others of apparently equal talent would be ignored.

But what could be a better mix than action and aesthetics? Everyone was alive. Each auction price was tallied and measured. Art reviews were either neutral or unfathomable. Collectors pretended to care about criticism, and artists pretended not to care about success, making them interlock like Velcro. Fund-raisers tripled, and MoMA, Dia, the Hammer, and the Guggenheim had benefactors lined up to get in. If you think this description is negative, I will remind you and myself of the particular ether that pervaded the contemporary art world's reach: vitality. This secular renaissance, this abundant artistic output, made news. It brought people to the arts, engendered thought, analysis, swagger, winners, and losers, and created a cache of art, whether on display or in storage, that will probably supply the cultural world with aesthetic grist for the next five hundred years.

60.

BARTON TALLEY, in an effort to get a piece of the booming market, made a lighthouse search around the globe for new artists, until his beam finally landed on China. China, whose artistic output for thousands of years relied on a tradition of calligraphy and flat perspective, seemed the unlikeliest place from which to emerge painting that would catch the attention of a western hemisphere art scene where the avant-garde was the norm.

But Chinese art was hot. Yue Minjun, who sold the painting *Execution* in 1995 for five thousand dollars, must have been flattered and frustrated when it sold in 2007 for 5.9 million dollars. The surprise in all this activity was that the Chinese painters were reviving a dormant subject matter: political commentary, which had not piqued collectors' interest for years. The message was, of course, diffused through the intangible glaze of artistic interpretation, making the artists somewhat safe from retribution by glaring Communist overlords.

Barton Talley had asked Lacey several times to accompany him on reconnaissance missions to China to uncover artists who might have star power, but she turned him down, unwilling to leave her gallery even for a week during its crucial early days. She regretted her decisions as she watched even an uptown gallery with a reputation for conservatism have a successful sale of a middling Chinese artist.

Proceeding parallel to the art boom was a real estate boom, inspired by crafty lenders who assured easy profits in home ownership, no money down. These weak paper promises to pay were sold off to investors in every corner of the world, and Wall Street saw a glut of money. Wads of cash fell off the money truck as it trundled through Chelsea, across 49th Street for a stop at Christie's, and onward to Madison Avenue and Sotheby's.

The publicity that convinced broke home owners that they could make nice profits flipping their houses was the same as that which motivated moneyed art collectors to go further into the market than was practical. The lure in art collecting and its financial rewards, not counting for a moment its aesthetic, cultural, and intellectual rewards, is like the trust in paper money: it makes no sense when you really think about it. New artistic images are so vulnerable to opinion that it wouldn't take much more than a whim for a small group of collectors to decide that a contemporary artist was not so wonderful anymore, was *so* last year. In the ebb and flow of artists' desirability, some collectors wondered how a beautiful painting, once it had fallen from favor, could turn ugly so quickly.

Lacey knew the contemporary market did not have the buoyancy of the modern art she had sold at Talley's. Even the lamest Picasso could coax a bid from someone, but work by an unknown artist was valueless until someone decided to buy it. This was rather like doing business from a cloud, but it was the business she was in, and she decided that if she didn't believe in it, neither would her customers. So in 2004, when Talley called her again, asking if she wanted to invest in a batch of pictures straight out of the studio by Feng Zhenj-Jie, a Chinese artist working in Beijing who painted Day-Glo images of glamour girls and was rumored to be sought after by several galleries, she listened.

She would need a million five, said Talley, a sum to be matched by him, to purchase a half-share of thirty paintings at approximately one hundred thousand dollars each. Talley believed that the pictures could be sold for a quarter of a million each, plus or minus depending on size. Lacey didn't really like Feng Zhenj-Jie's work; it seemed to belong to the school of *Playboy* more than anything else. But the images were strong. Talley said, "You can spot a painting by Feng Zhenj-Jie across a room and never quite forget it."

"Is that so good?" asked Lacey. "If you can remember it completely, there's nothing there when you go back."

"Lacey," said Talley, "we're talking about a moment. You buy the moment. There's no way to know if the moment will last. I think the moment is coming for Feng Zhenj-Jie. There's too much momentum. Everybody's talking Chinese."

"Problem," said Lacey. "I don't have a million five. I've got about five hundred thousand, but I operate on it. It's a cash pool I dip into, and it's absolutely necessary. Ever had a client want to sell a painting that you sold them and you have to act like it's the most desirable thing in the world so you give them their money back plus?"

"Of course."

"That's why I need that cash." Lacey declined the offer.

"You shouldn't be afraid of these deals, Lacey, my advice to you."

"Odd, isn't it?" she said. "You sell the conservative paintings and are risky in business, and I sell the risky paintings and I'm conservative in business."

One year later, Feng Zhenj-Jie set an auction record of three hundred fifty thousand dollars. He became an auction regular with consistent prices while Lacey sat by.

She did, however, sell her uptown apartment for a nice profit and buy a loft in SoHo on margin. The new place was better suited to the display of her artists and better suited for the occasional art parties she threw—all promotional and therefore all deductible. Decorative sparseness was a practical aesthetic, requiring less expenditure on furniture and fixtures while still keeping up with the Joneses, whose imagined apartment was also bare.

61.

LACEY WAS NOW THIRTY-FIVE. If her inner light had softened, her ambition had not. But in New York, one's sense of competition had to be practical: there was always someone doing better than you, always. Tanya Ross had acceded to department head, but Lacey still figured she had outdone Tanya simply because her name was in lights. There were rival dealers she couldn't quite topple, like Andrea Rosen and Marianne Boesky—both dealers operating within blocks of her and with nicer galleries. And of course there was Gagosian, who could, it seemed, like a quantum particle, be in two places at once, emerging from the back room of either his uptown or his downtown gallery whenever an important client strolled in. There was no place within Lacey that could properly couch her envy. She just burned up inside and that was that.

Agent Parks became a physical comfort for Lacey; there was evening activity between them that could be categorized as convenient, though there was a humor gap that Lacey could see and he could not. She never took him out to the art parties, and he never wanted to go out to the art parties. After all, he was an investigator of the very people he might meet, and he liked the surreptitiousness that guided their hours together. His business was clandestine encounters; why not have the same in his personal life, too?

He was one year younger than Lacey, with a tight, wiry body that was fun for her to explore. He kept himself in shape as part of his job, though the art world seldom required him to climb over chain-link fences or race along rooftops. Lacey liked to say to him, "Fuck me, Agent Parks," and when it was all over there was no awkward silence, because Agent Parks was not trying to make Lacey his girlfriend. He was not swooning over her, or worrying if he was saying the right thing, or going out of his way to be nice. Out of professional responsibility, he even kept secrets from her that were about people she knew, no matter how much she prodded him. He was a jock with a lust for Lacey and a job situated squarely in the art world, a trifecta of qualities that could never be printed in the personals section of *The New York Review of Books* but was nonetheless desirable in this combination.

In January 2006, Agent Parks went to Lacey's gallery, showed his badge to the receptionist, and asked if Miss Yeager was in. Lacey emerged from her office, and Parks held up a manila envelope. "I'd like to discuss an issue in private with you," he said.

Lacey took him in the office and closed the door. He whispered, "Shhhh." Agent Parks bent her over the desk, made a few clothing adjustments—he left his overcoat on—and quickly inserted himself into her. This visit had happened only a few times in their two-year-long relationship, and what appealed to Lacey about it was that Parks didn't seem to care whether she was in the mood or not. It was just urgent, and he needed it done. With her palms on the desk and her hair grazing its surface, Lacey's eyes were positioned directly over a pile of unopened mail. The pieces tended to move around as she raised and lowered her body on the desk, and one time, as she arched her back slightly, her blouse buttons brushed aside a few envelopes, revealing something unusual in this pile of announcements and bills: a corner of an envelope, handwritten. She used the momentum that was pushing her from behind to shift the envelopes that covered it and read who'd sent it. "Claire," it said, then above it in engraved letters: "The Carlyle Hotel." She grabbed it in her fist, not because of its sender, but because she had to grab on to something when Agent Parks intensified from behind.

She had not heard from Patrice Claire in years. She had heard about him, and no doubt he had heard about her, but there had been no direct communication. She was not curious about this letter. In fact, it bothered her. Inside, she guessed, was something quasi-romantic, something thought-out and carefully written, with probably either a request for an explanation, which she didn't have, or a request to meet, which she knew would be excruciating. Then Agent Parks came inside the condom that was inside Lacey and let her know it by stopping mid-stroke and squeezing her waist with both hands.

On his way out, the receptionist said to him, in complete ignorance, "That was quick. " He smiled, touched the brim of his fedora between his first finger and thumb, and left.

Lacey knew that at some point she would have to open the letter, so she picked it up, along with a few art magazines, and took it home. She dressed to go out, pausing first to vibrate herself in order to release the head of steam that Agent Parks had built up in her. She walked several blocks in a freezing wind before she found a taxi to take her to an artist's studio. She spent a half hour looking at work she instantly knew she hated, but she had to invest the time since she and the artist had a mutual friend.

Back home, she poured herself a glass of white wine and sat at the kitchen table in front of the day's mail from the gallery. Patrice's letter was on top, and she was still loath to read it because she knew that whatever was in it would mean more work for her, another ego to soothe. But with the wineglass on her right, easily grasped, she pared back the flap of the envelope and slid out a solitary card. In Patrice's handwriting, it read, "Dear Lacey, You should know that your Aivazovsky is worth much more than you paid for it, Patrice."

She turned the card over: nothing. She smelled it and wasn't sure if it carried Patrice's aroma. She put it back in the envelope, then took a sip from her glass. She got up from her chair and thought, Where is that painting?

She went to a hall closet, where a dozen framed things, wrapped in cardboard and tied with string, were filed as rejects. She searched through them and finally came across the picture. She had wrapped it for the move and never unwrapped it. She had meant to get to it, to sell it, but it was too much trouble, and she was always so preoccupied. She snipped the twine with scissors, took the picture back to her bedroom, and hung it in place of a small Amy Arras across from her bed. It looked better than she remembered, especially now that it was in a spot that had been professionally lit. Lacey figured it might now be worth double or triple what she had paid for it.

She called the Carlyle and asked for Patrice Claire, even though it was past ten p.m. The operator said, "Just a minute," and a full minute later, she came back on and said, "He's not in, can I take a message?" She left her name, but Patrice never called back.

Unlike the glory and wonder of the Warhol, there was no sentimental attachment to the Aivazovsky, but Lacey still waited a few days before pursuing the sale of the picture. She thought it would be more likely to find an enthusiastic customer in Europe, so she found a house in Sweden, the Stockholms Auktionsverk. She had her gallery photographer come to the loft and photograph the picture, then she e-mailed the image and information about where she got it—Patrice Claire's name gave it good provenance—and waited.

The picture hung in its spot across from the bed, in limbo, an ugly puppy about to be sold. But one night Agent Parks (she just couldn't call him Bob), after a wrestling bout in the clean linens of her bed, observed the picture. "What's that?" he said. "That's new, right?"

"Not really, it was put away."

"What is it?"

"It's Russian. Nineteenth century. Artist's name unpronounceable."
He walked up to it. "He's painting like Rembrandt. You know the
one that was stolen? *The Storm on the Sea of Galilee*? With the ship?
This has the same surface."

"You know the surface of the Rembrandt?"

"Yeah. I've seen so many photos, transparencies. Plus I saw it, quickly,
in a locker at the train station. It was a bargaining chip, but I couldn't
tell if it was the real thing. They called the wrong dude. They thought
I was a reporter. They wanted to give the pictures back in trade for no
prosecution. But how can the government agree to that? They can't say
it's fine to steal a bunch of pictures as long as they are returned. Then
the Rembrandt went underground again. Too bad. I've begun to feel
for those pictures.

"The Rembrandt *Galilee* has a layer of varnish over it," he continued, "like you're looking at it through amber, but I don't think it's the
varnish that gives you that feeling. It's somehow in the paint. This has
it, too." He moved in close to the picture, moving his head from side to
side to avoid the shadows from the overhead spotlight.

"You know about varnish?"

"Yeah. I had a quickie course when I started in this department."

"Who teaches art courses at the FBI?"

"We had someone from Sotheby's. Ross somebody?"

"Tanya?"

"Miss Ross, is all I know."

"So you didn't fuck her."

"How do you figure that?"

"Well, you called her Miss Ross."

"You call me Agent Parks. But no, I didn't. I didn't even think about
it. Not my type, I guess. Too sane." He smiled at her.

"I'm selling it," she said.

"Really? I like it."

"Tell me why you like it."

"Well, it's pretty. Kind of lonely looking. And it's symbolic, don't you think?"

"Symbolic?"

"That's where something in the picture stands for something else. Like truth or something."

"Thank you. So what's symbolic about it?"

"Remember, this is not my best subject."

"I'll remember."

"Well, the water, to me, represents the earth and all the things that happen on the earth, reality. And the moonlight represents our dreams and our minds."

"And..."

"And the reflection...well, I guess the reflection represents art. It's what lies between our dreams and reality."

62.

THE NEXT DAY, Lacey received an e-mail from the Stockholms Auktionsverk saying they could give an estimate on the picture at somewhere between one hundred fifty thousand and two hundred fifty thousand dollars, and that the wide range could be adjusted after they saw the picture.

None of Lacey's huge returns in the art market had been based on wise investing: one had been bought to show off, one was bought out of her surprising response to it, and a third was essentially stolen. But in an exploding market, it was hard to make a mistake. The Russians had come in the way they came into Poland, and while raiding the modern masters, paying huge sums for Lucian Freud and Francis Bacon, they eventually looked to their own nineteenth-century artists, whose prices rose with every fall of the gavel. Aivazovsky was one of the three or four nineteenth-century Russian artists who qualified as collectable. Except for one gigantic spike for the rarest bird of all, Kazimir Malevich, who sold at sixty million dollars, the Russians' own great modern movements of suprematism and constructivism attracted little attention because the market was flooded with homegrown fakes.

Too late for the fall sales, the Aivazovsky would be sold in the spring of 2007, almost eight months away. Lacey called the art movers, and the work was sent off to Sweden.

Ben and Belinda Boggs continued to befriend Lacey, which she sometimes viewed as her punishment for leaving Barton Talley, for moving downtown, for opening a gallery, for having ambition. They also bought pictures from her and gave her pictures to sell. There was a monthly train ride to Connecticut for an art dinner at their home, with guests numbering about forty. Dinner was inevitably accompanied by tours of the house, gallery, and sculpture garden, which she had memorized, and each repetitive tour was excruciating. She was running out of things to say, and she did not, absolutely did not, want to climb the stairs one more time and see their horse photos. The only light for her was the occasional presence of Barton Talley himself, who was often her dinner partner. Whenever Belinda started a soliloquy, Lacey would turn to him with a neutral stare that was code for an expression of disgust.

At one of these dinners, Belinda started in: "Oh, oh, stop me if I told you this. We were hosting a big gala event and we were showing our collection and we had the Beuys felt suit...well, Ben had a new tuxedo..."

Lacey turned to Talley with the blank stare and he gave the blank stare back. But this time, Lacey whispered, "Can we stop her with a gun?" and Talley snickered. Fortunately, there were ten seats between them and the hostess.

Belinda went on, soon to be interrupted by Ben: "Honey, you left out the part..." Finally, Talley turned to Lacey.

"Lacey, you know the artist Hon See?"

"Yet another Chinese," said Lacey. "The one who does large paintings of news stories."

"Yes, up-and-coming. Another opportunity. A collector in Singapore has thirty works. We could buy all of them and dole them out, a few yearly. An annuity."

Lacey remembered the missed opportunity with Feng Zhenj-Jie and viewed Talley as a dealer who never made mistakes. "Oh God, Barton,

I just can't do it. I'm in the same situation. I exist on the cash I have. How much do I need?"

"A million should do it. I'm putting in a million, and Stephen Bravo's putting in a million."

The difference between Bravo and Talley putting in a million and her putting in a million was that her cash was all she had and theirs was tip money.

"I can't. I just can't."

"…we steamed the suit and gave it to a gallery in Tulsa," said Belinda, eliciting courteous smiles from those who had heard the story before, which was nearly everybody.

After dinner, valet parkers pulled cars around, and Talley offered her a ride back to the city, liberating her from returning in the minivan that had ferried her and a few of the other lesser lights to the dinner.

In the car, Talley and Lacey reminisced. "You've done well, Lacey."

"The truth is, I've done just well enough," she said.

"It's a tough business."

"I miss the old pictures. Picasso drawings. Klees. Remember that small Corot landscape you had? So beautiful."

"Sold to the Met," he said.

"Thank you for hiring me."

"You were an asset."

"I might not have come to you highly recommended."

"You mean because of the Sotheby's thing?"

"What did they tell you?"

"Not much. They said you were bright and fast. And that there might have been a bidding issue, but they didn't know. Just that they had to let you go."

"That's what they said?"

"Yes. Was there a bidding issue?"

"I helped a friend."

"Was the friend you helped yourself?"

Lacey didn't answer, but Talley didn't care. He went on:

"When you start in the art business, you can see that there are ways to illegitimately cut corners. And because you're so desperate to make a sale, you do. Then you come to a crossroads and you decide the type of dealer you're going to be. I cut a few corners early on, then I realized being straightforward was so much easier. So whatever you did, I hope you moved on."

"That's what I learned from you," said Lacey, "and yes, I moved on."

There was silence in the car for several miles. Then:

"And oh, remember that FBI guy?" said Lacey. "On the Gardner thing you got me into?"

"I think so."

"I'm dating him."

"You never throw anything away, do you, Lacey?"

"All the time," she said.

63.

IT WAS FIVE PM one April day in 2007, and Lacey was sitting at her desk, fretting that she could not, or best not, participate in Talley's Hon See deal, worrying that the outlay could put her in jeopardy, and hating that she had to miss this big league opportunity that would put her in Talley and Bravo's world. Then the phone rang. It was Stockholms Auktionverks calling, the voice said.

"Is this Miss Yeager?" The accent was difficult and the connection worse.

"Yes."

"We have your auction results for today's sale. Lot 363, the Aivazovsky, sold for five million ten thousand Swedish kronor."

Her heart leapt when she heard "five million," but then she came to her senses.

"How much is a krona?"

"How much is a krona?" the voice responded.

"How much is a krona in dollars?"

"Ah, I see. Let me calculate that for you." And then: "That would be approximately seven hundred thousand U.S. dollars."

Lacey hung up the phone and thought that there were still a few surprises left in the art market: with the sale of one painting, she had paid for her entire gallery and its inventory. She called Barton Talley's cell and caught him in an elevator.

"Is the Hon See deal still open?"

"I'm meeting with Stephen Bravo now, to finalize."

"Is it still open?"

"We bought part of it, but we could buy the whole thing if you want in."

"Let's take the whole thing."

"Can you be at Bravo's at six? This will take some rejiggering."

"I'll be there."

~

Lacey didn't let Bravo's private elevator or the three hundred feet of art reference library in his Manhattan office intimidate her. She entered as Talley was listening to the Los Angeles art dealer on the phone. Bravo signaled her to sit down.

"We'll confirm it tomorrow," he said. "Yes, it's a done deal, but we'll confirm it tomorrow... How much more done could it be? Because we've got a third party and we've got to talk at least once. It's not done, but it's done."

Where would the pictures go? Half stored at Bravo's and half at Talley's gallery. They would wait until the fall 2007 auctions were over: there was a sensational Hon See coming up that would likely set a record, since everything was setting records. It was decided that the show would be split between Talley, uptown, and Lacey, downtown. This hadn't often been done before and would indicate that Hon See was a master in either milieu. Stephen Bravo would sell the pictures to select clients out of his back room in Los Angeles. The first show, they decided, would open in late September 2008, perfect for the fall gallery openings and in plenty of time to massage the market into a Hon See frame of mind.

64.

LACEY'S BUSINESS CONTINUED strong through 2007 and 2008, strong enough that she did not wish she could dip into her now invested, and therefore impossible to retrieve, backup fund. The fall sale saw a Hon See bring one hundred fifty thousand, and in the spring of 2008, a Hon See again brought one hundred thirty thousand dollars. Though it was less than the previous season, the price was solid, making the pictures worth at least what had been paid for them.

During the summer, Lacey prepared for her opening show, now set for September 18. She had tiny reproductions of the Hon See pictures made and paid an architecture student to render a two-foot-square model of her gallery. She could move the small images around and design the best layout for the show. Some of the pictures were floor to ceiling, while the smallest was thirty-six inches square, and Lacey thought the show was going to look handsome.

She ordered champagne and sent out pre-invitations saying, "Save the date," followed up by a formal and more exquisite foldout that made the night seem extraordinarily special. Talley did the same, and both their addresses were on the invitation, a coup for Lacey, as she was now linked with one of the most prestigious galleries in Manhattan. Ben and Belinda were invited, of course, and had accepted. Hundreds of others, too, had told Lacey they were going to both openings, uptown and down, and the evening, intended to flush art sales from the distant bushes, was turning into a soiree. Already there were holds on three pictures, at two hundred fifty per, minus a ten percent courtesy discount, and with two holds at Talley's end, she was at least one-third out of her investment.

On the Sunday before the opening, Lacey celebrated with Angela and Sharon, both of whom were coincidentally in Manhattan for the weekend. For this rare girls' night out, she bought dinner, and they seemed happy for her. Sharon, continuing on with a decent man and pregnant with a second baby, and Angela, who was accompanying her famous writer boss on a promotional tour, seemed happy with their lives far away from Manhattan. Lacey went to bed that night with visions of sugar plums dancing in her head.

Monday morning would be a day spent adjusting the show, sprucing up the gallery, and doing touch-ups on the shoe-level scrapes that had inevitably bruised the white walls. The gallery would be officially closed until opening night, and Lacey knew there would be urgent calls made by collectors trying to get an early peek. Monday noon she called Talley, but he was unavailable. "Have him call me," she said. By two there was no call back, so she called again. This time he took the call, but breathlessly.

"Have you been watching the stock market?" he asked.

"I hate the stock market. Why would I watch it?"

"It's down over five hundred points. Lehman Brothers is bankrupt, Merrill Lynch is sold, and AIG is bankrupt."

Lacey didn't quite know what all this meant, but Talley's voice was shaking.

"They're already calling it Black Monday," he said.

The next day, Tuesday, the stock market just quivered, but on Wednesday it fell four hundred fifty points. Investors, meaning not just high-end Wall Street pros but every civilian with a few thousand dollars, pulled their money and bought T-bills and T-bonds, and they certainly didn't buy art. There was no credit, which the U.S. mainstream had relied on for at least thirty years. Only the credit card system was still operating, and with usurious interest rates, those companies had little to worry about. Several were taking three percent of every purchase and eighteen percent on every unpaid debt.

Thursday, the day of Lacey's opening, the stock market gained a bit, and she called Barton Talley.

"Up today," she said.

"Lacey, still not good."

"But it's up."

"Even a dead cat bounces."

Opening night, Lacey swung open her doors to a few students. The only thing missing in Chelsea was tumbleweeds. There were a few stragglers, who looked like scavengers prowling for bodies from which to pluck watches and gold teeth after the big shoot-out.

By eight p.m., Lacey's receptionist was afraid to look at her. Talley called, reporting that there were a few people there, but all they talked about was the collapse. "Lacey," he said, "I've never heard anyone talk about global financial disaster and then say, 'I'll take it.'"

"But there's a market," Lacey insisted. "What about the last Hon See that sold at auction? Just four months ago."

"We bought it. Bravo and I bought to keep the prices up. We were the only bidders."

The last Monday in September, the Dow fell seven hundred seventy-eight points and continued its slide through the week.

Overnight, the Arabs, the Russians, and the Asians left the art market. The holds on the Hon Sees were released, with, "Sorry, can't do it right now," and, "I'm going to wait and see." Lacey's show hung for another month to cobweb silence.

Art as an aesthetic principle was supported by thousands of years of discernment and psychic rewards, but art as a commodity was held up by air. The loss of confidence that affected banks and financial instruments was now affecting cherubs, cupids, and flattened popes. The objects hadn't changed: what was there before was there after. But a vacancy was created when the clamoring crowds deserted and retrenched.

Art magazines and auction catalogs thinned. Darwinism swept through Chelsea, killing off a few species, and only the ones with the long necks that could reach the leaves at the tops of the trees survived. There was still some business, but not for Lacey, and negotiations got tougher and tougher up and down the street as collectors, even the ones unaffected, wanted bargains. Lacey was willing to give bargains, but no one wanted what she had to offer.

She needed an influx of buoyant money, but in her heart, she didn't know if it would be wise to keep the gallery afloat. She might just be incurring more debt by delaying the inevitable. She called Barton Talley. He could meet her at his gallery later that day.

The taxi ride uptown turned into a coincidental Grand Tour of her life in the art world: through Chelsea, past Christie's, and up Madison where all the galleries hid. Upon arriving at Talley's, Lacey pushed the doorbell as she had so long ago. It clicked and she muscled it open. She threw her weight against the inner door when there was a second click, and she saw Donna, older, shopworn, still feigning efficiency, with her thumb pressing on the door buzzer long after Lacey had entered the gallery.

"Hi, Lacey. Can I offer you something to drink?"

"Is there any poison?" said Lacey.

"Sorry?"

"I'm here to see Barton."

"I'll see if he's in."

Then she heard Donna say over the phone, "Are you in for Lacey Yeager?"

Donna looked up at Lacey and said, "Go on up."

The nostalgia continued for Lacey as she recalled her initial ascent of these stairs almost a dozen years ago, where she had encountered Agent Parks, now her boyfriend. She recalled her accidental peek at the Vermeer copy at the wrong end of the hall, and her first entrance into Talley's expert world. Her time in this gallery was the best of it, she thought, and as she walked down the hall, she recalled her footsteps years ago when she headed excitedly toward the window to look for Patrice Claire. Her memory couldn't quite trace what had led to this now funereal march to Talley's office; she just knew she had come, and gone, a long way.

"In here, Lacey," she heard Talley say.

She entered the office. "Well," she said, "I've come full circle."

"I've been through troughs before. They keep the boom times from looking like a Ponzi scheme. You want a drink?"

She said yes, and Talley poured.

"Lacey, I've seen a lot of beginners in the art business. You were the smartest one of all of them. You seemed to know things before you knew them."

"I just paid attention."

"Are you looking for investors?"

"What for? The fever is over, and without the fever…"

"What about dealing privately? No rent, except your apartment. You develop clients who trust you," said Talley.

"I've still got a gallery. I can work harder."

"Can you?"

"No, actually, I can't."

"So why'd you make the trip up here?"

"Oh, I suppose to say thank you, now that I've had a cocktail."

"I liked you, Lacey. You were always fascinating to me. And you brought in a lot of clients. Especially single ones." Talley laughed.

"And some married ones," Lacey said. "But, I'm looking you in the eye and saying thank you."

"It was fun. Fun and business. What's better?"

"I guess I got more out of it than you."

"In what way?"

"I had sex, fun, and business."

Talley laughed again. "Well, maybe I had a little of that, too."

"What's on the walls?" asked Lacey.

"We're low. Nobody wants to sell in down times. We've got a few things," Talley indicated the few drawings on the office wall. Then he pointed behind her. "What do you think of that?"

Lacey turned in her chair and saw against the velvet easel a painting in a gilded frame, overframed, in fact, for its diminutive size. There was a jab of recognition for this old friend in spiffy new duds. It was her grandmother's Maxfield Parrish.

"It was traded by some collectors to another dealer, and I got it in trade. It's a gem, don't you think? The condition is flawless, like it has been under glass."

Lacey got up and walked over to it. It was indeed a gem. She wondered if Talley was feeling her out, but he seemed innocent and she was content to believe he was.

"It is a gem," she agreed.

"The picture's right," said Talley, meaning that it was a genuine Parrish, "but we have provenance issues. We can trace it back to Sotheby's and there's a block. Can't trace it back to the artist. Doesn't really matter. It's real."

"Yes," said Lacey, "it's real."

"You know Parrish's work?"

Lacey turned toward him, taking a sip of her drink. "The girl in the picture. That's my grandmother."

"What?"

His disbelief assured Lacey that this was a coincidence and that Talley was not on FBI detail. "Kitty Owen, that's her, was my grandmother."

"My God. Well, there is a resemblance in the face."

"And ass, just so you know," said Lacey.

"Well, how lucky for you," he said with a smile.

Lacey stared at the picture, got lost in it, in fact.

Talley broke the spell. "They want a million six for it. Won't get it now. But it is a top Parrish."

"Well, let me know who ends up with it. Maybe one day I could buy it back."

"Back?"

"Buy it. Just buy it," she said.

65.

HER CASH POOL DRAINED, Lacey held on through the new year, finally accepting that her lease was worth more than her gallery and its inventory. In June 2009, she sold it at a loss to a restaurateur. The Hon Sees were sold to a speculator for nine hundred thousand dollars, less than one-third the cost, returning three hundred thousand of her million-dollar investment, which she used to the pay the capital gains tax on the Aivazovsky, which she had forgotten about. Her loft was destined for foreclosure.

Months earlier, on the drive home from Connecticut when she confirmed her misstep to Barton Talley, she didn't realize that, as discreet as he was, he still saw Cherry Finch and that pillow talk had leaked the confirmation of Lacey's grift to her, and thus to the world. The moment was so slight that even Talley didn't understand that he had passed along the information. When Lacey announced that she would become an "art adviser," working from home and taking ten percent from every sale advised, this little negative, that she was a bit of a crook, was made clear to clients by her rivals, even if they were crooks themselves.

Ben and Belinda Boggs were among the first to recoil from Lacey, sensing that she was an outcast. They also rehung their entire art collection, placing into deep storage objects that the new, dismal market shouted they had overpaid for, and pulling out more classic objects, including the Beuys felt suit, bought when prices were sensible. They hoped this would peg them as astute collectors.

Lacey's larger secret, that the auctioned Parrish had been purloined from her own grandmother, remained secret, and Lacey remained curiously, disturbingly, guilt-free.

66.

NOT MANY ART world denizens wanted to talk to me after the crash, fearing journalists, fearing would-be novelists, fearing parody and revenge for the free-spending years. I had drinks with Lacey once before I lost contact with her, and I told her of my intent to write this book. I offered to change her name. "How about Alison Ames?" I said.

"If I had to hear the name Alison Ames in my head for three hundred pages, I'd go insane," she said.

"It won't be all flattering," I said.

"I'm not trying to be a good little girl," she said.

Lacey seemed not to care that her life might be mirrored in a book, that she might not be portrayed as a heroine, and that art world readers would certainly deduce that it was about her. She seemed to have the attitude that of course she would be the subject of a book.

"My mother is ill, so I'm going back to Atlanta for a while."

"I'm sorry."

"*You're* sorry? She's so nuts about Jesus that I can hardly speak to her."

This was the mother whom Lacey had maneuvered out of six hundred thousand dollars that was presumably hers.

"Lacey," I said, "you're going to have to do something in Atlanta besides caretake."

"Elton John is disposing of some of his photography collection and I've been asked to help, so I can do two things at once. Help Mom.

Help Elton. And the High Museum there is good; I bet I can worm my way in somehow." On the word *worm*, she twisted her baby finger through the air, but it seemed a tired gesture.

"How'd you get into the Elton John situation?"

"I don't know. They called, saying someone recommended me."

I wondered who that might be, perhaps a sympathetic Barton Talley.

"Are you seeing anyone?" I asked.

"I'm seeing a guy who's got me figured out. He never says I love you."

"That's good?"

"I love him for it."

"Will he go with you to Atlanta?"

"He travels, he's FBI."

"FBI?"

"What did I say?" she said.

"Do you think it will last?"

"Daniel, there's no way it's going to last." Then she paused, staring at me. "Goddamn it, the art world ran out on me."

"You're still in the art world even if you're in Atlanta," I said.

"Paris doesn't qualify as being in the art world, why should Atlanta? I know I'm in purgatory." She sipped her coffee. "I'm going to take the Parrish print back to my mother. She says she'd like to see it."

It wasn't clear to me whether Lacey remembered that while under the influence she had told me about her larceny.

Lacey looked around the walls of the restaurant. "God, I've seen thousands of paintings. High and low. Remember the Avery I told you about? I'd like to see it again. It's like a first love; it might be nice to say hello."

Her energy seemed drained, but I knew it was not a permanent state. She even laughed a bit, saying, "Damn it, why didn't I try to seduce Rauschenberg? He might have given me a silk screen."

"Rauschenberg was gay and near death," I said.

"You don't know my powers," she said.

67.

ART WAS STILL ART whether it was tied to money or not. People continued to attend art fairs, museums, galleries. They thought about it, they chatted about it, they pontificated about it, but the financial race over it had stalled. Most art enthusiasts who resided outside of New York or Los Angeles didn't know or care about the market's collapse. The collectors stood back and tried to remember how to love art the old-fashioned way, and the dealers developed strategies—that finally included discounts—on how to survive the trough. A Pilot Mouse work died at auction. He was a symbol of the bubble, and the bubble had burst.

New York City's Armory Show of 2009 was just barely breathing, and collectors who asked prices always feigned disbelief and shock, trying to indicate lower, lower. There was acting on both sides, with the dealers citing sales and European notice, real or not. Two giant hangars housed the works for sale, connected by a membrane of jerry-built steel stairs, which allowed only ten people on at a time, for fear of another kind of art world collapse. The Modernist galleries were on one side and everything else on the other. Gold frames to the left; no frames to the right. The Nathansons would peer at a Miró gouache, then time-travel—to next door—and be puzzled by the extreme art of the present month.

As a writer—though one now fearing at all times for my reputation—I covered this waterfront, also attending the Miami Basel art fair in the fall. This fair was always a big draw, recession or not, and the gallerygoers included the sandals-and-T-shirt crowd out for an afternoon of eyeballing. I did not see Hinton Alberg there, and the usual party festivities were thinned out. I did see Patrice Claire, affectionate with a woman in her late forties who had streaks of gray in her black hair, and overheard them speaking French. I caught them at the drinks bar and introduced myself, reminding him that we had met before with Lacey Yeager and that I was a writer for *ARTnews*. Would he allow me to interview him, I asked, just to get his take on the fair?

No, he didn't want to comment; forgive him, he said. He was, characteristically, friendly toward me.

"How is Lacey?" he asked.

"Well, she closed her gallery in June, and she's moved to Atlanta."

"I think I heard that," he said.

"Too bad for her," I said. "I can't think of a personality less suited to becoming marginalized."

Patrice drank a sip of afternoon champagne and turned toward the woman with him, speaking as he turned his head back to me, which meant he was addressing the air: "I think Lacey is the kind of person who will always be okay."

68.

TWO MONTHS LATER, my article about Miami was published in *ARTnews*, and I received this handwritten card:

> *Dear Daniel,*
> *It was so lovely to finally read an essay about art that did not men-*
> *tion money. Congratulations on a refreshing take on things, and I*
> *hope you're doing well.*
> *Tanya Ross*

I could not tell if this was exactly what it was or something more. I wrote her back a handwritten card saying that it was nice to hear from her and that I had been working on a book, and if she had the time, I would love to get her comments. I couched the request as a favor, saying I could use her expertise to root out factual errors I might have made describing the workings of Sotheby's and, of course, wanting her general reaction. She responded yes and sent me an address, which was the same as when I was seeing her. Which made me have hope that she was still living alone.

My real wish, of course, is to have her read this story and understand that my small crime is now the stuff of novels—which I'm hoping might ameliorate it—and to make it clear that my loss of her is the most damage that has been done in my eighteen years of knowing

Lacey. If her response is not the one hoped for, I have thought of converting the book to nonfiction—which they tell me sells better—and leaving Lacey's name unchanged. But I'm not sure if that would ruin her or make her famous. I will determine which to do at a later point.

I sent Tanya the manuscript, but I have not yet heard from her.

PHOTO CREDITS AND COPYRIGHTS

293

Page 86. *The Bay of Naples by Moonlight,* by Ivan Aivazovsky: Copyright © Anatoly Sapronenkov/SuperStock.

Page 97. *Still Life with Wine Bottles,* by Giorgio Morandi: Copyright © 2010 Artists Rights Society (ARS), New York/SIAE, Rome. Photo: Gagosian Gallery.

Page 101. *Flowers,* by Andy Warhol: Copyright © 2010 The Andy Warhol Foundation for the Visual Arts, Inc./Artists Rights Society (ARS), New York. Photo: The Andy Warhol Foundation, Inc./Art.

Page 114. *Untitled,* by Tom Friedman. Art and photo are copyright © Tom Friedman. Courtesy Gagosian Gallery.

Page 126. *El Jaleo,* by John Singer Sargent: Copyright © Isabella Stewart Gardner Museum, Boston, MA, USA/The Bridgeman Art Library International.

Page 148. *Woman with Pears,* by Pablo Picasso: Copyright © 2010 Estate of Pablo Picasso/Artists Rights Society (ARS), New York. Photo: Copyright © The Museum of Modern Art/Licensed by SCALA/Art Resource, NY.

Page 149. *Marilyn,* by Andy Warhol: Copyright © 2010 The Andy Warhol Foundation for the Visual Arts, Inc./Artists Rights Society (ARS), New York. Photo: The Andy Warhol Foundation, Inc./Art Resource, NY.

Page 163. *Three Parts of an X,* by Robert Gober. Art and photo are copyright © Robert Gober. Courtesy Matthew Marks Gallery, New York.

Page 166. *Initiation,* by Wilfredo Lam: Copyright © 2010 Artists Rights Society (ARS), New York/ADAGP, Paris. Photo: CNAC/MNAM/ Dist. Réunion des Musées Nationaux/Art Resource, NY.

Page 182. *La Nona Ora,* by Maurizio Cattelan. Courtesy of the artist and Marian Goodman Gallery, New York.

Page 222. *Betwixt the Torus and the Sphere,* by Richard Serra: Copyright © 2010 Richard Serra/Artists Rights Society (ARS), New

York. Photo: Copyright © Richard Serra. Courtesy Gagosian Gallery. Photo by Robert Mckeever.

Page 227. *Felt Suit,* by Joseph Beuys: Copyright © 2010 Artists Rights Society (ARS), New York/VG Bild-Kunst, Bonn. Photo: Tate, London/Art Resource, NY.

Page 234. *Eine Kleine Nachtmusik,* by Dorothea Tanning: Copyright © 2010 Artists Rights Society (ARS), New York/ADAGP. Photo: Tate, London/Art Resource, NY.

All photos of artwork are used by permission.